Jean Joseph Languet

The Life of the Blessed Margaret Mary Alacoque

Religious of the Order of the Visitation. Second Edition

Jean Joseph Languet

The Life of the Blessed Margaret Mary Alacoque
Religious of the Order of the Visitation. Second Edition

ISBN/EAN: 9783337054120

Printed in Europe, USA, Canada, Australia, Japan

Cover: Foto ©Raphael Reischuk / pixelio.de

More available books at **www.hansebooks.com**

THE LIFE

OF THE

BLESSED MARGARET MARY ALACOQUE,

RELIGIOUS OF THE ORDER OF THE VISITATION.

"Gaude Maria Virgo, cunctas hæreses sola interemisti in universo mundo."—*Antiph. Ecclesiæ.*

SECOND EDITION.

LONDON:

THOMAS BAKER,

1, SOHO SQUARE.

MDCCCLXXIV.

Nihil Obstat.

Die XVII. Oct. MDCCCLXXIII.

J. E. Bowden, *Congr. Orat.*

Censor Deputatus.

Imprimatur.

Henricus E. *Archiep. Westmonast.*

We hereby approve and sanction the Series of Lives of the Canonized and Beatified Saints, the Servants of God declared Venerable, and others commonly reputed to have died in the odour of sanctity, now in course of publication by the Congregation of the Oratory of St. Philip Neri, and we cordially recommend it to the Faithful, as calculated to promote the glory of God and of His Saints, the increase of devotion, and the spread of our holy Religion.

Given at Westminster, the Feast of the Nativity of our B. Lady, A. D. 1851.

N. CARD. WISEMAN.

We very gladly approve and sanction the continuation of the Series of the Lives of the Saints, begun by the Reverend Fathers of the Oratory, with the approbation and sanction of our lamented Predecessor, being deeply convinced that, in the last twenty years, the Lives hitherto published have promoted a deep and solid piety among the Faithful in England.

✠ HENRY EDWARD,
ARCHBISHOP OF WESTMINSTER.

June 12, 1872.

TO

THE NUNS OF ENGLAND,

WHO SHIELD THEIR COUNTRY BY THEIR PRAYERS,

AND BY THEIR MEEK AUSTERITIES

MAKE REPARATION FOR ITS SINS;

AND TO

THE SISTERS OF MERCY,

WHOSE CHARITY IS THEIR INCLOSURE,

WHILE FOR THE LOVE OF THEIR HEAVENLY SPOUSE

IN HIS POOR AND SUFFERING MEMBERS

THEY DENY THEMSELVES

THE PEACE AND PROTECTION OF THE CLOISTER.

Daughters of Mary! in retreats obscure,
Lost to man's thought and eye, amid the trees
And unfrequented fields, on bended knees
Sueing for England's pardon, lives so pure
Mingle in heaven and God's approval share
With that uncloistered love, whose willing feet
Are borne through jeering crowd and gazing street
To scenes of lonely want and pining care.
For you the holy past is now unfurled,
That with its bright examples you may feed
The spirit of devotion. While the world
Honours your goodness with its hatred, you,
Still to your high and calm vocation true,
May win fresh light and strength from what you read.

F. W. FABER.

ST. WILFRID'S,
FEAST OF OUR LADY OF REDEMPTION,
M. D. CCC. XLVII.

PREFACE.

———

THE Life of the Ven. Margaret Mary
Alacoque, Religious of the Order of
the Visitation, of the Monastery of
Paray-le-Monial en Charolois, is tran-
slated from the French Life written by
Mgr. Jean Joseph Languet, Bishop of
Soissons, and published at Paris, A. D.
1729.

London,
The Oratory, Octave of the Sacred Heart, 1850.

PREFACE TO THE SECOND EDITION.

MOTHER MARGARET MARY ALACOQUE was solemnly beatified by Our Holy Father Pius IX., happily reigning, on the 18th of September, 1864.

In order to bring her life into the compass of one volume, it has been abridged, though very slightly, and a few of her letters have been omitted.

The Oratory, London,
Feast of St. Francis of Sales, 1874.

CONTENTS.

BOOK I.

PAGE

Her birth, education, and youth 1

BOOK II.

Her entrance into religion, and the virtues which she practised in the cloister 51

BOOK III.

Her employments in religion; the extraordinary graces which she received; and the opposition she met with 128

BOOK IV.

Of the particular graces Sister Margaret received touching the devotion to the Sacred Heart of our Lord, and the contradictions she met with on the part of Mother de Saumaise, superior of the monastery 164

BOOK V.

The Reverend Mother Greffier is superior. She subjects Sister Margaret to new trials concerning her extraordinary graces, and the devotion to the Sacred Heart of Jesus Christ 213

BOOK VI.

Mother Melin is superior. Sister Margaret is chosen mistress of the novices. Her conduct in this employment. First beginning of the devotion to the Sacred Heart of our Lord Jesus Christ. The opposition it met with 261

BOOK VII.

PAGE

The admirable vow which she made. The establishment
of the devotion to the Heart of our Lord in the Community of Paray. The fruits which she derived from
this devotion. Several instructions and practices prescribed by Sister Margaret   332

BOOK VIII.

Several miraculous favours bestowed by God on Sister
Margaret. Her gift of prophecy, and supernatural
lights upon divers subjects. Wonderful progress of
the devotion to the Heart of Jesus   396

BOOK IX.

She is made assistant. Her last sickness and death, and
the miracles performed at her tomb   437

BOOK X.

Collection of some of her writings of devotion   464

THE LIFE

OF THE

BLESSED MARGARET MARY ALACOQUE,

RELIGIOUS OF THE VISITATION OF ST. MARY,

WHO DIED IN THE ODOUR OF SANCTITY AT PARAY LE MONIAL, IN BURGUNDY.

BOOK I.

HER BIRTH, EDUCATION, AND YOUTH.

In the middle of the seventeenth century, the province of Burgundy, and more especially the diocese of Autun, which forms a part of it, saw with wonder and admiration the sublime graces with which Almighty God favoured Sister Margaret of the Blessed Sacrament, a Carmelite nun of the monastery of Beaune. This holy soul had been drawn to God from her earliest infancy in an extraordinary manner, and endowed with the most wonderful gifts of prayer. Her life was passed in practising austere penance, and in the most intimate communication of the grace of God. Miracles and the gift of prophecy rendered her holiness more marked and conspicuous. In a word, her reputation, no less than her words, excited the faithful more particularly to honour Jesus Christ in the mystery of His Infancy, and to bring into esteem this touching and instructive devotion.

1

The world was about to be deprived of this prodigy of grace, when it pleased God to produce another in the same province and diocese, in the person of a daughter no less favoured by Him. This was the Venerable Mother Margaret, who came into the world some months before the death of the other Margaret, whose sanctity has been made known by so many prodigies, and whose life has been written by the celebrated Father Amelotte, priest of the Oratory. Both have had, with the same name, country, and diocese, a conformity of much greater value, in a similar communication of the sublime graces of God, and in the execution of His designs for the instruction and edification of the faithful. If the one was endowed with a sublime gift of prayer from her infancy, the other was also raised to that miraculous prayer in her tenderest years; if the one was all her life the victim of austerity or suffering through her continual infirmities, the other was no less exercised in almost inconceivable rigours and bodily weakness. If one excited the faithful to pious and useful devotion towards the holy Childhood of Jesus Christ, the other was prepared by God to awaken in the faithful the love of our Blessed Lord, by opening their eyes to the infinite treasures they would find in His Heart, and engaging them to honour that Divine Heart, by offering it all the fervour of their own adoring and grateful hearts. In short, the resemblance between these two Margarets was perfect; and it would seem that Sister Margaret was the first in the order of time, that the world might be prepared, by witnessing the wonders of her life, to give a more ready credence to those we are about to relate, in the life of one whom God raised up to succeed her; thus perpetuating in the same country living models of the most sublime sanctity.

It was on the 22nd of July 1647, that the subject of this history came into the world at Lauthecour, in the parish of Veroure, in the diocese of Autun, that part of Burgundy which is called the County of Charolois. Her father, Claude Alacoque, was a man of probity and piety. His well-known character had obtained the esteem and confidence of the surrounding nobility, and the administration of justice in the greater part of the neighbouring lordships was entrusted to him. His means were adequate to his situation in life, to enable him to live comfortably, and supply all the wants of his family, and he never forgot to assist the poor with a liberality very unusual amongst those who possess small fortunes. This good use of his property drew upon him the blessing of God in his marriage with Philiberte Lamyn, by whom he had four sons and one daughter. The daughter was baptised three days after her birth, on the 25th of July 1647, and named Margaret, after Madame Margaret of St. Amour, wife of M. de Fautrieres de Corcheval, lord of the parish of Veroure.

God awaited not the lapse of years to attract the heart of the young Margaret to Himself. He anticipated the age of reason, inspiring her with the fear of sin before she could know what it was. For this purpose He made use of the holy education given her by her parents. She was but three years old when she showed a wonderful aversion to sin. The very name of sin, and the idea of offending God, filled her with horror; and her parents took advantage of this happy disposition, to repress the little vivacities of childhood, telling her that they would offend God if they gratified those inclinations in her which they believed they ought to check. Thereupon, the little Margaret would immediately master her natural vivacity, and sacrifice to the fear of displeasing God all those little caprices of the will which are so common, and so little under the control of reason at that tender age.

A heart so pure, and taught by God to hate sin before knowing it, learnt also from Him to love purity, and to consecrate her chastity at a time when the young Margaret could know only the names of these virtues. But in pious families, where masters and servants delight to talk of Christian virtues, children have a great advantage over those who hear only from the lips of their parents profane and often criminal words. The latter gather their first ideas of the world and sin from these thoughtless conversations, whilst the former, on the contrary, receive the first seeds of virtue from the family discourse, of the master who teaches, or the servants who surround them. It was thus with the little Margaret. Although not yet four years old, she already loved chastity. The grace of that virtue was communicated to her in an admirable manner; she felt drawn to engage herself to keep it all her life, and often pronounced in her heart these words, of which she knew neither the sense nor the merit, "My God, I consecrate my purity to Thee; I make a vow of perpetual chastity." She made this vow more explicitly one day that she felt strongly drawn to do so, and she chose for it the time of holy Mass, and the moment of consecration. The impression she then felt in her soul was so sweet, so consoling, and so strong, that the remembrance of it lasted through life, and neither succession of years, nor variety of occupations, could ever efface it from her mind.

When she was four years old, Madame de Fautrieres, her god-mother, wished to have the care of her for some time, and desired her attendants to teach her little god-daughter to read, and to say the catechism, and the usual prayers of Christians. In this house were two women of very opposite characters and merit. One of them had much piety, but her austere and stern virtue was not calculated to win the heart of a young child; the other had more gentleness, caresses were more natural to her, but her piety was not equal to her agreeable qualities. Though the little Margaret was so young, she was not attracted by the winning smiles of her more worldly friend, but attached herself strongly to the one whose true piety cheered her, and whose rough manners could not repulse her. It was thus that the Spirit of God already governed her heart, and repressed in her the natural inclinations that all children are but too apt to feel towards those who flatter them.

But in her docile heart the Divine Spirit soon wrought other and greater marvels. The little Margaret had only learnt the first elements of Christian doctrine, such as are taught to children when beginning to speak, but she found in them subjects of reflection and interior discourse with God. She was taught that God, though present everywhere, is more particularly so in our churches, and that Jesus Christ truly resides there in the Blessed

Sacrament. No sooner had she learnt this truth, than she felt attracted to go frequently to the church. The house in which she lived was near it, which gave her the opportunity of satisfying this desire, and she became skilful in eluding the attention of those who took charge of her, and running to the church without their knowledge. There she remained modestly on her knees, her hands joined, revolving in her mind with simplicity the truths she had been taught, and feeling her heart burn with love for Jesus Christ, whom she knew to be there present. This exercise never wearied her; and every moment that was spent by other children in amusements, was employed by her in this manner. Sometimes she remained whole hours in the church, and when she could not be found elsewhere, there she was sure to be. She was still more devoted to hearing Mass; and without well comprehending the nature of that august sacrifice, she felt powerfully drawn to adore Jesus Christ in it, and, in order her posture might be humble and penitent, she generally remained with her knees bare upon the ground, even in the most rigorous season of winter.

To this attraction for Jesus Christ was united a great love of solitude. Children in general love activity, games, dissipation, and amusements; this child loved to hide herself from others, and to be alone with God. They in their earliest years love to form little projects, according to their various dispositions, as to what they shall do when grown up; she would retire into some deep grotto or thick wood, and there remain in perfect solitude; and as St. Teresa in her infancy, fired by the desire of martyrdom, longed to seek among the Moors the opportu-

nity of suffering death, so did our little Margaret
long to fly into the first solitary place to devote herself entirely to prayer. This is what she afterwards
acknowledged when reviewing in her mind the graces
with which God had favoured her, either in order to
thank Him for them, or to give a relation of them to
those who required it from her. And she also
avowed, that what hindered her from putting this
design into execution, was the fear of meeting men
in her flight or in her solitude, because the sight
of men wounded her modesty, and terrified her
innocence.

A tender devotion to the Blessed Virgin was one
of the first-fruits of her infant fervour. This is one
of the characteristics of true piety, and God granted
it to her with His other favours. She delighted in
dwelling on the mysteries of the holy Mother of God,
on her virtues, and the graces which rendered her
blessed amongst women. In all her little distresses
she had recourse to her, and made her appeal with
the simplicity of a child, who pours out its sorrows
in the ear of a loving mother. She made a vow to
fast every Saturday in her honour, and when she
could read, to recite the little office of the Conception.
When she knew what the rosary was, she added that
also to her devotions, and that she might say it with
more fervour and respect, she often knelt down
when she thought no one perceived her, or kissed
the earth at every Ave she recited. The Blessed
Virgin, on the other hand, gave her at this early age
sensible proofs of her protection; and Sister Margaret afterwards declared, that she then delivered
her from three great perils, but without explaining
herself further.

All the world admired the gifts of God in this
child. She alone was ignorant of them. She had
been already taught an admirable manner of prayer,
and yet she believed she did not know how to pray.
She desired to learn this, seeking earnestly for some
one to instruct her, and was in affliction at not finding this assistance. She knew not what prayer was,
and yet its name alone awoke feelings of transport
in her heart. She reproached herself for not doing
what she had heard was practised by the Saints.
She laid before her God in prayer the desire that
she had to learn to pray, and with a lively ardour
she promised to spend in praying all the time she
could steal from her occupations. It was thus that
this poor child thirsted for the good she already possessed, which was hidden from her by her humility,
and expressed her desire with simplicity to all who
were placed over her. But it was in vain for her to
ask what this prayer was, nobody could or would
satisfy her. They laughed at her question and her
desire, which they attributed to the curiosity natural
to her age. God, who had given her an attraction
for it, and who had already sown the first-fruits of it
in her heart, gave her Himself the practical experience of it, and from that time forwards conducted
her to a sublime manner of prayer, and imparted to
her the most tender and familiar communications.
He instructed her Himself in an ineffable manner,
which the modesty of this holy soul has only imperfectly disclosed to us. All that she has manifested
to those who obliged her by obedience to speak is,
that having addressed her Divine Master in prayer,
earnestly entreating Him to deign to teach her how
to pray, He instructed her to prostrate herself hum-

bly before His Divine Majesty, to adore Him in an
exterior and interior state of profound nothingness,
to ask mercy for her sins, to weep for them in His
presence, and afterwards lay before Him with simplicity and confidence all the desires of her heart.
He drew her to the particular consideration of the
mysteries of Jesus Christ, and of the actions of His
holy life. Sometimes the Son of God presented
Himself to her in the mystery on which He wished
her to meditate. He turned her mind to the consideration of its consoling or instructive circumstances, and often kept all the powers of her soul so
absorbed in Him, and in the consideration of the
Divine Truths, that He left no room for the distractions so common to the mind of man, and still more
to the thoughtlessness of childhood.

Margaret was only eight years old when her father
died, leaving his sorrowing wife in distressed circumstances. Margaret was then at home, but her mother
was so much occupied with other affairs, that she
left her child too much in the care of a servant, who
was incapable alike of correcting or improving her.
Margaret's education suffered from this, and her
fervour relaxed a little. Although God condescended
to instruct her Himself, yet it was His Will that
according to the usual course, the care of her relations should concur with His graces for her sanctification. Madame Alacoque felt this, and to
supply that attention which her affairs did not
allow her to bestow, she placed her daughter in the
hands of the Sisters of St. Clare, in the town of
Charolles.

Her entrance into this house was a happy opportunity for the little Margaret to renew her fervour.

The eminent piety of these nuns, their austerity, prayers, and spirit of recollection, made all the impression that good example never fails to produce upon pure and docile minds. Margaret, edified and confused at finding herself so far removed from the fervour she witnessed, regarded these sisters as so many Saints. She desired to imitate their manner of life, and at that time conceived her first desire of becoming a religious. Her views were fixed upon this house because she knew no other; yet she sometimes regretted that they did not lead more solitary lives; and at the age when company and amusement are most loved, she found too much of them for her taste amongst these austere religious. If she was edified by their holy lives, the sisters were no less so by the wisdom, modesty, and recollection which they saw in her. Her love of prayer, her humility and obedience appeared to them beyond her years; and finding her so much advanced in reason, knowledge, and grace, they thought it right no longer to defer her first communion. She made it at nine years of age, and we may imagine what was the fervour and consolation of this holy soul that God had long prepared by such singular graces.

Notwithstanding these graces and this fervour, the young Margaret was not dead to everything. Her natural disposition led her to pleasure, and her love of solitude did not spring from a morose or melancholy disposition. She was of a gay, cheerful spirit, and this temper, which the world calls happy, might perhaps have drawn her into evil, if grace had not taken command of her, and if God had not furnished her by His Providence with the means of detaching herself from the diversions of which she began to taste the sweetness. Notwithstanding the attraction God had given her for prayer, she often followed her natural bent for pleasure; she sometimes gave herself up to the games and amusements of her age with her companions, and with all the vivacity of her ardent character. But God corrected her of this too human inclination in two ways. The first was by shedding a sensible bitterness over all those pleasures for which she felt so much attraction. This was one of the fruits of her first communion; the grace of God pursued her, as it were, when she sought these amusements; it urged her incessantly by stinging remorse and interior reproaches, which deprived her of all relish for diversion.

The other means employed by God to detach her from pleasure, was a violent sickness, which He destined in His mercy, not only to produce the fruit we have already described, but also to make her bear some portion of the sorrows of His Passion, and to crucify her with Him from her childhood. This illness was very long and painful. It began by rheumatism complicated with paralysis, which for four years kept her on a bed of pain. During this time she experienced all the sufferings of illness, and all the severity of medical treatment. She could neither walk, sleep, nor eat, and could scarcely move. She became so emaciated that her bones pierced the skin. After two years her mother removed her from the convent, hoping that her own attentions might be more conducive to the health of her daughter than those of the nuns. But by changing her dwelling, she could neither change nor soften her condition; the little Margaret continued to endure the same suffering for two years longer.

God, who had His own views in this illness, had them also in her recovery, and it was His Will that the sick girl should understand that both proceeded from Him. He decreed that her cure should be effected through the intercession of the Blessed Virgin, to whom He inspired the young child to dedicate herself by vow. She made this vow, promising that if the Blessed Virgin would procure her recovery, she would consecrate herself absolutely to her service. The vow was answered quickly, to show that the cure came from Heaven. In a few days Margaret recovered her health entirely; but what was more precious than her health was the singular protection that she experienced from this moment on the part of the Blessed Virgin. She had in her childhood devoted herself to the service of the holy Virgin, who acknowledged this fresh proof of her devotion by the graces she obtained for her of God, and also by supernatural visits and communications. In the recital of her life given under obedience to her director, of which we shall often have occasion to speak, she relates with much simplicity the circumstances attending this miraculous cure, and the results which followed it. "From this time," said she, "the Blessed Virgin made herself mistress of my heart, and looking upon me as her own, she governed me as one dedicated to her. She taught me to do the Will of God; she reproved me for my faults; and one day that I had happened to say the rosary in a sitting posture, she presented herself before me, and gave me this reprimand, which has never been effaced from my memory, though I was at that time very young : 'My child, I am astonished that you serve me so negligently.' "

The young Margaret profited by her recovery to return to her exercises of prayer, and to add to them those of mortification. The attractions which God poured into her soul were so delightful, that she felt no pleasure but in His presence. She regularly gave two hours in the morning and two in the evening to meditation, being then about thirteen years old. That these long prayers might not hinder her from performing the services required of her in the house, she rose before day to her morning meditation, and in the night she made that of the evening. Her love of prayer often induced her to pass the night in contemplation, and it was only by reasoning and doing violence to herself, that she withdrew herself from this holy exercise, to give to her body the necessary repose.

Her fervour in the church was still greater, because of the presence of Jesus Christ Who resides there in the Blessed Sacrament. She employed all the little address of which she was capable, to obtain from those on whom she depended permission to spend now and then a quarter of an hour there in the course of the day. She dared not communicate often, but she felt a kind of envy towards those who had the happiness of doing so ; and to recompense herself in some sort for the privation she suffered, she loved to approach the altar, as if to unite herself more closely to her Divine Master : and the thought which often filled her mind was, as she herself has said, " To consume myself by love in His presence, as the wax which I see burning upon the altar."

Her mortification at this tender age was as in-

conceivable as the gift of prayer to which she was
raised. She fasted regularly three times a week,
and it often happened that she even passed whole
days without eating. She had constantly recourse
to hair-cloths, disciplines, and small chains of iron,
to macerate her body. She lay upon the bare
ground, and often rose in the middle of the night to
pray. Whatever care she might take to conceal
these austerities, the servants perceived them : her
mother feared she might go too far, and to restrain
her ardour, obliged her to sleep in her own room.
To the fervour of her daughter this was a mortification greater than any she had practised ; but she
sacrificed all her good desires to obedience. God
supplied these austerities by pains of a different
nature. Besides a violent pain in the side with
which she was seized, and which she long endured
without making it known, there broke out such
terrible ulcers in her legs that she was unable
to conceal them. But being ingenious in procuring sufferings, she profited by this to obtain
leave from her mother to sleep in her room alone.
Her object was to be at liberty to take up again her
old practices of austerity. She did so, and took no
care to apply remedies to the disease from which she
suffered. In answer to her mother's earnest entreaties, she replied, " Be assured, my dear mother, that
it is God who has sent me this little suffering, and
He will Himself remove it without human remedies.
And," she added with much humility, " God, seeing
that I should not make a proper use of this trial,
has so spared me, that I do not feel so much pain
as you would suppose from appearances ; for if I

suffered much, I should be weak enough to show it."

These words neither satisfied nor persuaded her mother. To her entreaties she added commands, and insisted on her daughter's trying some remedy. The surgeon who was consulted gave no hope of a cure. It was then winter, and he said that nothing could be done before the spring; all he suggested was to try bleeding and other remedies, which had no effect. Margaret then said to her mother, "You see the utter weakness of human remedies. I have obeyed your commands. Remember what I said; God, Who has sent me this light affliction, will cure me before the expiration of another month. To console you in the grief which this little suffering causes you, I will join my weak prayers to yours, and you will obtain from God a recovery which will be no otherwise advantageous, than to make you happy."

The mother and daughter made a novena together. The brother of Sister Margaret, who deposed to this fact, of which he was a witness, does not say what was the object of their devotion; but he relates that the prediction of the young Margaret was accomplished before the end of the novena. Without any remedy her ulcers disappeared, and that so completely, that there were no traces of them left to show where they had been. She was delivered at the same time of the pain in her side. Feeling what God had done in her, she called her mother, and showed her in secret her perfect cure. The mother and daughter prostrated themselves before a crucifix, thanking God for so signal a favour. Then her mother, fearing that fresh austerities would give

rise to new diseases, said, " My dear child, since God
has granted you the restoration to health, which I
have so long prayed for, take care of it that you may
support me in my old age. In His name I ask you
to grant me this satisfaction." " Do not be uneasy,"
replied Margaret, " God will give me strength sufficient to serve you." And during the few years that
Madame Alacoque lived after this time, though her
daughter never ceased to practise the most astonishing austerities, her health was perfect, and her
mother received from her all the assistance she could
hope for.

A fervour so great, and one favoured by such
manifest miracles, ought, it would seem, to have
been perpetual; but it happened otherwise with the
young Margaret. After so many austerities and
graces, with the return of health there awoke within
her once more the love of the world and of pleasure,
and by degrees she gave herself up to her former
amusements. Little infidelities led to greater ones ;
she was not displeased as formerly with the company
of worldly persons, nor did she dislike the pleasures
which offered themselves. The vows which she had
made in her childhood, and that which had procured
her first recovery, seemed by degrees to be effaced
from her mind, or to leave only a slight impression.
Vanity crept into her heart, nor was she insensible
to flattery. The regard that her mother and brothers had for her served to nourish her self-love still
more, and the liberty she enjoyed was only a means
of gratifying her natural love for the diversions of
the world. This change in a person so favoured by
God was something astonishing; but it ought not to
appear so to us, who experience so often, notwith-

standing the abundant graces of God, such strange vicissitudes of fervour and coldness?

To tell the truth, in this state of relaxation the young girl did nothing contrary to the most exact decorum. In the eyes of her family her life appeared holy and edifying, but her soul was not strictly united with God; and He who searches the heart found there vanity, infidelity, dissipation, and love of the things of the world. These faults caused her eventually many tears and much penance, but she did not then feel what an unhappiness it is not to respond to the graces of God, and to what danger one is exposed in giving to the world any portion of a heart that God wishes to possess entirely. One of the greatest faults that she committed at this time, and that she related with much grief, was that at the time of Carnival she permitted herself to be persuaded to accompany her brothers and relations to a masked ball. How many times in the course of her life did she reproach herself for this sin, which the world considers so pardonable! She afterwards acknowledged, that the cause of her having fallen into these imperfections was that she confessed but seldom, for want of some one to whom she could have recourse to aid her in the practice of virtue.

God, Who had resolved to reign alone in that heart on which He had showered so many favours, prepared the young girl by fresh crosses to enter into herself; no longer, however, by bodily suffering, for her prediction was accomplished, but by the most severe treatment and bitter mortification that a young person of her age could possibly experience. To deprive her of that liberty which had been the

2

occasion of her loss of fervour, He permitted that she should be a slave in her own house.

Her mother finding herself overburdened with the care of her family, the education of her children, and the trouble attending the management of a farm, felt obliged to seek assistance, and to entrust some persons whom she took into her house with a share of her domestic affairs. They were of low condition, and taking advantage of the increasing age of their good mistress, and of the confidence she reposed in them, soon exercised an absolute authority over her and her family, and reduced the mother and children to a state approaching captivity. This was the more trying, as these persons were as coarse as they were uneducated. It was difficult to say whether vulgarity or dishonesty predominated in them. Under the pretence of economy they refused the most necessary things both to the mother and the children; they reproached them harshly with those things which they obtained with many entreaties; they exacted from them an unlimited subjection and compliance with all their demands; and under the pretext of serving them faithfully, reduced them to servitude themselves.

Margaret was particularly ill-treated. They could not endure her sweetness, charity, and devotion; they thwarted her incessantly in all her wishes; her practices of piety were the object of the continual raillery and bitter reproaches of these tyrants of her liberty; and though she submitted to them in all things, and used every endeavour to please them, she could never succeed in softening the asperity of their tempers. We cannot better describe her situation at this time than by repeating her own words:

"We had no longer any power," she said, "in our own house, and we dared not do anything without permission. It was a continual war. Everything was under lock and key, so that I could not even dress myself to go to holy Mass without asking for my hood and cloak. It was now that I began to feel my captivity; I yielded to it entirely, and so humbled myself that I would do nothing, not even go out, without the consent of three persons. From that time all my affections turned to seeking all my pleasure and consolation in the Blessed Sacrament of the altar. But being some distance from the village church, I could not go there without the consent of these persons; and if I could find one willing that I should go, I was sure to meet with opposition from another. Often when I showed my grief by my tears, they accused me of having made some assignation, and said it was their duty to put a stop to my hypocrisy in pretending that I wished to go to Mass or Benediction. I, who felt so great a horror of anything of the kind, that I would rather have consented to have my body torn into a thousand pieces, took refuge in some corner of the garden or stable, or in some other secret place, where, throwing myself on my knees, I poured out my heart with my tears before my God, imploring the intercession of the Blessed Virgin, my good Mother, in whom I placed entire confidence. Sometimes I remained there whole days without eating or drinking; indeed this was common with me. Sometimes the poor people of the village, out of compassion, would bring me in the evening a little milk or fruit. When I returned to the house, it was with such fear and trembling, that I was like a criminal who had just received sentence

of condemnation. I should have felt it a happiness
to beg my bread rather than live in this way, for
often I dared not take a piece of bread from the
table. The moment I returned the attack recom-
menced worse than before; and I was reproached
with having neglected my household duties, and the
care of the children of these dear benefactors to my
soul; and without giving me time to say a single
word, they set me to work with the servants, after
which I passed the night as I had passed the day, in
weeping at the foot of my crucifix."

In the midst of these trials, Margaret dared not
complain of those who made her experience them.
She even felt scrupulous of blaming them in her
heart, and in imagining they did wrong in treating
her so harshly. She did not even dare to speak of
their conduct in private with her mother, for fear of
wounding charity; and she went no farther than to
look upon these cruel and unjust persons "as
salutary instruments employed by God to accomplish His holy Will in her." These are the words of
this patient soul. At another time she said, "God
made use of them as instruments of His Divine
Justice, to punish me for the insult I had offered
Him by my sins. They were virtuous persons who
did not think they were doing wrong in so treating
us; I firmly believed so, since it was my God who
thus willed it, and I bore them no ill-will for their
conduct.

Our Divine Saviour recompensed so heroic a
patience by extraordinary graces. All those that
we receive from Him, take their source in His cross;
and to whomsoever He gives a more abundant share
in that cross, He also gives a greater share of His

favours. This was what was experienced by the young and holy Margaret. God had afflicted her when her liberty was a hindrance to her fervour; He comforted her when her captivity taught her a continual lesson of patience and humility. Hear again the simple and ingenuous recital she gave of these singular favours, as well as the admirable lessons which Jesus crucified taught His servant, whom He willed to resemble Him by sufferings and patience :—

"It was at this time," said she, "that my Divine Master disclosed to me, without my comprehending the manner of His doing so, that it was His wish to be the absolute Master of my heart, and to render my life in all things conformable to His suffering life : that He longed to make Himself present to my soul, so as to enable me to act as He Himself had acted in the midst of the cruel sufferings that He endured for my love. From that moment my soul was so deeply impressed by this, that I could have wished my sufferings not to cease for a single instant. After this He was always present to me in spirit, under the form of a crucifix, or an Ecce homo, or carrying the cross. These things made me experience so much compassion for Him, and love for His sufferings, that all my sorrow became light in comparison with the desire I felt to suffer, in order to be like my suffering Jesus. I was afflicted when, as it sometimes happened, the hands which were raised to strike me were restrained, and did not exert their utmost severity. I felt continually urged to render all sorts of services and good offices to these true friends of my soul. I would willingly have sacrificed myself for them, not having any greater pleasure

than to do them good and speak well of them. It
was not I who did all this that I write, and shall
have still to write (much against my inclination ;) it
was my sovereign Master who had taken possession
of my will, and who would not allow me to form any
complaint, murmur, or feeling of resentment against
these persons, nor even permit me to be pitied, or
meet with any sympathy in my sufferings. He told
me that to those who had ill-treated Him, He had
behaved with the like meekness, and when I could
not help others speaking of them to me, He wished
me to excuse them, and lay all the blame on myself;
adding that my sins deserved a much greater punishment."

She spoke also of the state of her mind in the
midst of so many trials. "The only kind of prayer
with which I was acquainted, was that taught me by
my Divine Master, and consisted in abandoning
myself to all His holy movements, whenever I could
shut myself up in some little corner with Him. But
scarcely any time was left for this enjoyment; for
while the daylight lasted I was at work with the
servants, and when evening came I found that
nothing I had done had given satisfaction. They
abused me with such severity, that I had not the
heart to eat; and I retreated to any place where I
could find a moment's peace. I often complained to
my Divine Master, that I feared I did not please
Him in everything, for it seemed to me that there
was too much of my own will in all that I did,
as I found pleasure in mortifications, and I was
afraid I did not act from obedience. 'Alas, my
Lord,' I said to Him, 'give me some one that may
lead me to Thee.' 'Am I not sufficient?' said He

to me one day. 'What dost thou fear? Can a child so loved perish in the arms of her Almighty Father?'"

The sufferings which Margaret endured on her own account were nothing compared with what she felt at seeing her mother so treated by those who ought to have been under her authority. She loved her mother tenderly, and through that tender love and compassion made all her trials her own. "The most cruel of my crosses," said she again, "was the not being able to alleviate my mother's sufferings. They were a hundred times harder to endure than my own. Yet I did not allow myself the consolation of saying a word to her on the subject, for fear of displeasing God by taking pleasure in speaking of our troubles. It was during her illnesses that my trial was the greatest. They gave her up entirely to my poor care and services, and everything being under lock and key, I was often obliged to go out and beg for eggs and such little things required by the sick. It was no little suffering to my natural timidity, to be compelled thus to seek assistance from the villagers, who often said more to me than I liked to hear." These poor people were aware of her life of slavery; and wishing to show their compassion for her, they spoke with severity of the hardheartedness of those who reduced both mother and daughter to poverty in their own house. But these expressions of pity wounded the delicacy of Margaret's charity; she refused to her sorrows that feeble alleviation which would have seemed innocent to another less faithful than herself.

The troubles of the mother and daughter were increased by an illness with which the former was at this time attacked. It was erysipelas in the face; her head was swelled in a frightful manner; the inflammation soon became excessive, and fever ensued. The life of the sick woman appeared in evident danger, but this seemed to be a thing of perfect indifference to the servants, and the uneasiness and anxiety of her daughter was to them a subject of ridicule and reproach. She never went to bed, and scarcely slept or ate; she watched her mother night and day, and yet they complained of her, and her uselessness. All the relief they granted the sick woman was to be bled by a common surgeon, who passed by chance, and who, on leaving the house, when he saw that they were not much inclined to pay him for his trouble, said that his patient could not recover except by miracle. Yet the miracle was granted to the prayers of the young Margaret. She complained to Jesus Christ alone of her sorrow, and being at Mass on the day of the Circumcision, she with simplicity entreated our Lord to be Himself both Physician and Remedy to her poor mother. She was still praying, when an abscess which had formed on the invalid's cheek suddenly burst, and Margaret found on her return a large wound formed by the opening of this abscess. Without experience, advice, or anything to apply to it, she set to work to heal the wound: she cut away the mortified flesh, and put to it what chance, or rather, the goodness of God, suggested, and in a few days she had the happiness of seeing her mother entirely cured.

From the persecution which Margaret had so long borne, she became somewhat relieved when she reached the age of eighteen, but it was only to find herself exposed to another trial, less

grievous, indeed, in the eyes of the world, but more
dangerous to the purity of her soul. It was of such
a nature, that this young girl, who had been so
patient and fervent in adversity, was on the point of
losing all her fervour, and, as she has since acknowledged, was in evident danger of hazarding her salvation, by not corresponding to the grace which
attracted her to God. Her relations and the friends
of her family now thought of settling her in life.
She had several highly desirable offers of marriage;
for although she had little money, her gentleness
and piety, the sweetness of her temper, and her
prudence in domestic affairs, attracted the esteem
and affection of many who hoped to find their happiness in marrying her. By this means much company was drawn to the house, and quite changed
its aspect. Everything was done to give pleasure to
the visitors, and Margaret was expected to contribute by her presence to the general entertainment,
and to enter into all the amusements common on
such occasions. She naturally loved pleasure and
company, and had with difficulty deprived herself of
them, so that it was a very dangerous temptation to
find herself obliged to take part in these amusements. To this was added another, which to her
affectionate heart was a very powerful one.

She tenderly loved her mother, who was not ignorant of the wishes her daughter had formed in her
heart, and was greatly alarmed by them; for she
feared to lose with her her principal stay and resource. From the time of the second miraculous
cure, of which we have spoken, she conjured her in
the name of everything she held most holy, not to
abandon her. "My dear child," she would say to

her, "since God has granted you the health for
which I so long entreated Him, and has spared you
to support me in my old age, I beg of you in His
name not to quit me." In addition to this, she earnestly desired to settle her daughter in marriage,
thinking this to be the only means of releasing herself from the captivity in which she was held, not
having the strength of mind boldly to shake off the
galling yoke under which she groaned. She supposed
that by marrying her daughter she would secure a
home for herself; and that by abandoning the property to her sons, she would at the same time free
herself from all embarrassment. With these views
she pressed her daughter to consent to marry; she
used the most lively solicitations and most tender
entreaties; she mingled tears with her words, and
never ceased attacking the heart of the young girl
in its most vulnerable part. "You witness," said
she, "my sufferings; I have no other hope of ever
escaping from the situation in which I am placed.
Will you refuse me this consolation? If you leave
me I shall die of grief, and you will be the cause of
it."

What cannot affection achieve in a heart that is
capable of feeling it? The reiterated solicitations of
the mother began to make some impression upon the
daughter, and to this temptation the devil added
another still more insidious. He made use of piety
itself to entrap a heart which lived only on devotion.
He presented the religious life to her view as a state
so holy and perfect that it would be presumption in
her to engage in it; he represented to her that this
life demanded a virtue so pure, and a perfection so
consummate, that she could never attain it. "What

art thou thinking of in wishing to be a religious?"
said he to her interiorly, "thou wilt make thyself an
object of laughter to all the world; thou wilt never
persevere, and what will be thy confusion when thou
quittest the habit and the convent! Where wilt
thou hide thyself after that?" She herself thus
relates the thoughts and fears that the tempter suggested. He said to her also, that if she were in
the cloister, she would no longer have liberty to
practise those austerities and works of charity
towards the poor, to which she was accustomed;
that everything in the cloister being regulated by
the will of another, she would not be free to do what
she believed to be necessary to her sanctification.
What made the poor girl's situation the more dangerous was that, in the midst of so many temptations and perplexities, she had no one from whom
she could receive light, or to whom she might make
known her temptations, so as to learn the remedy
for them.

These attacks made but too much impression upon
a heart little used to the stratagems of the demon.
He often transforms himself into an angel of light,
and when his temptations are cloaked with the
appearance of piety, they are only the more seduc-
tive; and with this truth Margaret was now to be
made acquainted. The first effect on her heart of this
temptation was to throw a doubt upon the vow of
chastity, that she had formerly made. It appeared
to her that this vow could not be a strict engagement; that when she made it she was too young to
engage herself knowingly, and that at most a dispensation would be necessary, which could not be

refused to the pressing necessity she was under of assisting her mother.

These thoughts were only doubts, and doubts combated by grace, but from these doubts and this uncertainty she passed to a still greater neglect of duty. She began a second time to enjoy the world and to be pleased with company, and to yield somewhat to the natural inclination she felt towards pleasure. The world pleased her, as she pleased the world, and she took more trouble than formerly about her dress and appearance. She gave less time to prayer, and much more to visiting and to the society of those who sought her company; and these vain compliances were the second step she was led to take on this dangerous road. How astonishing is it to see a young girl favoured by so many graces, drawn to God by such gentle movements of His love, and even by miracles, open her heart so easily to temptation! Let the most fervent souls learn from this to be humble and to distrust themselves.

It was not that Margaret fell into any grave fault, nor that others perceived any relaxation of her piety. If she had not herself revealed her trials, and so humbly confessed her weakness, we should never have known them. Some persons, who frequently saw her at this time, and who were living a few years ago, have testified to the decorum of her conduct, and even to the modesty apparent in her dress, manners, and conversation. "She often retired from company, to perform her pious exercises," says one of these witnesses, in a memoir that he has written of her; "and she employed several little stratagems to get rid of her companions, for fear of being remarked by them. They saw how much she was distressed, when in her presence anything was said which could possibly displease God. On such occasions, she skilfully turned the discourse upon other matters, insensibly and without affectation leading it to something pious, and when worldly subjects were spoken of, she appeared absent, not paying attention to the matter of the conversation. Her modesty in dress," continues the same witness, " was equal to her piety. Her mother left to her the choice of her attire, and Margaret always preferred what was most simple and modest. With respect to the offers she received, she appeared unwilling to accept any, however advantageous they might be; from which it began to be suspected that her taste led her to the religious life."

Thus all that the world saw was edifying. But this well-regulated exterior concealed an inclination for vanity and pleasure, which was not yet subdued. Margaret herself was ashamed of her relapse, her combats, doubts, weakness, and her inclination for the world and its frivolous amusements. These faults, which she afterwards expiated by so many tears, would, without doubt, appear trifling to the daughters of the world, who make dress a matter of duty, and think it becoming to enter into all passing enjoyments with relish. But the spirit of faith judges differently. What in this young girl appeared to the eyes of men to be pious and holy, was not sufficiently holy and pure for the eyes of God. He made His faithless spouse well understand this. He wished to possess her heart entirely, and the smallest attachment to creatures offended

His jealousy; and He punished these faults by interior reproaches, and by the alarms with which her conscience was troubled. He pursued her in the midst of company and diversions, and permitted her to enjoy nothing without a mixture of secret bitterness within her; and that poor soul, which belonged too much to God to dare to quit Him, but too little to satisfy Him entirely, could neither taste in peace the passing enjoyments of the world, nor the pure consolations of divine love.

In this agitation of mind she endeavoured to relieve herself, and at the same time to satisfy both God and the world, by overwhelming her body in secret with excessive mortifications, whilst she gave herself up exteriorly to every amusement which presented itself. She encircled her waist with a knotted cord, fastened so tightly that she could neither eat nor breathe without pain, and she even placed small chains of iron around her arms. In a short time these cords and chains cut so deeply into her flesh, that she could not take them off without the greatest pain. She either lay upon the floor, or strewed her bed with rough and pointed sticks, and often passed the whole night with scarcely any sleep, weeping before the crucifix over her wretched state, and seeking to drown her misery in her tears. While praying she would discipline herself even to blood, pitilessly lashing her weak frame. Thus her days were passed in anxiety and remorse, and her nights in austerities; and these austerities were excessive, indiscreet, and without the merit of holy obedience.

This was not what God demanded of her, neither did she find in all these practices the slightest alleviation of her pain. It is thus that we often deceive ourselves, giving to God what He does not exact from us, whilst we refuse Him the chief thing, the only thing, so to speak, that He requires. Every other sacrifice costs us less than that which God expects of our fidelity, and it is that alone which can work a true conversion and procure for us peace of heart. So it was with this young girl. God did not ask for her blood, but her will. It was not the immolation of her body He then required of her, but the remains of her vanity, her attachment to the world, and the too tender affection for her mother, which still occupied the heart of His faithless spouse.

Yet all unfaithful as she was to the call of God, He did not cease to favour her with singular graces. Sometimes He touched her heart so deeply, that she felt forced to leave her companions suddenly, and fly to some church or secret place, where she might weep undisturbed over her weakness, and mourn before her Spouse. Then He would reproach her interiorly with her ingratitude, and severely reprimand her for her cowardice. These reproaches were like burning arrows, which pierced her heart and gave her continual suffering. She would often throw herself upon the ground weeping, her face buried in her hands, and would end her prayer by a severe discipline; yet the very next day she would return as before to those amusements which gave so much displeasure to her God. One evening, when she had retired to her room, and was taking off the dress which she had worn with some little satisfaction during the day, the Son of God appeared to her, in the state in which He was after His cruel

scourging, His sacred Body bruised, torn, and
bleeding. He told her that it was her vanity which
had reduced Him to this state; that by her irresolu-
tion she was losing time, of which He should exact
a rigorous account at her death, and that she was
betraying Him by her infidelity. He made her
ashamed of her ingratitude, and compared it with
all the proofs of love He had given her, in order to
induce her to make herself in all things agreeable to
Him. These reproaches threw Margaret into a
state of inexpressible grief and confusion, and at the
same time what she had seen was impressed in such
a lively manner upon her soul, that she never afterwards lost the remembrance of it. But as she still
did not break her chains, this only served to augment her tears and interior pains, which were so
great that the rigour she exercised upon herself, and the contradictions she met with in the
house, of which we have often spoken, appeared to
her refreshing in comparison with what she suffered within her own heart. Let those who read
this learn to yield easily to the sweet invitations of
the grace of God, and willingly to sacrifice to Him
whatever He requires of them. We hesitate to do
this only because we dread a little pain, and yet in
this refusal we find greater pain than it would give
us to accomplish the Will of God: we do not
enjoy the pleasure we wished to preserve, and we
lose by this attachment to our own wills the sweet
consolation we should find in pleasing God.

This is what Margaret then experienced, and the
portrait she has drawn of her sufferings excites the
compassion of those who see the struggles that went
on within her heart. In the midst of her resistance

to the divine Will, the fear of offending God and the
horror of sin, with which she had been so deeply
impressed in her childhood, were incessantly before
her eyes; and she believed herself guilty of sins of
which she exaggerated to herself the enormity.
She knew how injurious it was to the Majesty of
God to resist His Will; she felt all the shame of her
ingratitude, and was sometimes astonished, as she
afterwards declared, that hell did not open under
her feet, and bury her alive in punishment for her
unfaithfulness. Notwithstanding this anguish, she
could not yet determine to take a courageous part,
to break her chains at once, and to follow absolutely
and without delay the voice of God.

Margaret bore her grief in silence; her family
were ignorant of it, though they saw that she was
pining away visibly; her mother was uneasy at seeing her grow pale and thin, without being able to
penetrate the cause of it, and her daughter could
not take her into her confidence, nor find any consolation in her counsels. She had not even the
relief of confessing often, not having any confessor
near her, to whom she could or dared open her heart.
She could only groan in secret, pray, and entreat
God to put an end to her struggles, and to place her
Himself in the way of holiness; and even while she
asked this, she feared to obtain what she requested. She often read the Lives of the Saints
for her encouragement, but at the sight of their
generous sacrifices she was disheartened, and despaired of ever being able to imitate them. She
wished to be holy, but she did not wish to make the
efforts that the saints did. Sometimes in taking up
their lives she said to herself, "I will look for a life

3

very easy to imitate, that I may conform myself
to it." She sought in vain; the saints became
saints only by doing violence to themselves, and
sacrificing without reserve all that was most dear to
them.

This was the part that Margaret chose at last.
After much resistance, she resolved to sacrifice
everything to follow the voice of the Lord, and she
formed the design of becoming a religious whatever
it might cost her. It was during holy Communion
that God worked this change in her heart, and filled
it suddenly with the calm which He alone can produce. He made His doubting spouse see that He
deserved to be preferred to all those worldly lovers
who sought her; that He was the most amiable, the
most rich, the most perfect of all the children of
men; and that having promised herself to Him for
so many years, it was strange that she should wish
to break with Him to make another alliance.
"Know," said He to her, "that if thou insultest Me
by such preference, I will abandon thee for ever,
but if thou remainest faithful to Me I will never
quit thee, and I will Myself be thy strength and thy
victory to triumph over thine enemies. I excuse
thine ignorance, because thou dost not yet know
Me, but if thou wilt follow Me, I will teach thee to
know Me, and I will manifest Myself to thee."
These favours were followed by the courageous
resolution that Margaret took of absolutely renouncing every offer in order to follow the voice of God;
and her resolution was followed by an interior calm,
the like of which she had not experienced for a long
time. "It seemed to me," said she, "that heavy
chains were removed from me, or that I was restored

to the light of day, after a long and gloomy night." All that had terrified her in the religious life, now appeared to her as nothing, or as mere trifles which deserved no attention; and the doubts which she had entertained of herself gave place to a tender and absolute confidence in the goodness of God.

To these consolations, which Jesus Christ poured into the heart of His spouse, He added singular favours and new communications. He one day showed her in prayer the beauty of the virtues of poverty, chastity, and obedience, and in what manner the holy engagements taken in religion for the practice of these virtues conduce to true holiness. Another time when she was melted into tears before the Blessed Sacrament, at the sight of the ingratitude she had shown to God, and her long delay to follow His voice, and was expressing to Him her astonishment that so much unfaithfulness had not offended His goodness, He replied, showing Himself to her at the same time to comfort her, " It was that I designed to make thee a compound of mercy and love." Another time He said to her, " I chose thee for My spouse, and we promised fidelity to each other when thou madest Me the vow of chastity. It was I who urged thee to make it before the world had any share in thy heart; but it was thy whole heart that I wanted, unsullied with any earthly affection; and to preserve it such, I took all malice from thy heart, that it might not be corrupted; and then I placed thee as a deposit in the bosom of My holy Mother, that she might form thee according to My designs." The holy soul, who gives the detail of these graces, avows also that she owed to the protection of the Blessed Virgin the coura-

geous resolution which she took to consecrate herself to God in religion. She declared this so deci-
dedly, that her mother did not dare to speak to her
further on the subject, nor even to weep in her presence, though she often did so in secret. Margaret
then asked that all those who frequented the house
to solicit her hand should be immediately dismissed,
and they were obliged to yield to her resolution.
Her brother in vain offered her a share of his property to increase her dowry, and marry her to a man
of condition; she would not listen to him: that
heart, before so tender and so timid, had become
like a rock which the waves dash over on all sides
without being able to injure it.

Then God added to her courage a disgust for all
the vanities and diversions of the world. Her natural inclination was not destroyed; she was still
easily led to innocent pleasures; but far from being
engrossed with them, her heart could no longer find
satisfaction in them. That mournful representation
of Jesus scourged and torn by blows, which had been
so deeply imprinted on her soul ever since the moment
of which we have before spoken, seemed to pursue
her in the midst of these trifling diversions, and to
make her this reproach: "Seekest thou pleasure in
these things? Did I ever seek the like? Thou
seest the state to which I was reduced to save thy
soul and gain thy heart! wilt thou still refuse Me
any portion of that heart which already belongs to
Me?"

The good works to which she consecrated herself
whilst waiting to put her design into execution,
were the proof of her victory and the fruit of her
fidelity. She was particularly attracted to the prac-

tice of two virtues, which served as preparation to the religious life. The first was a great charity towards her neighbour, and especially the poor ; she conceived so tender an affection for them, and so lively a compassion for their sufferings, that she found no pleasure but in visiting them, taking care of them and assisting them, and she would have wished to have no other employment, no other conversation. She would willingly have deprived herself of everything she possessed in order to succour them, and not being able to do more than distribute amongst them the little money left at her disposal, she consecrated it entirely to their service, and thus began to practise the virtue of poverty.

She carried her views still farther. In the assistance she afforded the unfortunate, she endeavoured to join the spiritual alms of instruction to corporal alms, and to make the one relished through the other. She attached herself particularly to those forsaken little children who are ignorant of God, who know only how to beg their bread, and to whom religious instruction would be more necessary than alms. She attracted these little ones by the hope of charity, assembling them in her house and teaching them to know God, to pray to Him, and to fear to offend Him; and she endeavoured to kindle in their little hearts some sparks of the Divine love with which her own was consumed. This charitable care drew forth new contradictions on the part of those imperious and capricious persons of whom so much has been said. They complained incessantly and bitterly of the inconvenience caused by these children. Under pretence of economy, they took pleasure in putting

obstacles in the way of Margaret's pious designs.
They reproached her with giving to these children all
that she could get. In this they were deceived; her
prudent charity, and the delicacy of her conscience,
would not allow her to take anything furtively,
under pretence of alms-giving. So far from it, she
did not even give to the poor what was her own
without the permission of her mother, which she
invariably asked. Sometimes she met with a refusal,
but this did not discourage her. She waited quietly
for a little time, and then returning gently to the
charge, using that address and those caresses which
charity inspired, she obtained for the poor all the
favours she had asked.

These pious exercises increased her charity, and
led her to make further efforts. She began to comfort and visit the sick, and to dress the wounds of
the poor. The desire of conquering herself influenced
her as well as the motive of charity, for she had a
great repugnance to seeing and handling wounds.
But remembering the interior combats from which
she had been so lately delivered, the fear of being
unfaithful to grace made her resolve not to listen to
her natural inclinations or repugnance, and to mortify them on every occasion. Although she could
not see a wound or an ulcer without becoming faint,
in a short time she ventured to kiss them, and afterwards it cost her nothing to dress them. She did
this as well as she could, for she had neither experience nor remedies of any kind; at most she was
acquainted with those little prescriptions which
are known to simple country people, but her
faith and charity supplied everything, and God
blessed her endeavours so abundantly that these

poor people were soon cured, and believed they owed
to her that health which they would scarcely have
recovered under more scientific treatment.

The second virtue which her Divine Director inspired her to practise, in order to prepare her more
particularly for the religious life, was an exact and
universal obedience towards all those who had any
authority over her, even those rude and imperious servants who usurped an authority over her, and made it
almost intolerable by their vulgarity. "My Divine
Master," said she, "impressed in my soul so great
a fear of doing my own will, and of following
it in anything, that I thought whatever I did would
only be agreeable to Him through obedience. This
gave me a great desire to do all my actions through
obedience and love, yet I knew not how to practise
either." Truly she only knew what her Divine
Master had taught her Himself, but He had taught
her to practise obedience in a most sublime and perfect manner. She excepted nothing from the laws
of obedience; she submitted to every one, and
obeyed even those whom she was entitled to command. "I would do nothing," said she, "without permission, not only from my mother, but from all with
whom I lived, and to whom I subjected myself. It
is true this was often a severe trial to me," (without
doubt, because of the contradictions that her charity
met with, and the ridicule her humility drew upon
her,) "but," continued she, "I thought it my duty
to submit to all those whom I felt the greatest dislike to obeying." It is easy to imagine how much
torture and constraint such universal and implicit
obedience would draw on her. The servants took
advantage of it to arrogate to themselves still more

authority over her, and delighted in opposing her, even in the most just and reasonable things. This would have been to others a reason for throwing off so grievous a yoke, but the faithful disciple of Jesus, "obedient even unto death," thought only of pleasing Him and conquering herself; and in these two motives she found wherewith to render even contradiction amiable. She wished, besides, to exercise herself in the first of those virtues belonging to the state she was so anxious to embrace, namely, universal obedience; and she understood already what so many old religious comprehend with difficulty, and still less practise, that he has not the spirit of religion who sets bounds to his obedience, and releases himself from the yoke of his superiors, under pretence of this yoke being too heavy, and that they abuse their authority.

Margaret thus prepared herself to consecrate her liberty to God in the cloister, and her family became at length reconciled to her resolution. The only question now was, what house she should choose for her retreat. One of her uncles, who was also her guardian, invited her to Macon, where she met with a cousin, who was in the Ursuline convent of that city. This sister, who was full of high esteem for her own state and love of her community, learning from the young girl the desire she felt to become a religious, thought it her duty to persuade her to enter that convent. With this object she used all the entreaties, kind offices, and tenderness of which she was capable, and engaged their common uncle to join her, and exert the authority which his relationship and age gave him over his young and docile niece. The nun even offered to divide with her the pension that her family had agreed to pay, and to persuade the community to dispense with a fourth part of the portion they were accustomed to receive with postulants. Margaret could with difficulty resist these solicitations. Her friendship for so kind a relation, and her respect for him whom she obeyed as her father, made her lean towards this convent, yet no interior attraction induced her to remain there. She seemed to hear a voice in the very depths of her soul, which said, "It is not here that I would have thee stay." She was faithful to that divine voice, and fearing to mix human motives with the holy resolution she had taken, she said to her cousin, "If I enter your house it will be for the love of you; I wish to go where I have neither relations nor acquaintances, that I may be a religious from no other motive than the love of God."

The same interior voice which removed her from this convent, inspired her with an inclination for the order of the Visitation of St. Mary, and her Divine Spouse made her feel that it was there He would wish her to remain. She knew no house of the order; she hardly knew the name of this Congregation, but she judged that an order which bore the name of the Holy Virgin must be particularly devout towards the Mother of God; and she conceived that in entering it she would find the opportunity of consecrating herself to her service, whose powerful protection she had so often experienced. Her uncle suspected her design; and whether from prejudice, interest, or some antipathy, he determined, as did all her other relations, to prevent her from putting it into execution. In her presence they gave frightful descriptions of this institute; they related tales con-

cerning it well calculated to discourage a young
person: they ridiculed its practices in a way that
would have disgusted a heart less constant and
faithful. They took especial care to prevent her
going to see the convent of the Visitation at Macon;
and as Margaret concealed her inclinations, and perhaps her uneasiness, by a profound silence as to her
views, her uncle thought that they were either weakened or changed; reckoning also that his authority
over a ward always docile to his wishes, would put
an end to her determination, and settle her choice,
he himself took the necessary measures for her
reception by the Ursulines; he agreed about her
portion, and regulated her pension, not doubting but
that his wishes would be acquiesced in.

The embarrassment of poor Margaret was very
great. She saw these proceedings, and dared not
interpose. She feared on one side to be unfaithful
to the voice of God; on the other she made a scruple
of failing in deference to the will of her guardian;
and in this state of uncertainty she was nearly compelled to enter into the Ursuline order. How blind
are those parents who wish to decide by their inclination or their prejudice, the destiny of children
confided to their care! What obstacles do they not
often place in the way of their perfection by mere
human views! Margaret had recourse to God in
this difficulty, and He delivered her by His providence. They urged her to enter the convent of the
Ursulines, under the specious pretext of trying if
this house was suited to her; but suddenly they
learned that one of her brothers was ill, and that
her mother was still more so. This news interrupted
all their proceedings: she was obliged to return

immediately, and travel all night to be as quickly as possible with her sick mother, who was cured by her presence. The illness was caused by grief for her absence, and her return brought health and joy with it. Margaret remained for some time with her mother to take care of her, and though the sacrifice she wished to make was thus delayed, yet the time was not lost for her.

It was in the year 1669, or thereabouts, that she received the Sacrament of Confirmation from the hands of Mgr. John de Meaupou, bishop of Chalons-sur-Saone, who then visited Veroure. To the name of Margaret she added that of Mary, as a new inducement to honour more particularly the most Blessed Virgin. The effusion of the Holy Spirit into a soul so well prepared to receive Him, increased her fervour, and the desire she felt to consecrate herself to God.

She already regarded herself as a victim dedicated and set apart for sacrifice; in this spirit she redoubled her austerities and prayers, and felt her ardent love of God and her desire of pleasing and suffering for Him increased within her. The Carnival was kept some months after this. These days of pleasure were passed by her in severe penance; she fasted, as much as she could without being perceived, on bread and water, and gave secretly to the poor what was intended for her meals. Every day she disciplined herself with so much rigour as to bathe herself in blood, and was deeply afflicted when she thought of the outrage done to God in these days of licentiousness by the sins of men, who think everything is permitted to them at such a time. She was desirous to expiate these faults, in which

she had no share, and would willingly have cut herself in pieces, if we may use the expression, to repair
by her love and penance the injury done to Jesus
Christ at this season of debauchery. Lent succceded, and was passed in the performance of the
same austerities.

These severities took their source in the lively desire which Jesus Christ had impressed on the heart
of His spouse, to imitate the suffering life He led
upon earth. This desire was so intense, that all her
austerities, and the contradictions she met with from
others, seemed as nothing, and could not satisfy her
ardent love of suffering. Sometimes she would say
with transport, throwing herself at the feet of her
crucifix, "My dear Saviour, how happy should I be
if Thou wouldst imprint in me the image of Thy
grief and Passion!" "That is what I mean to do,"
replied her Divine Spouse, "provided that thou dost
not resist Me, and on thy part correspondest with
Me." We shall see in the sequel how this promise
was accomplished, and how He satisfied the desire of
His spouse. What occasioned her more pain than
either penance or contradiction, was the little facility
which she had for approaching holy Communion.
This was an additional reason for wishing to enter a
convent. Such is ordinarily the effect of Divine
love on a heart which is inflamed by it. It produces
an ardent desire to be more closely united by the
Holy Eucharist to Him, Who is in this adorable
Sacrament, only to prove and communicate His love.
Such were the thoughts of the fervent Margaret;
but those who exercised an absolute dominion over
her, took upon themselves to regulate her devotions,

and abusing her docility, forbade her to approach
the holy table so frequently.

Not daring to fail in the obedience she had prescribed to herself, she was eager to derive at least
from those communions they allowed her all the
fruit she could. The days she approached the holy
table were to her days of joy and consolation, which
amply repaid her for all her sufferings. From the
preceding evening, the mere thought that she was
soon to receive Jesus Christ filled her soul with
transport, and scarcely left her sufficient liberty and
attention of mind to perform the work exacted from
her. " On the eve of communion," said she, " I felt
myself lost in so profound a silence, that it was
doing violence to myself to utter a word, so deep a
sense had I of the greatness of the action I was
about to perform. When it was over I could
have wished neither to eat nor drink, nor see any
one, nor speak, so great was the consolation and
peace that I felt within me. I concealed myself then
as much as possible, that I might learn in silence to
love my Sovereign Good. He pressed me to return
love for love, but I thought that whatever I could
do, I should never be able to love Him if He did not
teach me to pray." Nothing more clearly shows the
vehemence of holy love, than this desire of loving
God, this fear of not loving Him, or of not loving
Him enough, this eagerness to learn to love Him
more. Divine love is that wisdom of which the
Scripture speaks : " They that eat Me, shall yet
hunger ; and they that drink Me, shall yet thirst."
(Eccles. xxiv. 29.)

The tender and ardent love of this young girl
caused her another trouble, which was a fresh mark

of the purity and liveliness of her devotion towards
God. She began to see more clearly that the purest
and most agreeable sacrifice that we are able to offer,
is that of our own will. Upon this principle she no
longer set any value upon anything that was not
regulated by obedience, and this became a source of
great uneasiness to her. She had a scruple as to
the enjoyment she found in prayer, abstinence, and
mortification. She feared that she did not please
God in thus following her own will. This made her
ardently desire, whilst waiting for her entrance into
religion, to find a guide to whom she could submit
herself, and by whose direction she might regulate
her actions. She desired this no less from another
motive. She hoped that a director would teach her
to pray; for she believed she could not pray, though
she already did so in a sublime manner. She asked
this favour of God with great urgency, and having
been long deprived of such assistance, she attributed
this to her faults. "Ah! Lord Jesus," she said
tenderly, "give me some one to conduct me to
Thee!"

He granted her a part of what she desired with so
much humility. A religious of the order of St.
Francis, of eminent piety, passed through Veroure,
and at the entreaty of the inhabitants, stayed there
for some time. The jubilee granted by Clement X.
in the year 1670, upon his elevation to the pontifi-
cate, had just awakened their devotion. Every one
was anxious to receive the benefit of it, by a general
confession to this good Father, whom they justly
regarded as a very holy man. Margaret prepared
herself for this duty with a care corresponding to
her fervour. It was with the most intense bitterness

of soul that she reviewed all the years of her past life. Each of her infidelities to divine grace appeared to her a crime, and one which ought to be expiated by the most poignant sorrow. Her tears never ceased to flow, and yet she complained of not weeping enough. What a reproach to us who find ourselves dry and insensible in the tribunal of penance, in presence of the great sins of which we accuse ourselves, whilst the purest souls are penetrated with the most lively grief! That which proves still more the vehemence and sincerity of the contrition of this fervent penitent is, that instead of experiencing that weakness so common to penitents who would wish to hide their sins, and who with difficulty can resolve to accuse themselves unreservedly in the secrecy of the tribunal, she would have sincerely wished to publish her faults to all the world, that she might feel the shame and confusion of them.

It gave her much affliction not to discover in herself the numberless crimes she believed she had committed. This she thought was an effect of her blindness which made her ignorant of her sins; to remedy this pretended blindness which she imputed to herself, and to escape the danger of omitting anything in her confession, she determined in the simplicity of her heart, to accuse herself of the greater part of those sins which she found described in the books used preparatory to confession. She mentioned all these sins as if she had committed them, saying to herself, "Perhaps I am guilty of them without knowing it, and even if I have not committed them, it is just that I should have the shame of accusing myself of them, to satisfy the justice of God for so many other sins

which have escaped my notice." The confessor soon
perceived his penitent's simplicity, and obliged her
to omit these false charges, explaining to her that
the accusations of a penitent ought to be simple and
sincere, without exaggerating or diminishing his
sins. The advice of the confessor was a new subject of humiliation for her; she grieved deeply
before God for this fault, fearing she had displeased
Him on this occasion. But our Lord took care to
appease her scruple Himself, telling her that He
forgave everything to a will free from evil intention.

This good religious gave his attention for some
time to the conduct of a soul which appeared to him
so highly favoured by God. He instructed her in
the method of mental prayer; he gave her much
excellent advice upon the state of her soul, and left
her full of consolation and peace. He rendered her
another service, in persuading her family no longer
to oppose her desire of entering into religion. He
made her mother and relations see the fault they
were committing by putting obstacles in the way of
her wishes. His counsel had its effect, but they still
wished to place her in the Ursuline convent. Margaret was not alarmed at these fresh attempts; she
had addressed herself to the Blessed Virgin, to
obtain a deliverance from these importunate solicitations, and she had been assured in prayer that she
should obtain the liberty she desired. This promise
strengthened her resolution, and when her brother
spoke to her one day on the subject of the Ursulines,
she resolutely replied, "No, that shall never be. I
will go into a convent of the nuns of St. Mary, that
is a long way off, where I shall have no acquaint-

ances.. I wish to be a religious for God alone ; I wish to quit the world entirely, to hide myself in some corner where I may forget it, and be forgotten by it for ever."

She did not then know either the town of Paray-le-Monial, or the monastery of the Visitation in that place. She had there neither relation, acquaintance, nor connexion. She heard this house, which is in the same province of Charolois, spoken of, and she immediately thought of retiring thither. Accompanied by one of her brothers, she went to Paray to present herself to the convent. No sooner did she enter the parlour, than she felt a most lively attraction for the house. Her Divine Spouse said to her interiorly, " It is here I would wish thee to remain." The idea of having found, after so many struggles and delays, what she desired, inspired her with such a transport of joy, that some of the sisters were surprised, and feared that her gaiety proceeded from levity and dissipation. But the Mother Margaret Jerome Hersant, who was then superior of the house, judged differently. She was a religious of consummate virtue and prudence, and had been professed in the convent of the Visitation in the Rue Saint Antoine at Paris ; while her reputation in the order had induced the nuns of Paray to elect her as their superior. Her heart was burning with an ardent love for God, and she had received from Him a rare discernment of spirits. She soon discovered that God had prepared a treasure for the house of Paray in the person of the postulant, and was no less desirous to receive Margaret on trial, than she herself was to be admitted.

Some little delay was still necessary ; Margaret

4

was to return to her family, to set her temporal affairs in order, to take leave of her mother, and receive her blessing. Never was there so much tenderness, desolation, and grief on one side, and on the other so much firmness, as was seen in this separation. Her good mother was bathed in tears, and could not speak; her relations and all the members of her household wept with her; and her daughter, formerly so easily moved, was like one of those large trees that the winds and storms attack on every side, whilst it remains unshaken, because its roots are deeply planted in the soil. With a serene countenance, on which joy was depicted, she embraced some and consoled others, and made all feel that grace alone was the source of her firmness and courage. She at length departed, with the joy of a captive who, released from slavery, returns to the house of her husband, to enjoy his presence, to share in his riches and glory, and to give herself up in freedom to all his affection and tenderness.

The pleasure she then experienced can only be thoroughly understood by those who, like her, have tasted the happiness of consecrating themselves courageously to the service of God. Yet this joy, so lively and so pure, suddenly disappeared, when she was about to enter the convent. Satan made a last effort to trouble or delay a sacrifice he had so long endeavoured to prevent. The young girl was suddenly seized with a secret but strong impression of horror and terror, so that her whole frame trembled. Whatever she had formerly heard against the Institute of the Visitation, now presented itself to her mind. All the repugnance she had formerly felt, her interior pains and struggles, again assailed her; but she who had courageously triumphed over natural tenderness, triumphed also over this new effort of the enemy of our salvation. She rose above these vain terrors, and at the very moment she entered the house, she felt all her peace of mind return. She said with the prophet, " The Lord has broken the bonds of my captivity; He has clothed me with the garment of praise. It is here that He wishes me to dwell, and to be the place of my rest for ever."

BOOK II.

HER ENTRANCE INTO RELIGION, AND THE VIRTUES WHICH SHE PRACTISED IN THE CLOISTER.

It was on the 25th of May, in the year 1671, that Margaret Alacoque entered the convent of the Visitation of St. Mary, at Paray-le-Monial in the Charolois, when she was about twenty-three years of age, and began her probation. She was placed under the care of Mother Anne Frances Thouvant, mistress of the novices, who possessed a rare and solid piety, and a strict fidelity to the practices of her rule, and to the smallest duties of her state. She had already been superior, and her merit caused her in the sequel to be elected again. One of the most remarkable of her good qualities was a particular talent for fortifying souls under difficulties, and she had also a spirit of discernment which could distinguish readily and with certainty between that which proceeded from God in the conduct of souls, and that which

was only the effect of illusion, or of those passing
fervours which have no other foundation than imagination or self-love.

Under the eye of so enlightened a mistress, the
young postulant made that progress in virtue which
might be expected from one of her fervent spirit.
From the first God had engraved deeply on her
mind this idea, the impression of which was never
effaced as long as she lived, viz., that a religious
house is a holy place; that those who inhabit it are
destined, not to serve God with a common degree of
virtue, but to become true saints; and that, in
order to become such, they must renounce themselves and sacrifice their entire will without reserve.
The people of this province corrupted the name of
the daughters of the Visitation into that of the Saint
Maries. Margaret took this literally, and thought
they were thus named because they were all saints,
and being ashamed that she was not yet a saint, she
conceived that if she did not become one, she should
be wanting to her vocation. This idea of acquiring
sanctity was always uppermost in her mind, and she
used it on every occasion as a decisive argument for
overcoming the natural repugnance which stood in
the way of her perfection.

Though her Divine Spouse continued to favour her
with the same graces and supernatural communications with which He had before honoured her, it
was with this difference, that formerly He taught
her Himself what she was to do to please Him,
because she was then almost destitute of any external spiritual assistance; but when she had entered
religion, all the instructions she received from her
Divine Master tended only to keep her in depend-

ence and obedience, and to teach her to have no other rule of conduct than the will and orders of her superiors.

During the first days of her retreat, she was often awakened in the morning by a voice which distinctly pronounced these words of the Psalmist: "Dilexisti justitiam, et odisti iniquitatem; propterea unxit te Deus. Thou hast loved justice and hated iniquity: therefore God hath anointed thee." Or these, "Audi filia et vide, et inclina aurem tuam. Hearken, O daughter, and see, and incline thine ear." Or these others, "Thou hast reformed thy path and thy way, O Jerusalem! the Lord will guide thee." She did not understand these words, especially when they were spoken in Latin, but she immediately repeated them to her mistress, with the same simplicity that the young Samuel related to the high-priest Heli what he had heard in the night; and this judicious mistress, recognizing the voice of God, explained to her pupil the sense of the words she had heard, and the fruit she was to derive from them, and taught her as Heli did Samuel, to say with submission, "Speak, Lord, for Thy servant heareth."

The first care of the postulant was to ask her mistress to teach her to pray. She always thought that she did not know how, and was extremely afflicted at her ignorance. This humble demand, coming from a person already raised to so high a gift of contemplation, gave great consolation to her mistress. She saw in this a proof of the simplicity and modesty of a soul highly favoured by God; and, as if fearing to put her hand to a picture which God Himself had begun to sketch, she said to Margaret, "Go, place yourself in the presence of God, and tell Him that it

is your wish to be before Him as the canvass before
the painter." The postulant understood nothing of
these words, but without replying, or even daring to
ask the meaning of what was said, she went before
the Blessed Sacrament to say what she had been
ordered. Whilst she reflected with simplicity upon
the meaning of what had been prescribed to her, her
beloved Lord said to her, "Come, I will teach it to
thee." And He immediately made her understand
that this canvass was her soul, upon which He wished
to paint the features of His suffering life; a life which
was passed in love and privation, in occupation and
silence, in short, in sacrifice even to its consummation. That He would imprint that very same life on
her soul, after having purified it from all spot and
affection for earthly things, and also of love of self
and of creatures, to which her too complying disposition still inclined her. This was the lesson our
Lord taught her, and at the same moment, it seemed
to His disciple, that her Divine Master despoiled her
of all her affections, emptied her heart of self-love,
and illuminated her soul with an ardent desire of
loving and suffering.

From this moment her wish to love and to suffer
became so intense, that it allowed her no repose.
Her thoughts were incessantly occupied in considering how she could fulfil these desires, and how she
could by suffering increase and satisfy her love.
She imagined and invented all kinds of means, but
dared not put them in practice of her own authority.
She proposed her plans with simplicity to her mistress, and endeavoured by earnest entreaties to obtain her permission to practise the austerities she
had devised. She concealed none of her wishes, and

generally performed with great docility whatever her mistress prescribed. It was, in fact, the constant practice of this good disciple, to give an account of everything to her mistress, to obey her implicitly, and to submit to the direction of obedience even the lights she received from God in prayer. Nothing could more satisfactorily prove that the extraordinary things which occurred to her did not proceed either from illusions of the devil, from imagination or hypocrisy, than the simplicity with which she gave an account to her superiors of what passed within her, and her punctual fidelity in executing whatever obedience prescribed. She listened to her mistress as to Jesus Christ Himself, and received her words as oracles; and the principle of this entire confidence and blind submission was the fear she continually felt of being deceived. Whence it arose that though her eagerness to mortify herself and to suffer was so great, yet her desire to obey and to practise implicit submission was still greater.

However, on one occasion, by a subterfuge suggested by a desire of suffering, she resolved to prolong some austerity that had been permitted her farther than exact obedience allowed. Although her motive was good, this excess did not please God, who loves the simplicity of obedience better than the most heroic sacrifices. The holy founder of the Visitation, for whom she had conceived a great devotion since her entry into religion, appeared to her to reprove her for this fault. He spoke to her severely, and uttered words which remained deeply engraved in the heart of the postulant, who repeated them afterwards to her mistress. " What!" said he, " do you think to please God in passing the limits of obe-

dience? Remember, that obedience is the chief virtue
of this Congregation, and not austerities."

After three months of trial and fervour, Margaret
was admitted to receive the holy habit of religion as
a novice on St. Louis' day in the same year, 1671.
This was to her a day of rejoicing and blessing, both
on account of the transports with which her soul
was inebriated, and the singular graces with which
God favoured her. She was obliged to give an
account of them in writing, and the following is a
part of her relation: " Our Lord," said she, "manifested to me that this was the day of our spiritual
betrothal, that this engagement gave Him a new empire over me, and that I contracted also at the same
time a double engagement of loving Him with a love
of preference. He afterwards caused me to understand that He wished to make me taste all that was
most delightful in the sweetness of the caresses of His
love. From this moment His divine caresses were
so excessive, that they often carried me, as it were,
out of myself, and almost made me incapable of
exterior actions; and this was a subject of such
strange confusion to me, that I dared not appear in
public." The reason was that these supernatural
and ravishing effusions of the graces of God appeared in her outward conduct, and began from this
time to be remarked in the house.

Our Lord told her also at the same time, that she
must make a solitude in her heart, and that He
would come and keep her company, and teach her to
love Him. She endeavoured, therefore, to shut herself up in this kind of retreat, and to entertain herself with God whenever her employments did not
compel her to leave it; and besides the usual times

of prayer prescribed by the rule, she devoted to it
all the time that the other exercises left free. These
prayers, in which she enjoyed an admirable repose in
God, occasioned her also some trials.

In the first place, she found a great difficulty in
presenting herself before God to pray in the manner
her mistress had prescribed, and often she could not
apply herself to the matter which had been given for
her meditation. Her heart, from the beginning, was
as it were laid hold of by the presence of God, and
this presence, which filled her soul, rendered her
incapable of anything but loving and desiring to
suffer for Him. At other times she found herself
deprived of these impressions of love and tenderness,
and of the consolation with which these feelings
filled her heart, and feeling unable even to keep
herself in the presence of God, she lovingly complained to her Beloved of the strange changes which
she experienced, and told Him of the distress that
these different dispositions caused her. He showed
her that this uneasiness arose from seeking herself in
the consolations she enjoyed, that He still saw in her
too much curiosity, and that this curiosity put her
in danger of going astray if she did not correct it.
He told her that for Him to fix His dwelling in a
soul, He required an understanding without curiosity, a mind without self-judgment, a judgment
without self-will, and a heart which aspires to no
other movements than those of His love. He added
by way of reproach, " If I would have thee in My
presence deaf, blind, and dumb, oughtest thou not to
be content ?"

Our Lord then began to shew His spouse more
distinctly that we were to suffer, and to be an image

of His crucified life. On All Souls' day she was deeply penetrated with grief in considering the many ways in which she believed she had abused the favours of God, as well in the use of the Sacraments, as in the practice of prayer; for she always thought herself ignorant and but little advanced in this holy exercise; besides which, she saw in herself and in all her actions nothing but infidelity, ingratitude, and abuse of grace. Desiring then to expiate the many faults of which she believed herself to be guilty, she offered herself to God, to be in His sight a holocaust of sorrow and expiation. Our Lord appeared to accept her sacrifice, and said to her, "Remember it is a crucified God Whom thou desirest to espouse; for this reason thou must conform thyself to Him by bidding adieu to all the pleasures of life, for henceforth there will be none for thee which will not be connected with My cross." He afterwards placed before her eyes His Sacred Humanity attached to the cross for the salvation of all men, and He desired her to attach herself from that time to the cross which He prepared for her. "It will be so hard," added He, "that if thou art not supported by My all-powerful arm, it would be impossible for thee not to give way."

The novice gave an account of all these things to her mistress with her usual simplicity; but though this enlightened religious could not help recognising the hand of God in all that she heard, yet she was alarmed at these extraordinary communications, because she feared they might make the young novice depart from the spirit of the Institute, which wisely treads the more common ways. She consulted the superior, and both declared to the novice, that if she did not renounce these extraordinary ways, they could not receive her to make her profession. They required from her that she should confine herself to the ordinary method of prayer, and that in making it she should reject every other thought and light. The novice made efforts to obey. She regarded the fate with which they threatened her as the greatest of all misfortunes, and besides, she feared being under a delusion. We may judge what was her anxiety and trouble in this condition. She could not pretend not to know the voice of God, which had conducted her from her childhood, and yet through obedience she turned away her mind from all the lights she received, and made all the efforts of which she was capable, to subject and limit herself to the methodical acts prescribed to her.

The superior employed another expedient, either to distract her mind from those interior lights, which often enraptured her in spite of all efforts, or to try if her prayer proceeded from God. She placed her as assistant to another sister in one of the busiest offices of the house. The sister was told to make her work incessantly, scarcely to allow her any relaxation, and to occupy her particularly during the time of prayer. The docile novice obeyed with all simplicity. They only permitted her to hear the subject of the meditation read with the companions, and she was then sent to sweep the house till Prime. When she afterwards asked permission of her mistress to make at some other time the hour of prayer she thought she had lost, she was severely rebuked, and told that she ought to make her prayer while at her work; and to try her fidelity, she was expected to give an account every day of the prayer she thus

made. She gave this account with the utmost simplicity, and at the same time discovered to her mistress the joy she felt at being thus rebuked and contradicted, and how much it pleased her Divine
Spouse. She expressed her joy and satisfaction in
a kind of poetry that she made with great facility,
in the uncouth rhyme of which she depicted in a
lively manner the dispositions of her soul :

> " Plus l'on contredit mon amour
> Plus cet unique bien m'enflamme.
> Que l'on m'afflige nuit et jour,
> On ne peut l'ôter à mon ame.
> Oui, plus je souffre de douleur,
> Plus mon Dieu s'unit à mon cœur."

They tried her with no less attention and severity
with respect to the practice of mortification. Her
eagerness to suffer led her incessantly to ask permission of her mistress to practise some austerity,
which was almost always refused; but in place of
the penances she wished to practise, they ordered
her others so humiliating and so contrary to her
very sensitive nature, that she had need of all her
courage to support her in the violence she did to her
feelings, though she never gave any outward sign of
what she endured. She called her Divine Master to
her assistance. "Alas, my Lord!" said she to Him,
"come to my aid : Thou art the cause of my trouble." "Acknowledge," said He to her interiorly,
"that thou canst do nothing without Me. I will
never fail to assist thee, provided that, lost in the
sentiment of thy nothingness and weakness, thou
ever leanest upon My strength."
She particularly felt the effect of this promise on

an occasion which was very trying to her, and when she would not have been able naturally to overcome the difficulty. She had from her birth an insurmountable repugnance to eating cheese. This kind of antipathy often arises from delicacy or bad habits, but with Sister Margaret it was not only a natural, but even an hereditary dislike, in which all her family had shared from their childhood. Her brother, who feared his sister might be obliged to conquer a repugnance which he knew to be naturally insurmountable, had warned the superiors of it when she entered religion. He told them that all the attempts which had been made during the infancy of his sister had only injured her health, and that when she had been deceived, to make her overcome her dislike, her stomach could not bear that kind of food. He had even carried his precautions for his sister so far as to obtain a promise from the superior and the mistress of the novices that they would never constrain her on this point. However, as they were determined to humble the novice on every occasion, it sometimes happened that the mistress taunted her for not having the resolution to conquer herself upon so easy a matter. It also chanced one day, that in distributing the portions to the sisters, they placed some cheese before her as before the others. She thought that perhaps this was done designedly, and that she was expected to do violence to herself by eating it; instead of murmuring against conduct which might naturally appear to her harsh, she thought it her duty to submit. The very idea of doing so made her tremble, yet she thought it a point of duty to obey and to eat; but her strength

failed her, and she was upon the point of fainting
when she was perceived, and the sisters ran to assist
her.

Though the mistress admired the fervour of her
novice, she appeared to take no notice of it; on the
contrary, she reproached her as if she had undertaken to conquer herself from a feeling of pride, and
had given way for want of courage; and she forbade
her henceforth to undertake such practices without
permission. The humble novice was greatly confused at her weakness, which she attributed to pure
cowardice, and her fervour led her to suppose that it
was her duty to overcome herself on this point,
though it might cost her her life. For three days
she continually reproached herself, but she still felt
the most extreme natural repugnance to this kind of
food, her dislike to which had been increased by the
efforts she had made, and by what she had suffered
in consequence. In this struggle with herself she
had recourse to God, and prostrate before the Blessed
Sacrament, she said to her Lord with many tears,
"Alas! ought there, then, to be any exception to my
sacrifice? Ought not the holocaust to be entirely
consumed? Ought there to be in me any natural
inclination unsubdued? Yes, my God, I must conquer, or die." Resolved to make another trial,
animated with confidence in God, and full of the
thought that love requires the sacrifice of everything, she hastened to find her mistress, and to ask
permission to make another attempt. The mistress
ought perhaps to have refused her; for to attain
perfection it is sufficient to subdue those likings and
antipathies which it is quite possible for us to master; and it is not necessary to overcome natural

aversions which are merely physical, without either sin or danger of any kind. But the mistress believed she ought to encourage the efforts of her novice, either because she did not think the dislike insurmountable, or because she was well pleased that her fervent disciple should be humbled if she did not succeed. But Margaret, more courageous than they had supposed her, vanquished herself entirely. What it had cost her to do so was known by the faintness she experienced the whole of the day, and the violent pains which ensued. She renewed her attempt the next day, and also the following days, with equal dislike and the same result; but her courage never slackened, and during a considerable time she continued to do the same violence to herself whenever occasion offered, without her ever being able to accustom herself to a species of nourishment which her stomach could neither digest nor endure. At length the fear that such violent efforts would seriously injure her health, obliged the superiors, though somewhat late, to forbid her absolutely and for ever to continue the practice. But what cost her so many struggles and so much pain was liberally recompensed on the part of God, by the caresses and favours she received from Him in prayer. They were at the same time so tender and so consoling, that she was constrained to say to Him in the transports of her love, "Suspend, O my God, these torrents that overwhelm me, or increase my capacity to receive them."

About the same time she had to gain another victory over herself, which, though in appearance easier, cost her scarcely fewer struggles than the preceding. Its object was the particular friend-

ship and tender affection she felt for one of the
sisters, in whom she thought she discovered more
virtue and piety than in the others. Those who are
versed in the maxims of spiritual life, are aware
that these particular friendships, which are often
formed from pious and holy motives, are nevertheless contrary to perfection and universal charity.
Our Lord reproached His spouse interiorly for this
friendship which she cultivated. Whether the inclinations of the heart are more difficult to destroy
than the antipathies of the senses, or that God willed
that the novice, by a victory still more marked, and
by more laborious struggles, should be guarded
against a fault to which her tender and affectionate
disposition naturally inclined her, she was certainly
less faithful on this occasion than on the preceding,
for it was three months before she gained the
victory over herself that her Lord required. He
made known to her in the meantime in prayer, that
this affection divided her heart, robbed Him of a
part of that love she owed to Him alone, and put an
obstacle to those graces He wished to bestow on her.
At length she entirely broke this tie, and vanquished
her inclinations for ever, but not until her divine
Master had told her reproachfully, that He cared
not for a divided heart, and that if she withdrew her
affection from Him to bestow it on creatures, He
would withdraw Himself from her.

The time of the noviciate gradually passed away,
and that of her profession approached. To satisfy
herself fully as to the spirit which animated the
novice, the superior multiplied and redoubled her
trials, which consisted principally in trying if her
obedience was absolute and without reserve, and if

her humility was as constant as it ought to be in a person so highly favoured. This is a touchstone by which it may be easily and infallibly discovered, whether such extraordinary lights are from God, or the effect of illusion, a subtle pride, or a weak imagination. When humility and obedience do not eminently adorn the soul, these lights ought to be suspected, however sublime they may appear; on the contrary, where humility without affectation, and obedience without delay, reserve, or murmuring exists, there is the true spirit of God. To these tests the fervent novice was over and over again submitted; but to be more fully satisfied on the matter, they told her plainly that they did not think her fitted for the order of the Visitation; that they feared all extraordinary ways there, because they so often proceeded from error and illusion. Without being disturbed at this reproach, she went in all simplicity to relate it to our Lord in prayer, and said to Him tenderly, "Alas! my Lord, Thou wilt then be the cause of their sending me away." Upon which He replied, "Tell thy superior she has nothing to fear in receiving thee; that I will answer for thee, and that if she considers My guarantee sufficient, I will be thy caution." The novice ingenuously related to the mother-superior what had been said to her. "Well, then," said she, "ask our Lord, as a proof of the security of His promise, to make you useful to the community, by the practice of all its observances." Margaret repeated to her Lord what she had been commanded, and He said to her in return, "Well, My child, I will grant it to thee, for I will make thee more useful to your community than they think, but in a manner known only to

Myself. I will dispense My favours to thee, according to the spirit of thy rule, the will of thy superiors, and thine own weakness. Thou must look with suspicion on whatever draws thee from the exact observance of the rule; it is My Will that thou prefer it before everything else. Moreover, I am content that thou prefer the will of thy superiors to Mine, whenever they forbid thee to do what I shall order thee. Permit them to do with thee whatever they will; I shall know how to make My designs succeed, even by means which may seem in opposition to them. I reserve to Myself the guidance of thy interior, and particularly of thy heart. I have established there the empire of My love, and I will never yield it to any other."

The mother-superior and mistress of the novices were the more satisfied with this assurance, as the effects followed the promise in so clear a manner, that they could not doubt that He who is Truth itself had made it. And when they saw the continual tranquillity of heart possessed by the novice in the midst of the many trials to which she was daily exposed, and her inviolable attachment to the most trifling practices of obedience, they recognized still more clearly the words of God within her.

A trifling occurrence at this time served to show to what a length she carried the simplicity of this obedience, and deserves to be related, as a proof how dear this virtue was to the heart of Margaret. They kept in the convent enclosure an ass with her foal, which were left to graze at liberty, but the novices were requested to watch that these animals did not stray into the kitchen-garden. Our novice took to herself, as if it regarded her alone, the order given to

the community, and set herself to perform this duty
most faithfully. It was no longer in the church and
before the Blessed Sacrament that she passed the
moments of leisure that the ordinary occupations of
the rule allowed, as she had done before; all this
free time was spent in running after these animals,
which gave her plenty of exercise. It was not
wished that they should be tied up, nor inclosed with
hurdles, but that they should be in a certain part of the
garden allotted to them; and as her superiors took
pleasure in seeing how far the simplicity of her obedience would extend, they permitted her to be occupied for a long time every day with these animals,
who escaped her continually, and got into the
kitchen-garden whenever any other business called
her away. During this time, the days of her retreat
preparatory to her profession arrived. As the order
which had been given her was not revoked, she
thought obedience obliged her to the same watchfulness, and that she might perform what she was required
in the retreat, she occupied her thoughts with God,
and communed with Him even while engaged in this
troublesome duty, saying to herself, " Since Saul
found the kingdom of Israel while seeking his asses,
I must gain the kingdom of heaven while running after the like animals." After a day or two
this trial was put an end to, and she was desired to
give an account in writing of her interior dispositions in this humble employment. She thus
describes her feelings: " I was so happy in this
occupation, that I should not have cared if it had
lasted all my life. My Sovereign Lord kept me
such faithful company, that all my running about
did not deprive me of His presence, and I experienced

as much consolation and satisfaction as if I had been
before the Blessed Sacrament; I received greater
graces at that time than I ever had before, especially
in the knowledge our Lord imparted to me of the
mystery of His Passion and death; but this is an
abyss which I am unable to enter into in words. It
is this which has given me such an excessive love for
the cross, that I cannot live a moment without suffering, and suffering in silence, devoid of all consolation, support, or compassion from any one. Happy
should I be if I could die with the God of my soul,
crushed under the cross of opprobrium, humiliation,
sorrow, oblivion, and contempt. In the evening,
though very much fatigued with so much exercise, I
enjoyed so much peace, that my only uneasiness
arose from not loving my God enough, and all
night I was agitated by this thought. One evening, not being able to sleep, (for she already suffered
in silence many infirmities,) and wishing to relieve
myself by turning in my bed, my Divine Master said
these words to me: ' When I carried My cross, I
did not change from one side to the other, to relieve
Myself.' "

In this same relation she gives an account of the
other occupations of her retreat, of her prayers and
the feelings of her heart. We will quote a part of it:
"Every morning when I awake, it seems to me that
my God is present, to Whom my heart is united, as
to its principle, and its only fulness. This gives me
so ardent a desire to go to Him, that the moments
employed in dressing appear to be hours. Most
frequently I go to my prayer with no other preparation than that which my God Himself makes within
me. I generally present myself as a person sick and

languid before a Physician Who is all-powerful, and
without Whom I can neither find rest nor relief. I
place myself at His feet as a living victim, with no
other wish than to be immolated and sacrificed, in
order to be consumed as a holocaust in the pure
flames of His love. I feel my heart lose itself there
as in a burning furnace, so that I seem as if I no
longer had possession of it. It sometimes seems as
if my spirit were disengaged from my body, to unite
and lose itself in the immense greatness of God, so
that I am unable to apply it to the subject of meditation I had prepared. It is content to rest on that
object alone, where it finds such fulness of delight
that it is indifferent to everything else. My understanding is sometimes so dazzled, that no other light
or knowledge pierces it than that which the Sun of
Justice communicates, and then I have no other impression nor inclination than that of loving God. I
am often so much overcome, that I would give my life
a thousand times to prove to Him the fervour which
consumes me. The time of my prayer appears to me
so short, that I cannot help complaining to God,
and saying to Him, 'Beloved of my soul, when will
these moments, which now distress me by their swift
flight, no longer have power to limit my happiness?'
On other occasions I pass this time in suffering with
my suffering Jesus. In this state my heart and understanding rejoice in loving Him; my inferior
nature finds no relish in all this; it neither sees nor
knows what passes in the higher part of my soul.
God then fills me with His Divine Presence in a
sensible manner; He discovers to my soul the beau-
ties of His love; that sight enchains all the powers
of my soul, and holds me so mute in the presence of

God, that I am unable to testify my love by making
repeated acts, which is sometimes a cruel torment to
me.

"Although there is an inexpressible sweetness in
this state, I do not cease making efforts to be
released from it, but all in vain; it appears to me
that our Lord takes pleasure in seeing my struggles
and their futility. I say to Him tenderly, 'Ah, my
God, dost Thou not perceive the ardour with which
my heart seeks and desires Thee?' This is what I
usually do in prayer, not, however, that it is any
work of mine, but that my Divine Master works in
me. I usually conclude without being conscious of
what I have been doing, and without forming any
resolution or request, or making any offering, except
that which I make of my Jesus to the Eternal
Father in this manner: 'My God, instead of thanksgiving for all the benefits Thou hast conferred upon
me, instead of prayers, instead of offerings, instead
of adoration and resolutions, I offer Thee Thy well-
beloved Son; I offer Him to Thee as my love and
my all. Receive Him, Eternal Father, to supply for
all my deficiencies, and whatever Thou desirest of
me, since I have nothing to offer Thee which is not
unworthy of Thee, excepting Jesus my Saviour,
of Whom Thou givest me the possession and enjoyment."

We have not ventured to retrench anything from
this account, for it shows to the life, the sublimity of
Margaret's prayer, the fervour of her heart, and the
abundance of the lights and graces bestowed upon
her by God. For the same reason, and to contribute
to the edification of our readers, we will transcribe

what she wrote down of her resolutions during the same retreat :

"Here are my resolutions, which are to last to the end of my life, since my Beloved dictated them to me Himself. After having received Him in the Holy Communion, He said to me, 'Behold the wound in My side, that thou mayest make there thy dwelling, now and for ever: it is there that thou wilt be able to preserve the robe of innocence with which I have clothed thy soul. Thou shalt live henceforth the life of a man-God: thou shalt live as no longer having life, that I may live perfectly in thee: thou shalt think of thy body and of all which may happen to it, no more than if it no longer existed. For this purpose thy powers and thy senses must be buried in Me, that thou mayest be deaf, dumb, and blind to all earthly things. Thou must will as having no longer a will of thy own, without desire, private judgment, affection, or any wish save that of My good pleasure, in which all thy delight ought to consist. Seek nothing out of Me, if thou dost not wish to insult My power, and to offend Me, since I am willing to be everything to thee. Thou shalt often be delivered up to the fury of thine enemies; but fear nothing, I will surround thee with My power, and I will be Myself the reward of thy victories. Take care never to consider thyself as having a separate existence from Me. Let to love and to suffer blindly be thy motto. One only heart, one only love, one only God.' "

What follows was written by Sister Margaret with her own blood:

"I, a poor and miserable nothing, vow to my God to submit and sacrifice myself to whatever He

desires of me, immolating my heart as a holocaust
to the accomplishment of His good Will, without
any condition but that of His greater glory and His
pure love. I consecrate and abandon to Him all
my being and every moment of my life. I am for
ever bound to my Beloved, as His servant, His
slave, His creature, since He is everything to me.
His unworthy spouse Sister Margaret, dead to the
world. All in God, in myself nothing. All to God,
and nothing to myself. All for God, and nothing
for myself."

These last words must not be taken in a strict
theological sense. Sister Margaret, carried away by
the fervour of her love, seems to have looked in this
prayer more to rhythm and rhyme than to exact
theology. If she said, "All for God's sake, and
nothing for self," it was without excluding the
object of Christian hope, namely, the graces of God
in this world, and eternal happiness in the other,
which we ought to desire for ourselves in every state
of perfection. She only excluded that human motive
of self-love, which in seeking the glory of God, seeks
also itself: Sister Margaret wished to retain nothing of
this. It was in the same sense that she said, "All in
God, and nothing in myself. All for God, and nothing
for myself." She was not ignorant, that according to
the expression of St. Augustine, the gifts of God
become by His grace our own merit; she simply
wished that whatever was in her, might so be of
God, in God, and for God, that vanity and self-love
might appropriate nothing to themselves to the prejudice of His glory.

A virtue so sublime, joined to a constant mortification, a blind obedience, and an exact fidelity, at

length obtained the novice's admission to make profession on the 6th of November, 1672, in the
hands of Mother Mary Frances de Saumaise, of the
Convent of Dijon, who had been that same year
elected superior at Paray. It is well known throughout the order of the Visitation what a high reputation this holy superior enjoyed, and how she governed several convents of the order. Doubtless it
was by a disposition of the Providence of God, that
during the whole of Sister Margaret's life the convent she inhabited was governed by superiors taken
from different houses, in order that the sublime
ways in which God conducted His servant might be
tried in different manners, and by different persons,
all prejudiced, as much as prudence allows, against
extraordinary ways, and all attentive in examining
those of the novice. We shall see in the account of
the remainder of her life with what care and discretion these superiors acted towards her, and in the
end the uniform and unquestionable testimony they
rendered to her high virtue.

If God imparted to Sister Margaret at the time of
her taking the habit the abundance of His graces
and consolations, which we have already related,
those with which He favoured her on her profession
were still more wonderful, and beyond description.
He gave His servant to understand that her cloth-
ing held the place of betrothal in the design He had
formed of taking her for His spouse, and that it was
as His spouse that He now received her at her profession, and in giving her this title He inebriated
her, as it were, with His sweetest consolations. A
less perfect soul would have abandoned herself to
these happy transports of joy, and would have said

with St. Peter upon Mount Thabor, "Lord, it is
good for us to be here." But the holy lover of the
cross of Jesus Christ was alarmed at feeling nothing
but consolation, and even gently reproached her
Divine Master with it; but He showed her that joys
and sorrows have each a time appointed by His good
Providence, that it was His desire she should leave
Him to act according to His Will, and that she
should abandon herself to His conduct without resistance, and with no other view than that of pleasing Him, should she even become the sport of His
love, of which He might dispose as absolutely as
children dispose of the little objects of their amusement. Such was the simple but clear idea that God
impressed on her mind of the dependence and entire
abandonment she was to feel to the Will. of her
heavenly Spouse.

The most signal grace He then bestowed on Sister
Margaret, was that of gratifying her with His Divine
presence in a manner that she had not yet experienced. She saw Him with the eyes of her soul, she
felt Him, as it were, near her. " I knew Him much
better," said she, " than if I had seen and felt Him
with my corporal senses ; for my senses would have
been distracted, and diverted me from that presence ;
but the exterior senses did not divert me from this
interior sight, which occupied my soul, as the presence of a friend attaches and transports those who
enjoy the delight of his conversation."

This continual sight imprinted in her soul a great
reverence for the ever-present God, and produced a
kind of deep and interior annihilation, so that she
regarded herself as if returned to the original nothingness in which she was before His grace had

created her.   To satisfy this feeling, she would have
wished to be continually before her Spouse, either
prostrate, or at least on her knees to adore Him.
When alone in her cell she was always in one or
other of these positions, whenever her employment,
the weakness of her health, or obedience did not forbid it.   Every other posture more agreeable but less
respectful, was a restraint to her, and she never
allowed herself to sit, excepting when she was
obliged to do so in company.

This divine presence usually produced another
effect, equally sanctifying, in her.   The sight of the
holiness of God made her apply herself incessantly
to the discovery of all her weaknesses, faults, and
infidelities.   Her feeling at the sight of her defects,
as visible in the light of God's perfections, was so
keen, that in considering her nothingness, she could
scarcely bear with herself.   The shame and confusion with which she was filled, made her avoid appearing in the presence of any one, except when
compelled by necessity.   She had then all the feeling of one guilty of some enormous crime, who believes that whoever he meets is about to reproach
him with it, who casts his eyes to the ground, and
appears oppressed with shame and fear.   Such was
the state of the humble spouse of Jesus Christ; all
the injuries, reproaches, corrections, or contempt
bestowed upon her, she felt to be just, and she
thought herself worthy of them.   Far from complaining, she experienced a kind of rejoicing in these
things, since what others called punishments just
suited the idea she had of herself, and assisted her
in abasing herself still lower at the feet of Him
before Whom she reckoned herself as nothing.

It is easy from this to form some judgment as to the extent and depth of her humility. It is this virtue which makes saints, and which distinguishes them from those who are humble only in appearance; it is this virtue which is in the saints the cause or the occasion of the most extraordinary graces. Those which Sister Margaret received, however wonderful and miraculous they may appear, served only to increase the low opinion she entertained of herself. So sincerely did she believe that all creatures had a right to treat her with contempt, that she was afflicted at not being sufficiently despised. She asked her superiors in all sincerity to humble her often, and the proof of her good faith in this point is clear, for what she requested was readily granted. In fact, her superiors were always very liberal to her in this kind of favour, in order either to be more certainly assured of the truth of the supernatural favours received by her from God, or to prevent the vanity which these graces might occasion in her. We see by the notes that one of her superiors has left on the subject, that Sister Margaret wished to be permitted to do imperfect and foolish things in the presence of the sisters, that she might draw upon herself reproach and contempt. She would have done this several times, if this enlightened superior had not made her understand that it was contrary to the spirit of St. Francis of Sales, whose precept is, " Do good in the spirit of simplicity, without pretending to be foolish or wise, either to gain esteem, or court contempt."

We may be permitted to pause here for a moment, to entreat people of the world who read these pages, not to speak against those things of which

they are ignorant. They will not believe them because they are above their comprehension, but let
them remember that the wisdom of God is a hidden
treasure, that the human understanding cannot
attain to it, and that the spirit of man cannot conceive what God has prepared for those who love
Him.

Besides, the prodigies of the early life of Sister
Margaret ought to render credible those which follow. She, who before the age of twelve years had
practised the surprising mortifications we have related, who from that time lived in so much purity
and fervour, and to whom in her childhood the heroic
practice of every Christian virtue was familiar, may
she not be allowed at the age of twenty-five to be
raised to an interior life so sublime as to surpass the
understanding of man? It is to disparage the
riches of the goodness of God to circumscribe His
graces within the bounds of our weak capacity.
Let critics first begin to seek God, to know Him
and to love Him, and then, experiencing something
of His heavenly consolations, they will learn to form
a more just idea of those sublime graces which God,
infinite in His liberality as in His other attributes,
prepares for fervent and courageous souls; they will
see that those wonderful communications of which
examples are given in the Lives of Saints honoured
by the Church, are neither impossible to the Lord,
nor unworthy of His goodness. But to return to
the virtues of Sister Margaret.

That profound humility of which I have spoken,
gave rise to the ardent desire she possessed of being
hidden and forgotten by everybody. The first care
she took in entering religion was to forbid herself

the remembrance of all she had left in the world, and to hold no intercourse with it either by letter or conversation. The parlour soon became so irksome to her, that she regarded it as a place of punishment. This repugnance increased in proportion to her union with God; it became at length so strong, that it often supplied matter for most painful sacrifices. Nothing short of an express order from the superior could determine her either to go to the parlour or write a letter. Feeling this extreme dislike, she began to fear lest it might draw her into some act of disobedience; thus, distrustful of herself and of her obedience upon this point, she threw herself upon her knees before God, humbly beseeching Him not to permit her to be wanting in obedience, however painful the commands of her superiors might be to her.

Her horror of the parlour and of all intercourse with the world, was partly caused by the flattering compliments and empty praises that politeness induces men to utter at the expense of truth. Penetrated with a deep feeling of her own nothingness and numberless faults, she thought that all that was either said or written in esteem for her character, was an injury done to truth. Several persons, owing to the reputation of her singular holiness, came to see her, either from curiosity, or to consult her on matters of importance; others wrote to her requesting her advice, and to all this much praise was added. These praises and marks of esteem, which might have given pleasure to other hearts, were to her a grievous punishment and trial. "O my God," she would sometimes say, "rather arm all the fury of hell against me, than the tongues of men with their vain praises and empty applause. Rather than this, let every contradiction and confusion overwhelm me." A religious of another convent having written to her in high terms of commendation, in order to obtain her opinion upon a subject, in Margaret's idea little worthy of the sanctity of the religious profession, she answered her in these words : "My only desire is to be blind and ignorant in whatever regards creatures, and thoroughly to learn this lesson, of which I stand of so much need, namely, that a good religious must leave everything to find God, be ignorant of everything in order to know Him, forget everything to possess Him, and do and suffer everything that she may learn to love Him ; and I assure you, nothing short of obedience could have induced me to answer your letter."

The love of humiliation and of the hidden life sometimes led her to entreat God to efface her from the memory of all creatures, or that He would make her ingratitude, her sins and defects known to the whole world in all their deformity, so that no one might even think of her without feelings of horror and contempt. She particularly asked Him with much earnestness, that He would be pleased to conceal all the favours with which He honoured her, and to make nothing appear but what would lessen her in the eyes of all, and turn to her own confusion. We shall see in the sequel how fully this petition was granted ; and the superior to whom she gave an account of the request she had made to her Spouse, and of the promise she had drawn from Him on this subject, could never cease from admiring the fulfilment of it on those occasions, when what was calculated to procure for her the veneration of the whole world, only served to draw on her reproach and shame.

When obliged to give an account of the singular graces she received from God, either to her superiors in obedience to the rule, or to her confessors in order to obtain their advice, she experienced a great fear lest her recital might attract their esteem, and took especial care to make at the same time a sincere and humble confession of all the infidelities, ingratitude, and sin of which she had been guilty. She obliged to strict secrecy all those to whom she was compelled to make known what passed within her, and exacted from them a promise that they would burn all the letters and writings in which she related the wonderful communications received by her from God. These precautions, however, were generally of no avail; the greater part of her memoirs and letters have been kept by her superiors, for they considered themselves less bound to yield to the humility of Sister Margaret, than to give glory to God and edification to man, by manifesting the singular favours bestowed upon His spouse by her merciful Saviour.

It was partly from this view, and at the same time to examine more closely, and ascertain more certainly, whether it was the Spirit of God which guided Sister Margaret, that one of her directors obliged her towards the end of her life, by an express command, to put into writing an account of all the favours she had received from God from her infancy. It is impossible to express the distress and confusion with which she was filled on receiving this command; her repugnance was so excessive, that notwithstanding her spirit of obedience, she delayed for some time to do what she was required. Our Lord Himself reproached her for this, and when she excused herself by alleging how impossible it was for her to remember all that had passed during so many years, He said, "Knowest thou not that I am the Eternal Memory of My Father, in Whom the future and the past are as if they were present?" And when having begun to write, she still hesitated, He said to her, "Go on, my child; proceed, thy repugnance will make the account neither more nor less. My Will must be accomplished." He at the same time discovered to her His designs in prompting her confessor to issue his command. "It is in the first place," said He, "to show thee that I laugh at all the precautions thou hast taken to hide the profusion of graces with which I have enriched so miserable a creature, and that it is My Will that these precautions should be useless. Secondly, I wish to teach thee that thou oughtest not to appropriate to thyself these favours, which are intended for others also; I wish to make use of thy heart as of a channel, to spread them in other souls according to My pleasure. In the third place, I desire to show that My favours and graces will endure the test of all kinds of examination and trial; and that I am faithful to My promises, the Eternal Truth Who cannot lie." He added also, "Why dost thou refuse to obey My voice, and to write down what proceeds from Me, and not from thyself, as thou art but an instrument in My hands? Consider what thou art and what thou deservest, and thou wilt know whence comes the good that thou possessest."

Sister Margaret no longer ventured to resist the Will of God, but she obeyed with an earnest desire that

6

this recital, from the sincere confession with which it was accompanied, of what she called her crime and abuse of the favours of God, might prevent those who should read it from conceiving any esteem of her character. " O my Lord !" said she "grant me at least the grace to die, rather than relate anything but what may conduce to Thy glory and my own confusion. And oh that Thou woulds not permit this account to be seen by any other than he whom thou wishest to examine it, lest it should hinder me from being buried in an eternal forgetful. ness and contempt of all creatures. Oh my God grant this consolation to Thy poor slave !"

In a letter that she wrote to the same director, who had exacted an obedience so painful to her humility, she thus expressed herself: "I am then obliged, Rev. Father, by your commands, to relate the favours bestowed on me by my Saviour, of which I would never willingly have spoken. Never do I think of them without suffering intense pain at the remembrance of my ingratitude. It would have already precipitated me into hell, if the mercy of my divine Saviour had not disarmed His justice in my regard; and to speak sincerely, I never reflect on these great favours without fearing, that after having deceived myself, I may be also deceiving those to whom I am obliged to speak of them. I beg incessantly of God that He would grant me the grace to be unknown, annihilated, and buried in eternal forgetfulness; I should regard this favour as greater than all those I have already received."

These humble desires were not granted, as we have already said. God has willed that the trea- sures He confided to this holy daughter should be manifested after her death. The papers in her own handwriting remained in the possession of her superiors, and are carefully preserved in the monastery of Paray. In perusing them, we have been struck with admiration at the profusion of graces with which it pleased God to load this holy religious, and also with the care taken by this humble servant of God to make known and even to exaggerate her resistance and her faults. The style of writing, so simple and ingenuous, so humble and full of unction, shows with what spirit this saintly religious was animated. The grace and supernatural operation of God are clearly visible: and even were there no evident miracles worked by God through her, no accomplishment of prophecies uttered by her, nor the constant testimony of so many enlightened persons who acknowledged her sanctity, the style alone of these papers would make the most incredulous feel the heroic virtue of her by whom they were written. It is thus that light manifests itself, and has no need of foreign aid to make its rays visible.

One so humble could not but be perfectly obedient. These two sister virtues, humility and obedience, are inseparable, and Margaret possessed the one in equal perfection with the other. It is through obedience that it may be safely ascertained whether the spirit which conducts souls by ways so sublime is truly the spirit of God, or whether it does not rather proceed from hypocrisy, illusion of the devil, or the imagination of a brain puffed up with pride. Sister Margaret was not spared upon this point. Her obedience was put to all kinds of trials throughout the whole of her life, and remained firm and un-

alterable. Her superiors always found her full of
a blind submission to their will, and a continual distrust of her own illuminations; and if through inad-
vertence she ever failed in obedience, she was always
the first to accuse and humble herself for it, and often
said that nothing appeared to her so horrible in the
house of God as a self-willed religious.

All her superiors, one after another, have given
their testimony to the perfection of her obedience,
and have even thought fit to leave it in writing for
the assurance and information of their successors.
One of them reproaches herself for the too great
severity she thinks she used towards her. She
thought it her duty not to spare her, in order to try
her completely, and avows that she never found the
least resistance in this humble and obedient religious.
The following was written by her after the death of
this servant of God, to a religious of the house of
Paray :

"Do not doubt, my much honoured and loved
sister, that I have sincerely sympathised with you in
the very great loss your dear community has sustained
in the death of a sister that I always regarded as a
chosen soul, and a channel of the graces of God in
favour of souls who are willing to profit by them. I
esteem myself happy that God raised in her heart
so much affection for me. It was neither my mild-
ness nor any favours I ever showed her, which procured me this advantage. I saw that it was our
Lord's Will that she should always gather myrrh,
and to satisfy the desires of this holy soul, who so
ardently sighed for contempt and suffering, as well as
to put her to the proof, I have often given full scope
to her desire for mortification, though my esteem and

compassion were always leagued together against me in my conduct towards her. But in whatever manner I received her confidence and blamed her conduct, never did I see the least feeling contrary to the submission, profound respect, and charitable affection which she believed due to me, not only as her superior, but also as her good mother; and never did I perceive in her a feeling towards her neighbour in the slightest degree opposed to perfect charity, whatever contradiction or mark of contempt she received from them. You know that nothing in the way of trial was wanting to her; God permitting it to be thus for her sanctification. I believe her to have obtained a high seat amongst the blessed in heaven."

It was God Himself who prescribed to His servant this blind, entire, universal obedience towards her superiors. He exacted from her, that she should not only sacrifice her own will, but also her lights and her judgment; and more than this, whatever He Himself commanded, He did not wish to interfere with the ordinary rules of obedience; and He required that she should even submit to her superiors the divine lights with which He had favoured her. Upon this subject she thus writes: "Though my Divine Saviour constituted Himself my Master and Director, yet He did not wish me to obey His commands without the consent of my superior, to whom He wished me to yield, if I may say so, a more implicit obedience than to Himself. What He particularly taught me, was to distrust myself, as the most cruel and powerful enemy I could possibly have; but He promised that if I placed all my confidence in Him, and obeyed perfectly, depending

in all things on the will of my superiors, He would
protect me. Moreover, He forbade me to trouble
myself about anything that might happen to me,
and to regard all the events of life as occurring in
the order of His providence and Will, Who can,
when it pleases Him, turn all things to His glory.
Finding myself engaged in an employment which
often deprived me of leisure to meditate with the
community, a slight feeling of discontent arose in my
mind one Easter-day. I was immediately reproved
by my Divine Master, Who said, ' Know that the
prayer of submission and of sacrifice is more agreeable to Me than contemplation and every other
meditation, however holy it may appear.' This impressed on my soul so deep a feeling of peace, that
from that time I have never been troubled in the
least by anything my superiors required of me."

Another time He gave her this instruction, which
ought to terrify all those religious who neglect obedience, which is the essential virtue of their state:
" Listen well to these words from the lips of Truth.
All religious separated and disunited from their
superiors, ought to regard themselves as vessels of
reprobation, in which the best waters turn to corruption, the rays of the sun of grace producing on
them the same effect as the natural sun produces upon
muddy waters. These souls are rejected from My
Heart. The nearer they endeavour to approach to
Me by the means of sacraments, prayer, and other
exercises, the farther I remove Myself from them,
through the horror I feel towards them; they will
go from one hell to another. Such disunion has
already ruined numbers, and will ruin many more in
the end, since every superior holds My place,

whether he be good or bad. For this reason, when the inferior thinks only of resisting authority, he is covering himself with so many mortal wounds. It is in vain for him to knock at the door of My mercy; he will not be listened to, unless I hear the voice of his superior."

She was never tempted to fail in the most exact obedience, excepting when urged by her intense desire of suffering; then it sometimes happened that her love of mortification led her not indeed to violate the orders of her superiors, but only not to wait their permission before mortifying herself. Her Divine Master again reproved her for this very severely. "Thou deceivest thyself," said He to her one day, "in thinking to please Me by practising this kind of mortification, chosen by self-will, which would rather have the will of superiors bend before it than bend itself. Know that I reject all such things like fruits that self-will has turned to rottenness, for self-will in a religious soul excites My abhorrence. It is more agreeable to Me that such a soul should remain in ease and quiet through obedience, than load itself through caprice with austerities and fasts."

Sister Margaret had not received this lesson when she one day in the beginning of her noviciate ventured to prolong a penance beyond the appointed time. God then said to her as if He were angry with her, "What thou didst at first was for Me, what thou art now doing is for the devil." Another time when doing the same penance for the souls in purgatory, with the same disregard to obedience, these suffering souls seemed to surround her, complaining that she injured them and increased their sufferings by her ill-regulated mortifications. These warnings made her resolve never to pass the bounds of the most exact obedience. The remainder of her life will show how faithfully she kept this resolution.

In order to show the perfection of her obedience, it will be sufficient to add, that she regarded the smallest observances laid down in the rules of the community, as so many laws and precepts, and that from her first entrance into religion until the end of her life, she made it an inviolable law to keep them with the most extreme exactness. Indeed, she succeeded so well, and fulfilled them so completely to the letter, that if it were possible to err in the simplicity of obedience, it might be said that she sometimes carried it to excess. The instant the bell rang, she suddenly interrupted her employment, to obey the order of God, intimated by the sound; and this fidelity, which the ancient fathers of the desert so carefully recommend, and for which they are so much praised themselves, was renewed by Sister Margaret several times in the course of each day. To leave imperfect a half-formed syllable or letter, to cut short a conversation the moment the bell interfered, and many other such little sacrifices, were daily and habitual practices with her. This exact obedience occupied her thoughts so much, that she often forgot to pay that attention to other things which she ought to have done, which omissions drew upon her the frequent railleries of those imperfect religious, who loved to find fault with one whose perfections they could not imitate. Sometimes they also attracted severe corrections from her superiors and those in office, and then she never attempted to excuse or justify herself, but always allowed that she was wrong, and profoundly humbled herself for the fault. Besides which, every humiliation and contradiction which befell her for having practised obedience too strictly, appeared to her more valuable than any other, and she regarded it as a recompense bestowed by God.

Of all the observances of the house, those for which she felt most attraction were silence and poverty. United continually to God, it was more difficult for her to turn away from Him to discourse with her sisters, than it is for a dissipated soul to command her tongue. When she was obliged to converse, it was only of God that she spoke ; it was painful to her to enter on vain and useless subjects. Yet she found even in this holy disposition a motive of self-abasement, and she sometimes said, " From the great talker that I once was, I am now become so ignorant that I know nothing, and cannot tell what to say, and am no longer able to learn anything. Yet," she added, " I desire to learn nothing but Jesus Christ crucified."

As to poverty, she practised it all her life in its fullest perfection. When she entered religion she refused a pension which her relations wished to have settled on her for life, regarding it with horror, as contrary to the spirit of true poverty, and of confidence in the providence of God. She was not satisfied with merely possessing nothing, but believed that it belonged to her state of life to feel and to bear the inconveniences of poverty, and to bear them, too, without complaint. Never was she known to be discontented with what was given her, either in dress, food, or the furniture of her room, but she received with gratitude whatever was provided for her, both in sickness and in health, receiving all as if it were not her due; and when she was in want of anything, she bore the privation in peace, saying that it became the state of poverty to be without the comforts of life, and that the wish of those who of themselves have embraced poverty through love of Jesus Christ, is to delight in experiencing the inconveniences and difficulties of that condition. "It is not to be truly poor," she added, "to make a vow of poverty, and yet to want for nothing." Whence it happened, that when she had freedom of choice, her inclination always led her to prefer the meanest, oldest, and worst, either in dress, furniture, or anything appertaining to her use.

The spirit of poverty made her labour beyond her health and strength, and it was surprising to see that with health so weak, and so great a taste for prayer, she could accomplish all the work with which she was burdened; on this subject the sisters said amongst themselves, that her good angel must do the greater part of her work. The true secret by which she gained her end, was in never losing a single moment when she was not engaged in prayer, always having work of some kind in her hand, carrying it even into the parlour, thinking herself obliged, as a poor person, to gain her living by her labour. To this readiness to do her own work, she added great charity in assisting others in theirs, and sometimes went to offer her services to the sisters in the kitchen, to help them in carrying wood, washing plates, and sharing with them the most fatiguing duties, which practice she observed to the end of her life. Even when she became assistant, she still, when the opportunity presented itself, did the same, and she sought with eagerness this kind of work, stimulated thereunto in an equal degree by the spirit of charity, and by that of holy poverty.

If obedience was a certain proof of the truth of the extraordinary graces received from God by Sister Margaret, an ardent love for Jesus Christ was the fruit of them. This love was tender, generous, compassionate, constant, heroic; in a word, it comprised all the most admirable qualities, and the liveliest affections. This love began, as it were, with her life. We have seen how from her infancy she was captivated with this burning love without knowing it herself; it increased with her years and her different situations in life, and was still more lively and tender when she consecrated herself to Jesus Christ in religion, and when she received the title of His spouse. She fulfilled the duties of this high calling with all the vivacity of feeling and affection of which her heart was capable. We do not undertake to describe them, for the tongue of a seraph would be necessary to speak worthily on such a subject; and her letters and writings breathe those divine transports that could only be described by one who had experienced them in a like degree. Yet she was uneasy even about her affection; she feared that she did not love enough, and afflicted herself before God on this account; she accused herself of it to her confessors and superiors; and all her desires tended only to love God still more, Whose love for us is infinite as His being, and Who deserves to be loved in the same measure as He loves us. Nothing can be more tender or more heroic than the following, which Sister Margaret wrote one day to the director of her conscience: "I know not," said she, "if I deceive myself; but it appears to me, that my greatest pleasure would consist in loving my amiable Saviour with a love as ardent as that of the seraphim; and I should not be distressed, it seems to me, if it were even in hell, so that I might love Him. The thought that there will be one place in the world where throughout eternity an infinite number of souls bought by the Precious Blood of Jesus Christ, will never love this loving Redeemer, sometimes causes me the most excessive grief. I could wish, my Divine Saviour, if it were Thy Will, to suffer all the torments of hell, provided that I might love Thee as much as all the miserable beings who will suffer eternally, and who will never love Thee, would have been able to love Thee in heaven. What! is it possible that there is a place where during eternity Jesus Christ will not be loved? Truly, if all mankind did but know the desire that I have to suffer and to be despised for the love of Jesus Christ, I doubt not that charity would induce them to satisfy me on this point."

From this ardent love naturally proceeded the delight she took in conversing with God. All times, places, and occupations, furnished her with an incentive, or rather, with the means thereunto, because she everywhere felt His presence, and raised the affections of her heart to Him. But her greatest pleasure was to discourse with God in church, where He is present in a more particular manner. She found nothing to compare with the happiness of throwing herself at the feet of Jesus Christ, Who from love of us truly resides upon our altars in the Blessed Sacrament. This miracle of the love of

Jesus for men excited in her heart the most lively feelings of gratitude and love. Her chief consolation was to remain in church before this august Sacrament; every free moment of time was passed there; and our Lord drew her so powerfully to this holy spot, that she felt within her unspeakable pain, when she in the slightest degree resisted this interior attraction. This also she felt when obliged to leave the church to go to her other occupations; her heart seemed torn and divided when drawn from the object of her love. At these times she addressed herself to her Divine Spouse, entreating Him tenderly to accompany her where she was summoned by obedience, and not to quit her, since she only quitted Him to obey and please Him.

As on festivals she was not employed in house work, she passed almost the whole of the day in the church, without experiencing the least decrease in the profound interior and exterior recollection, or rather annihilation, which seemed to possess her whole being, remaining always on her knees, her hands joined, her body immoveable and without support, notwithstanding her many infirmities, and the great weakness to which these infirmities generally reduced her. In this holy occupation, the least look, a momentary distraction, a more agreeable, or less uneasy posture, were in her view enormous crimes, of which she accused herself with the deepest feelings of humility and confusion. She thought that they ought to be expiated by penances, which she demanded of her superior, and she related these faults to her with the same earnestness that indignation kindles in uncharitable persons, when they recount and exaggerate the faults of others. She

has herself told us how she learnt to deplore so
deeply these faults, which our little faith induces us
to call light ones. "My Divine Master," said she,
"has never ceased reproving me for my faults, and
showing to me their deformity. But there is nothing
which displeases Him so much, and for which He
reproves me with so much severity, as a want of
attention and respect before the Blessed Sacrament,
especially in the time of office and prayer. Alas! of
how many precious graces have I deprived myself by
a distraction, a curious look, by sometimes putting
myself in a posture a little more convenient and less
respectful! The grief I felt when I perceived that
I had displeased Him in anything, obliged me to go
promptly and ask for some penance. For this Divine Saviour has made known to me several times
that the smallest penance done through obedience is
more agreeable to Him than the greatest austerities
of my own choosing." What follows in the same
paper regards obedience, and shows the pure ideas
with which God inspired His servant upon the practice of this virtue. We will transcribe it, that nothing may be lost of the salutary instructions this
holy religious received from God. "I can assure
you also," she goes on to say, "that my Divine
Saviour has repeated to me a hundred times, that
there is nothing so hurtful to people in religion as
the want of obedience, however slight, either to
superiors or to the rules; and the least answer on
this point showing any mark of repugnance, is an
insupportable defect in the eyes of God." Such
was the perfection of the obedience of Sister Margaret, and the source whence she had derived it.

We will return to what regards her devotion towards God and our Lord Jesus Christ.

One Holy Thursday, a few days after her recovery from a severe illness, while still feeling all the languor of an imperfect convalescence, she asked her superior's permission to pass the whole of the night before the Blessed Sacrament. There was no apparent likelihood of her being able to remain there so long, but her fervour made her forget her weakness. The superior only gave her permission to stay from half-past seven till the hour of rest, which was long for a weak person; but it was too short to satisfy the ardour of Sister Margaret. She urged her superior with further entreaties, assuring her that God would give her strength, and that she should not be inconvenienced by it, adding, that she ought to be there part of the time for herself, and the rest for the souls in purgatory, for whom she felt moved to pray and suffer extraordinarily. At length her solicitations overcame the discretion of the superior, and she consented to her wish. Sister Margaret repaired to the choir at half-past seven, and from that time until the next day she remained on her knees, her hands joined, without support, and motionless; and when the community assembled on the Friday morning at the hour of prime, she. tranquilly took her place in the choir with the others, without appearing either exhausted or wearied.

But if her exterior recollection was astonishing, what passed in her soul during that night was still more so. Her superior demanded an account of it, and the sister told her with great simplicity, that she had suffered much with our Lord, Who had done her the favour to make her participate in His grief and agony in the Garden of Olives, and in this state it seemed every moment as if her soul was being torn from her body, but that God and His love had supported her.

This was not the only time that she thus passed the entire night of Holy Thursday before the Blessed Sacrament. After having once received permission she requested it every year, and managed so well that she generally obtained it; so that this practice, which seemed to pass the bounds of human strength, especially in a person of weak health, became her usual custom on this holy festival. The religious who came at the different hours of the night to adore the Blessed Sacrament, were witnesses of the constancy of Sister Margaret in her prayers; some of them even watched her several times to see if she changed her posture, or gave herself any support when she was alone; and all testified to the immoveable constancy with which she passed the whole of the night; and they have declared it in their depositions, when by order of the Bishop of Autun, a judicial information of the virtues of this servant of God was taken in the year 1715.

Two of these religious relate a circumstance which will be no less edifying and perhaps more useful, since obedience, according to the teaching of Holy Scripture, is better than sacrifice. A young sister wishing to try whether vanity or singularity had any share in this practice, asked permission of the superior to go in the middle of this holy night and interrupt Sister Margaret's prayer. In consequence of the permission which she obtained, she went and said to her in a low voice, "Our mother orders you to go and warm yourself." The servant of God did not hesitate an instant to obey, but went immediately to the common-room fire, remained there a quarter of an hour, and then returned to resume her place before the Blessed Sacrament.

Another sister made the same trial the following year, without the knowledge or order of her superiors, as she has herself confessed in deposing to this fact. Charity prevented Sister Margaret from suspecting that she announced to her an order from the superior which the superior had never given, and she obeyed with the same promptitude. A third related in her deposition that curiosity one day led her to say to the servant of God, "Sister, how can you possibly remain so long in so fatiguing a posture?" To which Sister Margaret replied confidingly, "I am unconscious at the time of possessing a body; the sufferings of Jesus Christ so completely occupy my mind that I can think of nothing else."

The holy and painful exercises to which Sister Margaret abandoned herself from the very beginning of her religious life, caused it to be feared that her health would be seriously injured, weakened as it was already by the austerities of her youth. She was urged to moderate them, or to take some respite. Sometimes jealousy united with charity, or assumed its appearance, in lecturing Margaret on discretion and prudence. Tepid nuns reproached her with wishing to pass for being more devout than her sisters; some taxed her with hypocrisy; others, while praising her fervour, condemned her indiscretion. She received all this with the most perfect humility, and believing it to be her duty to defer to the advice

7

of some of the elder nuns on her too great assiduity
at church, and regarding herself as an object of
scandal to her sisters, she resolved henceforth to
remain in her room. But our Lord reproached her
for this, and seeing that she wished to resist the
interior attraction which would have led her before
the Blessed Sacrament, He said to her in a voice
full of severity, "Learn that if thou withdrawest
from My presence, thou wilt repent it, and so will
all those who are the cause of it. I will hide My
presence from them, and they shall not find Me when
they seek Me."

We may judge by her delight when before the
Blessed Sacrament, what her feelings would be with
respect to holy communion. She often said to her
superior that she always felt herself famishing with
two kinds of hunger, which appeared to her insatiable, the one for suffering, the other for communicating, or, to make use of one of her familiar expressions, "To receive the God of her heart, and the
heart of her God." " I have so great a desire to
communicate," said she in one of the writings of
which we have spoken, " that if it were necessary to
walk barefoot through the flames, it seems to me the
pain would cost me nothing in comparison of what I
should feel in the privation of so great a good.
Nothing is capable of giving me such sensible joy as
this Bread of love. After having received it, I remain as if annihilated before my God, but with a
joy which so ravishes my whole being, that sometimes for several minutes my whole interior is in
profound silence, listening to the voice of Him Who
is the delight and satisfaction of my soul."

To prepare for the happiness of communion she

purified her soul by penance, with a care which equalled the ardour of her love for Jesus Christ. Her examination of conscience was often so rigorous as to fill her with trouble and fear, so great was her dread of carrying the least spot to holy communion. What vices had a soul so pure to reproach herself with? It was this which caused her trouble. She perceived little or no sin to accuse herself of, and she thought it was her blindness and hardness of heart which concealed it from her view. In this mistaken notion of her blindness, she condemned herself for sins which she could not discover, yet of which she believed herself to be guilty. God took care to relieve her from this anxiety, saying to her one day when she was more than usually distressed in her examination of conscience, " Why dost thou torment thyself? Do what is in thy power. I love nothing so much as a contrite and humble heart, which sincerely resolves to displease Me no more, and accuses itself without disguise."

On the eve of her communions, her soul was transported with joy; almost the whole night was passed in tender colloquies with her beloved Lord; even during her sleep she thought of the happiness of receiving Him, and seemed to discourse with Him as if in prayer. It is not surprising that after this her heart was so consumed with the divine fire of the love of God, that she could not restrain its ardour: it was also in the holy communion that our Lord communicated Himself to her in a more intimate manner, and bestowed upon her His most signal favours and miraculous graces. Then, annihilated before God, and entirely occupied with the sweetness of His presence, she often exclaimed aloud

in a sudden transport, "O Love! O Love! O the
excess of the love of God towards so miserable
a creature!" Again, she relates of one of these
wonderful conmunications of God in the holy
communion; "My Sovereign once asked me this
question after holy communion : 'Which wouldest
thou prefer, to receive Me once unworthily, and
afterwards be admitted into heaven, or be deprived
of receiving Me that I might be more glorified, and
after this privation, be swallowed up in hell?'
Love," continued she, "immediately made the choice
and the answer. I said to Him with all the warmth
of my heart, 'O my Lord, open this abyss, and the
desire of Thy glory will soon precipitate me into it.'
So much pain did it cause me," she adds, "to think
that this Bread of life should be eaten unworthily."
Let the false mystics who believe it to be a virtue to
acquiesce in one's own damnation, draw no argument from this impossible supposition of the excess
of love; Sister Margaret would have preferred the
fires of hell to sin, but never would she have
agreed to cease from loving God.

God Himself had produced the infinite horror she
felt for an unworthy communion, by showing her
one day under a sensible form the ill-treatment that
souls receiving Him in sin exercise upon His
sacred Body. She saw It tied and bound, and
trampled under the feet of sacrilegious profaners,
and the Son of God said to her in a tone of extreme
grief, "See how sinners treat Me, and to what
degree they despise Me."

Lukewarm and incredulous souls will find it difficult to conceive how a heart can experience such
lively affection for our Lord, and receive from Him

such singular favours; but the miracle, if I may so
call it, of the penance and mortification of Sister
Margaret renders credible that of her love. "Works
are the proof of love," said St. Gregory; and according to the same principle, miraculous austerities
serve as proofs of the miracles of Divine love. Now
the constant and fervent mortification of this courageous soul was a kind of miracle.

We have seen that she began from her earliest
years to equal by the inventions of her fervour the
greatest austerities of saints famous for their penance. In her youth she practised inconceivable
mortifications, and when she became a religious, her
ardour for austerities did not diminish, but became more meritorious because regulated by obedience, and less imprudent because directed by the
authority of her superiors, who often saw excess in
what Margaret regarded as light sufferings. Hair-
shirts, frequent and bloody disciplines, girdles of
iron studded with very sharp points, and a thousand
other inventions to torment and punish her body,
were daily practices with her, or at least the object
of her desires, and of the continual requests she
made to her superiors. To induce them to consent
to her wishes, she had always plausible reasons to
allege, and she was most desirous to persuade them
that her health was not injured by such things.
Her humility supplied her with most urgent reasons. She had always some fault to expiate either
for herself or for others; she believed herself re-
sponsible to God, not only for the faults which she
committed, but for those to which she gave occasion.
She always allowed herself to be in the wrong, and
immediately asked for a penance in expiation of the

sin which she thus took upon herself. One of her superiors relates of herself, that when she arrived at Paray, being anxious to discover with what spirit Sister Margaret was animated, she at first readily granted her requests in order to try her perseverance. The following is what she tells us on this subject in the memoir she wrote after the death of the holy sister: "Finding myself without experience or assistance to guide her in such extraordinary ways, I trusted a little, I may say a great deal, to the assurances Sister Margaret gave me, that our Lord would cause me to act according to His holy Will in her regard. For this reason I fearlessly followed my natural inclination, which loves peace and tranquillity, and appeared to pay no attention to the extraordinary things done by this holy sister. I never alluded to her either to those within or out of the house; and if it happened that she did anything that displeased others, though it might have been by my order, or with my permission, I allowed her to be blamed, and even blamed her myself. When it was spoken of in her presence, she humbly acquiesced, and agreed that she was always in the wrong. According to her own account, it was always she who did all the evil, or who was the cause that God permitted it; for which reason she incessantly asked leave to do penance to satisfy the divine justice. If she had been permitted, she would have destroyed her poor body with watchings, disciplines, and other austerities, and even during the six years that I knew her, she enjoyed but five months of health."

Another of her superiors relates, that one of the reasons she often gave to obtain permission to practise fresh austerities, was the contradiction she experienced from several of the sisters, who never spared her in any way. In the same spirit as the prophet, who clothed himself with hair-cloth when his enemies persecuted him, she entreated to be allowed to practise austerities, either to expiate the faults she had committed, or those that others committed, of which she believed herself to be the cause.

As not nearly all that she asked in this way was granted, and as the discretion of her superiors repressed her ardour for penance, she incessantly employed a thousand other means to subdue her senses, weary her body, and mortify her feeling. Once, when in retreat, she covered her bed with pieces of broken earthenware. Whatever food was the most distasteful, she chose for herself. Spoiled fruit, portions either cold or ill-dressed, pieces of bread picked up from the ground and covered with dust, were for her the most exquisite repasts. She has often been seen to mix cold water with her portions, to make them insipid. Sometimes, when forced in the heat of summer to relieve the devouring thirst with which she was consumed, she took warm water into her mouth, to deprive herself of the pleasure she would have experienced in satisfying with cold water that thirst which she could no longer support.

During the greater part of her life she suffered intense thirst, like that felt in a high fever, and she admitted that nothing was ever able to satisfy it. To mortify herself still more in this matter, she resolved absolutely to abstain from drinking from the Thursday of every week till the Saturday. She practised this austerity for a long time, but it was at length discovered, and her superior, far from commending her, reproved her severely, forbade her to do it for the future, and even ordered her on each of those days to drink three or four times between meals. The sister humbled herself and obeyed, but in her obedience she found the means of a new mortification. She drank indifferently of every kind of water she could find, however unfit or disgusting it might be, even that which flowed from the washing-tub. This new kind of mortification was also remarked, and her superior reproving her for it, desired her to accuse herself of it, as of a fault against obedience, and gave her publicly a severe correction. She placed this mortification in the class of sins against obedience, quoting that beautiful maxim of St. Francis of Sales, that "the truly obedient soul conforms herself not only to the command, but even to the spirit and intention of him who gives it."

These extraordinary and heroic mortifications are not always a certain mark of sanctity; they are to be admired in this holy sister, but ought not to serve as rules for those who wish to walk in the way of perfection. Vanity, singularity, delusion, and a certain refinement of self-love which takes delight in itself, and finds satisfaction in extraordinary austerities, may sometimes be found in these practices. The great masters of the spiritual life warn us of the danger that persons encounter who give themselves up from taste and choice to the most rigorous mortifications. But what can never be suspected of delusion and self-love, and what appears most instructive in the life of Sister Margaret, is her having the same taste for mortifications and sufferings when they were not of her own choosing. On every occasion of humiliation, privation, or pain, which presented itself, she suffered without complaint or murmur, and without even showing the least alteration in her countenance.

Whatever she was ordered to do, or whatever was given for her use, she appeared equally content. The superior who has informed us of these particulars, adds that she never complained in her infirmities, and never asked for relief. She contented herself with receiving with gratitude and humility whatever was offered, but was equally content if nothing were given her. In the violent and frequent illnesses with which she was attacked, she endeavoured to follow the exercises of the community, and would have done so until she fainted, if care had not been taken of her, and that repose prescribed which was necessary. She never allowed herself to show her inclinations or natural repugnances, not even by certain motions or words, which so easily escape from mortified persons, or at least from those who think themselves such. She never considered her health or the delicacy of her constitution, but was always ready to undertake the hardest labour to assist her sisters, to suffer everything for them, and to sacrifice her repose and her life to accomplish the duty of obedience or charity.

Her fervour on this point extended so far, that she was distressed when attention was drawn to her infirmities, and compassion or pity excited by them. She then reproached herself with being too sensitive with regard to this slight consolation, and accused herself severely of being sensual, of having a repugnance to conquer herself, and, to use her own ex-

pression, of being too tender towards herself. One
winter, when she had the charge of the boarders, a
whitlow gathered on one of her fingers, which she
bore in silence for several weeks, notwithstanding
the great pain which it usually causes. She
passed almost all the nights sitting by the fire, not
being able to sleep, and abstaining from complaining
or making the least noise for fear of disturbing the
repose of the boarders, who slept in the same room.
She was at length observed by one amongst them,
who immediately informed the superior. Upon examining the wound, the superior asked her why she
had not mentioned it sooner ?   " Because, dear
mother," said she, "it was such a trifling thing, it
was not worth mentioning." The surgeon was summoned, and finding the whitlow both deep and dangerous, he made an incision down to the bone, which
Sister Margaret bore without making the slightest
movement. With the same resolution she endured
the painful dressings which were for a long time
necessary. The surgeon, astonished at her patience,
said, "It is an excellent thing to be holy, since holiness renders us insensible to pain." Some praised
her resolution, and others pitied her, but praise and
compassion were more bitter to her than the pain
she endured, and she showed her dislike of both.
Her superior having given her an opportunity of
expressing her feelings on this and some other troubles which she experienced about the same time, she
wrote to her in these words: " I assure you, my dear
mother, I feel no sweeter pleasure, than when you
speak to me of divine love in the midst of my sufferings. I consider myself unhappy in not having
yet been able to suffer anything with the purity

which love requires. I believe it is in punishment
for my sins, that I cannot have the least cross without its being published, and that God is often
offended by it. This is what afflicts me, and makes
me feel that all creatures ought to have a great
horror of me, and that every one has a right to be
revenged on me for the sins which I commit, or for
those of which I am the cause. I can truly say that
it is my happiness to have no other consolation on
the part of creatures than crosses and humiliations,
and never was I more rich in the possession of these
treasures. Return thanks for me to the Sacred
Heart of Jesus Christ, and beg of Him to give me
grace to make a holy use of His precious gifts.
Were it in my power to order things otherwise, I
would only remove what offends my God, and as to
all things else, I wish them to be as God wills and
permits them for my humiliation, for such is my
only joy in the adorable Heart of my Jesus. But
would you believe, my dear mother, that nature
is so pleased in receiving praise and compassion,
that I am prevented from reckoning as suffering
this pain in my hand, because I am told so incessantly
that I suffer a great deal. It seems that this should
be more truly said in derision at seeing me sensitive
to so trifling a pain. It has confirmed me in what I
had before experienced, that it is most agreeable to
nature to have such sympathy. It cannot resolve to
suffer without support and consolation the humiliations, contempt, and abandonment of all creatures.
Pure love, however, demands that it should do so;
without this, our sufferings do not deserve the
name."

Let us listen once more to the humble recital she

was obliged to make of an heroic action, in which, however, she saw nothing but imperfection and a blameable delicacy. "The sweetness of my love," said she, "urged me so strongly to suffer in return for His sufferings, that I could find no repose but when my body was weighed down with suffering, my mind full of confusion, and my whole being in humiliation and contempt. By the grace of God, nothing of this was wanting to me, for it pleased Him not to leave me a moment without either internal or external pain. When this salutary suffering diminished, I felt myself compelled to replace it by mortification. My sensitive and proud nature furnished me with sufficient matter, and it was the Will of my Spouse that I should lose no opportunity of mortifying it. When on account of the great violence I had to do to myself I failed in mortifying my inclinations on any point, my Divine Master made me suffer severely for it, and when He required anything of me, He pressed me so urgently that I could not resist Him, and chose for me whatever was opposed to my nature, and contrary to my inclinations, the reverse of which it was His Will that I should constantly follow. I was so very dainty that anything in the slightest degree unclean would completely disturb my stomach. He reproved me so severely upon this account, that once having to clean up what a sick person had vomited, I could not refrain from doing it with my tongue, saying to Jesus Christ, 'If I had a thousand bodies and a thousand lives, I would sacrifice them to Thy service, O my Spouse.' I found so much delight in this action that I wished to meet with a like occasion every day, to learn to conquer myself, and to have God as my only witness." We might recount many other such incidents attested by her superiors.

A courage so heroic in the practice of mortification of the senses, took its rise in her insatiable desire of suffering, a desire with which her love for Jesus Christ suffering inspired her, with the view of conforming herself to Him. She spoke with transport of Jesus dying for the love of us; and in speaking of suffering, she used words as impassioned as those which others employ in expressing their enjoyment of pleasure. She delighted in that saying of St. Teresa, "To suffer, or to die," which she repeated incessantly. She was frequently heard to say, that she would cheerfully live to the day of judgment in the greatest sufferings for God, but that to live without suffering appeared to her the most insupportable of all sufferings. These sentiments became as it were natural to her, and she could not understand how any one, although not animated by the love of Jesus Christ, could feel differently. "No," said she, one day, "it cannot be that a spouse of Jesus crucified should cease to love the cross and endeavour to shun it; is it not the same as flying from Him Who has borne it for the love of us, and Who made it the object of His desires?"

It is impossible to give a better description of her love for the cross of Jesus Christ, than by transcribing a letter she wrote to a holy religious of the Society of Jesus, in whom she placed confidence, and whom she consulted upon all that passed within her: "It seems to me, Father, that I shall never rest until I am in an abyss of humiliations and suffering, un-

known to all the world and buried in eternal oblivion; or if I am ever remembered, let it only be with
feelings of contempt, which may give me fresh occasion to humble myself.　Truly, if my desire of being
despised were known, I cannot doubt but that
charity would induce all the world to satisfy me in
this respect." In another letter to the same, she
again says, "Reverend Father, nothing is capable of
pleasing me in this world but the cross of my Divine
Master, a cross altogether similar to His, that is to
say, heavy, ignominious, without sweetness, without
consolation, without relief. Let others be supremely
happy in ascending Thabor with my Divine Master;
as for me, I am contented to know no other road
than that of Calvary even to my last hour; to be
amongst the thorns, the nails, the scourges, and the
cross, with no other pleasure, no other consolation
than that of finding none in this life. What happiness to be able to suffer always, in silence, and to die
at length upon the cross, loaded with every kind of
misery in body and mind, forgotten and despised, for
one without the other would not satisfy me. Return
thanks then for me, reverend Father, to our
Sovereign Master for honouring me so lovingly and
liberally with His precious cross, not leaving me a
single moment without suffering. Entreat this
loving Saviour not to be offended at the bad use I
have made until now of so great a favour. Let us
then never be weary of suffering in silence; the
cross is good at all times and in all places, for it
unites us to Jesus Christ suffering and dying. But
I see that I please myself too much in speaking of
sufferings, and yet I know not how to do otherwise;
for the ardent thirst I feel for them is a torment

that I am unable to describe. Yet I well know
that I am unable either to suffer or to love, which
shows me, that when I speak of either, it is but a
mark of my self-love and a secret pride which exists
within me. Ah, how much I fear that all these desires
of suffering may only proceed from the artifices of
the devil, who seeks to amuse me by vain and empty
sentiments. Tell me sincerely what you think about
it."

This humility is very remarkable, and gives a useful
lesson to those pious persons who are not sufficiently
distrustful of themselves and their fervour. We are
courageous in imagination; in prayer we believe
ourselves ready to bear anything; and we are
cowardly and discouraged when the opportunity of
suffering presents itself. Then those inclinations
and desires which amused the imagination, and
which perhaps were nourished by self-love, disappear; we can scarcely support pain and sorrow,
much less are we ready to bear neglect or contempt;
and the crosses desired only in appearance, and
borne with such real cowardice, leave to the soul
which thought itself so courageous, nothing but the
humbling experience of its own weakness.

Sister Margaret feared this delusion of self-love,
and yet she had less reason to fear than we have. It
was in the midst of all kinds of trials that she
loved suffering, and spoke of it with so much
eloquence. The constant fulfilment of her wishes,
whilst they still continued as ardent as ever, was a
certain proof of their sincerity. Her whole life was
passed in suffering. God, Who produced within
her this fervent love of the cross, was careful to
satisfy it, and at the same time to support her

whom He had associated to Jesus suffering, for
without a miracle she would have been unable to
endure all that she underwent. Her illnesses were
incessant, and she was afflicted with constant acute
pain in the head, occasioned by some wounds of
which we shall speak hereafter. When she recovered from one illness, another followed: her interior
pains equalled those of her body; she experienced
distastes, repugnances, and aversions, which can only
be conceived by those who have undergone similar
trials. The devil often attacked her furiously; and
in the midst of these afflictions, which sometimes
came upon her all at once, she seldom met with sympathy or consolation from her sisters, for God permitted her for a long time to be as it were an object
of contradiction to all the house, as we shall relate
in the sequel.

The superiors under whom she lived, and who
were all persons of great virtue and singular prudence, also furnished her with continual opportunities of suffering, and of proving the inexhaustible
depths of patience and humility within her. They
generally began by being prejudiced against the extraordinary ways by which God conducted her;
however, they soon found by her exact obedience,
sometimes even by miracles, that these ways were
holy and the work of God; but they thought it their
duty to co-operate in His work by keeping in humiliation and suffering the soul whom they saw so
clearly called to that state, and who had nothing to
fear so much as pride; for which reason they spared
her neither reprimands, reproaches, nor corrections. The humble and patient sister bore all with
equal peace and contentment of mind; far from

becoming weary of her trials and of this severe treatment, she incessantly urged her superiors to humble and mortify her, and to spare her in nothing. Instead of murmuring, which is so naturally excited in the heart, when we are corrected with severity by our superiors, she felt only a sincere tenderness for hers, and a heart-felt gratitude that she was treated according to her wish. It was this which attached her so strongly to Mother de Saumaise; the corrections which that wise superior so often bestowed on her, served only to increase Sister Margaret's confidence, which she preserved during her whole life; often consulting her by letter, when this good mother was called to other convents.

Mother Greffier, who succeeded Mother de Saumaise as superior, increased her trials. She took every occasion of humbling and mortifying Sister Margaret: she designedly interrupted her devotions; she often blamed her conduct publicly, and frequently while refusing the penances she requested, she imposed others more humiliating and more severe. Yet Sister Margaret was not only docile, but what was more admirable, her love and confidence towards her superior was increased in proportion to her severity. She went to her with the same freedom and frankness as if she were caressed and won by engaging manners. For three years she had been thus treated, when she wrote to Mother de Saumaise on the subject of this superior in these words: "I must tell you for your consolation, that God has given me a true mother, all goodness and charity to me." It was in the midst of these trials, so long and difficult to endure, in the midst of acute pain and continual infirmities, in the midst of the

8

contempt and opposition which she encountered
from the greater part of the community, that Sister
Margaret loved the cross and loved suffering.
Those who love like her, and under the same trials,
are safe from the danger of delusion.

Yet Sister Margaret greatly feared delusion for
herself, and in the uneasiness caused by her humility
she put her thoughts in writing for the information
of her superior, who answered her in the same way.
We will transcribe a part of these precious letters,
which will show what passed in the minds of both,
and especially will manifest the sincere humility of
the fervent sister, as well as the great discernment
and solid piety of her superior.

"As a general rule, my very dear sister," said this
wise superior, "attach yourself to God, and not to
His sensible favours. He gives them gratuitously
to whom He pleases; but He will only give Himself
eternally to the heart which truly loves Him. May
our Lord Jesus Christ, who afflicts you according to
His good pleasure, both in body and mind, be also,
by His grace, the strength and consolation of your
whole being, spiritual and corporal. I see nothing
in the disposition you manifest which ought to excite fear; suffer or enjoy in peace the crosses or
holy afflictions that God sends to your soul. As to
your mortifications, I would willingly give you a
large portion of that food of the religious soul, if
God gave you better health; but your infirmities
shake my resolution to that effect whenever I am
disposed to gratify your spiritual hunger. Entreat,
then, our Lord either to give me less tenderness for
your weakness, or you greater strength; or to dispense with my treating you according to your

demerits, on occasions when you give me an opportunity of correcting and humbling you."

We see from other writings of the same superior, that besides the trials and oppositions which Margaret bore so courageously, the fear she felt of being under a delusion was an inward sorrow which it required no less constancy to support. A false virtue takes delight and feels complacency in itself; but true virtue, which is founded upon humility, is suspicious of itself, and finds motives for humiliation even in the extraordinary graces bestowed by God. Unenlightened persons, and those who loved to find fault with everything, treated as hypocrisy, delusion, or even as the work of the devil, all that they found extraordinary in the conduct of Sister Margaret. They accused her in the most severe manner of these things. Instead of being irritated by these insults, the humble servant of God, always ready to prefer the judgment of others to her own, entered into their ideas, and, distrustful of herself, feared that in reality it was all delusion, and that she was in error, and even guilty of hypocrisy; and this interior trouble crucified her anew, and often greatly distressed her. We perceive this in some answers to letters sent her by the same superior, which deserve our attention.

" Remember, my dear child, what I have already said to give rest to your mind. Your last letter satisfies me still more that there is nothing evil in the spirit which leads you. If it is the devil who wishes to deceive you, he will not succeed, unless you become vain-glorious, and full of self-esteem through the desire of being known, and esteemed on account of the graces you receive. Keep your-

self humble within yourself, and be constant in
suffering abjection and humiliations, which are sometimes the more felt as they are inconsiderable and
little remarkable in appearance. It little matters
whether it be an angel or a demon which teaches
and leads you, provided it be in the right way, and
that you arrive at the perfection which God demands
of you. The intention of the devil would undoubtedly be bad, but yours is to love God, to
be humble and annihilated in body and soul, suffering in both whatever God shall see fit to inflict; and
this intention will cause everything to turn to your
good, and our Lord to be glorified in all."

We see by the tone of the superior's letter, that
she did not wish to relieve the servant of God from
all her trials, but to keep her in a humble frame
of mind. It is with this view that she adds as if
doubtfully, "I am supposing that what happens to
you is from God: it may be so, because He is rich
in mercies, and glories in bestowing them upon
the most miserable. That being so, it remains for
you to endeavour to attain the deepest humility,
which will keep you little and low in your own eyes,
deriving satisfaction from being humbled, abased,
and despised by every one. As long as you feel this
desire in the higher part of your soul, fear nothing ;
but endeavour to preserve it, and to bear courageously the humiliations, contempt, and abjections
you may meet with. Jesus Christ received and suffered such things, to make them serve to our sanctification : receive them in like manner, and endure
them in order to conform yourself to His holy Will.
As for everything else, remain in peace."

. From this same superior we learn the fact we are

about to relate, which shows the height of the
courage and patience of Sister Margaret.   One
day when she was drawing water from the well
belonging to the house, the pail, when quite full,
slipped from her hands, and falling with all the
rapidity produced by its weight, turned with violence
a long iron handle which served to draw the water.
This struck Sister Margaret severely on the head,
threw her to the ground, and knocked out some
teeth with so much violence, that a piece of her gum
hung bleeding from her mouth.   Sister Margaret
arose calmly, and without uttering a single word of
complaint, only begging some of the boarders who
saw the accident to cut off this piece of flesh, and
presenting her scissors for the purpose.   The children, frightened at the accident, and still more so at
the operation she proposed to them, ran away ; the
sister endeavoured to do it herself, and cut off, as
well as she could, the piece of flesh with her scissors,
as tranquilly as if she had been only cutting a piece
from her gown.   So painful an accident, in addition
to the operation so awkwardly performed, could not
fail to cause great pain, which could scarcely be
relieved by remedies.   It came on with violence
every time she attempted to eat.   The same accident
produced extreme pain in her temple, which seized
her periodically every day, and was like the most
acute tooth-ache.   Her only alleviation, said the
Mother Greffier, was to leave the community exercise, with permission to walk in the garden till the
excess of pain had passed off; immediately after
which she tranquilly returned to her place as if she
had suffered nothing.

This pain was the more distressing on account of

her having already suffered frequent and almost insupportable pain in the head, caused by accidents in which she had received severe blows, and from which she had never recovered. Once when she was carrying a heavy weight upstairs, she fell and struck her head violently against the wall. Another time a pole fell upon her head and bruised it severely. A third time she inadvertently hit herself against a beam in the barn; and these different accidents happening very near the same time, left an habitual pain, which to one less mortified would have appeared a grievous calamity. "But with whatever evils she was afflicted, she bore all without a complaint," says the superior who has left us her memoir, "never asking for any remedies, and always following the usual routine of the community and its exercises, unless the acuteness of the pain constrained her to rest awhile; even this was commonly not her own doing; it was necessary for others to think of it for her."

Another of her superiors has borne the same testimony to her patience and courage, namely, the Mother de Saumaise, who directed her in the first years of her profession. "For the space of six years," said she, "in which I knew our Sister Margaret Mary, I can assure you that I never saw in her for an instant the slightest wavering in her resolution of consecrating herself to God by the religious profession, that He might reign in her before everything, above everything, and in everything. She never allowed herself any pleasure, either of the body, the mind, or the senses. This fidelity drew down from the Divine Goodness very singular favours, which inspired her with a fervent desire for crosses, humiliations, and sufferings. It might be said without exaggeration, that no ambitious man was ever more greedy of honours and dignities than she was of suffering, which she accounted her greatest joy, though naturally she was very sensitive to every kind of pain or grief."

It was to prepare her for one of these accidents of which we have spoken that our Lord conferred on her the following favour, which she has herself related. Going to holy communion, the sacred Host appeared to her resplendent as the sun, so that she could scarcely endure its splendour. In the midst of this light she saw our Lord, Who, holding in His hand a crown of thorns, placed it on her head, saying, " My child, receive this crown as a sign of what will soon be given thee, to bring thee to greater conformity with Me." She did not at the time understand the meaning of these words, but fully comprehended them when she received those blows on the head of which we have already spoken; the prediction was accomplished, and the pain lasted all her life. It often seemed to her that her head was surrounded with sharp thorns, deeply driven in, which caused the pain she endured, and was sometimes so violent that she could neither sleep nor rest her head upon her pillow. This is what she herself says of it: " I return infinite thanks to my God, who bestows such great favours on me, His miserable victim. But, alas! victims, as I have often said, ought to be innocent, and I am a criminal. But I confess that I feel more indebted to my Sovereign for this precious crown than if He had presented me with all the diadems of the greatest monarchs of the earth ; and the more so because nobody can deprive me of it. It often places me under the happy necessity of watching and discoursing with the only object of my love, not being able to rest my head upon the pillow, in imitation of my good Master, who could find no rest for His adorable Head upon the bed of the cross. It makes me feel inconceivable joy and consolation when I see myself in some measure made conformable to Him. It is His Will that by this pain, and the merits of His crowning with thorns, to which I unite mine, I should demand of His Father the conversion of sinners and humility for myself, whose pride is so displeasing and injurious to Him."

If the accomplishment of the promise made by Jesus Christ to Sister Margaret bears testimony to the truth of that singular favour which she received from our Lord, these heroic sentiments of courage and fervour under such continual sufferings, render another testimony which appears to us no less convincing. God alone could inspire a love so generous and so strong, a love beyond all the sentiments of nature. The most sublime human wisdom could only inspire the sufferer with patience and tranquillity; but God, by the power of His grace, raises the spirit of man even to a feeling of satisfaction and joy while enduring pain, and still more, makes him sincerely prefer sufferings and crosses to all the pleasures and honours of the world. This is what our Lord implanted in the heart of His servant; and this miracle of His grace renders credible all the other wonders we shall relate. Our Lord Jesus Christ exacted of this faithful lover of His cross, that she should be in all things His victim.

He gave her one day these two lessons. In the

first place, He enjoined her to be employed in one
continual act of sacrifice, for which purpose He
augmented her natural sensibility and the repugnance she felt within herself, so that she could do
nothing without effort and violence, thus giving her
an opportunity of acquiring merit even in the most
common and indifferent things. This she confessed
to having experienced to the letter. Secondly, He
made her understand that she should no longer taste
any delight but in affliction and the cross ; and that
He would make her experience a continual martyrdom in whatever causes joy and pleasure to others.
These predictions were accomplished exactly, and to
their utmost extent. Whatever might be called
pleasure, consolation, or human support, became a
torment to her ; from this moment she dreaded the
refectory and the repose of the night, so that their
approach made her shed tears. The parlour was
insupportable to her; she never visited it without
such extreme dislike, as to be reduced to the necessity of throwing herself upon her knees, earnestly to
beg strength of God to conquer herself. The little
extraordinary recreations which are sometimes
granted in communities, appeared punishments to
her. "At such times I suffer more," said she to her
superior, "than if I were in a burning fever." Yet
she did everything like the others, and concealed
her martyrdom under the appearance of contentment and peace. God exacted this of her, and she
carefully obeyed ; but she sometimes cried out, " O,
my God ! how dearly bought is this pleasure !"

Thus God accomplished His work in her. De-
signing to raise her to the most sublime favours, He
laid the foundations of them by the deep humiliation

in which He kept her; and to render her fit for His
designs, He made the virtues of humility and patience natural to her.

In order to raise her ardent love of humiliations
and suffering to a more sublime and perfect degree,
He willed that she should honour the mystery of
His cross in a more particular manner. One day
when engaged in spiritual reading, in order to have
something to contribute to the conference which is
held in the community after vespers, her beloved
Lord presented Himself to her, and said, " I wish to
make thee read in the Book of Life, which contains
the science of love." Then showing her His Sacred
Heart pierced for our salvation, she saw there these
words: " My love reigns in suffering, it triumphs in
humility, it rejoices in union." This occurred at the
beginning of her religious life.

Another time whilst considering our Lord hanging
upon the cross, and consummating His life in the
midst of sorrow and humiliation, she felt at the sight
a great desire to suffer something after His example.
Then our Lord seemed to give her His cross, and to
say to her, " Receive, My daughter, the cross which
I give thee, and plant it in thy heart, having it
always before thine eyes, and bearing it always in
thine arms. It will make thee feel the most intense
torments. They will be unknown and continual;
hunger, without being satisfied; thirst, never to be
quenched; heat, without refreshment." She comprehended not these words, and said with all simplicity to our Lord, as St. Paul at his conversion,
" Lord, what wilt Thou have me to do?" Then He
said to her, " To carry My cross in thy heart, is to
be crucified in everything. To bear it in thine arms,

is lovingly to embrace all the crosses which present themselves, as the most precious token of My love that I can give thee in this life. The continual hunger will be for suffering, to honour what I had to suffer for My Eternal Father. The thirst will be for Me, and for the salvation of souls, in memory of what I suffered upon the wood of the cross."

Thus God willed that her love and her sufferings should have no bounds, and also that they should serve for the conversion of sinners. He made her understand this more expressly about the same time, that is, in the first years of her profession. She thus relates what passed within her: "One Friday, during holy Mass, I felt a great desire to honour the sufferings of my crucified Spouse. He told me lovingly, that He desired me to come every Friday, a certain number of times during the day and night, to adore Him upon the wood of His cross, which is the throne of His mercy, prostrating myself humbly at His feet, and keeping myself there in the very dispositions of the Blessed Virgin at the time of His Passion, offering these holy dispositions to the Eternal Father, with the sufferings of His Son, to demand the conversion of all the hardened and unfaithful hearts which resist the movements of His grace; and He added, that He would be merciful at the hour of death to those who are faithful to this practice." This may teach pious souls who serve God in seclusion, that although by their state they are not employed in labouring for the salvation of souls by the ministry of the word and instruction, they may yet contribute much to it by the loving homage which they pay to Jesus crucified for the salvation of the world, by the care which they take to conform themselves to His sufferings, and by expiating by their austerities the crimes which are committed against His Divine Goodness; in fine, by the prayers which they offer for the salvation of all infidels and sinners, in union with the offering of His sufferings and death that Jesus made for them to His Father.

In the midst of these crosses, afflictions, and austerities, Sister Margaret enjoyed intervals of delight and consolation, which can neither be expressed nor described. God communicated Himself to her in different ways, and though to suffer and to love were the greatest of all pleasures to her, yet He shed into her soul that superabundance of consolation and joy of which St. Paul speaks, and with which He crowns even in this life the heroic mortification of those who give themselves up to Him without reserve. He frequently treated thus His faithful spouse. He moreover took care to prepare her for the new trials He destined for her, by communicating a greater abundance of those heavenly joys of which people of the world neither know anything, nor are even able to conceive. But what raised the generosity of this faithful lover of the cross to its greatest height, was that she did not become attached to these sensible sweetnesses; she was even sometimes afflicted at their frequent recurrence, and entreated God to deprive her of them. "O my Love," she would then say, "to Thee I sacrifice all these delights; keep them for those holy souls who glorify Thee more than I do. I wish but for Thee alone, and for Thee upon the cross, where I desire to love Thee only for Thyself!"

We shall still more clearly perceive the preference

she gave to suffering in what we are about to relate,
simply copying her own words: "On one occasion,"
said she, "the only-Beloved of my soul presented
Himself before me, bearing in His Hand the picture
of a life, the happiest it is possible to imagine for a
religious soul; a life all peace, with interior and
exterior consolations, perfect health, the esteem of
all men, and everything else delightful to nature.
In the other Hand was the picture of a life poor
and abject, a life altogether crucified by every kind
of humiliation and contempt, always in suffering
both in body and mind. In presenting these two
pictures to me, He said, ' Choose, My child, that
which is most agreeable to thee; I will bestow on
thee the same graces in the one as in the other.' I
prostrated myself at His feet in adoration, and said,
' O my Lord, I only wish for Thee, and the choice
that Thou wilt make for me.' He pressed me anew
to choose, but I still said to Him, ' Thou art sufficient for me, O my God! Do with me what will
glorify Thee the most, without regarding my interests or satisfaction; please Thyself, and that is
sufficient for me.' Then He told me that with Mary
I had chosen the better part, which should not be
taken away from me, but should be my inheritance
for ever. Afterwards presenting to me the picture
of the crucified life, ' Behold,' said He, ' that which I
have chosen for thee, and which is the most agreeable to Me, as well for the accomplishment of My
designs, as to render thee conformable to Me. The
other is a life of 'enjoyment, not of merit; it is reserved for eternity.' I accepted then this picture of
death and of crucifixion, kissing the Hand of Him
Who presented it to me, and though my whole

frame trembled, I embraced it with all the affection of which my heart was capable, and pressing it to my bosom, I felt it so strongly imprinted in me, that I seemed to be composed of whatever I had seen there represented, and I found such a change in my whole being that I no longer knew myself. But I leave the judgment of all to my superior, from whom I must neither conceal anything, nor omit any part of what she ordered me to relate."

Let those who read this prove their love in this manner. There are few even among the just who would have had the courage to make such a choice. What Sister Margaret did on this occasion was verified throughout her life, which was a continual tissue of affliction, suffering, contempt, and infirmity, as it had been several times announced to her by our Lord. Her superiors, to whom she confided these predictions, were also witnesses of their fulfilment, in a manner which surpassed their expectation, and each one has separately borne testimony to this fact, which is above all suspicion. God had His designs in making His servant pass through so many troubles and trials. He made her a miracle of suffering and patience, to prepare her by sorrow and humiliation for the wonderful graces He intended to bestow on her, and to tranquillise the minds of the most incredulous as to the truth of the favours with which He honoured her. For the same reason we have given this lengthy account of the virtues of this holy nun, especially of her humility and love of the cross, before relating the singular graces with which God has favoured her. However incredible what we are going to say may appear to people of the world, it will seem so no longer when her mortification and

humility are considered ; because it is to the humble
that God delights to communicate Himself, and because the supernatural communications of God are
miracles less wonderful than that a child of Adam
should be humble without murmuring in the midst
of humiliations, and in extreme and continual suffering should not only be content to suffer, but carry
within her a species of hunger and thirst for suffering. The nature of man which leads him to seek
himself, to relieve himself, and to complain, is no
less difficult to conquer than that of the elements ;
God alone can work these miracles. Of all the marvels, then, which we have related, the most difficult
to believe are not apparitions, ecstacies, supernatural
communications, and discourses with God; we see
many examples of these in Holy Scripture, and in
the authorised histories of the Saints. An heroic
constancy, capable of suffering continually without
complaining, without seeking relief in the midst of
the most extreme suffering; an insatiable desire of
crosses and mortifications ; a spirit which seeks itself
in nothing, and which denies itself always, and in
everything ; a heart humble enough to love to be
despised and forgotten, to wish this sincerely, and to
bear it joyfully, to distrust itself, and to prefer in
everything the judgment of its superiors to its own,
seems a miracle so great, that all the rest can only
be regarded as the consequence and recompense of a
life so perfect and so divine.

BOOK III.

HER EMPLOYMENTS IN RELIGION. THE EXTRAORDI-NARY GRACES WHICH SHE RECEIVED, AND THE OPPOSITION SHE MET WITH.

The fervour which filled the heart of Sister Margaret at the time of her religious profession, was not one of those transitory emotions which subsist and flourish for a few months, and then decay and fade away. " The path of the just," says the Scripture, " as a shining light, goeth forward and increaseth even to perfect day." It was thus with our fervent nun. After her profession she was placed, according to custom, in the different offices of the community. In these she soon found opportunities of satisfying her love of humiliations and suffering. Her practice in every employment, when she had the liberty of choice, was to undertake whatever was most painful and disagreeable. One holding any office held in her mind the place of superior, and received from her the most implicit and blind obedience. She submitted equally to those among the sisters who, being of the same age and standing as herself, were appointed to serve as assistants in the same offices. Persuaded that she was the least and most despicable of all, she always reckoned herself as the last; and the other sisters generally took advantage of the humble opinion she had of herself, and made her practise it to the letter. Far from murmuring at this, she carried her principle of

universal obedience to such an extent, that she considered as commands the smallest wishes of those to
whom she voluntarily submitted, according to those
words of the Apostle, ".Submit yourself to every
creature for the love of God."

However well regulated the house where she was
might be, there were but too many of those nuns,
who, after having renounced all, think they may
still indulge their fancies. If Sister Margaret found
gentle and charitable officers, she also met with
those who were severe and sharp, and of that hard
disposition which can feel no sympathy with others.
They abused her ready willingness, and took advantage
of her humility to reproach her; they insulted her
simplicity, and sometimes even criticised severely her
conduct, practices, and scrupulous exactness in the
smallest observances. All endeavoured to avoid
being under officers of this character, and used every
effort not to be associated with them, so that Sister
Margaret, who desired nothing and refused nothing,
generally found herself destined by obedience and
the will of the superior to be under those officers
whose temper and rule no one else was willing to
submit to.

The first employment given her was that of assistant in the infirmary, under an infirmarian exceedingly zealous in her charge, active, and fervent, but
who exhausted her charity in favour of the sick, so
that there remained little for the sisters who were
subordinate to her. If she was quick in action, her
temper was not less so, and could not accommodate
itself to the quiet manner of Sister Margaret, which
she made a continual subject of reproof. She became a severe critic of her devotions, her recollected

9

demeanour, and her assiduous prayers; and this
new Martha, as hurried and eager as the one of the
Gospel, ceased not to blame the tranquillity and
peace of Mary. She believed she did everything
and her assistant nothing, and complained that what
the latter did was done either badly, or too slowly.
When Sister Margaret wished to go to the church,
the infirmarian took pleasure in detaining her, and
giving her some occupation. When she thought she
had accomplished her task, the infirmarian made her
do it over again, adding reprimands for her ignorance
or want of skill. With such a mistress it would
have been much to suffer in silence, to obey with
simplicity, and not to be disheartened; but Sister
Margaret did not thus limit her practice of patience;
she entered fully into her superior's way of thinking,
and really considering herself unskilful and idle,
believed herself highly favoured in not receiving
worse treatment.

After a year of trial in this employment, she was
sent to assist in the education of the boarders.
Sister Margaret had a natural dislike to children,
and consequently little relish for the constant care
they require. It was a long time before any one
knew of this aversion. She never showed it, excepting when obliged to give an account of her
interior dispositions to her superiors. It is only
through this superior that we know what violence
Sister Margaret did to her feelings in subjecting
herself to this employment, and fulfilling it with as
good a grace as if it had been exactly to her taste.
In this occupation her principal care was to inspire
the hearts of these little children with a love of
virtue, and to gain for God those young hearts

which the world and sin had not yet seduced. She
sought opportunities of enkindling in them some
sparks of that divine fire with which she was consumed. All her words breathed fervour and love
of God; even in the recreations and games of
these little children, she knew how to introduce this
subject without wearying them, and she had a wonderful art of sanctifying even their amusements.
She first attracted their confidence by her sweetness, by the affection she showed for them, by her
attention in serving and in satisfying them in whatever was not against the rule, and by her compassionate care to relieve and comfort them in their
wants or distresses. One of them had an abscess on
her foot, which was frightful to look upon. Sister
Margaret dressed it every day, but in doing so was
overcome by a feeling of sickness, which she was
unable to control. Either from a wish to conquer
her repugnance, or a hope of procuring a more
speedy relief to the little sufferer, charity and mortification made her do what the love of gain has sometimes led mercenary souls to practise for the cure of
wounds. She sucked the foot of this young patient,
and that for several days, and she would have continued to do this longer, had it not come to the
knowledge of the superior, who forbade it.

If Sister Margaret attracted the affection and
confidence of the young girls she was appointed to
govern, it was without prejudice to another of her
duties, which consisted in reproving and correcting
them for their faults. She was attentive to everything, and let no fault pass without notice and
warning to the one who committed it. She seasoned
her words either with gentleness or severity, accord-

ing to the case; and as bad temper or anger had
nothing to do with her corrections, they were always efficacious.   This is of much importance to
those engaged in the education of children, for the
want of keeping one's temper from being ruffled
whilst reproving, correcting, or punishing, is the
great cause of their labours being for the most part
useless. A word said without anger, and accompanied by reasons which awaken the minds of these
little creatures, has more effect than punishments
bestowed in impatience and anger.   But what is
still more to be imitated in Sister Margaret, and
what cannot be too much recommended to those who
have the same charge, is that she drew down the
blessing of God upon her labours, by assiduous
prayer and practices of penance; believing it as
much her duty to sanctify these young scholars by
her prayers, as to edify them by her conduct, and to
serve them by her exertions. In concert with the
principal mistress of the children, and the others
who assisted in this duty, she passed the afternoons
of festivals and Sundays before the Blessed Sacrament, offering to God those young hearts which
were under her charge, to draw down upon them the
blessing of God, and to entreat that by His grace
He would preserve them from sin. She often communicated for this intention, and performed other
practices of fervour and penance with the same
intention. If those entrusted with the education of
young people would do the same, they would see
more fruit result from their efforts, which are now
but too often useless.

Sister Margaret was made to pass through most of
the offices of the house; and as she was the resource of

the superior, when in their distribution she was wearied and embarrassed by the likes and dislikes of the other nuns, the servant of God was moved from one employment to another; she was placed and displaced without hesitation, because she was always contented and obedient, and had no other principle than that of St. Francis of Sales, namely, "to desire nothing, and to refuse nothing." If she had had any choice or inclination, it would have been for that employment which was the most neglected, despised, and laborious. Notwithstanding her infirmities, she was made assistant in the dispensary and refectory. These duties were too fatiguing for her health, but her courage and love of the cross of Jesus Christ gave her strength; and full of the desire of suffering, and of being the victim of charity towards her sisters, she took charge of whatever was most laborious, that she might relieve others at her own expence. She endeavoured to please every one as much as was in her power, which was no easy task in a large community, for amongst a great number of nuns, some are always to be found of indocile and unmortified dispositions, who indemnify themselves by murmuring if they are not treated according to their wish, and revenge themselves by complaints against those above them. Sister Margaret provided everything quietly, and without complaining of reproaches, avoided what gave occasion to them, or bore them with patience; she regarded herself as the servant of the servants of God, and imposed on herself the submission, vigilance, and humility that masters and mistresses love to find in their servants. With this feeling she endured everything in silence, as an affectionate servant is wont to bear the humours of his master without answering; and putting herself in this humble rank in relation to her sisters, she destined to her own use whatever was poorest, most disagreeable, and contemptible. If a portion of food was bad or ill-dressed, or if it had fallen on the ground, she laid it aside and reserved it for herself, taking care to derive profit from the opportunity which thus presented itself of mortifying her natural delicacy.

In the midst of these numerous exterior occupations, Sister Margaret never lost the intimate union of her soul with God. Her prayer was almost continual, as were also the graces she received from the communications of the Holy Spirit; it was thence that she acquired strength to fulfil perfectly such different functions, and learnt the fidelity with which she ought to devote herself to them. God Himself instructed her in these different duties; He indicated her defects, and reproved her for them; He taught her how to expiate them, and how to conquer in everything her natural antipathies. We have before related what she suffered from her involuntary antipathies, and how God permitted, for her greater trial, that this repugnance should increase miraculously, so that she should do nothing without a struggle. According to the promise He has made the just, not to suffer them to be tempted above their strength, He did not abandon her in these combats, but supported her by His presence, by the supernatural light which He communicated to her, and by the favours with which He solaced her. One day, when more than usually pressed by these feelings, so that it appeared to her impossible to resolve to obey, so strong was her repugnance, our Lord

showed her His Sacred Body covered with the
wounds He received in His Passion, and reproached
her with her cowardice in delaying to overcome herself for the love of Him. "What wilt Thou have
me to do?" said she to her Beloved. "My will is
stronger than I am." "Place it," said our Lord,
"place it in the wound of My Heart, and it will find
there strength to overcome itself." "O my God!"
cried she, with transport, "place it there so deeply,
and inclose it so well, that it may never move
thence!"

This kind of instruction and reproof were frequent, almost continual. God was jealous of the
purity of her soul, and allowed no fault to pass
without reproof and punishment. When she had
committed any, He made her feel such a lively impression of His anger that she has declared that
nothing ever caused her such sensible affliction, and
that the most rigid penance would have appeared
much more tolerable. At the beginning of her religious life, our Lord had promised to treat her in
this manner. One day when she had fallen through
self-love into the fault of dissimulation, by using in
conversation some little artifice contrary to simplicity, she was severely reproved by her Divine
Master, Who said to her, "Learn that I am holy,
and that I teach holiness. I am pure, and cannot
endure the slightest spot. Thou must act then in
My presence with simplicity of heart, for the smallest insincerity is disagreeable to Me. I would have
thee know, that if the excess of My love has induced
Me to become thy Master, to teach and mould thee
according to My designs, I cannot endure cowardly
and lukewarm souls; if I am gentle in bearing thy

weakness, I shall be no less severe and exact in punishing thy infidelity."

Another time she permitted in herself some slight movement of vanity; this fault cost her also many tears, and many reproaches on the part of her Divine Spouse. "O dust and ashes," said He as in anger, "what art thou? and for what dost thou glorify thyself? Of thyself thou art nothing and dust. Thou oughtest never to lose sight of this, nor to go out of the depths of this abyss."

In giving an account of her dispositions to her superiors, this holy religious said that the faults which our Lord reproved and punished most severely in her, were want of respect and attention before the Blessed Sacrament, particularly in the time of prayer and during the office; deficiencies in uprightness and purity of intention; vain curiosity; sins against charity and humility; above all, those of disobedience, even the least reply to the injunctions of superiors; showing repugnance or discontent, and infidelity to the rule. When any faults of this nature escaped her, she had no other means of appeasing her Spouse than by going immediately to accuse herself and ask for a penance; it was only by this humiliation that her Divine Master received her into His favour again. Then filled with the impression of His anger and His holiness, she accused herself in the most humiliating terms, and it was plain that she spoke from a heart deeply penetrated and confounded. What appear to us light imperfections, were in her sight atrocious crimes; she spoke of them as such, and begged for penances proportioned to the idea which she had formed of their enormity. Such was the impression which the lively idea of the holiness of God and His infinite horror of all sin caused within her.

To keep her in this state of humility, and of horror at whatever could sully the purity of her soul, He one day represented to her as in a picture, what she was in His sight when in a state of sin. This picture terrified her to such a degree, that she herself has said that she would have fainted upon the spot if she had not been supported by God. Every time that her heart felt motions of vain complacency, God recalled this picture to her memory and placed it before her eyes. No torment was so insupportable to her as this; it inspired her with a hatred of herself which she found it impossible to express, and if not held back by obedience and discretion, she would have satisfied this hatred by every kind of austerity. From this partly arose her patience and content under ill treatment or severe bodily suffering, for she regarded these trials as the just punishment of her sins, and she always believed sincerely that she merited a great deal more. Let us see how she expresses her interior dispositions at the sight of those faults of which Jesus Christ made her feel the enormity: "A thousand times I have felt astonished that I was not annihilated after falling into so many sins; yet great as they were, He never deprived me of His loving presence, but rendered it so terrible to me when I had in anything displeased Him, that there was no torment which would not have been delightful in comparison; and I would have readily sacrificed a thousand lives rather than bear this Divine Presence, and appear before the holiness of God having my soul sullied with sin. If it had been possible I would have hidden myself at these times;

but it was in vain, all my efforts were useless;
everywhere I found that which I fled from, and the
anguish I endured made me fancy myself in purgatory. All within was suffering, and suffering without any alleviation, so that I cried out in the bitterness of my soul, 'Ah, how terrible a thing it is to
fall into the hands of the living God!' "

Such is the description given by this holy soul of
the dreadful state to which she was reduced at the
sight of an irritated God; and we may ask, if this
presence of God was so painful to His cherished
spouse, who had only committed slight faults, what
will it be to the reprobate at the day of judgment?
They will in vain call upon the mountains to fall
on them and hide them, but they will not be able
to avoid that terrible look.

To impress on her heart a horror of the lightest
faults, our Lord showed her, in His Divine Person,
two kinds of holiness; a holiness of love and a holiness of justice. "The holiness of love," said the
servant of God, "is full of unction and consolation;
it has also its pain, but this ineffable pain produces
joy and satisfaction. This holiness communicated to
a soul inspires her with so great a desire of union
with God, that she feels no repose either night or
day. Her Spouse manifests Himself to her, discovers the treasures with which He enriches her,
and the infinite love with which He anticipates her
needs, notwithstanding the small return she makes.
In this way He urges her so vehemently to love
Him, that love itself can alone describe what the
soul then feels. With regard to the holiness of
justice," said she, "it is a strange torment to feel
the impressions of it." She declared she had no

words to express it; it is the anger of God, as infinite as His love, which is the root of it; and this
anger rushes like a torrent into the mind and heart
of the faithless spouse, to whom He deigns to manifest it; so that she cannot conceal the sins and
faults which irritate this avenging God. "I would
throw myself willingly," says Sister Margaret, "into
every imaginable suffering, rather than appear before this terrible holiness of God with a single
sin."

Her holy guardian angel also, who often gratified
her by his sensible presence, would not allow her to
commit any fault without notice, and punished her
for those which had escaped her observation. He
taught her never to forget the respect due to the
Divine Majesty present in every place, which ought
everywhere to engage our attention. She often saw
him prostrate before God, inviting her to follow his
example in continual adoration, and to throw herself
at His feet whenever she was able to do so. She
once wished to interfere in the marriage of one of
her relations, who was the subject of conversation in
the parlour, but her guardian angel reproved her
severely for it, and made her feel how unworthy it
would be of a religious, who belongs entirely to God
and not to her family; he told her that if she ever
interfered in such affairs, she would never be allowed
to see him again.

If God punished her faults so severely, He did
not fail to reward by singular favours the heroic
virtues she so steadily practised. These favours of
love were so many lessons to her, and would be
equally instructive to us were we but willing to
study them. It is remarkable that these graces and

miraculous communications were invariably accompanied by some salutary instruction, from which we, like Sister Margaret, may draw fruit for our own perfection, and it was partly the value of these heavenly lessons which induced her superiors to require her to put them in writing.

One All Saints' day, while making her meditation upon the glory of the blessed, God caused her to hear in the depth of her heart these mysterious words:

> " Rien de souillé dans l' innocence :
> Rien ne se perd dans la puissance :
> Rien ne passe en ce beau sejour,
> Tout s'y consomme dans l' amour."

These words were at first an enigma to her, but after having meditated on them attentively, and humbled herself for her ignorance and inability to understand them, she obtained the following explanation. Our Lord taught her in the first place, that the purity which God forms in His saints in heaven, towards which they ought to tend by the innocence of their lives, is such, that it tolerates no stain ; and that to merit the purity of heaven, the slightest spot must be dreaded in the road which leads to it; which is expressed by these words: " Rien de souillé dans l' innocence."

Secondly, by these words, " Rien ne se perd dans la puissance," she was given to understand, that the infinite power of God collects all the merits and desires of the just, that He may give them in heaven an infinite recompense, worthy of His magnificence ; that this ought to produce in the hearts of the saints upon earth, a generous abandonment of everything to Him, and a sacrifice of all human consolation, since they can never lose anything by giving all to God, Who repays more than a hundredfold what we give up for Him.

The other words, " Rien ne passe en ce beau sejour, tout s'y consomme dans l'amour," are easily understood, and show the happiness of the saints in its two most beautiful and delightful characteristics, the ravishing love in which they are immersed, and the unchangeableness of God in which they participate, inasmuch as their bliss will be eternal without a shadow of change.

Shortly after this, Sister Margaret lost her voice, which prevented her from singing the office with the nuns. This incapacity to join with the rest of the sisters in singing the praises of God, was a great affliction to her. From this infirmity she was wonderfully delivered on the vigil of the Visitation of the Blessed Virgin, the account of which we cannot do better than give in her own words : " After having long been unable to sing the office, which was a great trial to me, as well on account of the pleasure I took in praising God, as because I regarded it as a just punishment of my negligence, and therefore was humbled by it exceedingly ; I made several useless attempts on the eve of the Visitation to sing the Invitatory, but could not even follow the choir in the psalms. At the first verse of the 'Te Deum,' I felt a power go through me to which all my faculties were instantly directed in a spirit of homage and adoration. I then perceived a light brilliant as the sun rest on my bosom. This made me say interiorly and in silence, ' My Lord, and my God, what excess of love thus lowers Thine infinite greatness?' He then answered, 'I come, My daughter, to ask thee why thou so often entreatest Me not to approach thee.' 'Thou knowest,' said I, 'O my Saviour, it is because I am not worthy to approach Thee, still less to touch Thee.' 'Know,' replied He, 'that the more thou withdrawest thus into thine own nothingness, the more My greatness lowers itself to find thee.' Then fearing that it might be an angel of Satan who thus spoke to me, I made this request : 'If it be Thou, O my God, enable me to sing Thy praises.' I immediately felt my voice free and stronger than ever, and followed the 'Te Deum' and the rest of Matins with the choir without my attention being distracted from the office by the caresses with which His goodness honoured me. I only felt that my whole interior was powerfully united to the Divine presence, and occupied in honouring it. At length He said to me, 'I wished to try the motive that ani-mates thee in singing My praises, for if thou hadst for a single moment been less attentive, I should have withdrawn from thee.' " We see here the humble distrust of Sister Margaret, who, submitting her own light to those who attributed what passed within her to delusion, kept herself on her guard against the supernatural favours which she received from God.

Not long afterwards she again lost her voice. When she begged our Lord to restore it, He replied that her voice did not belong to her, but to Him ; that He had only lent it to her for a time to deprive her of the uneasiness she felt upon fearing that His visit was an illusion, and to oblige her to trust in Him ; and that she ought to be equally satisfied, either to possess or to lose the use of her voice.

She profited from this lesson, which produced in her a great indifference to all the providence of God concerning her ; and upon this subject she said that there was nothing more profitable for a soul than to abandon itself entirely to the Will of its heavenly Father.

We have related how great had always been her devotion to the Blessed Virgin through whom God several times bestowed on her His singular favours. The Mother of God appeared to her one day, and showed her the same favour which she had formerly done to St. Antony of Padua. She appeared carrying her Divine Son in her bosom, presented Him to her faithful disciple, and permitted her to caress Him and to hold Him in her arms. It would be impossible to express the feelings of her heart at this moment, so full was it of tenderness, gratitude, and joy ; to recount them worthily would require a heart as full of divine love as hers.

It was not for herself alone that the Blessed Virgin thus favoured her ; she sometimes endowed her with supernatural knowledge of the state of holiness or tepidity of her other servants in the same monastery, either to induce her to pray to God for them with more fervour, or that she might, as occasion offered, insinuate to them what would be useful to their perfection. On one feast of the Assumption the Blessed Virgin showed her a sort of crown, which she had made of all those religious who were devoted to her, and with which she wished to be adorned as with flowers in the presence of the heavenly court ; but she added, that wishing to ascend to heaven with these flowers around her head, the greater part were found too much attached to earth,

and fell from the rest, fifteen only remaining firm;
and that of these fifteen there were found but five
who were perfect and pure enough to be received
into the number of the spouses of her Son. "The
Blessed Virgin wished," says Sister Margaret, "to
teach me by this how important it is for a religious
to be detached from everything, and especially from
self, if she would have her conversation in heaven."

On a different occasion the Blessed Virgin showed
her under another figure the holiness of these five
spouses. She represented the Sacred Heart of Jesus
Christ as a fountain of living water; five channels
conducted these waters of salvation into the hearts
of these five religious, and it seemed that our Lord
regarded with complacency these hearts which He
had chosen, in order to fill them from this divine
abundance. There were beneath several other
hearts, which also received plentifully of these saving waters, but lost by their own fault this precious
treasure of graces, though abundantly supplied to
them.

Our Lord Himself authorised the devotion of
Sister Margaret to His holy Mother, and taught her
how she might draw more fruit from it by studying
the holy dispositions of the heart of the ever Blessed
Virgin, and conforming her own to it. Once,
amongst other favours, He prescribed to her, for
three different exercises, three very holy dispositions,
in imitation of the Blessed Virgin in the mysteries
of her life.

The first of these exercises was that of holy Mass.
He taught her to hear it with the dispositions of the
Blessed Virgin, when she was upon Calvary, near
His cross, offering His Passion and His sufferings to

the Eternal Father for the conversion of all hardened and unfaithful hearts.

He taught her in the second place to go to Holy Communion, offering to Him the interior dispositions of the Blessed Virgin at the moment of His Incarnation in her womb, entering as well as she could into the holy transports of His Mother at that happy moment, and asking grace through her intercession.

Lastly, He taught her to pray after the example of that prayer which arose from the heart of the Blessed Virgin, when she was presented to God in the temple, uniting herself to her interior dispositions in that consecration of herself, and begging to participate in them.

We may add here the account of an instructive favour she received from St. Francis of Sales soon after her profession, in which the daughters of that great saint will find a very important lesson for themselves. Just before the day of his festival, he made her understand while praying, that the virtues for which he had always wished to see his daughters remarkable, were those which had united him most closely to God during his life, viz., charity and humility. He added that he had reason to complain of several of his daughters who were at variance amongst themselves. "We fail," continued he, "in charity towards God, when in our actions we regard creatures, and seek only their approbation, without considering that by this conduct we render ourselves extremely displeasing in the sight of God." He added that particular friendships destroyed common charity and silence. With respect to humility, he taught her that we lose it for want of keeping a

10

strict watch over our own defects, whence it happens that at the least sign we judge evil of our neighbour, and put a wrong construction upon his intentions. He showed much dislike of these failings, which he attributed to the too great gentleness of superiors, arising from too much complacency towards creatures, and only to be remedied by loving severity and continual watchfulness. "In fine," said the holy founder, "I will come on the day of my festival, to make choice of my true daughters, namely, such as possess my spirit. I will write them in my heart, in order to offer them incessantly at the throne of the majesty of God, as an odour of sweetness."

The signal favours that Sister Margaret so frequently received from heaven were soon an occasion of suffering and pain to her; and God, by these first gifts of His consoling grace, prepared her to endure with greater courage the state of suffering to which He destined her, that she might be raised by this path to the highest perfection. The humble sister never failed to give an account of all that passed within her to Mother de Saumaise, her superior, with the utmost simplicity. The prudent superior, either fearing delusion in these extraordinary ways, or wishing to test more certainly the truth of what she was told, appeared to make light of them, and forbade her to think anything more of them. This was an occasion of inexpressible suffering to Sister Margaret; for on the one hand it was her principle to prefer obedience to everything, even to that which had been taught her by our Lord Himself, as we have already seen; on the other it was difficult to doubt the truth of these divine favours, after so long and so frequent experience of them; and besides, these extraordinary communications from God attracted all the powers of her soul to Him with so much force, that it seemed to Sister Margaret impossible to resist His operation. Then complaining tenderly of the pain which His goodness caused her, and laying her embarrassment and uneasiness before her Spouse, she said, "O my only Love, why dost Thou not leave me to the common life of the daughters of St. Mary? Hast Thou brought me into this holy house that I may be lost? Give Thy precious graces to those favoured souls who will correspond with them better than I, and who will glorify Thee more, since I can only resist Thee, and am compelled to do so through obedience; I wish for nothing but Thy cross and Thy love, and that will suffice to make me a good religious." Our Lord reassured her, and told her that it would be in vain f r her and her superior to resist His Will. "Fight, My daughter," said He, "I am content; we shall see which will gain the victory, the Creator or the creature, strength or weakness; but he who shall be conqueror shall be so for ever." He then added, "Understand that I am not displeased with these struggles and oppositions that thou offerest Me through obedience. I love obedience. It was for obedience that I offered up My life; but I will teach thee that I am the absolute Master of My gifts and of the creatures of My hand, and that nothing shall pre ent Me from accomplishing My designs. It is for this reason that I wish thee not only to do what thy superiors direct, but also to do nothing that I shall order thee, without their consent. Without obedience no one can please Me."

Sister Margaret gave an account of this new favour to Mother de Saumaise, who was well pleased to be thus assured of the obedience of her spiritual daughter. It was a day for communion, and she told her while communicating to make an offer of herself to God, abandoning herself entirely to His divine power to do and suffer whatsoever it should please Him to ordain. The sister was wonderfully consoled at this command, which she joyfully obeyed, making before holy communion, with all possible fervour, the sacrifice which had been prescribed to her. After communion, whilst enjoying the happiness of possessing our Lord, He desired her to repeat the sacrifice she had made of her whole self. Margaret repeated her sacrifice with renewed fervour, but added, "Provided, my Sovereign Lord, that Thou allowest none of Thy extraordinary communications to me to be known, unless they cause me humiliation, render me abject and more despicable in the eyes of creatures, and destroy their esteem of me. For, alas! O my God! I feel my weakness; I fear to betray Thee, and that Thy gifts would not be safe with me." Our Lord reassured her, promised to be Himself the guardian of His gifts to her, and that it was His Will to make her, as it were, powerless to resist Him. But still she entreated Him to give her suffering, and to exchange her consolations and favours for crosses and humiliations. "Wherefore," said she, "O my God, wilt Thou let me always live without suffering?" She considered trifling all that she had hitherto suffered from austerities and penances, and from the infirmities which had increased upon her; they all appeared as nothing in comparison of the burning desire for the cross, which love had enkindled within her. Our Lord then satisfied her desire, showing her a cross so large that she could not discover the end of it. This cross appeared covered with flowers, the marvellous beauty of which delighted her eyes; but under them were concealed thorns, nails, and sharp points of every kind. "Behold," said her Lord, "the bed of My chaste spouses, where I will cause thee to feel the perfect delights of My pure love. By degrees these flowers will fall and the thorns alone remain; I cover them at present with these flowers on account of thy weakness, but thou wilt soon feel their sharpness so acutely, that thou wilt need all the power of My love to aid thee to support the pain."

Sister Margaret's joy was extreme at these words, which would have frightened a less courageous soul. She thought, in her fervent love for the cross, that she would never have suffering enough to satisfy her thirst, which from this time began to be so pressing, that she had no relief from it night or day; and what to others appeared delightful and easy, was to her more painful than pain itself. Austerities and penances were her ambition, and of these she could never obtain enough to satisfy her desire. The cross which now appeared to her the most desirable was a pure cross, without consolation, relief, or compassion on the part of man. Our Lord soon accomplished His prediction, and in a manner granted what she had herself desired; that is to say, He never allowed the supernatural favours with which He honoured her to appear, except when they produced the effect of humbling His servant in the eyes of men.

In short, her continual practice of prayer, her
strict union with God, the austerity of her penitential life, the exactness of her regularity, and the
humility and simplicity of her obedience, instead of
attracting the admiration of all who witnessed them,
by the especial permission of God appeared to the
eyes of the greater number as natural virtues, or the
effects of singularity. ᵃ She was certainly regarded
as one regular in all her duties ; but this very regularity, which they treated as scrupulousness and
littleness of mind, gave rise to a feeling of contempt
for her.   If some of the more enlightened amongst
them, such as the superior, discovered the eminent
sanctity of Margaret, the rest could scarcely endure
her.   The imperfect could not relish her fervour,
which condemned their own coldness, and the fervent
thought it their duty to blame what seemed extraordinary and out of the common course.   From different motives all criticised her actions, and objected
to her conduct.   Either from antipathy, prejudice,
or mistaken zeal, they found something to blame in
whatever she said or did ; her silence was attributed
to stupidity, her mortification passed for dangerous
singularity, and her charity for littleness of mind.
Her maladies were attributed to hypochrondria, her
communions and prayers were suspected of delusion,
and even her humility and recollection of spirit
were found fault with.   She had not even a single
friend who pitied her situation or defended her
cause, as God permitted that those who esteemed
her the most should pass her over as did the others ;
and although the house possessed several holy and
fervent religious, nevertheless God permitted, by a
particular disposition of His Providence, that the

most devout should concur, through motives which appeared to them just and pious, in keeping her in contempt and humiliation.

If she was thus treated by the most spiritual, those who were less faithful to their vocation treated her still worse, and often said the most severe things even in the presence of the servant of God. It was not only in private that they passed these unjust and disadvantageous judgments upon her conduct, but they uttered their reproaches publicly in her presence when conversing together.

A religious who had been in the convent-school under Sister Margaret, has deposed in the information taken on her life and virtues, that seeing her so often treated as a visionary and a hypocrite, she one day said to her in confidence, that she was astonished they had so little regard for her and treated her so ill; but that the humble mistress answered, "My child, these persons know me better than I know myself, therefore thank God with me for the favours which He sends me."

Another has deposed, that being indignant at the cutting railleries that were uttered even in the presence of this holy soul, she sometimes said to her, "You are very good to bear all this;" to which Sister Margaret one day replied, "My dear child, let us go before the Blessed Sacrament to ask forgiveness of our faults, and at the same time, we will pray for those who have given me the opportunity of suffering something for Jesus Christ."

Her modesty and sweetness emboldened the indiscreet to utter unsparingly the most bitter words, which they called truths. They thought they did not wound charity because they never ruffled her patience, and they found in her pretended stupidity a reason for speaking harshly to her. There were in the house several very good sisters, who giving way to prejudice, thought themselves even obliged in conscience to say seriously to Sister Margaret, that she was under a delusion, that she ruined herself by her singularities, and that her conduct was a sort of scandal. In whatever way she received these constant reproofs, she was generally blamed, whether she humbly accused and condemned herself, or modestly gave a reason for her conduct; the one was looked upon as hypocrisy, the other as pride. God permitted them to treat her thus, that His spouse might share His fate when on earth, in being like Him an object of contradiction; He permitted it also to render her virtues, which had been put to such trials, more conspicuous.

Sister Margaret, in the midst of these reproaches and contempt, which made her like to Jesus Christ, despised and reviled, resembled Him no less in the patience and sweetness with which she bore them. She received everything peacefully, listened to all with joy, neither avoided those who insulted her, nor retired from the recreations of the community, though it was at these times that her humility was put to the greatest proof. No complaint, reproach, or murmur ever issued from her mouth; her heart was not even moved or excited against her neighbour either to resentment or coldness. "I admired," said the superior, "I admired her disposition, ever undisturbed, always ready to converse with, and to be employed with persons who declared themselves against her, and who most highly disapproved of her conduct; she was just the same with them as with those who showed her the greatest friendship. Never," she continues, " did I perceive that she made the least complaint, or that her heart cherished the slightest feeling of resentment against them ; and she never found herself so little esteemed by any one as not to believe that she was thought better of than she deserved."

The only thing which distressed Sister Margaret in these contradictions, was her fear that they might give offence to God. But without passing any disadvantageous judgment upon her sisters, she imputed the fault to herself alone, and accused herself in all humility of giving occasion to them. Her suffering did not end here ; she took against herself the part of those who reproached her or gave her advice ; and reflecting upon her unfaithfulness and upon what she called her crimes, she feared to be in reality, what they had cruelly enough called her, a hypocrite and a visionary, and she with difficulty avoided doubting the truth of the wonderful communications with which God had favoured her ; she could not conceive that such unusual graces should be imparted to a creature so unworthy and so vile, and recalling to mind what had been told her of the illusions of the devil and the danger of extraordinary ways, she was filled with those inexpressible fears of which we have before spoken ; and these distressing fears, joined to her infirmities and the persecution she experienced, made her whole life one of suffering and of participation in that heavy cross which our Lord had promised her.

Mother de Saumaise had formed a more favourable opinion of Sister Margaret than these unjust or imperfect nuns. A witness of her obedience, humi-

lity, and patience, she could not doubt that the
Spirit of God would guide securely in the ways of
perfection this highly-favoured religious; she found
that these miraculous graces had no other effect
upon her than to make her advance in the heroic
virtues of Christian life; in fine, she saw daily the
sensible accomplishment of the predictions and promises made by the Holy Spirit to His spouse. By
marks like these it may be surely discovered whether
such operations are supernatural and divine, or the
work of the imagination, or the stratagems of Satan.
Yet she had difficulty in believing what it may be
said she saw with her own eyes: the truth, evident
as it appeared to her, was still mixed with that
kind of uncertainty to which our natural incredulity inclines us in the midst of the most clearly
proved miracles; and because the conduct which
God held towards His servant, appeared to the
superior not conformable to the spirit of the order of
the Visitation, she thought it her duty to behave
towards Sister Margaret nearly in the same manner
as the others, either for the purpose of more securely
trying her virtue, or that she might not authorise in
the house what appeared singular in a life more
angelic than human.

We may imagine what an increase of suffering it
was for Sister Margaret to be opposed by her superior, whom she wished to obey in everything, and to
be obliged at the same time to fight both against
herself and against God. In truth, God often drew
her Himself out of the common way in her prayers,
her spiritual readings, and her other exercises.
When she wished to apply herself to the reading
prescribed by the rule, He attracted her strongly to

Himself; and He made Himself so completely master of her interior and exterior senses, that she was
incapable of resisting the power He exercised over
them. In communion she could force herself through
obedience to perform the acts which had been prescribed to her, when suddenly God would occupy her
mind with the thoughts which He thought proper
to inspire her with. In these moments she seemed
unable to do anything but to wish ardently to
love, suffer, and to give herself up to Jesus Christ as
His suffering likeness, and to entreat Him to finish
what He had begun in her, by allowing her complete participation in His cross.

Mother de Saumaise thought it a duty which she
owed to prudence, and to her love for the plain and
simple spirit of her order, to give no outward sign of
what she thought in her heart of the sanctity of this
her daughter, and she resolved to continue to act
towards Sister Margaret as if she thought nothing
of all that she saw, and gave no credit to the
recitals made her by the holy religious. She treated
these communications with God as the reveries and
visions of an over-heated imagination, and obliged
her strictly to obey the rule in every respect, reproving and imposing a penance on her whenever
she failed to do so; she even took part with the
other religious against her, and as Sister Margaret
always accused herself as guilty of all that was
alleged against her, the whole weight of authority,
as it were, fell upon her. Thus appearing to be
wrong always, and in everything, she bore the punishment of faults which she had never committed.

These trials and sufferings were greatly increased
by the extraordinary graces which God communi-

cated to her with regard to the devotion of the
Sacred Heart of Jesus Christ, which it was His
Will to make known by her means. Of this devotion we shall speak later; in the meanwhile we
cannot conclude the present book better than by
transcribing two fragments which remain to us of
the retreats she made in the first years of her profession. We shall thus see what were the graces
with which God favoured her, the fervour with which
she corresponded to them, and the instructions, salutary and useful to all spiritual persons, which she
derived from these supernatural communications.

RETREAT OF THE YEAR 1678.

Vive Jésus ! Behold what my divine Master
taught me in my Retreat of the year 1678. When
I complained that He gave me too great an abundance of consolations, and that I felt unable to bear
them, He told me that they were given to strengthen
me against what I should afterwards have to support. " Eat and drink," said He, " at the table of
My delights, to refresh thyself, that thou mayest
walk courageously, for thou wilt have to take a long
and painful journey, and wilt have frequent need to
take breath and to repose in My heart, which will
always be open to thee, so long as thou advancest in
this way. I desire thy heart to be an asylum for
Me, where I may retire to take My pleasure when
sinners persecute Me, and reject Me from their
hearts. When I make thee understand that the
Divine Justice is irritated against them, thou shalt
come and receive Me in the Holy Communion, and
having placed Me upon the throne of thy heart,

thou shalt adore Me, prostrating thyself at My feet; thou shalt offer Me to My Eternal Father, in the way that I will teach thee, in order to appease His just anger, and move His mercy to pardon them; and thou shalt offer no resistance to My Will when I make it known to thee, nor to the way in which I shall dispose of thee through obedience, for it is My Will that thou serve as an instrument to draw many hearts to love Me." "But I cannot comprehend, O my God, how this will be accomplished." "By My almighty power, which made all things out of nothing. Never forget thine own nothingness, and that thou art the victim of My heart, and must always be ready to be immolated in the cause of charity; for this reason My love will never be idle within thee, but will make thee always ready either to work or suffer, without receiving any reward, if such is My good pleasure.

"The workman's tool has no part in the work that is done; yet as I have promised thee, so shalt thou possess the treasures of My heart, and I shall permit thee to distribute them at thy will to those persons who are fitted to receive them: be not sparing of them, for they are infinite.

"Thou canst not please Me better than by adhering strictly to thy rule, and faithfully observing it, the slightest departure from it being a great defect in My eyes; and the religious who imagines she can find Me in any other way than that of the exact observance of her rule, deceives herself and removes herself from Me. Preserve in purity the temple of the Lord, for wherever He is He will assist thee by a special presence of protection and love. I am thy director, to whom thou shouldst abandon thyself entirely without the least care or solicitude, since thou canst never fail of help until My heart is wanting in power. I will take care to recompense or avenge whatever shall be done unto thee; I will even remember those who commend themselves to thy prayers, that thou mayest be free to occupy and employ thyself entirely in My love. I have still a painful and heavy cross to lay upon thy weak shoulders, but I am powerful enough to support thee; fear nothing, and leave Me to do whatever I will with thee, without doing anything either to hide thyself and be despised, or to put thyself forward for esteem. I will not permit Satan to tempt thee except by the three ways with which he had the boldness to attack Me: but fear nothing, trust in Me, I am thy protector and thy security; I have established My kingdom of peace in thy soul, which no one shall have power to disturb, and that of My love in thy heart, which will produce in thee a joy of which none shall deprive thee."

Some time afterwards, when I was in great suffering, our Lord came to console me, saying, "Be not afflicted, My daughter, for I will provide thee with a faithful guardian who shall accompany thee everywhere, and assist thee in all thy distress, and who will prevent thine enemy from prevailing against thee; further, all the faults into which he shall hope to make thee fall shall turn to his own confusion." This favour gave me so much courage that I seemed no longer to fear anything; for this faithful guardian of my soul assisted me with so much love, that he delivered me from every trouble. I did not see him sensibly, but when my Lord hid His presence from me, in order to plunge me into most painful grief by the contemplation of the holiness of His justice, it was then that he comforted me by his familiar conversation.

He once said to me, "I wish to tell you who I am, that you may know the love which your Spouse bears for you. I am one of those who stand nearest to the throne of the Divine Majesty, and who participate the most intimately in the fire of the Sacred Heart of Jesus; and I am sent for the purpose of communicating it to you, as far as you are capable of receiving it."

Another time he told me that there was nothing so liable to illusion and deception as visions; that it was by their means that Satan seduced so many, disguising himself as an angel of light, to give them a thousand false raptures; that he often endeavoured to lay in wait to deceive me, but that he would be driven away by the words, "Per signum Crucis, &c.," which verse I was to say to prevent him from succeeding.

On another occasion he said to me, "Take great care that no favour or familiar caress you may receive from our God ever make you forget who He is, and what you are; for otherwise, I should myself endeavour to annihilate you." When our Lord honoured me with His divine presence, I no longer perceived that of my holy angel. Having asked him the reason of this, he told me that during that time he prostrated himself in profound respect, to render homage to the infinite greatness that condescended to visit my littleness; and in fact I saw him thus when I was favoured with the loving caresses of my celestial Spouse. I found him always ready to assist me in my necessities, and he never refused me anything that I asked of him.

RETREAT OF THE YEAR 1684.

In my retreat of the year 1684, my Sovereign Master did me the favour to impart to me His graces in such profusion, that I find it difficult to describe them. In order to obey, I will only say that several days before entering upon this retreat, my God so impressed me with the spirit and desire of it, that my whole spiritual and corporal being did nothing but sigh after this happiness; as He powerfully drew up all my faculties within Himself, I could only abandon myself to the sovereign power which kept me buried within itself. The first day He presented to me His Sacred Heart, as a furnace into which I felt myself thrown; and I was at first penetrated and consumed by such a burning heat, that I thought I should have been reduced to ashes. These words were said to me, "See the divine purgatory of My love, in which thou must be purified during the whole of this life; then I will find for thee a habitation of light, and also of union and transformation." I have so powerfully experienced this during all the time of my retreat, that sometimes I know not whether I am in heaven or on earth, so much am I filled with and buried in my God; this caused me pain at first, because it prevented me from thinking of my sins, but the night before my confession I felt myself awakened, and all my sins were represented to me as if they were written, so that I had only to read them when confessing, and that with so many tears and so much contrition, that it seemed as if my poor heart would break with regret for having offended that infinite Goodness which did not cease to make itself sensibly present to my soul. During all this time my sorrow increased beyond expression, and there was no sort of penance and punishment to which I would not have willingly condemned myself; but after the three first days my most cruel torment was the privation of holy Communion. I was placed in an habitation of glory and light, where my poor nothingness has been loaded with so many favours, that one hour of such enjoyment would be sufficient recompense for the torments of all the martyrs. In the first place, Jesus espoused my soul in the excess of His charity, but with an unspeakable union, changing my heart into a flame of the burning fire of His pure love, that it might consume all the terrestrial love which approached it; making me understand that having destined me to render continual homage to His state of Host and Victim in the ever-blessed Sacrament, I was continually to immolate my being to Him by love, adoration, self-annihilation, and conformity to the death-like life which He leads in the holy Eucharist, and to practise my vows by taking example from it, in which He is so utterly destitute of everything, as to receive from His creatures whatever they wish to give Him and render to Him.

In like manner, by my vow of poverty, I was not only to be despoiled of property and all the conveniences of life, but also of all pleasure, consolation, desire, affection, and love of self, submitting to be neglected or attended to, as if I were dead or insensible to everything.

11

Who is there more obedient than my Jesus in the holy Eucharist, in which He is at the instant that the sacramental words are pronounced, whether the priest be good or bad, or whatever use he may wish to make of Him ; suffering Himself to be carried to those whose hearts are sullied with sin, of which He has so great a horror? In the same manner, in imitation of Him, He wishes me to abandon myself into the hands of my superiors, whoever they may be, to be disposed of according to their pleasure, without showing the least repugnance to anything, however contrary it may be to my own inclination, which I desire to oppose in all things, saying, " My Jesus has been obedient even to the death of the cross ; I wish then to obey even to the last sigh of my life, to render homage to the obedience of Jesus in the Host, whose whiteness teaches me that it must be a pure victim which is immolated to Him, without spot, pure in body and heart, in intention and affection, in order to possess Him. To be transformed into Him, it is necessary to lead a life without curiosity, a life of love and of privation, rejoicing to be despised and forgotten, in order to repair the forgetfulness and contempt that my Jesus receives in the Host. My interior and exterior silence shall honour His. When I speak, it shall be to render homage to the Word of the Father, the Divine Word who is hidden in the Host. When I take my food, I will unite it to that divine nourishment with which He feeds our souls in the holy Eucharist, begging Him to cause each morsel to become a spiritual communion, to unite and transform me entirely into Himself. My repose shall be taken in honour of that which He takes in the sacred Host. My trials and mortifications shall be offered in reparation for the insults He receives in the holy Eucharist. I will unite all my prayers with those which the Sacred Heart of Jesus makes for us in the Blessed Sacrament; in the same manner I will unite the recital of the divine office with the praises which that adorable Heart gives there to His Eternal Father; and in making genuflexions, I will think of those which were made to Him mockingly in His Passion, and I will say, "May all bend before Thee, O greatness of God sovereignly abased in the Host! May all hearts love Thee, may all spirits adore Thee, and may all wills be submissive to Thee!" In kissing the ground, I will say, "I render homage to Thine infinite greatness, confessing that Thou art everything, and that I am nothing." In whatever I do or suffer, I will enter into this Sacred Heart, to copy from it His intentions, to unite myself to Him, and to beg for His assistance. I will offer every action to this divine Heart, that whatever He may find defective may be repaired, especially in my prayers. When I have committed faults, after having punished myself by penance, I will offer to the Eternal Father one of the virtues of this divine Heart, to expiate the outrage that I have done Him, and thus pay my debt by degrees; and in the evening I will place in this adorable Heart all that I have done during the day, that He may purify my actions from whatever has sullied and rendered them imperfect, and make them worthy of being appropriated by, and placed within, His divine Heart; leaving to Him to dispose of everything according to His desire, reserving to myself only the power of loving and pleasing Him; since He has given me to understand that I have no pretension to merit in anything I do or suffer, having sacrificed it to the advantage and good of the community. After all that I have said, I trembled with fear lest I should not be able to put it in practice, but on going to Holy Communion our Lord showed me that it was He Himself who had impressed upon my heart the holy life which He leads in the blessed Eucharist, a death-like life of sacrifice, and that He would Himself give me strength to do what He required of me.

BOOK IV.

OF THE PARTICULAR GRACES SISTER MARGARET RE- CEIVED TOUCHING THE DEVOTION TO THE SACRED HEART OF OUR LORD, AND THE CONTRADICTIONS SHE MET WITH ON THE PART OF MOTHER DE SAU- MAISE, SUPERIOR OF THE MONASTERY.

Before entering upon what passed in Sister Margaret regarding her devotion towards the Sacred Heart of our Lord Jesus Christ, we must beg the reader to recall to mind what we have already said of the solid proofs of her sanctity, and of the utility of this devotion, proofs which preclude and dispel every doubt. Repetition of them would not convince those who are determined to yield neither to force of reasoning, evidence of facts, weight of authority, nor the most incontestable miracles; for it is upon such solid foundations as these that this devotion is everywhere established at the present day, in consequence of the revelations which it pleased God to make to His servant. There are no longer found any to oppose this devotion, save some incredulous minds, accustomed to believe nothing but what they can see with their own eyes, to reject without examination whatever passes the bounds of their own understanding, and to disfigure by unseemly scoffing all in religion that is worthy of our reverence. The criticism of such persons, laden with sin, is as unworthy of consideration as their approbation would be; as they have generally little religion, they ought to have still less authority. The mysteries of God are hidden, according to Scripture, from the mind where pride dwells, and its own incredulity is the veil which conceals them most effectually from its view; but these same mysteries which God hides from the wise of this world, from the prudent according to the flesh, He in His goodness manifests to the little and the simple. It is for those whose humility places them in this rank that we write, and we shall be plentifully rewarded if we can contribute to their edification.

The object of the devotion to the Sacred Heart is the immense love that Jesus has had for men, for whose salvation He delivered Himself up to death; a love of which He has given so precious a pledge in the mystery of the Eucharist. The end proposed is in the first place, to acknowledge, as much as lies in our power, by every kind of homage, and particularly by an affectionate and grateful love, the tenderness of Jesus towards us, especially in the Blessed Sacrament of the Altar. Secondly, to repair, according to our ability, the outrages and indignities to which He submitted for love of us during His mortal life, and

to which He is still exposed in the Blessed Sacrament; thus the whole of this devotion consists in
ardently loving Jesus Christ, Whom we have ever
present with us in the holy Eucharist, and in showing forth and proving this love by different external practices. Happy are the devotions which only
tend to nourish this love, to excite in us a deep
regret at seeing Jesus so little known and so little
loved by His own children, and to lead us, as far as
we can, to make amends by greater fervour for the
little gratitude He finds in those who do not know
this divine mystery, or who, knowing it, neglect and
forget it.

It is to make the object of this devotion known
that we represent it by the Heart of Jesus Christ,
because the heart is the natural symbol of love, and
consequently ought to be that of a devotion which
is all love. Love is its object, love its motive, and
love its end. Now the heart and love are sy-
nonymous amongst men, and the heart is recognised by them as the representation of love. It is
thus that under the name and symbol of the sacred
Wounds of Jesus Christ the Church honours His
sufferings, and in the same spirit we find in the
representation of the Heart of Jesus Christ, and in
the symbol of that adorable Heart, the remembrance
of His love, and a fit object to awaken our tenderness and gratitude.

Sister Margaret had scarcely been professed two
years, but her union with God was so complete, that
every day she received fresh favours; while those
which were conferred on her at that time in relation to the Heart of Jesus Christ, surpassed all that
had been previously bestowed. One day, when she

was before the Blessed Sacrament, consecrating there
the little time allowed her from the continual occupations by which her attention was distracted, she
was deeply penetrated with a feeling of the presence
of God. Abandoning her mind to the impression
with which it was filled, and her heart to the force
of that love with which it was inflamed, her exterior
senses were so absorbed that she forgot herself and
the place where she then was. At this moment
Jesus Christ showed Himself to her under a sensible
form, and caused the head of His servant to repose
sweetly upon His breast. It was in this precious
moment that He for the first time discovered to her
the unspeakable secrets of His divine Heart, and
the treasures of love with which it is consumed for
men. Then filling the heart of His servant with a
love in some sort proportioned to His own, He said,
"Behold My Heart, Which is so inflamed with love
for men and for thee in particular, that being unable
to contain within itself the fires of its love, it is
compelled to spread them by thy means. It wishes
to manifest itself to men, that they may be enriched
by these precious treasures, which I discover to thee,
and which contain sanctifying graces capable of drawing them from perdition. I have chosen thee," He
added, "as an abyss of unworthiness and ignorance,
for the accomplishment of this great design, in order
that all may be done by Me." Afterwards the Son
of God demanded of His servant the surrender of
her heart as the price of the present He had just
made her. The sister offered it to Him with all the
ardour of which she was capable, and prayed her
Divine Master to condescend to take possession of
it. It seemed to her, that the Son of God then in

reality took her heart, and placed it within His own, which she saw through the wound in His side, and which appeared to her brilliant as the sun, or as a burning furnace, whilst her own seemed but a little atom in the midst of it. Afterwards, our Lord appeared to draw it from Him so inflamed that it resembled a furnace, and replacing it in the side of His servant, He said, " Behold, My beloved, a precious token of My love, which encloses within thy bosom a small spark of My charity to serve thee as a heart, and to consume thee to the last moments of thy life. Hitherto," He added, " thou hast taken the name of My slave, henceforth I will give thee that of the beloved disciple of My heart."

It was now His Will to leave her a sensible mark of the favour she had just received, both to perpetuate the remembrance and consolation she had derived from it, and to be a testimony to her superior, as He at the same time declared to her; in order that when she related what had passed, it might not be rejected as imaginary. This mark was a continual pain in the place where our Lord seemed to her to have opened her side, to take from it her heart, and where He also replaced it. To this pain was added an intense and very sensible heat in the breast, which nothing was able to cool or to diminish. Our Lord, who had predicted that she would suffer this pain and burning heat, also ordered her, when she found herself excessively oppressed by it, to ask her superior with simplicity to allow her to be bled. He foretold her that this request and these bleedings, which would become frequent, would draw on her much humiliation, contradiction, and raillery, but that this heat and pain, which she was hence-

forth to feel, could only be relieved by this means.
In fine, He added that He prescribed this remedy
for the very purpose of procuring humiliations for
her, and the event verified the prediction, as we shall
hereafter see.

This ecstasy lasted a considerable time, and the
impression of it remained with Sister Margaret in so
striking a manner, that for several days she felt as if
inebriated and out of herself, so that she could with
difficulty either speak, eat, or attend to her usual
employments, and only succeeded in doing so by
extraordinary violence to herself.   This state, the
cause of which all around her were ignorant of, was
a fresh subject for humiliation and reproach, and
the epithets, silly and stupid, were lavishly bestowed
on her by some of the nuns who possessed but little
charity.   It was no less difficult for her to obtain
rest; the precious wound she had received in her
side caused such acute pain and intense heat, that she
felt devoured by an internal fire which deprived her of
sleep.   As our Lord had foretold, this pain continued
during the whole of her life, but she especially felt
it on the first Friday of every month, a day on which,
as we shall see, Jesus Christ enjoined her to honour
more particularly His Sacred Heart.   On this day
the pain and the favours which she had originally
received were renewed; the divine Heart of her heavenly Spouse was shown to her like a sun blazing
with the most brilliant light, the concentrated rays of
which fell directly upon her heart.   "Then," said she,
" my heart felt consumed by a fire so ardent that it
seemed as if it would reduce me to ashes.   It was
particularly at these times that my Divine Master

taught me His Will, and discovered to me all the
secrets of His adorable Heart."

According to the rules of obedience which our
Lord had prescribed to Sister Margaret, she was
compelled to give an account to her superior of this
ecstasy, and what she had experienced during it.
She did so without delay, but besides the difficulty
she felt in explaining herself, on account of the spiritual inebriation (if we may use the expression) which
she still experienced, she was much confused in relating such singular graces, of which she at the same
time felt so unworthy. "I should have preferred,"
said she, in writing down the dispositions of her soul
on this occasion, "I should have preferred a thousand times to tell all my sins to the whole world,
and to read my general confession in the public
refectory: this would have been a great consolation,
if I might have been permitted to do it, in order to
show the depth of corruption within me, and that
none of the graces which I received should ever be
attributed to myself." Notwithstanding her repugnance, she was obliged to yield to the duty of obedience, and then it was a fresh humiliation to find
herself treated openly as a visionary, and the divine
illuminations taxed with being mere imaginations.
The pain in her side was most acute, but no more
regard was paid to her infirmity than to her ecstasy;
both were equally despised. The pain, however,
increased with time; she complained no more, but it
was at length perceived that she grew weak, and
the nuns began to fear for her life, and to think of
applying remedies. In order to obey the command
of God, she said with all simplicity to her superior,
that bleeding would relieve her. This request was

turned into ridicule; the physician assured her that the remedy would be injurious, and in order to apply others which he prescribed, she was placed in the infirmary. These human remedies had no other effect than to increase the evil, and to excite so continual a vomiting as to prevent her from retaining any nourishment, by which she was in a few days reduced to a state of extreme weakness. The invalid endured all without complaint, without refusing any of the remedies prescribed, and without again speaking of the bleeding which she knew to be her only remedy. She soon found herself reduced to the greatest extremities; she could with difficulty speak; respiration became more and more difficult through the excessive oppression, and she had no longer strength to bear the frequent returns of vomiting.

In this state, when, according to the rules of medicine, bleeding would have been more hurtful than salutary, the superior determined that it ought to be tried. The physician could with difficulty be induced to consent; but he judged that in a case where there was no hope, the risk might be run of trying such a remedy. The superior proposed it to the sister, who said with her usual sweetness, "I know this is the only thing which can relieve me, but I do not desire it if your charity does not desire it for me; for my Jesus makes you wish for me whatever He wishes. I am well satisfied to suffer as much as He pleases." This is a good lesson for those who are uneasy in sickness, and weary every one by their eagerness to find remedies which may relieve them. They then bled Sister Margaret slightly, and had scarcely drawn one cup of blood, when God willed that His prediction should be ac-

complished in so marked a manner that it could not
be called into question. The vomiting ceased instantly, the speech and respiration became free, and
the arm was hardly bandaged when the invalid found
herself so strong, as to be able to leave the infirmary
and follow the exercises of the community, which
she would have done if she had not been forbidden.

So singular an event and so marked an accomplishment of Sister Margaret's prediction, determined the superior not to refuse her the same relief from time to time when her pain required it;
but the greater part of the nuns, who were still
ignorant of this prodigy, continued to feel the same
prejudice against her. Those who could neither
appreciate her piety nor her character, made these
frequent bleedings a subject of continual raillery;
thus for the entire fulfilment of the prediction, this
remedy was a frequent occasion of contradiction and
humiliation. These nuns did not hesitate to regard
her as an imaginary invalid, a hypochondriac, and
her remedy as wholly fanciful: the most indiscreet
said as much in her presence, sometimes making a
jest of her, and at other times reproaching or remon-
strating with her.

The superior, who was filled with admiration at
Margaret's patience, and also at the fulfilment of
the words of Jesus Christ, thought it her duty to
spare the humble sister this kind of confusion and
contradiction, and on one occasion caused her to be
bled secretly in her cell by one of the religious; but
our Lord, who did not wish His spouse to have even
this slight alleviation, permitted her that day to fall
into a swoon during mass in the midst of the com-

munity. The cause of this accident was soon divined, so that the incredulous continued to scoff, and Sister Margaret to suffer with her accustomed sweetness.

The Son of God supported His servant in the midst of these trials by abundance of grace, and by manifesting more and more to her the treasures of His Divine Heart; He Himself taught her the practices she was henceforth to follow in honouring it, in relating which we cannot do better than copy the account she was obliged through obedience to give of these heavenly favours : " One day when I was before the Blessed Sacrament exposed upon the altar," (it was some time after the wonderful cure we have related,) " after having felt myself entirely drawn into myself, by the absorption of all my powers and senses, my Divine Master Jesus Christ appeared to me in the splendour of His glory, with His five wounds brilliant as five suns. From His Sacred Humanity flames issued on every side, but especially from His adorable Side, which resembled a furnace. In the midst of it He showed me His loving Heart, which was the source of these flames. It was then that He discovered to me the inexplicable wonders of His love, and the excess to which He carried His love for men, from whom He received only contempt and ingratitude. ' It is this,' said He to me, ' which I feel more deeply than all that I suffered in My Passion ; for if they would return My love I should reckon all that I have done for them as nothing, and if possible, I should even wish to do more; instead of which, I meet with coldness and repulses from all men in return for all My anxiety to do them good. At least then,' added He, 'do thou give Me satisfaction by atoning for their ingratitude as far as thou art capable.' I then laid before Him my inability, to which He replied, 'Stay, behold what will supply for all thy deficiencies;' and at the same time opening His Divine Heart, there issued from it a flame so ardent that I thought I should have been consumed, and I was so entirely penetrated with it, that not being able to endure it, I entreated Him to have compassion on my weakness. 'I will be thy strength,' said He, 'fear nothing; but be attentive to My voice and to what I require of thee, to fit thee for the accomplishment of My designs.' "

He afterwards prescribed the manner in which she was to honour His love and His Sacred Heart. "'In the first place,' said He, 'thou shalt receive Me in the Holy Sacrament as often as obedience will permit, notwithstanding all the mortifications and humiliations which will arise on that account," (alluding to the raillery she met with from the imperfect nuns, no less on account of her frequent communions than of her bleedings, as they took occasion to turn all that she did into ridicule.) "'Thou shouldst receive these humiliations,' added He, 'as pledges of My love. Thou shalt communicate, especially on the first Friday in every month, and on every Thursday night I will make thee participate in that mortal sadness which it was My Will to suffer in the garden of Olives. By this sadness thou wilt be reduced, without knowing how, to an agony more insupportable than death. To accompany Me in that humble prayer which I offered to My Father in the midst of My anguish, thou shalt rise between eleven and twelve o'clock, in order to prostrate thyself with Me for an hour, with thy face towards the ground, as well to appease the divine anger of My Father in asking pardon for sinners, as to share, and in some way soften, the bitterness which I felt in being at that time abandoned by My apostles; an abandonment which obliged Me to reproach them with having been unable to watch one hour with Me. During this hour thou shalt do as I will teach thee. Now listen, My daughter; believe not lightly every spirit, and place no confidence in thyself. Satan is raging to deceive thee, for which reason do nothing without the approbation of those who direct thee.'" Such were the precautions which the Son of God Himself taught His servant. The weapon with which He furnished her, to render useless all the stratagems of hell, was the salutary shield of obedience. Thus the Son of God subjects His divine lights to those which we receive through the voice of obedience; and by this it is easy to recognise the spirit of God.

This ecstasy lasted so long, that the sisters, astonished to see her before the Blessed Sacrament far beyond the time allowed her, went to call her away, and make her rise, but seeing that, still absorbed in the union which she enjoyed with God, she could neither speak nor reply, and that she had difficulty in supporting herself, they dragged her to the superior, and accused her as if she had been guilty of a great fault. The superior understood that something extraordinary had occurred, but pretending to be ignorant of it, or to look upon it as nothing, she treated her with severity, and spoke to her in the most humiliating way. Sister Margaret received these reproaches and instructions upon her knees,

without attempting to defend herself, and she afterwards confessed that she received them with a sensible joy, seeing what she had demanded of God
accomplished in her, namely, that the singular graces
which He bestowed on her might turn to her humiliation. The more God lavished His favours on this
holy soul, the more her humility increased. She
saw in herself nothing but unworthiness and misery
when compared with so many graces, and this idea
threw her into the deepest confusion: thus to humble her was to satisfy her, and in this spirit she wel-
comed whatever her superior judged proper to say
to her, however severe and unpalatable. Afterwards, she was ordered to relate what had passed
within her before the Blessed Sacrament. She
obeyed with simplicity, but still the superior took
occasion to humble her, treating the whole as imaginary, and even forbidding her to practise what she
said had been prescribed by our Lord. Sister Margaret made no reply, but, according to the instruction of her Divine Master, submitted to whatever
the superior ordered.

The sisters were not present when Sister Margaret
gave an account of her vision, but for a long time
they saw the effect it had produced, in the profound
recollection she preserved at all times and in every
place, and in the effort it cost her to give her attention to exterior actions. The most holy were edified
at beholding in her a certain air of interior recollection, such as may exist in a soul absorbed, as it
were, in God; but the foolish seeing her in this
state, took occasion to annoy her by disturbing her,
and to humble her by taking notice of all the mis-
takes she made on account of her absence of mind.

The only things which grieved her were the many obstacles placed in the way of her desire to honour the Sacred Heart of Jesus Christ, but this trouble was made known to God alone. She addressed herself to Him, laying before Him the resistance which was made to His Will, and calling earnestly upon Him to overcome it according to His eternal designs. "Leave them alone;" replied He one day, "since I am for thee, what canst thou fear? Heaven and earth shall pass away, but My words shall not pass away. They never fail of effect." This prediction was soon afterwards verified, and the superior, notwithstanding her prudent resistance, was at length obliged to allow Margaret to put in execution, at least in part, what she had been commanded. The following were the means employed by God to obtain this end.

The ardour of divine love which devoured the heart of Sister Margaret, and which had been sensibly communicated to her in her ecstasy, was so vehement that it made an impression on her body, and being unable to support the fire which consumed her, she fell into a constant fever. The pleasure she found in suffering prevented her from speaking or complaining, but her exhaustion betrayed her. After some time her strength failed her, and when she could no longer support herself, she was obliged to confess that she was ill. The physician easily discovered the cause of her extreme weakness, and declared that she had brought it on herself by concealing her pain. He endeavoured to relieve her, but all his efforts were in vain, as the fever neither ceased nor diminished. Margaret endured it more than sixty days, with every kind of pain added to

12

the burning fever. Instead of being overcome, she found delight in suffering without measure. "Never," said she, "had I felt so many consolations. The devouring fire which consumed me was fed only by the cross and every kind of suffering. No pain that I felt was equal to that caused by my not having enough to suffer." At length her life was despaired of, and they thought her end approaching. Her strength diminished visibly, and she frequently fainted away. It was in one of these swoons, which ought rather to be called an ecstasy, that she received the following favour.

The Three Persons of the Blessed Trinity appeared to her under the form of three young men in white garments all resplendent with light, of the same age, the same stature, and the same beauty. The Eternal Father bore in His Hands a large cross studded with sharp-pointed nails, and hung about with all the instruments of the Passion of Jesus Christ. He presented this cross to Sister Margaret, saying, "Behold, My daughter, I make to thee the same present as to My beloved Son." "And I," said Jesus Christ, "wish to attach thee to it, as I was Myself attached, and I will keep thee company faithfully." The Holy Spirit added that for His part, being Himself fire and love, He would consume and purify her upon this cross. In the moment of her transport, Margaret did not comprehend the extent of suffering which this vision announced to her, and which this symbol designated; but she felt so sweet a joy and consolation as to indemnify her for the extreme pain of her disease.

The superior, to whom she gave an account as usual of all she had seen, had too much compassion to mortify and humble her in the dying situation in which she believed her to be, but ordered her to ask of God the restoration of her health. She obeyed with simplicity, but her desire of suffering made her dread lest her prayer should be answered. The Mother added, that if Sister Margaret obtained her recovery from God, she should understand by that sign that all which passed within her was from Him, and that she would grant her permission to execute what our Lord had prescribed to her in honour of His Sacred Heart, particularly the prayer during the night and Communion on the first Friday in each month. She obeyed without hesitation, representing to our Lord all the wishes of the superior; and God, Who desired to give an undoubted testimony to the holiness of His servant, and render incontestable the singular graces with which He favoured her, immediately heard the request of His spouse and the wish of the superior. This miraculous cure was effected through the ministry of the Blessed Virgin, who gratified her servant by being sensibly present to her during another ecstasy on the same day. After a long conversation and indescribable caresses, she said to Sister Margaret, "Let the health which I bestow on you on the part of my Son, encourage you, my daughter, for you have still a long and painful journey to take, always remaining on the cross, amidst the nails, the scourges, and the thorns. But fear nothing; I promise you my protection, and I will never forsake you." Margaret arose the same day, and to the astonishment of the community, she, who had appeared to have scarcely a breath of life remaining in her, was now able to walk without help.

So visible a miracle, of which the superior had
been the occasion and the witness, and of which she
has left her testimony in writing, had the effect
upon her mind which it was so well calculated to
produce. She no longer felt any scruple as to the
truth of those graces bestowed by God upon His
servant, but her conviction threw her into another
difficulty, and exposed Sister Margaret to a new
kind of suffering. The humble superior thought
herself incapable of conducting one so highly
favoured by God, and of leading her in such sublime
paths. She thought it her duty to seek assistance
in the advice of others. For this purpose she
obliged Sister Margaret to break the silence which
until this time she had maintained with regard to
these singular favours. Her superior was the only
person to whom she had opened her heart, both from
humility, fearing it might produce esteem, and also
in obedience to the same superior, who had forbidden her to speak on the subject, treating the whole
as illusion and folly. She was now commanded to
confer upon the state of her soul with some persons
of piety who were at Paray, and to relate to them
the singular favours she had received from God.
She obeyed, but it was with a repugnance, the bitterness of which had no alleviation.

Her conferences with these directors, to whom she
spoke separately and at different times, were the
cause of fresh humiliation. They were but little
experienced in spiritual ways, and formed their judgment as the greater part of the world do, condemning
without examination whatever wears the appearance
of miracle, singularity, or supernatural operation; for
to spare themselves the trouble of sifting and examin-

ing the matter, or in order by a bold and hasty decision to hide their ignorance of spiritual ways, they
no sooner heard than they condemned and despised
the whole affair. Such were the directors of this
little town, but slightly acquainted with the science
of the mysteries of God and of His grace. At Sister
Margaret's first recital they were prejudiced against
her; they shook their heads, regarded her as a
visionary, and ordered her to take broth; and the
oracle they pronounced was a condemnation of her
attraction to prayer, and a prohibition both to
the superior and the sister henceforth to pay any
attention to these marvels, however evident they
might be. Then they congratulated themselves upon
the supposed wisdom of their decision.

We may imagine what a trial it was to a mind so
convinced by its own experience, to acquiesce and obey
against that conviction; or rather, we may judge of
the perfection of Sister Margaret's obedience, by
her submission without murmur or reply to this
imprudent decision, of which she felt deeply the
falsity and error. She submitted to what was
ordered, and even carried her obedience so far as to
justify to her own mind the mistake of these directors,
and to acquiesce in all the humiliating and contemptuous things they had uttered, by condemning herself as one given up to the illusions of the devil in
punishment for her sins. "I made," said she,
"every effort to resist all these attractions, believing
myself to be assuredly in error, but not being able
to succeed, I gave myself up for lost, since I was
told that they were not from the Spirit of God, and
yet it was impossible for me to resist that Spirit
which attracted me."

In this fear, and in the midst of the strange agitation which arose within her in this violent struggle,
she addressed herself to our Lord, to find in Him
her consolation.   Then this Divine Spouse, who had
taken pleasure in seeing to what a height she carried the exactness of her obedience, reassured her,
telling her that He would soon extricate her from
her difficulties without her being wanting in the
obedience and submission which she owed to His
ministers.   He told her that by the secret arrangements of His providence He would shortly cause
one of His faithful servants to come to Paray, who
would console her in her troubles, and conduct her
in the holy ways which He would appoint.   He
added, that He wished her to manifest to His servant,
according to the knowledge which He would then
give her, all the treasures of His Divine Heart which
she had seen, and all the secrets which had been imparted to her.

Margaret communicated to her superior the prediction which had been made to her, and they soon
witnessed its accomplishment.   The faithful servant
whom God had promised was the Reverend Father
de la Colombiere, of the Society of Jesus.   This
father, who was so celebrated in that age for the
eloquence of his preaching and for the holy unction
which is found in all his works of piety, was still more
famous for the holiness and austerity of his life, his
apostolic labours, and the persecutions he suffered
for the faith in an heretical country.   It was he
whom God had destined to conduct His servant, to
manifest her holiness, and to co-operate with her in
the establishment of the devotion to the Heart of our
Lord.

This religious was sent by his superiors to Paray in 1675, to superintend the small house which the Jesuits have in that town. Soon after his arrival, he went to the monastery of the Visitation to pay his respects to the superior and the community. When Sister Margaret came into the parlour with the other nuns, it was said to her interiorly, "This is he whom I send thee." She concealed, however, this interior feeling, and was not eager to make herself known. Some days after, this father came to give an exhortation to the community. He was not acquainted with Sister Margaret, nor had he heard her spoken of; but during the exhortation he remarked a nun amongst the rest, in whom he saw something so recollected and divine, that after it was over he asked the mother-superior who that religious was whom he had remarked in such a place. The superior merely mentioned her name, speaking highly of her, but in a general way, without discovering the supernatural things which passed within her.

Soon afterwards the Ember-week of Lent arrived, and Father de la Colombiere was appointed extraordinary-confessor to the community. Sister Margaret went to him in her turn in the confessional, but as she had no order from her superior to open her mind to him, she refrained, notwithstanding her interior attraction, from making known to him her situation and her difficulties, and confined herself to a simple confession. The superior, before consulting this religious, wished to ascertain with greater certainty his knowledge of spiritual things; but having soon discovered the height of his sanctity and his experience in interior ways, she gave orders to Sister Margaret to communicate with him unreservedly.

Margaret then felt all imaginable repugnance to obey, either from her natural timidity, or from its being the Will of God that she should enjoy no consolation which was not mingled with suffering and victory. She overcame herself, however, and related with simplicity to Father de la Colombiere all that had passed within her, the different judgments that her superior and directors had formed, and the uneasiness and alarm which it had caused her; in a word, she described all the feelings of her heart.

Father de la Colombiere did not form his judgment hastily, but took time to study the operations of grace in this pure soul. He examined not once, but several times, her whole conduct; he often humbled her, and treated her in a severe and mortifying manner, more especially trying her obedience in several ways, for he knew that perfect obedience was the least equivocal mark of true holiness, and an infallible remedy against delusions. At length, after all the attention and care which might be expected from so prudent and holy a man, he could not avoid seeing in Sister Margaret clear proofs of the communication of God by supernatural means.

He then consoled her as to the uneasiness she felt, and assured her that demoniacal illusion had no share in what passed in her interior. He only warned her to guard her humility, by comparing her unworthiness and weakness with the graces God had bestowed on her, which she had not merited, and by considering that God loaded her with them continually instead of casting her off for her daily faults. He also gave her some advice as to vocal prayer, to which she applied herself with much difficulty, because she was strongly attracted to a more sublime prayer, which often hindered her from continuing what she had begun. This was a subject of scruple and trouble to her. He ordered her to confine herself to the vocal prayers of obligation, adding only the chaplet every day as far as she was able ; as to all the rest, he told her to allow herself to be directed without repugnance or scruple by the inspirations of the Spirit of God, according as it might please Him to communicate Himself to her.

She also consulted him upon a practice which several in the house condemned. She often felt urged interiorly to send spiritual letters to different persons, either to fortify them against the trials and temptations they experienced, or to induce them to make to God the sacrifices which He demanded of their fidelity. She only knew the necessities of the persons to whom she gave advice, by the same light which pressed her to give it ; but these inspired letters were not equally well received by all. Sometimes they reproved her for sending them, and took occasion to humble her, reproaching her with meddling with matters which did not concern her. As she willingly deferred to the opinion of others in opposition to her own lights, she began to fear that in reality there was temerity and indiscretion in the practice. The father reassured her ; he ordered her to continue to follow simply the movements of the Holy Spirit, whatever unpleasantness might happen to her on that account, to show these letters to her superior, and to be guided by her as to giving or withholding them, and lastly, told her to write down henceforth all that passed in her interior. This

order was very bitter to her ; she nevertheless obeyed, but posterity has not benefited by it, because to
reconcile obedience with humility, she had no sooner
written what she was ordered, than she immediately
threw it into the fire.

Margaret paid dearly for the consolations she experienced in the counsels of Father de la Colombiere.
According to our Lord's prediction, it was necessary
that everything should turn to her confusion and
the augmentation of her cross, in which Father
Colombiere bore his share. Their conversations at
the confessional were frequent during a certain time,
and sometimes very long, and both of them were
soon highly blamed. They said of Sister Margaret
that she wished to deceive this holy man, as she had
already deceived so many others, and that the countenance of this servant of God only tended to authorise her hypocrisy. Others said of Father de la
Colombiere, that he was no less visionary than his
penitent, that it showed much weakness in him to
amuse himself so long with a woman of so poor a
character and so little sense. The sister heard these
remarks, and more alive to what was said of her
director than of herself, she laid at the feet of her
Spouse all the bitterness which it caused her, and
complained of it to Him alone. The Son of God, to
fortify and support her, made her soon afterwards
understand in a miraculous manner the use He
would make of them both for the glory of His Heart,
and the share He would give them of the love with
which this divine Heart is inflamed.

This holy religious was saying the mass of the community in the church of the Visitation, when he felt
his heart burn with a new and inexplicable love for our

Lord Jesus Christ, at the sight of His goodness in communicating Himself to us in this divine sacrifice. Margaret knew by the Spirit of God what passed in the heart of Father de la Colombiere. When her turn came to communicate, our Lord at that moment showed her His divine Heart under the symbol of a burning furnace; she also saw two other hearts united with it and consumed in it; and at the same time she heard these words interiorly, "It is thus that My holy love unites these three hearts for ever;" and she understood that the two hearts consumed by this holy flame were the heart of Father de la Colombiere and her own. Our Lord told her also that He wished her to reveal to His servant what He had manifested to her concerning the admirable treasures contained in His Heart, and the love with which it is filled, that this holy religious might make it known to others, and disclose to the faithful the good they might derive from it. He added, that by their relation to this divine Heart, He wished them to be as brother and sister, who share equally the inheritance of their father; and that thus the treasures of grace which they would find in their union with Him should be shared. Margaret felt overcome with confusion at the kind of equality on which the Son of God seemed to place her with this father, whose sanctity she so much admired, whilst she regarded herself as an abyss of misery and sin. Our Lord replied to her, "The infinite riches of My Heart will equalise everything and supply everything."

The holy man was in his turn much confused, when the sister related to him what had passed; he thought himself very unworthy of being compared to a soul so favoured by God, and of whose holiness he had so high an idea, whilst he had a very mean opinion of himself. Such are the rivalries of the Saints, who dispute among themselves which is the lowest, and who, in opposition to the dictates of self-love, esteem themselves little, whilst they think highly of others, and seem to have eyes only for the virtues of their neighbours and for their own defects. Such was the disposition of these two faithful imitators of the humble Heart of Jesus Christ. Sister Margaret received nearly at the same time another singular favour, in which Father de la Colombiere had a large share, and which was, as it were, the first-fruits of the establishment of the devotion which had been up to this time so strongly opposed.

Being one day before the Blessed Sacrament during the Octave of its Feast, God bestowed exceeding graces of His love upon her, and made her feel an ardent desire to give Him a perfect return, by rendering Him love for love ; upon which our Lord said to her, " Thou canst not make Me a more acceptable return than by doing what I have so often asked." Then discovering to her His divine Heart, He said, " Behold this Heart, which has loved men so much that it has endured everything, given all its treasures, and made every effort to testify that love. In return I receive from the greater number only ingratitude, contempt, irreverence, sacrilege, and coldness in this sacrament of love. But what I feel the most deeply is, that there are hearts even, which are consecrated to Me, that treat Me thus. It is for this reason that I require that the first Friday after the Octave of the Blessed Sacrament, shall be set apart as a particular festival in honour of My

Heart, to make a reparation for all these indignities which are offered to it,' and as a day of communion, in order to atone for the unworthy treatment which it has received when exposed upon the altar. I promise that My Heart shall be opened to shed abundantly the influences of its divine love upon those who will pay it this honour, and lead others to do the same." "But, my Lord," replied Sister Margaret, "to whom art Thou speaking? To a creature so despicable, to so miserable a sinner, that her unworthiness will hinder the accomplishment of Thy designs." "What," replied our Lord, "dost thou not know that I make use of the weak to confound the strong; and that it is generally in the least and the poorest of spirit, that I make My power shine forth most strikingly, that they may attribute nothing to themselves?" "Give me, then," replied Margaret, "give me the means of doing what Thou commandest." Then He added, "Go to My servant,", (meaning Father de la Colombière,) "and tell him from Me to exert himself to the utmost to establish this devotion, and to give this gratification to My Heart. Let him not be discouraged by the difficulties he will encounter, for he shall succeed in the end; but let him also remember that he is all-powerful who places no confidence in himself but trusts entirely to Me."

Margaret, with her superior's permission, repeated what had passed to Father de la Colombiere. This father was not one of those light-minded persons who believe everything indiscriminately; but as he had carefully tried the holiness of Margaret, and recognized by clear and evident marks the truth of her communications with God, he could not refuse

what was commanded him by our Lord through the
ministry of His servant; he believed it his duty to
contribute to the establishment of this holy devotion, which was already authorized by so many miracles, and in which, moreover, there was nothing to
arouse suspicion. He began with himself; he wished
to be the first disciple of the Heart of Jesus Christ,
and the first adorer of His love according to the
rules given to Sister Margaret; and he therefore
consecrated himself wholly to this Sacred Heart, and
to the love which is its due; he offered all his
powers, and whatever he possessed, in its honour,
esteeming himself happy to be the victim of the love
of Jesus Christ. He made this consecration of himself to our Lord on the Friday after the Octave of
the Blessed Sacrament, June 21, 1675; a day which
we may regard as that on which this devotion made
its first conquest; a devotion which has since spread
throughout the world with abundant success and
fruit, as we shall see in the sequel.

From this day Father de la Colombiere experienced so many graces, and felt the fervour of his
love for Jesus Christ so much increased through this
devotion, that he was more and more confirmed by
his own experience in the opinion which he had conceived of it, as well as in that which he had formed of
the holiness of the servant of God, who had disclosed
to him this treasure. He spoke highly of it in the
journal of his spiritual retreat, which he made some
time afterwards, when occupied in the English missions. This journal, which was found amongst his
papers at his death, has been printed, and no one
can read it without being touched with the fervour
and unction which animated him. This is the testi-

mony which he renders to that devotion of which he had begun to understand the value at Paray: "At the end," said he, " of this retreat, being full of confidence in the mercy of my God, I have made a resolution to procure, by all possible means, the execution of what my Divine Master has ordered for the accomplishment of His desires, touching the devotion which He has suggested to a person to whom He communicates Himself most confidingly," (this was Sister Margaret,) " and for which He is pleased to make use of my weakness. I have already made known this devotion to several people in England. God, then, revealed His Will to that person, who, we have reason to think, after His own Heart, because of the great graces He has bestowed on her, and she explained it to me. I obliged her to write down what she told me, and I have given a general idea of it in this journal of my retreat, because God has willed, in the execution of His designs, to make use of my feeble endeavours."

This father did not wait until that time to spread the devotion to the Heart of Jesus Christ. He remained at Paray the whole of the year 1675, and part of 1676, during which time he directed many persons who applied to him to put in practice what had been prescribed by our Lord to His servant, and the result astonished even himself. By the practice of this devotion, several obtained the entire conversion of their hearts, and others found the means of advancing in perfection in the singular graces which they received from God.

Towards the month of September 1676, Father de la Colombiere was sent into England by his superiors, to labour in the difficult missions of that country.

A long time before this order had arrived, Sister
Margaret learned his destination from our Lord, and
predicted that he would leave France. She persisted
in assuring him of this, notwithstanding two succes-
sive orders which he received from his provincial to
repair to other posts for which he was destined; but
when he was preparing to execute the last of the
two orders, he received a third, which, by sending
him to England, verified the prediction of the servant
of God. This departure, though foreseen, was sensibly felt by Margaret, who lost in this holy man the
only director who had given her any consolation, or
reassured her in her interior troubles. She complained of it, however, only to her Spouse, for she
thought the spiritual direction of this true servant
of God necessary for her; but our Lord reproached
her, saying, "What! am I not sufficient for thee?
I who am thy beginning and thine end?"

Before his departure the father gave Sister Margaret spiritual advice. It was also the Will of God
that he should be warned by her of what was to
happen to him in England, in order to fortify him
against the snares which the devil would lay for him
in that laborious mission. The following is the
memorandum which she gave him, and the father,
who experienced its usefulness by its fulfilment, has
made mention of it in the journal of his retreat which
we have aleady quoted.

"The talent of Father de la Colombiere is to lead
souls to God, for which reason the devils will exert
all their efforts against him. Even persons consecrated to God will give him trouble, and will not
approve of what he will say in his sermons in order
to direct them to Him: but in these crosses the

goodness of God will be his support, so long as he continues to trust in Him.

"He ought to have a compassionate gentleness for sinners, and not be severe with them, except when God shall make known to him that it is His Will he should do so.

"Let him beware of drawing good from its source. This sentence is short, but contains much, of which God will discover to him the meaning according to the manner in which he applies it."

This memorandum, at once instructive and prophetic, was carefully preserved by the holy missionary; it served him as a precaution and guide on difficult occasions; he often felt the importance of the advice it contained, and experienced the truth of its predictions. Sister Margaret repeated this advice and warning in her letters after his departure, in clearer terms and greater detail. The third paragraph of the memorandum was not clear to the holy missionary, but God afterwards gave him the explanation of it, to lead him to practise in an heroic degree disinterestedness and poverty. Margaret from time to time sent letters to Father de la Colombiere through her superior, giving him the advice necessary for the position in which he was; she knew his needs as it pleased God to reveal them to her; and the mother-superior, through whose hands these letters and their answers from England passed, saw with astonishment the truth of what was revealed to the sister, and the accomplishment of what she had foretold. This superior has left us these facts in writing, of which account the following is a fragment, which deserves to be recorded:

13

" Our Lord one day revealed to Sister Margaret
the crosses and interior trials which Father de la
Colombiere endured in the country where his
superiors had sent him. She came to inform me of
this, presenting a letter to be forwarded to him. It
contained two very consoling things about his position, which Jesus Christ had dictated to her. As I
soon afterwards received letters from this great
servant of God, I knew by the requests he made that
he needed our prayers; and I thought this might
relate to what Sister Margaret had knowledge of.
I determined, therefore, to send the letter she had
placed in my hands. As I was copying it without
having mentioned it to any one, Sister Margaret came
to tell me that I had altered something in it which
did not please our Lord, Who wished it to remain as
He had caused it to be written. I reperused it, to
discover if I had made any mistake, and found that
I had in truth substituted for what she had written,
other words, which though very similar were less
forcible. Father de la Colombiere, after he received
this letter, wrote word that it had arrived just at the
right time, and that without its assistance he did not
know what he should have done."

These letters and several others signed and attested by this superior have been carefully preserved,
as well as the original letters of Father de la
Colombiere, which testify to the truth of the supernatural knowledge received by Sister Margaret for
the benefit of this holy missionary. He spoke of her
as follows in one of his letters to Mother de Saumaise, in 1678:

" It was not without reason that you informed me
that our Sister Margaret had been confirmed in her

opinion on the subject of the first article of the
paper you gave me on my departure. I needed this
just at the time you wrote to me, on account of the
ecclesiastic who caused me trouble concerning what
I said to draw souls to God. It was the only thing
of which I had not up to this time seen the accomplishment; but now it has happened as she
foretold. In the case of N., whom I mentioned
you the last time I wrote as having given himself
to God without its having caused me any annoyance,
I remembered it, thank God, most opportunely on
the very first occasion; for I was strongly tempted to
abandon everything from the fear of an outbreak
which might give scandal and wound charity."

In another letter of the 3rd of May, in the same
year, he said to Mother de Saumaise, "I do not
believe that without the letter containing the advice
of Sister Margaret, I could have borne the pains
which I have suffered, and which have never attacked
me with more violence than when pressed and overburdened with work."

On the 27th of June in the same year he writes
again: "The letter of our sister has caused me
much confusion, but I cannot sufficiently express
how exactly her advice was suited to my state; if she
could have seen into my interior she could not have
said anything more appropriate."

In another letter he said, "I cannot express to
you the great treasures I have discovered in what
you gave me on my departure from our Sister
Alacoque." (He speaks of the paper which is
given above.) "But what I can say is, that if the
evil spirit dictated it, it would be mightily against
himself, seeing that from it I have derived such great

assistance, that it has produced in me all the effect that the Holy Spirit is accustomed to produce."

Yet this holy missionary, who saw daily the truth of Sister Margaret's predictions, and who experienced also the value of her counsels, had not been able to comprehend the meaning of the third article of the paper. That mysterious advice, " not to draw good from its source," often occupied his thoughts without his being able to fathom its true application. God reserved the manifestation of it to Himself, to raise him by this means in His own time to a more heroic and entire detachment than that to which he had as yet attained. It was when the father was making a retreat of eight days in London, that its true meaning was made known to him. The following is what he himself relates in the journal we have already quoted :

" I perceived on the third day of my exercises, that the first point of the paper given me on my departure for London, which has been confirmed by a letter received two months ago, is only too true. For since my departure for Paris, the devil has laid five or six snares for me, which have greatly troubled me, and from which I could not have escaped without particular grace.

" On the fifth day God made known to me, if I mistake not, the meaning of this paragraph of the note which I brought from France : ' Let him beware of drawing good from its source. This sentence is short, but contains much, of which God will discover to him the meaning, according to the manner in which he applies it.' It is true that I have often examined this sentence without being able to discover its meaning. Having today remarked that God was to give me intelligence according to my application, I meditated on it for a long time without finding any other sense than this, that I ought to refer to God all the good that He may accomplish through me, since He is the only source of it all; but after having turned my thoughts from this consideration, suddenly a light came into my mind, by which I saw clearly that it cleared up a doubt respecting my pension, which had troubled me during the first two or three days of my exercises."

The father had hitherto received from his relations a considerable pension, which was of great assistance to him in his missions, and for the continuance of which he might have pleaded many pious reasons. But his love of perfection led him to feel troubled with regard to it; he feared that he had not sufficient confidence in the providence of God, and detachment from creatures; and that the spirit of poverty would not be perfected in his heart as long as he had this temporal resource. Whilst his judgment lay suspended between disinterestedness and prudence, the advice which he had received, and the light given him by God, determined him to make the generous sacrifice of this purely human assistance, and henceforth to have no other wealth or resource than the providence of God. Thus he gave up " drawing good from its source," that is to say, from his family, who had been the source of this provision. We may judge by the generous resolution taken by Father de la Colombiere, how pure and entire was his detachment, and how heroic his virtue; and from the merit of this holy religious we may estimate that of his penitent, in whom he saw so much sanctity.

It was this also which confirmed Mother de Saumaise in the firm persuasion at which she had
at length arrived, that what passed within her
spiritual daughter was the work of God. She was,
as we have seen, the confidant of the pious communications between these two disciples of the Heart
of Jesus Christ. Sister Margaret did not usually
write to Father de la Colombiere, but remitted to
her superior, as we have already said, short. papers
containing either the advice which she gave him
from God concerning himself, or that which she
requested of him for her own benefit; and it was to
the same superior that Father de la Colombiere
wrote in answer. Thus the pious intercourse
derived an additional merit from obedience, and
at the same time showed clearly to the mother-
superior, that the spirit which inspired the prophetic words of the sister was undoubtedly the Spirit
of God.

   It was this which induced her to yield credence to
a remarkable grace received at this time by Sister
Margaret relating to the community in which she
lived, a grace that only served to augment the feeling against her, and the ill-treatment she received
from her sisters. The community, notwithstanding
the care and attention of Mother de Saumaise, and
the good example of some of the elder sisters, had,
as may have been observed, fallen into a relaxed
state. God made known to Sister Margaret how
much He was irritated against the house, and the
danger in which it was of being abandoned if His
servant did not sacrifice herself for its good. "My
daughter," said He to her one day, "thou must be
the victim of immolation of My Heart, that by its

mediation thou mayest turn away the chastisements which the irritated justice of My Father is on the point of inflicting on thy community." At the same time He showed her in spirit the particular defects which existed in it, relaxation in the practice of the rule, intercourse with people of the world, murmurs against obedience, attachment to temporal things, the coldness for prayer and communion, vanity, &c.; and He also showed her what she must suffer in order to appease His anger, and to obtain for the house a return to its first fervour. She confessed, in the account she gave of this favour, that at the sight of the sufferings which were proposed to her she trembled all over, and she dared not make the sacrifice of herself which her Divine Spouse required. She only replied that, not being her own, she could not make this sacrifice without the consent of her superior. The fear that obedience might impose on her the necessity of doing what was required of her, which would cost her so much, made her commit another fault; she deferred giving an account of what had been shown her to her superior, and asking her permission to comply with what her Lord desired. But her Divine Spouse pursued her incessantly, reproaching her with cowardice and weakness. He pressed her so urgently that at length she went, bathed in tears, to relate to Mother de Saumaise what God exacted from her, and the fear with which she was overwhelmed. The mother believed it to be her duty to submit to the Spirit of God, and ordered the sister to sacrifice herself without reserve in all that God desired of her.

Sister Margaret's fear was so great that she still hesitated, and though she dare not refuse to make the sacrifice, she delayed it for several days, until at length on the eve of the Presentation, when praying with the community, and struggling against this repugnance, the wrath of God was suddenly made manifest to her under an appearance so terrible, that she was completely overwhelmed; and at the same time it was said to her, as to St. Paul, "It is hard for thee to kick against the goad." The Spirit of God added, "Since thou hast made so much resistance to avoid the humiliations that it was necessary for thee to suffer in this sacrifice, I will give thee double. I only asked of thee a secret sacrifice, but now it shall be public, in a manner and at a time beyond all human calculation. It shall be accompanied by circumstances so humiliating, that they will be a source of confusion to thee for the rest of thy life, as well in thy own sight as in that of others, in order to teach thee what it is to resist God." The sisters left the choir after prayer, but Sister Margaret remained there to give vent to her tears, until the bell rang for collation. She felt urged to go to the refectory, there to make aloud in presence of the community the sacrifice that God had required from her. The superior, whose permission she must first obtain, not being there on account of sickness, Margaret repaired to the infirmary to seek her, but was so much overcome, and her interior struggles were so violent, that she was unable to proceed. She stopped half way, completely overwhelmed, bathed in tears, and trembling from head to foot, repeating from time to time these words mingled with sighs, "My God, according to the greatness of Thy mercy, have pity upon me." One of the sisters finding her in this state about

eight o'clock, led her to the superior. She stood
there overpowered by the same transport of grief and
confusion, seeing nothing, and thinking of nothing
but the anger of God, the impression of which she
felt in an unspeakable manner. They questioned
her as to what had happened, how she felt, and what
she wished, but still silent, she continued on her
knees before the superior in terrible confusion; for
it seemed to her that all the world saw and knew
what passed within her, and was informed of her
struggles, her infidelity, and of the anger of God;
thus she remained in that silent confusion which
a criminal feels in the presence of his judge, to
whom he dare not confess the crime which yet he
cannot conceal.

The superior judged that something extraordinary
was passing in her soul, and knowing the power of
obedience over her, enjoined her to disclose her
trouble. Sister Margaret obeyed, and related simply how God had communicated to her His displeasure against the house, the sacrifice which He
exacted from her on that account, and the resistance
which she had made to His Will. In fine, she added
her submission to the Will of God, and her resolution to make, as she in reality did, the sacrifice
required of her. Mother de Saumaise was inspired
by God to submit to the warning given to His servant, and thought it her duty to direct all the community to appease His divine anger. She sent the
sister-assistant with orders from her to all the nuns,
then assembled for matins, to do a certain penance
which she prescribed that same night, because God
was highly incensed against them.

This sudden order caused great dismay in the

hearts of those sisters who were neither mortified
nor obedient; the number of these was great, and
they immediately conspired against Margaret, whom
they judged to be the cause of this alarm. Whilst
the more spiritual retired to their cells to practise
there what the superior had ordered, the others at
the conclusion of matins hastened to the infirmary,
where Sister Margaret still remained overwhelmed
with grief: they could learn nothing of what had
passed, excepting that Margaret had said that God
was highly irritated against the community, and this
only increased their indignation. They believed
themselves insulted by this warning, and in contempt of the rule of silence, and still more of charity,
they began to heap every kind of insult upon the
servant of God. They reproached her, ridiculed her,
and cross-questioned her in the most indiscreet manner; but still she answered nothing, and remained
motionless on her knees, with her hands clasped in
the midst of the crowd of rebellious sisters. However, they were at length obliged to leave the infirmary, as the bell for retiring was rung.

They agreed to conduct the servant of God to
her cell, but it was not charity which induced them
to undertake this charge; they rather dragged than
led her, for the weight of her grief had so crushed
her, that she could neither speak nor support herself. They dragged her thus, sometimes to one
place, sometimes to another, every one questioning
or quarrelling with her according to their fancy;
and as the holy religious was unable to speak, they
made a crime even of her silence. Some of them
said she had become foolish or stupid, and ought
be shut up; others that she was in a fit of apoplexy,

and wished to apply remedies. There were some who imagined her to be possessed, and made the sign of the cross over her, while reciting prayers to drive away the demon. A part of the night was passed in this way, and it was only put an end to by the weariness of the sisters, who at length retired to rest, while the remainder was passed by Margaret in deep sorrow, oppressed by the weight of God's anger, and quite unable either to lie down or sleep.

The next morning the mother-superior having learnt that Sister Margaret was still in the same state, sent her orders to go to mass and to communicate. Obedience had always a certain effect upon her. She did as she was commanded, and in the communion our Lord caused her to hear these words: "At length peace is established, and My holiness of justice is satisfied by the sacrifice which thou hast made to Me." But as David, after his sin had been pardoned, still expiated it by the afflictions prepared for him by God, so also the peace which God sent into the heart of His servant did not release her from the suffering and humiliating state to which He had reduced her. She was still overwhelmed with the impression of terror which she had felt at the sight of the terrible anger of God, and the shame of the remembrance of her infidelity increased her interior pain; her senses partook of the pain that her heart suffered; she could scarcely eat, sleep, or speak, and it was only by making extraordinary efforts that she could apply herself to the exercises and employment with which she was charged; for the sight of her state and of the anger of God never quitted her, and absorbed her senses

so that she seemed to possess the control of them no
longer. "My whole occupation," said she in the
account which she has given of this event, suppress-
ing the name of the community which had given rise
to it, "My whole occupation consisted in remaining
prostrate before my God, Whose sovereign greatness
kept me buried in a profound sense of my own
nothingness, continually weeping, sighing, and entreating Him, that in His mercy He would turn
away the scourges of His just anger."

In the meanwhile what had passed was discussed
in the house, and each one judged of it according to
her disposition. One endeavoured to divine what
was the subject of the anger of God, and of the
sacrifice which He required from His servant, forming conjectures at hazard. Some declared that this
pretended vision was an insult to the house and to
the whole order; others thought the sister very
proud to believe that she could sacrifice herself for
the good of others; some pretended that she failed
in charity, others in prudence. One questioned,
another mocked, a third blamed, a fourth turned her
into ridicule; some even insulted those who compas-
sionately undertook her defence. "Were we not
right," said several, "in always regarding her as a
visionary, who gives us dreams for revelations?"
The most charitable knew not what to say or to
think of an action which appeared to them so extraordinary. There were some also who said that it
was a pity she had become so foolish, and others
who persisted in believing seriously that she was
possessed, and that she ought to be exorcised, and
came devoutly to sprinkle her with holy water.

The idea which had before been taken up by some

that she was under a delusion, was revived, and she
was pitied for being thus the sport of the devil, by
whom, said they, she permits herself to be deceived.
Each in her own way furnished her with an occasion
of suffering and humiliation, some through piety,
and others from dislike or folly. The absence and
illness of the superior during the whole time that
this feeling against the servant of God lasted, gave
still greater liberty to those imperfect religious who
disliked her. To induce her to eat they were obliged
to employ the authority of obedience, which was
always efficacious with her; but the form of the
command shewed indiscretion of the sister who in
the absence of the superior took upon herself to
give it. Margaret was ordered to eat whatever was
presented to her. She thought this beyond her
power, nevertheless she complied, not once only, but
at every repast; and this obedience caused her fresh
suffering, as each meal was followed by violent
vomiting, which in a few days deranged her stomach
very much, and caused her excessive pain. The
order which had been given was changed, but too
late; the pain lasted for a long time, and added
languor and faintness to all the other interior and
exterior sufferings with which the servant of God
was overwhelmed.

This state and this kind of persecution lasted
several days, and was only put an end to by obedience. The mother-superior ordered Sister Margaret
to ask our Lord at the time of holy Communion to
restore her to her ordinary state. She obeyed immediately, and our Lord granted her prayer without
delay, assuring her of it interiorly, and telling her
that He would endue her with new vigour, in order

to immolate her afterwards by fresh sufferings.
Everything came to pass as He had said. From that
moment she recovered her liberty of acting, speaking, and eating, and she felt like a slave released
from his chains and set at liberty. As for the disposition of the greater part of the sisters towards
her, it did not change for a long time; and as Jesus
Christ had predicted to His servant, that which in
His sight was so meritorious, was for a length of time
in the eyes of those sisters, who were ignorant of
the mysteries of God, a matter of reproach, and also
for herself a subject of confusion.

Mother de Saumaise, however, judged very differently of all that had passed; she felt more than
any one the need there was of a renewal of fervour
amongst her spiritual daughters, and she could not
cease admiring the conduct of God towards His servant in sanctifying her by the way of the cross, and
making her by means of opprobrium and sorrow a
complete image of the Son of God. The experience
she continually had of the truth of the communications of the Spirit of God to this favoured soul,
induced her at length to permit Sister Margaret to
practise without reserve the devotions prescribed by
our Lord in honour of His adorable Heart.

This permission was a subject of indescribable joy
to our holy religious, and it was a fresh source of
graces and favours to her. She affirmed that whatever she had until then felt was nothing in comparison of what she now experienced in the holy Communion, and in the prayer during the night of the
first Thursday in the month until the Friday morning. It was in one of these prayers that God warned
His servant that Satan had demanded to have power

over her, as he formerly had over holy Job, that he might have permission to attack her by temptations and fresh contradictions, and even by exterior ill-treatment; that this had been granted him, with the exception of temptations against purity, by which God never permitted His servant to be in the least molested. He warned her that amongst other things she would be particularly tempted to despair, pride, and gluttony; He instructed her as to the vigilance with which she was to guard herself against the snares which would be spread for her, assuring her of ultimate success in these struggles, and adding that He would fight for her, surround her with His power, and be Himself the reward of her victory.

This prediction soon began to be accomplished. The devil waged against Margaret every kind of warfare, and this persecution lasted almost the whole of her life. As the first declaration of war, and with the design of intimidating her, he presented himself to her under the form of a hideous Moor; with his eyes darting fire, and grinding his teeth like a ferocious beast, he said to her furiously, "If I can once get thee in my power, I will make thee feel what I can do. I will injure thee in every way." Threats were followed by acts, and that in a manner so sensible, that the sisters were astonished at it. Sometimes the demon attacked Sister Margaret exteriorly, sometimes in the secrecy of her soul. Several times this invisible power was known violently to take away what was in her hands, and throw it on the ground, in order to cause her vexation or impatience, or to draw upon her confusion and reproach. Sometimes when seated with the sisters round the common fire, an invisible force would drag the seat upon which she was sitting violently from beneath her, and make her fall suddenly several times running. In 1715 there were still living three sisters who had witnessed this, and deposed juridically to the fact, as well as to the greater part of the things we have related. Once the devil precipitated her from the top of a staircase to the bottom, while carrying an earthen pot filled with fire, which was neither broken nor upset. The nuns who saw her fall expected to find her sorely bruised, but she had sustained no injury, and knew that her good angel had preserved her. In secret the devil ill-treated her more freely and more frequently, but he found in her the same patience as formerly in holy Job; she even denied herself the slight consolation of speaking or complaining of her trials.

She, however, faithfully disclosed to her superior the frightful temptations with which she was assailed interiorly. Sometimes she felt thoughts and movements of pride and vain-glory excited within her, and immediately afterwards would find herself plunged into sadness, disgust, and inconceivable despondency; the devil suggesting to her, that so wicked and unfaithful a creature as herself ought not to expect to have any part in Paradise, and that even now she had no share in the love of God. The darkness that by the permission of God Satan then spread over the soul of His servant was so thick, that she no longer perceived the ardent love with which she was inflamed for her Divine Spouse; she could only see what she regarded as sins, the enormity of which was magnified by the temptation, and everything which she did appeared to her to be faulty. She

took for sins the involuntary sentiments which the
devil excited in her, and every thought of pride or of
despair that he suggested pained her heart as if she
had consented to it.   One must have passed through
this state to understand its indescribable bitterness;
what Sister Margaret felt appeared to her inexplicable, though she did her best to make it known to her
superiors, two of whom successively were witnesses
to these interior pains, which lasted a long time.
She gave them an account of her state in writing,
and her superiors also sometimes answered her in the
same way.   From some of these notes, which Sister
Margaret kept for her own consolation, and which
were found after her death, we may form some
idea of the bitterness of the temptations which
tormented her.   Her superior speaks of them as
follows :

"I pray Jesus Christ our Saviour and almighty
Lord, to command the tempest to cease within you;
and I say to you in His name, remain in peace;
your soul is the portion of the Lord.   In spite of
your enemies you will ever love Him, rejoicing in
Him in eternity, and suffering for the love of Him
in this life whenever He gives you the opportunity."

In another note the superior thus consoled her:
"All that I can say, my child, touching your position and your sufferings, is, that you complain of a
superfluity of graces.   I should esteem it a great
favour if God caused me to feel a pain similar to
yours.   I have already told you that it is to think
or to speak evil of the goodness of God, to entertain
the thought that He will abandon to the privation
of His eternal love, a heart which aspires to love

14

Him alone in time and in eternity.   No, He never
has done it, nor will He ever do it.   He does not
condemn and abandon the poor and the miserable,
unless they are rendered such by their own malice.
If in doing you the favour to give you some extraordinary insight into His divine attributes, He at the
same time shows you something of your own unworthiness; if He makes you feel that your sins leave
you nothing to expect but the abyss of hell, you
must not make a bad use of this knowledge; it is
given you in order that you may confess the greatness of the divine mercy of our Lord, Who, by opposing His merits to your sins, wishes to save you from
them and from their punishment.   Thus you should
dispel all the desponding thoughts suggested to you
by these words: 'I will sing eternally the mercies
of the Lord, for He is good in all ages.'   Yet it is
necessary during this life to give something to His
justice; now what we owe to Him is patience,
humility, and submission of heart in the trials and
sufferings which befall us, of whatever nature they
may be.   Bear yours in this manner; you ought to
esteem and cherish them, because they are not such
as happen to the reprobate; great saints have suffered them, and you do not deserve to experience
them.   Receive them then, with thanksgiving, peace,
humility, sweetness, and patience; you will indeed
be happy, if they lead you to feel your own
nothingness, and no longer to seek yourself in anything."

While in this state Sister Margaret always desired
to be humbled and mortified.   She found in the
contempt she received a sort of relief, as it satisfied
the lively horror she had conceived of her sins, and

of the state in which she beheld her soul. She regarded herself as the object of God's anger and justice, and entreated the mother-superior to satisfy the craving she felt for mortifications; we will now see what answer this wise and experienced religious made to her request:

"I will take care to humble and mortify you at the time and in the manner I shall think best. Leave this to our Lord, in order that He may inspire me to do what will be useful to you. If it is His Will that your death should serve as an example of terror and fear to others, cheerfully submit to it; but your soul will not be lost, for He will save it by His holy mercy. No one is a hypocrite without the consent of his own will; he alone deceives his fellow creatures who wishes for their honour and esteem; you have no wish of the sort, do not, therefore, be troubled by the thought that you are a hypocrite."

By these answers we see in part what were the interior pains of this poor religious, when delivered over to the fury of Satan. He next tormented her with the temptation of gluttony, which was the more surprising, as she had always been conspicuous for temperance in eating and drinking. The devil made her feel an insatiable hunger, and at the same time represented to her imagination in the most lively manner the objects most calculated to excite her appetite. It was often in prayer and in her other spiritual exercises that her mind was filled with these importunate ideas. This hunger never left her excepting when she entered the refectory; then she was filled with a disgust for all food, and it was only by doing violence to herself that she managed to eat at all. Scarcely had she left the table when her hunger returned with double force; and thus her days were passed either in absolute disgust of food, or in an uncontrollable longing for it, with the continual punishment of never being able to satisfy either of these feelings.

The superior ordered her to come and ask permission to eat something when she was thus pressed with hunger. Sister Margaret knew well the utter uselessness of this remedy, but nevertheless obeyed, though this obedience caused her great confusion and shame; for when she came, the mother-superior reproached her in a humiliating manner for so unreasonable and ill-regulated an appetite, and to increase her confusion, ordered her to go and ask the procurator for something to eat, confessing her extreme hunger. The obedient sister performed with exactness what was required of her, and was not disheartened by these humiliating commands. It was by these exercises of humility and obedience that she was at length delivered from this temptation. The demon was baffled and ceased to torment her on a subject which only increased the merit of the servant of God.

BOOK V.

THE REVEREND MOTHER GREFFIER IS SUPERIOR. SHE
SUBJECTS SISTER MARGARET TO NEW TRIALS CON-
CERNING HER EXTRAORDINARY GRACES, AND THE
DEVOTION TO THE SACRED HEART OF JESUS CHRIST.

When the six years of the superiorship of the venerable Mother de Saumaise were over, she was elected
superior by the nuns at Moulins, and the community
of Paray chose the Mother Peronne Rosalie Greffier,
a professed nun of the monastery of Annecy, to fill
her place. She obeyed the call, and arrived at Paray
on the 17th of June, 1678.

No one could be better fitted to fill the place for
which Providence had destined her, and particularly
to test the extraordinary ways by which it pleased
God to conduct Sister Margaret. It was His Will
that these ways should be tried and approved by
different persons who were wise and experienced, free
from credulity or weakness, and conspicuous in the
order for their prudence. Thus a superior like
Mother de Saumaise was succeeded by another no
less holy and enlightened, who possessed all the
qualities which could be desired to try the virtue of
the servant of God in the surest manner. With
great elevation of mind, solid piety, very deli-
cate discernment, and much firmness, she combined
consummate experience in spiritual ways; added
to which, that nothing might be wanting in the
dispositions necessary for careful examination of

the conduct of Sister Margaret, this wise superior possessed, together with a great inclination to suspect anything extraordinary, and almost a species of incredulity towards it, the most perfect attachment to the spirit of the order of the Visitation, which is one of simplicity and obedience without singularity.

When Mother Greffier entered the monastery, she found the community very much divided in their opinion of Sister Margaret. Some, but it was the smallest number, began to overcome their prejudices against her; others spoke very badly of her; some taxed her with hypocrisy, others with delusion; the more moderate blamed what they called singularity in her conduct. The mother determined to judge for herself, and in order to do so, tried Sister Margaret by all the most approved means. Her first efforts were directed to humbling her profoundly and almost continually, even going beyond what Mother de Saumaise had already done. Her principal object was to put her obedience to the proof, well knowing that this was the touchstone of solid piety. She not only ascertained that her orders were exactly and promptly obeyed, but she sometimes took pleasure in giving contradictory commands, in putting difficulties and obstacles in her way, to see how her obedience would steer its course among these little embarrassments, and to discover if self-love would direct her in the choosing between opposite commands, or if vanity would not take advantage of them to find excuses for not obeying. These difficult and frequent trials served only to convince the superior that Margaret's obedience was perfect. The servant of God, to the best of her power, reconciled what appeared contradictory; she surmounted difficulties, and would disentangle herself from the snare without either complaining, murmuring, boasting, or excusing herself, so that nothing could be discovered but unhesitating obedience and most unaffected simplicity.

To the trial of her obedience the superior joined that of her humility, the other touchstone of real virtue; and she did this the more boldly because she well knew there was no fear of discouraging a person so greedy of crosses and humiliations as was this holy religious. She tried her by every kind of humiliation and penance, and far from being disconcerted by this increase of rigour, Sister Margaret felt intense joy in being filled with this bread for which her soul sighed incessantly. The peace of her heart is shown by her placing the same entire confidence in this austere superior as in the preceding one, whose removal natural feeling would have caused her to regret. She went to her with the same frankness and cordiality as to Mother de Saumaise; she disclosed to her as simply what passed within her, and gave her as exact an account of the extraordinary graces which she continued to receive from God. The mother always listened to her with much patience and charity, but showed in a marked manner that she made no account of these supernatural favours, appearing to place no faith in them, and always following the common rules in the advice or the permissions she gave her.

The contempt with which this new superior treated the extraordinary lights that Sister Margaret received, threw her into fresh trouble. Her doubts upon the state of her soul returned; she again suspected the truth of the favours she received from God; she more than ever feared that she was deceived by the devil, and was the sport of his illusions. It was sufficient for the superior to appear to believe or to doubt, to make Sister Margaret do the same, and we may form some judgment of her troubles, when these afflicting thoughts were added to the interior desolation with which she was oppressed. We cannot forbear to make a passing remark on the perfection of this obedience, which finds few imitators. We are apt to think we do much in obeying the orders of our superiors, while we allow ourselves to judge and blame them interiorly; but this holy soul carried her obedience so far as to be ready to sacrifice the most evident communications of God to the judgment of her superior.

Mother Greffier carried her trial of Sister Margaret so far as to forbid her the practices by which she honoured the Sacred Heart of our Lord, those practices which God Himself had prescribed, and which the preceding superior had permitted after so many precautions. Margaret obeyed without a murmur, but our Lord appeared to her, shewed anger at the prohibition, and ordered her to tell the mother-superior that He would satisfy Himself and punish her in a manner she would deeply feel. The superior paid no attention to this menace, and thought it her duty to disregard it; but shortly afterwards God deprived her of one of her nuns, for whom she had conceived a great esteem, and in whom she placed great confidence for the government of temporal affairs. This religious was carried off by an illness which appeared contagious, and made the superior apprehensive for the rest of the community. Mother Greffier, who has herself given the account of all these details, adds that this death, so afflicting to her, was accompanied with some peculiar circumstances which she did not think proper to make known, but which appeared to her clearly to verify the prediction made by the Son of God to His servant. After this she gave the permissions she had before refused, especially that of making the accustomed prayer on the night from Thursday to Friday; only, to spare the health of Sister Margaret, she forbade her to pass the hour of prayer prostrate on the ground, with her arms extended in the form of a cross, as she had been accustomed to do, and desired her to remain on her knees with her hands joined.

This event, added to the constant obedience and humility of Sister Margaret, sufficed to convince the superior of the reality of the extraordinary favours which she received from God; yet she dared not be precipitate in her judgment, because of the opposition she met with from several of the community, and from other good people, who persuaded themselves, as those who are not willing to examine anything profoundly almost always do, that there was nothing in this sister but weakness of imagination, delusion, or singularity. This difference between opinion and experience threw the mother into great perplexity, in which she was confirmed by the doubts of Margaret herself, who, in her humility, and in the midst of the strange temptations with which the devil tormented her, dared not persuade herself that God had really bestowed on her such great favours. But to reassure both the mother and daughter, God

made use of the same means which He had already
employed to enlighten Mother de Saumaise. Father
de la Colombiere was recalled from London by his
superior at this time ; he had permission to pass ten
or twelve days at Paray, and he arrived there pre-
cisely at the time when his presence and his guidance
were necessary to relieve Mother Greffier and Sister
Margaret from their uneasiness. In a short time he
calmed the suspicions of the superior, and made her
understand that there could be no illusion of the
devil in what was so admirable in Sister Margaret,
and that the hand of God was too clearly shown
there to be mistaken ; and that if she had acted pru-
dently in trying the dispositions of this sister,
there would be only suspicion and obstinacy in
pushing incredulity farther after such evident proofs
of her exalted virtues. " Be sure," added he, " that
humility, simplicity, and exact obedience were never
united with false virtues, nor can they ever be the
fruit of deceits of the devil."

In the conversation of this holy man Margaret
found great consolation in the midst of her troubles.
With the permission of her superior she had several
interviews with him, but as, according to our Lord's
prediction, she was never to have any consolation
without a mixture of bitterness, one of these conversations drew upon her a humiliation, which was
remarkable on account of the patience with which
she received it. The parlour being occupied, the
superior permitted her to discourse with Father de
la Colombiere in the confessional. The long time
she remained there caused some of the sisters, who,
as is too often the case in communities, were indiscreet and fond of criticising, to complain. The

superior knew this; she forgot, or thought proper
to conceal, the permission she had given, and severely
reproved the sister in chapter, as guilty of a great
fault, imposing a penance on her. It would have
been easy for Margaret to justify herself, by humbly
declaring the permission which had been given her,
but she chose rather to imitate the silence of Jesus
Christ when unjustly accused, and to submit to the
reproaches which were made to her; and her innocence would never have been known, if the superior
herself had not taken care in the end to inform the
sisters of it for their edification, and to commemo-
rate this fact in the memoirs she has left us of this
holy soul.

Such was the austere conduct of Mother Greffier
towards Sister Margaret during the whole time that
she was superior; she thought it necessary for the
good of the servant of God, that she should be
directed only by the way of humiliations and crosses.
This prudent superior did violence to her gentle and
charitable disposition, in order to conform herself to
the Will of God with regard to His spouse; and she
had the consolation of seeing that He blessed this
severity, as the humble religious became by it more
fervent and more holy. What Mother Greffier wrote
on this subject after Margaret's death has already
been related. The testimony of a person who carried her prudence to suspicion, and almost to severity, ought to have great weight with the incredulous. We may say of her, what St. Gregory said of
St. Thomas the Apostle, that in one sense, he had
contributed more by his incredulity to assure us of
the truth of the resurrection of Jesus Christ, than
the other apostles had by their faith. In truth, the

conviction of an incredulous person is the strongest
of all testimonies; the witness, therefore, which
Mother Greffier bears to the virtue of a religious
so severely tried by her, ought to overthrow all the
doubts which extraordinary favours raise in the
mind.

But what, in our opinion, adds a high degree of
certainty to the marvellous things related of this
sister, is, as we have before said, her confidence in a
superior so suspicious and so austere, a confidence
more wonderful than the greatest miracles: and this
has been remarked by Mother Greffier herself. Sister Margaret concealed nothing from her, and though
a thousand times repulsed when she related the
favours of Jesus Christ, or told of her own interior
sorrows, she still communicated them with the same
simplicity. The mother thought fit to order her to
describe in writing the state of her mind and her
troubles, as she had done with Mother de Saumaise ;
and as she wished only to prove and not to discourage her faithful disciple, she answered her with
charity. I will here introduce some of these answers, which will make known the merit of this
superior, and the height of her knowledge in the
ways of perfection:

. "I have already frequently told you that God is
the Master of His graces, and gives them to whom
He pleases. It is certain that you are more indebted to Him for those He bestows on you than
many others would be, because I see nothing in you
which can attract them, and therefore they proceed
only from His goodness and His infinite mercy.
Keep yourself humble in the spirit of simplicity, and
leave Him to do whatever He pleases in your soul.

When His light and His grace lead you to love and
esteem your vocation and your religious duties, it is
a good sign; when they inspire you with a love of
suffering, contempt, and abjection, be with regard to
them in the disposition of one who asks nothing and
refuses nothing, but receive with a loving simplicity
either enjoyment or privation, rejoicing equally in
one or the other, for they both come to you in the
order of Divine Providence. I do not mean that
this should dispense you from asking from God the
continuance of your health for the time marked out
in the inclosed obedience. Do not listen to your
difficulties thereupon." We will in the sequel relate
what was the occasion and the success of this demand for health that the superior prescribed to Sister Margaret, of which she again speaks in the following note:

"You please me, my dear sister, when you write
instead of speaking to me, as it is thus more easy for
me to answer what is right and fitting, because in
speaking my mind is distracted. I promise you that
I will humble and mortify you willingly and cheerfully at proper times, because you have need of this
assistance; it is charity to do this to you, and I
desire the good of your soul. Let not that, however, take away your confidence in coming to me, or
in writing to me, according as you may wish; I
shall always be anxious to serve you, for your soul
is dear to mine, notwithstanding all that may make
you disagreeable, a burden, or importunate to me.
I must imitate your heavenly Father, who bestows
His favours without any merit on your part. Come,
then, not only three times a day, but six if you will,
to receive the blessing you desire; I give it you with

all my heart. I command you once more, in virtue of holy obedience, and in honour of the submission of the adorable Heart of our Lord Jesus Christ to God His Father, that you ask the preservation of your health, that is to say, as much as is sufficient to follow the common order of the rule without need of dispensations, and also to be able for the time to come to accomplish the Will of God, and the order of obedience, with a good heart, in a proper manner, and a sweet and charitable concord between your neighbour and yourself."

In another note she thus writes: "Live at the mercy of Divine Providence, and receive indifferently, as from Him, joy and sorrow, peace and trouble, health and sickness. Ask nothing, and refuse nothing, but hold yourself ready to do and to suffer whatever Divine Providence may send you. The three desires which torment you are good, provided they do not influence your will in a direction contrary to the rule and to obedience, and that they leave you in a state of holy indifference. In this spirit endure the torment of these desires." We have before seen what these three desires were with which she was so ardently filled, after the example of our Lord, Who said, " I have a baptism wherewith I am to be baptised, and how am I straitened until it be accomplished!" The mother thus continues: "Whether these desires torment you or leave you in tranquillity, it ought to be the same thing to you, since you belong to God. If He wishes to mould you like soft wax, or to play with you as with a ball, what matters it? Abandon yourself for the love, through the love, and to the love of Jesus Christ. This is what I believe God expects from you, since

He loves to govern us, and we know not how to conduct ourselves. I do not think that the devil has anything to do with what you tell me in your letter. Be in peace.

" I am always firmly convinced, my dear sister, that the most secure ways of God are those which annihilate us, humble us, and make us suffer much in our souls and bodies. You ought to be indifferent as to what means Divine Providence employs for this end. When you hear words of raillery, contempt, scorn, or disapprobation directed against you, it is the exterior mark that He gives you of His design to perfect you in humility of heart. Do not make yourself uneasy as to natural antipathies; only be firm in desiring that notwithstanding this resistance, the good pleasure of God may reign in you above all, and overwhelm you, if it so pleases Him, with bitterness, anguish, humiliation, &c. You know that He is a kind Master, and that with one word He can cure all your evils. The time will come, my much-honoured sister, when you will reap in joy; the present is the time of sorrow. A little patience, and for a moment of crucifixion the Lord will reward you by an eternity of blessed enjoyment."

Mother Greffier has depicted her own character in this advice; and in so wisely pointing out the way of perfection she has shown us how far she had herself advanced in it. Her spiritual enlightenment, joined to her suspicion of all extraordinary ways, renders incontrovertible the testimony which she has so often borne since the death of the venerable Sister Margaret, not only to her virtue, but also to the supernatural and miraculous favours which she frequently received from God.

One of the graces which Sister Margaret most commonly received, was a knowledge of the interior state of certain persons. God manifested to her the secret sins into which these persons had fallen, and imposed on her the obligation of suffering for them, in order to obtain for them the grace of repentance. This knowledge was a source of great pain to Margaret, both on account of the horror which she felt towards sin itself, for she seemed to see it then as it is in the sight of God; and also from the terror into which she was thrown by the angry countenance of her Spouse. The bitterness and interior desolation with which God filled her soul, that she might bear in part the punishment due to those crimes which were revealed to her, was very grievous; and on one occasion this pain was so great as in a manner to make her experience the state of desolation of a guilty soul, at the moment when, separated from its body, it finds itself condemned by God.

It was more often in behalf of those religious souls who were imperfect in their state of life, that God exacted from her this kind of expiation. From the first years of her profession, Jesus Christ ordered her to sacrifice herself freely to Him, and to endure this kind of pain whenever it should please Him. He, at the same time, made known to her the sins which were the most displeasing to Him; and He included in them want of charity amongst the sisters; "For," said He, "this virtue springs from the Heart of God, and to sin against this divine virtue is to wound this Heart itself, which is all charity." He added, that He should already have cut off these half-rotten members, if His holy Mother, to whom these persons were still devout,

had not retarded the effects of His justice. Then
the sister offered herself to Him, to bear, according
to His Will, all the punishment these sins deserved,
that He might be glorified by the souls that offended
Him ; " Even," added she, " were these pains to last
to the day of judgment, provided that God be glorified by them, I should be content."

This knowledge and these generous sacrifices were
several times renewed, always with the same suffering and the same courage. Our Lord one day presented Himself to His servant, covered with wounds;
His Body appeared bathed in blood, His Heart
torn and withered by weariness and suffering. At
this sight she was seized with fear, and prostrated
herself before her Spouse, without daring to speak
to Him. " Behold," said He to her, " the state to
which My chosen people, whom I had destined to
appease My justice, have reduced Me! They persecute Me, and that secretly. If they do not amend
their lives, I will chastise them severely ; I will
withdraw My just ones, and immolate the rest to
My anger."

"Another time," said she, " as I was working
alone, a religious then living was placed before me,
and it was plainly said to me, 'Behold this nun, who
is a religious only in name, and whom I am on the
point of casting from My heart and abandoning to
herself.' I was at the same time seized with so
lively a terror, that I threw myself down with my
face to the ground, and remained there a long time
unable to rise. At last I offered myself to the
divine justice, to suffer whatever He pleased, that
this unfaithful religious might not be abandoned.
It suddenly seemed to me that the anger of God

15

was turned against me, and I found myself in a state of frightful and boundless anguish and desolation. I felt as if loaded with an enormous weight, and knew not where to look for comfort. If I raised my eyes, I saw God angry, and, as it were, armed with scourges ready to strike me; and if I turned away, I seemed to see hell opened to swallow me up. All was disorder and confusion in my soul; the devil attacked me at the same time with violent temptations to despair; I fled from Him who pursued me, and from whose eyes I could not conceal myself; there was no kind of torment which I would not have endured to avoid the terrible sight of Him; and as it seemed to me that my state was known to the whole world, I at the same time suffered an overpowering sense of confusion. In this state I could not pray, nor express my grief except by tears. I could only say, 'Ah, how terrible a thing it is to fall into the hands of the living God!' At other times, casting myself on the ground, I said, ' Strike, my God, burn, consume whatever pleases Thee; spare neither my body nor my life, my flesh, nor my blood, provided that Thou savest this soul eternally.' " She added that she could not long have endured this terrible state, if the mercy of God had not supported her, and the effort which she then made was so violent, that she had a severe illness, from which she recovered with difficulty.

On another occasion after the evening prayer, our Lord presented Himself to her, bearing in His hands a burden which He appeared anxious to place upon the shoulders of His servant. It was so enormous and so heavy that she thought it would crush her. Our Lord said, showing her a religious of

the house, "Art thou willing to bear the weight
of My divine justice? I am ready to lay it upon
this religious, a religious in name only, whom Thou
seest." Sister Margaret, terrified, threw herself on
the ground before her Divine Master, and said to
Him, "Rather consume me, even to the marrow of
my bones, than condemn this soul, which has cost
Thee so much Blood. Spare not my life; I sacrifice
it to Thy will." Afterwards, when rising to retire,
she felt pressed down by a weight so heavy that it
crushed her. She had great difficulty in walking,
and believed that she could not have moved if our
Lord had not Himself supported her. At the same
time she felt inwardly consumed as by a devouring
fire, which penetrated even to her bones, by which
she was soon so much weakened as to be confined to
her bed. She was bled, but without success; and
the physicians, who could not discover the cause of
her malady, knew not what remedy to apply. She
endured this sickness as long as the justice of God
required it for the conversion of the soul who occasioned her pains.

The sister did not become weary of these trials,
but bore them with the more courage, as she generally obtained from her Beloved the conversion of
those whose state He manifested to her. Our Lord
showed her in communion another religious who
had communicated with her, and of whom He said
that though she was not actually in a state of mortal
sin, she had yet in some sort renewed the sorrows of
His Passion, because she entertained some affection
which displeased Him. Sister Margaret mourned a
long time for her, and at length, on Easter day,
Jesus consoled her by saying that He had grant-

ed the favour which she had asked of Him. It
was sometimes for her greatest enemies that she
thus prayed and suffered; that is, for those who,
not being able to endure her regularity and fervour,
contradicted, ridiculed, and ill-treated her in every
possible way. Nothing can be more beautiful or
edifying than her account of the resistance which her
charity induced her to make to the justice of her
Beloved, who wished to punish several of these imperfect religious:

"Our Lord," said she, "often made me bear these
painful visitations. On one occasion having shown
me the punishment He was about to inflict upon
some souls, I threw myself at His sacred Feet, saying to Him, 'O, my Saviour, rather discharge upon
me Thine anger, and efface me from the Book of
Life, than condemn these souls who have cost Thee
so dear!' He answered me, 'But they love thee
not, and cease not to afflict thee.' 'It matters not,
my God, if only they love Thee: I will not cease
from imploring Thee to pardon them.' 'Leave Me,'
replied He, 'I can suffer them no longer.' Then
embracing His Feet and clasping them more tightly,
I exclaimed, 'My Lord, I will never quit Thee until
Thou hast pardoned them.' He said to me, 'I will
do so, if thou wilt answer to Me for them.' 'Yes,
my God; but I will pay Thee only with Thine own
property, with the treasures of Thy Sacred Heart.'
'Wherewith,' added she, 'our Lord expressed Himself satisfied.'"

It was thus that Moses disputed with God, as the
Scripture relates, and restrained, as it were, His
divine anger by fervent supplications, so that God
said to Him in wrath, "Leave Me, that I may exter-

minate this ungrateful people." Yet the prayers of
His servant triumphed over the divine wrath.
Sister Margaret received the same favour, and we
may judge thence of her fervour and familiarity
with God, and especially of the charity with which
her heart was inflamed, even towards those whom
she would have naturally had so many reasons not
to love.

It was not only the sins of religious which
were the object of her zeal and the subject of her
suffering; God also frequently exacted from her
that she should carry the weight of the sins of
seculars, and do penance for people in the world.
"Wilt thou," said He to her one day, "wilt thou
give Me thy heart as a place of repose for My suffering love, which all the world despises?" She answered with fervour, "My Lord, Thou knowest that
I am all Thine, do with me according to Thy Will."
He added, "Knowest thou why I give thee My
graces so abundantly? It is to make thee a sanctuary, and thy heart an altar, where the fire of My
love may burn continually. I have chosen this
altar, to offer sacrifice thereon to My Eternal Father,
to appease His justice, and whilst men offend Him,
to render Him infinite glory by the offering that
thou makest of Me, and by the union of thyself in
the same sacrifice."

It was during the carnival that she usually suffered most, as that is the time when people in the
world give themselves up to sin with greater
license. On one of these days of sin, her Divine
Spouse presented Himself to her in the state in
which He was when Pilate showed Him to the
people, to excite their compassion, saying to them,

"Behold the Man!" He appeared all torn with stripes and covered with wounds; His Blood flowed from every part; He bore upon His shoulders a heavy cross, and said with a sad and mournful voice, "Will no one have pity on Me and compassionate My grief? Behold the miserable state to which sinners reduce Me now!" The holy lover of Jesus Christ melted into tears at this touching spectacle, and offered herself as a consolation to her Divine Spouse. He accepted her offer, and put upon her shoulders the cross He bore. "Feeling myself crushed under the weight," said she in the account she gave of this favour, "I began to comprehend more fully the malice of sin. He showed me that it was not enough for me to carry this cross, but that He wished me to attach myself to it with Him, that I might keep Him faithful company, participating in His sorrows and in His ignominy. I abandoned myself," added she, "to whatever He wished to do with me. He fastened me, in fact, to His cross, by a violent illness, which made me feel the pain of that cross studded with sharp points."

From this day forth she was every year at the time of the carnival reduced to the same state of pain and sickness; and that it might be known that her infirmities proceeded from no natural cause, she was always perfectly cured on Ash Wednesday, and full of the strength and vigour needful to bear the Lenten fast, although the day before she had been reduced to extremity and in most acute suffering. After the experience of some years, the community were accustomed to predict with certainty her illness during the carnival, and her recovery on the first day of Lent.

It was at one of these seasons that she wrote thus to a father of the Society of Jesus, describing the state of suffering in which she then was: " Our Sovereign Master has permitted me to find much consolation in the letter you had the goodness to write to me, but only after having forbidden me for a long time to read it, because of a certain eagerness I felt to find comfort in it, in the state of suffering in which it is His pleasure to place me during the time of carnival, when so many sinners offend and forsake Him. This is a time of such great suffering and sorrow to me, that I can neither see nor relish anything but my Jesus crucified; and compassionating the grief of His Sacred Heart, I am penetrated with it in so lively a manner, that it serves as an instrument of the Divine Justice to torment me. I am unable to do anything but sacrifice myself to it as a victim of immolation; it seems to me that I suffer in so extraordinary a manner, that if His mercy did not fortify me, it would be impossible for me to support the weight of His rigorous justice for a moment. I did not think I could have written to you, for in my present state I could wish to say no more than those words of my dear Saviour, 'My soul is sorrowful, even unto death;' or, 'My God, My God, why hast Thou forsaken Me?'"

In the meanwhile Mother Greffier did not cease to try Sister Margaret, sometimes in one way, sometimes in another, in order to keep alive her fervour and patience. With this view she thought proper to forbid a second time the devotion that our Lord had prescribed for the first Friday of the month.

We do not find stated either the occasion or the
cause of this new trial; but whether it was through
the advice of directors, or on account of the frequent
illnesses of Sister Margaret, it is certain that those
practices from which she had derived so much fruit,
were forbidden, and even the communion which she
usually received on that day. The humble religious
bore this privation in silence, though it was the most
sensible and painful that could have been imposed
upon her; but our Lord had taught IIis servant
that obedience was always to be preferred to the
desire she felt to communicate. God, however, made
use, for the accomplishment of IIis designs, of
means very similar to that which He had formerly
employed on a like occasion, but attended with
circumstances still more marked and miraculous. A
young sister fell dangerously ill, and in a few days
she was at the last extremity; her death appeared
inevitable, for the physicians confessed their ignorance of her disease, and the most harmless remedies
only served to increase it. Sister Margaret, touched
with compassion for the state of this religious, earnestly entreated our Lord to grant her recovery.
He then made known that her sickness was due to
His anger against the superior, and that she would
not recover until the permission to communicate on
the first Friday of the month, which had been taken
away, was again granted.

Sister Margaret was much troubled by the knowledge thus given her by God. She dared not declare
to her superior what had been revealed, and yet our
Lord urged her to do so, and showed her how angry
He was with her for placing an obstacle in the way
of His designs. Sister Margaret, in her doubt,

which had no other motive, as we shall see, than the most wonderful humility, addressed herself to one of the elder nuns in whom she placed much confidence on account of her great virtue, and wrote to her the following letter :

"It is in the Sacred Heart of our Lord that I write you this, my dear sister, since it is His wish. Be not surprised that I address myself to you in the extreme difficulty in which I find myself with respect to Sister N. This morning, on rising, I seemed to hear distinctly these words, ' Say to thy superior that she has greatly offended Me, since, to please creatures, she has cut thee off from the communion which I ordered thee to make on the first Friday of every month, in order that by offering Me to My Eternal Father, His divine justice might be satisfied for the faults which are committed against charity, the victim of which I have chosen thee to be. For this reason I am resolved to sacrifice to Myself the victim who now suffers.' See, my dear sister, what torments and pursues me continually, so that I am unable to withdraw my thoughts from it, because it continually urges me to tell it to our mother. To speak candidly, I fear to do so because I believe that it is all a stratagem of the enemy, who wishes to make me singular by this communion, or that it is but an imagination and illusion; for it is not to a miserable hypocrite like myself that our Lord would show such favour. I conjure you, my dear sister, to tell me what you think on this subject, in order to relieve me from my difficulty. Do me this favour without flattering me, for I fear to resist God, and cannot express what I suffer from seeing our sister in this state. Ask Him to make known the truth

to you, and what it is His Will you should say to
me, after which I will endeavour to think no more
of it. I beg you will burn this note, and keep my
secret."

The sister kept the note instead of burning it,
as she was desired; but she induced Sister Margaret
to reveal the whole to her superior. She deferred
to this counsel, notwithstanding her repugnance,
and simply repeated what she had been told regarding the sick sister. The superior no longer hesitated to promise permission to make the communions and the forbidden devotions, provided Sister
Margaret obtained the recovery of the young religious who was then at the point of death, and given
over by the physicians. Sister Margaret prayed for
her, and immediately the sick religious was rescued
from the gates of death, her sudden cure appearing
to the physicians as unaccountable as her disease.
Nevertheless, perfect health was not yet restored to
this sister; God left her a part of her suffering,
although He released her from the danger of death;
for He wished that she should be indebted for her
entire cure to a second miracle, which should serve
to manifest still more clearly the truth of those
graces which He communicated to His servant.

Whether the superior forgot the promise she had
made to allow the communions, or whether she
thought her promise the same as a permission, she
said nothing more to Sister Margaret, who, punctual
and exact in obedience, dared not renew them, or
again ask the refused permission, but confined
herself to entreating God most earnestly that He
would finish His work in the suffering nun, and
restore her to perfect health. However, her illness

still continued, and the physicians agreed that they could give her no further remedies, having tried all those that their art could furnish. This state of things lasted some weeks. The servant of God, touched with compassion for the sick girl, thought that charity ought to outweigh the scruple which obedience suggested, and at length declared to the superior that it was our Lord's Will that the invalid should not recover until she permitted her to resume her communions.

The superior, who had been witness of the first miracle, now saw a second, which appeared to her as decided, because it was equally prompt; she granted the permission, and immediately the sick nun was entirely freed from those mysterious pains. They had no other source than the power of God, Who willed that His designs should be accomplished, and that it might be known that delusion or imagination had no part in what He wrought in His servant.

Notwithstanding these clear proofs, the superior did not discontinue the trials to which she subjected the servant of God from day to day. The illnesses with which she was continually afflicted, of the nature of which the physicians generally knew nothing, furnished her with several occasions of doing so.

It was while Sister Margaret was in the infirmary, that the days destined for the retreats customary in the order of the Visitation arrived. Each took the time appointed by the superior; in the case, however, of Sister Margaret it appeared that no time could be allotted to her, on account of her weakness, and no mention was made of her; but Mother Greffier thought it her duty to try the courage and

obedience of her sick daughter on this occasion.
She repaired to the infirmary, accompanied by some
sisters, in order to discharge her from it, under the
pretext that she made everybody the dupe of her
imaginary ailments, and desired her to go with the
others and make the retreat in her turn. Sister
Margaret was then in a high state of fever, and yet
the order to leave the infirmary was given her. This
would have been considered by most persons not an
excuse, but a just reason to allege for delay; yet
she instantly arose without murmur or complaint,
when the superior said to her, "Go, sister, place
yourself in retreat in your turn. I put you under
the care of our Lord Jesus Christ; may He direct,
govern, and cure you according to His Will." Sister Margaret obeyed without reply; she withdrew
into her cell, very well pleased to suffer, and to be
made over to the direction of her good Master. She
was no sooner there than our Lord presented Himself before her, while she was shivering with cold
and stretched upon the ground, as she was unable
to support herself. He raised her up, and said to
her, "See, thou art with Me and under My care.
For this reason I will restore thee in perfect health
to her who has placed thee in My hands." His
word was all-powerful; the shivering immediately
left her, and was not followed by perspiration or any
other inconvenience; and her health was so perfectly
restored that no appearance of having been ill remained; and from that moment she began the exercises of the retreat. She afterwards avowed to the
superior, that no retreat had ever been so delightful
to her, that she had never experienced so much joy
and sweetness, and that she could have imagined

herself in heaven, on account of the continual favours and caresses she received from our Lord and His holy Mother.

Mother Greffier witnessed a similar miraculous cure of this sister, of which she has certified, the particulars in writing. We will transcribe her own words:

" When visiting the infirmary where she was recovering from an illness, but before she had left her bed, (whether it was on a Saturday or the eve of some festival I do not remember,) she asked my permission to rise the next day to go to mass. I hesitated a little at this request, and she comprehended that I did not think her strong enough to bear the exertion. Upon which, replying to what I felt, she said to me in a winning manner, ' Dear mother, if it is your will it will be God's Will also, and He will give me strength.' I then gave orders to the infirmarian to give her some nourishment, and permit her to rise about the time of office in order that she might go to mass. In the evening our dear invalid said to the infirmarian, that if she pleased she should very much wish to go to holy mass fasting, that she might communicate, and that she hoped our Lord would give her sufficient strength. The infirmarian agreed to her desire, and thought that I should make no objection. She promised the sick sister to ask my permission, but forgot it until the next morning, when having allowed Sister Margaret to rise fasting, and earlier than I had said, she left the infirmary to seek me, to inform me of this arrangement, and to obtain my approval. It was permitted by God, that as she left the infirmary at one end I should enter at the other. Scarcely did I see that the

poor invalid had risen, and knew that she was fasting, with the intention of communicating, than,
without informing myself of the reason, I gave her
a sharp reprimand, exaggerating the defects of her
conduct, which I said was the effect of her self-will,
want of obedience, submission, simplicity, &c. At
length I said that she should go to mass and should
communicate, but that as self-will had given her
courage enough for that, I would also command in
my turn; that she was to take her bed down to her
cell, and her plate to the refectory, and from thence
go to the office when the bell rang, to remain there
and follow all the other exercises of the community
for five months, without during that time taking any
remedy or entering the infirmary, unless to see the
sick and assist them if the infirmarians had need of
her. She received my correction on her knees with
her hands joined, with a mild and tranquil air, and
after having heard my orders, before rising from the
ground, humbly asked my pardon and penance for
her fault, and immediately began to execute to the
letter all that I had said. Our Lord willed that she
should obey in everything, and promised her in
return her health, which continued good from that
day until the feast of the Presentation of our Lady,
which completed the five months. On this day our
Lord, when accepting the renewal of her vows,
renewed in her, as a grace, all her former suffering;
and that she might lose nothing by the five months
of health, He redoubled her pain, so that, although
previously she had been bled not oftener than once
in a fortnight or three weeks, on account of the pain
in her side, she could not now pass a week without
having recourse to bleeding."

The same superior, seeing how readily God honoured the obedience of His servant by these miraculous cures, thought on another occasion that she
might again make use of the same means to obtain a
fresh assurance that whatever supernatural passed
within her was truly from God. One day when the
servant of God was so strangely oppressed with the
pain in her side as to lose her speech, and very
nearly her breath also, Mother Greffier placed in
her hand an obedience, which several religious who
have attested this fact in the process, declared they
had seen. It was in these terms : " I command you
in virtue of holy obedience, to ask God to inform
me, since I am charged with the direction of you,
whether what passes, and has passed within you, is
caused by His supernatural power, or is simply
natural ; and as a sign that it is the work of God,
that He will suspend your bodily ailments for the
space of five months only, without your having need
during that time either of remedies, or of exemption
from the ordinary rule. But that if it is not the
extraordinary power of God, but only nature which
acts in you inwardly and outwardly, He will leave
you as usual, sometimes in one state, sometimes in
another. By this means we shall be assured of the
truth."

As soon as she had delivered this note, feeling
certain of the power of obedience over her spiritual
daughter, she made her leave the infirmary. Sister
Margaret obeyed without reply, and went immediately to present to our Lord in prayer the order
which she had received. This is the answer He
made her : " I promise it to thee, My daughter, as a
mark of the good Spirit who conducts thee. I would

have as readily granted as many years of health as she has demanded months; and she should in like manner have had any other assurances she might have requested."

The fulfilment soon followed the promise. While Margaret was at mass, it seemed to her that at the moment of the elevation of the sacred Host, all her infirmities were taken off from her like a garment, and from that moment she was in a robust state of health. Although tried by the ordinary labours of the house, her health did not fail her during the whole course of the five months. All the community, who had been informed of the order given her, and who were witnesses of the success of this trial, were filled with admiration; but their astonishment redoubled when they saw repeated the other miraculous proof that we have already related. On the day and at the hour of the expiration of the five months, Margaret was suddenly seized and cruelly tormented by oppression and her other usual infirmities. This was a remarkable proof; yet Mother Greffier still wished for another. It was not so much to satisfy herself as to disabuse the community of the prejudices that the greater part had conceived against the servant of God. She gave, then, to the sufferer a new obedience, which she wrote in these terms, beneath the last:

"Twenty-fifth of May. I confess that I have remarked in you that health which I commanded you to ask of God, and by this manifest sign I ought to be convinced that the incomprehensible mercy and goodness of the Sacred Heart of Jesus Christ, is the author of what has passed and is still passing in your soul. I am willing to believe this; but I com-

mand you once more to pray to God the Father,
through our Lord Jesus Christ, that for the love of
Him, and to free me from every doubt, He will continue your health for a whole year from the first
obedience. That passed, I will abandon your body
to whatever He shall please to do with it, but the
fulfilment of what I ask is necessary in order to
satisfy me entirely."

As God was not irritated when Gedeon, after the
first prodigy, asked a second to fortify his faith and
strengthen his confidence, so He was not offended
that Mother Greffier still demanded a fresh miracle
from Him, and granted it in reward of the praisewor-
thy motives by which it was dictated. Sister Margaret
left the infirmary, whither they had carried her, and
after having made known to God the wish of her
superior, she passed the whole year without requir-
ing bleeding or other remedies ; the whole community was witness of this third miracle, as it had been
of the two others. This fact, which is proved as
well by the original paper, which is still in existence,
as by the memoirs of Mother Greffier, was related to
us by some sisters of the convent who were living in
1714, and who had been witnesses of it. They also
deposed to the same in the juridical informations.
One of them relates that she then said to Mother
Greffier, "You ought to command Sister Margaret
not to re-enter the infirmary for two years, since
you have succceded so well." The wise superior
however would not tempt God, and answered, "This
is sufficient to convince me that our sister is guided
by God."

These singular favours sometimes emboldened the
mother to demand others of God through His ser-

16

vant. One of them deserves particular mention, because it makes us better acquainted with the dispositions of Sister Margaret's heart. A young religious had fallen into a lethargic sleep, and was thought to be in imminent danger of dying, without being able to receive the Sacraments of the Church. The superior seeing that the physicians had no longer any hope, addressed herself to Sister Margaret, and ordered her to ask from God for this poor sister the time she needed to confess and receive the last sacraments; and in order more readily to obtain this favour, she told her to offer to our Lord a promise to do whatever it should please Him in return. Sister Margaret obeyed, and the following are the three sacrifices which our Lord required from His spouse, sacrifices which show to what an extent this holy soul carried her detachment from the world, and all in which self-love most delights. Religious often take pleasure in conversing in the parlour with people of the world; they like to keep up their connexions abroad by letters; they are ambitious of employments in the house which occupy them according to their taste, and which give them some distinction or dispensation, or which procure them amusement. The absence of all these things in Sister Margaret amounted even to aversion and antipathy; and this repugnance formed the most ordinary matter of the struggles she maintained, and the occasion of her victories, sometimes even that of her want of fidelity.

Now this was the subject of the sacrifices which our Lord exacted from her. In the first place, He ordered her to accept all the employments that should be given her, without endeavouring to obtain a dispensation from them; the second was, never to refuse to write letters; and the third, to go into the parlour whenever she was summoned. This last sacrifice would have been none to a dissipated soul, which would enjoy the refreshment of conversing with people of the world, as a relief from the weariness of solitude, but it cost Margaret the greatest effort to obey. She, however, did obey, and to bind her to accomplish with greater fidelity what He had required, our Lord wished that she should oblige herself by vow. She obtained the permission of her superior, and the success of her prayer was as prompt as it had been on other occasions. The sick nun recovered her consciousness, had all the time necessary to receive the sacraments with devotion, and died in sentiments of great fervour and penance.

It was during the superiorship of Mother Greffier that God bestowed a new favour upon His servant, in which it was His Will that her wise superior should have a considerable share, either to convince her more fully of the truth of the wonders which He wrought in Sister Margaret, or to approve her prudent severity as well as to honour the humble submission of His servant. He required from Sister Margaret that she should make, in favour of her divine Spouse, a kind of mystical testament or donation of all she should do or suffer, and of all the prayers that should be made for her, before or after her death, in order to be disposed of according to His holy Will. For fear of weakening this favour by relating it imperfectly, we will simply transcribe what she has herself written in the account which was exacted from her humility; only adding the circumstances mentioned in the Memoirs of Mother Greffier:

"My sovereign Lord required me to make in His favour a written testament or donation, entire and without reserve, as I had already done by word of mouth, of whatever I could do or suffer, and of all the prayers and spiritual benefits that should be made or performed for me, whether during my life or after my death. He desired me to ask my superior if she would serve as notary in this act, for which He promised to reward her abundantly; and if she refused I was to apply to Father de la Colombiere. My superior, however, was willing to do it, and having presented it to the only Love of my soul, He expressed great satisfaction." This act, written by the hand of Mother Greffier, and signed with the blood of Sister Margaret, was conceived in the following terms:

"May Jesus live in the heart of His spouse, Sister Margaret Mary, for whom, and in virtue of the power that God has given me over her, I offer, dedicate, and consecrate purely and inviolably to the Sacred Heart of the adorable Jesus, all the good she shall be enabled to do during her life, and whatever shall be done for her after her death, that the Will of this divine Heart may dispose of it as He pleases, and in favour of whomsoever He may think fit, whether living or dead. Sister Margaret protests hereby that she freely and entirely despoils herself of everything, excepting her will to be for ever united to the Heart of her Jesus, and to love Him out of pure love of Himself. In testimony of which she and I sign this writing. Done the last day of December, 1678. Signed, Sister Peronne Rosalie

Greffier, at present superior, for whose conversion and final perseverance Sister Margaret will pray every day." Then follows the signature of Sister Margaret, written with her own blood, in this form, "Sister Margaret, disciple of the Divine Heart of the adorable Jesus."

Sister Margaret thus continues her recital: "My Divine Master expressed great satisfaction at this act, and told me that He would dispose of it according to His designs, and in favour of whom He pleased. But that since His love had despoiled me of every-thing, it was His Will that henceforth I should have no other riches than those of His Sacred Heart, of which He then made me a gift, causing me to write with my blood what He dictated."

This act, thus dictated and written, is couched in these terms:

" I constitute thee heir of My Heart and of all its treasures for time and for eternity, permitting thee to use them according to thy desire. I promise thee that thou shalt never be wanting in assistance until I shall fail in power. Thou shalt be for ever its beloved disciple, the sport of its good pleasure, and the holocaust of its love. It alone shall be the object of all thy desires ; it will repair and supply for thy defects, and will fulfil all thy obliga-tions."

Sister Margaret having written this consoling promise of the Son of God, thought she ought to consummate this exchange made with her Divine Spouse by a courageous act of love, and, as it were, water with her blood the holocaust she presented to Him. Taking, therefore, a penknife, she engraved upon her breast with that instrument the holy Name of Jesus, in characters large and deep, disregarding the evil effects that such an act might produce. The conclusion of what concerns this favour is thus related by her:

"My Saviour then said to me that He would take care to recompense a hundred fold all the good that should be done to me as if done to Himself, since I no longer wished to lay claim to it; and in order to recompense her who had drawn up the testament in His favour, He would bestow upon her the same reward as He had vouchsafed to St. Clare of Montefalco; that therefore He would add to her actions the infinite merit of His own, and by the love of His Sacred Heart He would make her deserve the same crown."

These words of the Son of God declare the merit of this worthy superior; and the holiness in which the remainder of her days was passed, evidently shows that she experienced the effects of this promise. Those who would condemn her on account of the prudent severity which she used towards Sister Margaret, should reform their judgment upon that of the Son of God. What follows in the recital of the Sister is again very remarkable, since it shows with what tenderness, and, if we may use such an expression, in what good faith she loved a superior, who on many occasions seemed to spare her but little. She thus continues:

"This promise of the Son of God in favour of my superior gave me great consolation, because I loved her much, and because she nourished my soul abundantly with the delicious bread of mortification and humiliation. This bread was so agreeable to the taste of my Sovereign Master, that to give Him this pleasure I could have wished that everybody might partake of it."

Such was the relish of the servant of God for suffering; a relish which was always maintained with the same fervour, in the midst of the various kinds of pain which she endured. Her infirmities were almost continual, and the contradictions she met with from her sisters no less so, whilst interior temptations soon succeeded to the passing consolations with which God favoured her. The superior always treated her outwardly in an austere manner, and believed that her sublime virtue should be supported by continual trials. Yet Margaret, not content with the many troubles which overwhelmed her, sometimes in succession and sometimes altogether, sought to increase the weight of her cross by voluntary mortifications. She prayed her superior to permit them, and urged her by assiduous and repeated entreaties to do so; and though in everything else she carried her obedience to such an extent as never to venture a reply, in this matter she went beyond the bounds of that scrupulous obedience, and endeavoured as much as possible to extort from her by frequent solicitations the permission which she desired to macerate her weak body, and to add fresh pain to that of her maladies.

When these austerities were denied her, she carefully husbanded the occasions of suffering she met with, and failed not to prolong them if she could, as she practised with regard to the wounds made upon her breast by engraving there the holy Name of Jesus. We dare scarcely repeat what is found in the depositions which confirm this act, so astonishing is it. But why conceal the wonders of divine love

though they be not imitable, and why hide what
God has honoured with many miracles? Sister
Margaret, then, having remarked that this wound of
love was closed too soon, judged proper to render it
more lasting and more painful. In another excess
of fervour she took a lighted taper and with its
flames slowly renewed the marks of the holy Name
of Jesus upon her breast. This astonishing operation, which might be called imprudent, was performed so severely, and with such courage, that
Sister Margaret bore the wound and the pain for
nearly a whole year; so that the first wound, made
on the last day of December of the year 1678, was
still fresh and bleeding in the autumn of the following year.

This season was the time of retreat, and Margaret's
turn having come, she entered upon it with great
fervour; but as she examined her conscience with
wonderful exactness, she made a scruple of having
so long kept the pain of this wound secret, not having mentioned it to her superior, and immediately
went to accuse herself of it. The superior fearing
the consequences of an evil which had lasted so
long, told the sister she must use some remedies for
its cure, and ordered her to apply whatever was
recommended by the infirmarian, whom she would
send to her.

The obligation thus imposed on Sister Margaret
to disclose this wound to another, sensibly afflicted
her modesty. She went immediately to pour out
her heart to her Lord, saying to Him, " Oh, my only
Love, wilt Thou allow others to see the wound which
I have made for the love of Thee ? Art not Thou
powerful to cure me, Thou who art the sovereign

remedy of all evils?" Our Lord heard her desire,
and promised her that she should be cured the next
day.   Accordingly it so happened; her wounds,
though deep and of long standing, closed and dried
up during the night in such a manner, that the next
day nothing remained but large marks which
covered the scars and served to show the extent of
the injury.

The next day Sister Margaret not having found
time to inform the superior of her cure, the mother
sent a religious with a note in her hand, telling her
she was to show the wound to her. Sister Margaret
thought the miraculous cure dispensed her from
obeying; and bashfulness and modesty gaining the
victory over the exactness of obedience, she thanked
the sister for her good offices, saying that she no
longer needed them, for she was cured, and begging
her at least to wait till she had given the superior
an account of her recovery. She then hastened to
find Mother Greffier, to tell her that she had not
executed the orders contained in her note, because
she was cured. Though the mother-superior was
filled with admiration at so prompt a recovery, she
seemed to pay more attention to the conduct of
Sister Margaret than to her cure. She took the opportunity of humbling her, exaggerating the fault she
had committed against the exactness and promptitude which obedience requires, and even punished
her by depriving her that day of holy Communion,
which, to this ardent lover of Jesus Christ, was the
most rigorous penance which could have been imposed; in fine, she ordered her to execute what had
been commanded, and to show the infirmary sister
her wound, as it then was. Sister Margaret, who

has related this with her usual simplicity and humility, adds, that she was punished still more for this fault by our Lord than by her superior. When she presented herself to Him in prayer, He made her the same reproaches. "To punish me," said she, "for this delay of obedience, He humbled me under His sacred Feet for about five days, during which I did nothing but weep. He showed me several times how disagreeable the least defect in the obedience of a religious is to Him. At length, after having made me feel the punishment, He Himself dried up my tears, and on the last day of the retreat, which had been for me a solitude of grief, He restored joy to my soul, but added, that in punishment of my fault, not only the sacred Name, of which the engraving had cost me so dear, should no more be seen, but that the former one should disappear also, though at that time it was clearly marked by its scar."

Mother Greffier, and the sisters who knew what had passed, saw with astonishment the accomplishment of this double miracle. Sister Margaret had at length executed what had been prescribed her, and shown her bosom, cut and burnt, to Sister Des Ecures, then infirmarian, who found it cured. She saw those wounds, before so deep and old, covered with large dry marks, which left no other appearance than the form, distinctly marked, of the Name of Jesus, in large characters, like those printed in capitals in large books. It is thus that she who saw them expresses herself in the account she gave to the superior. This same sister and another religious, (for this astonishing event could not be hidden, and the whole community was soon informed

of it,) had, after the death of Sister Margaret, the
curiosity to look, when putting on her shroud,
whether the Name of Jesus was entirely effaced,
according to the prophecy, which was known to
them; and they found that the word of the Son of
God was accomplished to the letter; there no longer
remained upon the bosom of His servant any trace
of those large wounds, or even the smallest scar,
though such injuries, formed by steel, increased by
fire, and lasting several months, would naturally
leave very deep marks.

God made use of another means to manifest the
sanctity of His servant, which her humility was unable to conceal. It was more than two years since
Father de la Colombiere had left Paray for England;
but the health of this holy religious being very indifferent, his superiors recalled him for change of air,
and sent him to Paray, hoping that the air of that
country would be beneficial to him. He arrived in
the month of August, 1681. If it was a consolation
to Sister Margaret to see for the third time one who
had been her guide in the ways of perfection, it was
one she was not long permitted to enjoy, for she was
soon afterwards deprived of it by the death of this
great servant of God. He remained at Paray about
six months without deriving any relief from the
change. The physicians, seeing all their remedies
were useless, advised him to try his native air; the
superiors gave their consent, and the father prepared
to set out. The day of his departure was fixed,
when the servant of God sent to entreat him not to
leave Paray if he could remain there without failing
in the obedience he owed to his superiors. The
holy missionary desired to know what were the mo-

tives of this proposition. Margaret, with the permission of her superior, wrote as answer these few words: "He has told me that He wishes the sacrifice of your life here." Father de la Colombiere understood the meaning of these prophetic words, yet he thought that obedience required him to prepare for his departure. But on the eve of the day which he had fixed for leaving, the fever seized him, and carried him off in less than a week. He died a holy death on the 15th of February, 1682. When he was taken ill, he sent the note he had received from Sister Margaret to the superior of the house of Paray, and by this means we know the prediction which was made so clearly by the servant of God, and its accomplishment. Sister Margaret made every effort during the illness of Father de la Colombiere, and after his death, to recover possession of this note; but the superior of the Jesuits, who knew its value and had seen its accomplishment, replied that he would rather sacrifice all the archives of the house than that prophecy. Thus, notwithstanding the sister's humility, her prediction and its fulfilment were known to all the world, and established by certain evidence. This event served not a little to remove the unjust prejudices which several persons had conceived against the holy nun.

As soon as Father de la Colombiere had expired, (at about five o'clock in the morning,) a devout person came to announce his death to Sister Margaret. The holy religious, without being moved, or uttering any regrets, said simply to this person, "Go, and pray to God for him, and cause all to pray for the repose of his soul." This same day in the evening, she wrote a note to the same person in these terms:

"Cease to afflict yourself: invoke him: fear nothing. He is more powerful to assist you than ever." These expressions give us cause to presume that she had been supernaturally informed of the death of this holy man, and of the state of his soul.

The peace and tranquillity of Sister Margaret, at the death of a director who had been so useful to her, was another kind of miracle which will appear no less surprising to persons who have a lively, and sometimes inordinate attachment, to their director. Sister Margaret loved nothing except in God and for God; He was everything to her, and consumed in her by the fire of His love every sort of attachment. The superior herself was surprised at her tranquillity at the death of this holy missionary, and still more that she asked no permission to perform some extraordinary penance for the repose of his soul, as she was accustomed to do on the death of those she had known, and for whom she thought it her duty to interest herself. The superior asked her the cause of this, when she simply replied, "There is no need of it. He is in a state to pray to God for us, being placed in heaven by the goodness and mercy of the Sacred Heart of our Lord Jesus Christ. Only," added she, " to satisfy for some negligence in his practice of divine love, his soul was deprived of the sight of God from the time of its departure, until his body was laid in the tomb."

It was about this time that Sister Margaret received from God three singular graces, the recital of which will be very instructive to pious persons. The sovereign Pontiff granted a general Jubilee, on occasion of the inroads of the Turks into Germany. When it was opened at Paray, Sister Margaret applied herself to gain it with all the fervour of which her heart was capable. Our Lord showed Himself to her as a judge, and an angry judge, and at this sight His servant was seized with terror. He at the same time made her understand that His justice was not so much irritated by the disorders committed by the infidels in their conquests, as by the crimes of His chosen people, who revolted against Him, and made use of their familiarity with Him to persecute Him. It was thus that He designated persons particularly consecrated to God, whose offences are the most grievous to Him. He added, that as long as these more favoured souls had been faithful, He had compelled His justice to give place to His mercy, that His people might be spared, and that one just soul could obtain pardon for a thousand criminal ones; "But if they do not all amend," continued He in a severe and terrible tone, "I will make them feel the weight of My avenging justice." At this moment the bell for matins rang, and Sister Margaret hurried to the choir, but the vision did not cease. Jesus Christ continued to speak to His servant, and said to her, "Weep and sigh continually for My Blood which is uselessly shed for so many souls, who make so great an abuse of it in these indulgences; they are contented to cut down the bad weeds which have grown in their hearts, without wishing to draw them up by the roots. But unhappy are those souls which remain uncleansed and dry in the midst of, and at the very fountain of, these living waters; they will never be either washed from their stains or find their thirst satisfied." The servant of God in the terror with which she was seized, and the grief which she felt, addressed herself to Jesus Christ; and speaking of His Sacred Heart, she said to Him, "My Lord and my God, Thy mercy must place here all unfaithful souls, in order that they may be sanctified and glorify Thee eternally." "I will do so," replied the sovereign Judge, "if thou wilt be answerable for their perfect amendment." "But," she replied in her fervour, "Thou knowest, my God, that that is not in my power, unless Thou dost Thyself accomplish it by rendering efficacious the merits of Thy Passion."

In the same rapture our Lord showed her what it would be most meritorious for her to do during the holy season of the Jubilee, namely, in the first place, to offer to the Eternal Father the ample satisfaction which He made for sinners to the Divine Justice upon the tree of the cross, praying Him to render the merit of His Precious Blood efficacious in all the criminal souls in whom sin has caused death; in order that rising again to grace they might glorify God eternally.

Secondly, to offer to Him the infinite ardour of the Heart of Jesus Christ, in satisfaction for the tepidity and cowardice of His chosen people; entreating Him, that by the ardent love which caused the Son of God to suffer death, it would please Him to warm these cold hearts in His service, and inflame them with that same love, that they might love and glorify Him eternally.

Thirdly, to present to Him the submission of the will of His Son to His Divine Will, in order to obtain by the merit of this precious obedience, the perfect accomplishment of His holy Will on earth.

The second remarkable grace of which we have

spoken, regards more particularly the Sacred Heart
of Jesus Christ. We cannot better describe it than
by quoting what Margaret wrote in the account her
superiors required of her: " One day during the
time of work, I withdrew into a little court near the
Blessed Sacrament, where, doing my work on my
knees, I felt myself absorbed interiorly and exteriorly. At the same time I saw before me the
loving Heart of my adorable Jesus, more brilliant
than the sun. It appeared as if in the midst of
flames, which were those of His love. He was
surrounded by seraphim, who sang these words in
admirable harmony: 'Love triumphs; love rejoices; love rejoices in God.' When these blessed
spirits invited me to join in their canticle of praise
to the Heart of Jesus Christ, I dared not do it; but
they reproved me, and told me they were come for
the purpose of associating themselves with me in
offering a continual homage of love, adoration, and
praise to this Sacred Heart. For this object, they
would take my place before the Blessed Sacrament,
that through their mediation I might be able to love
without interruption; and they would participate
in the love that caused me to suffer in the same
manner as I, in their persons, should share in their
joyful love. It appeared to me as if they wrote this
compact in letters of gold on the Sacred Heart, in
the unfading characters of love. This communication lasted about two or three hours; I have felt all
my life the effects of it, both in the assistance I have
received from this association, and in the sweetness
it has produced, and still continues to produce in
me. I was overcome with confusion, yet in addressing these holy angels, I called them my divine asso-

ciates. This favour gave me so great a desire to obtain purity of intention, and so high an idea of what is necessary in order to converse with God, that all things appeared impure to me, in comparison with the fervour of the Seraphim."

The third favour which she received about the same time was the return of her interior trials, and God, in order that she might be prepared, forewarned her of them. We have already related her former trials of this nature, which had been a little relieved to give place to other pains. Now that the prodigies God performed in her were more striking, He doubled her preceding trials, to serve as a counterpoise to these favours, and to keep her soul in a more profound interior annihilation. He prepared her for this fresh combat by predicting it Himself, as we will relate in the words of the servant of God herself:

"The Sovereign of my soul, Who is pleased to pour forth the treasures of His mercy on the most unworthy subjects, honoured me with a visit, for the purpose of telling me how much I had to endure during the remainder of my life in the execution of His designs. Profoundly annihilated, and prostrate in His presence, I could not persuade myself that God would ever deign to make me capable of suffering anything for His love. Yet the desire of suffering increased in me to such an extent, that I should have been delighted to find all instruments of punishment employed in torturing me. Then He clearly disclosed to me all the humiliating and afflicting things which were to befall me from that moment until my death. What very much consoled me was that in showing me this I was so strongly

17

impressed, that all these sufferings which were at that time only in the imagination, seemed to be as sensible as if I were really enduring them."

For the accomplishment of this prediction, it was the Will of God that Sister Margaret should feel with renewed force the repugnance already mentioned, and which, arising interiorly, made the practice of every kind of virtue most irksome. She especially felt this with regard to going to the parlour, and to the vow she had formerly made upon this matter. Ever oppressed by this inconceivable aversion, and at the same time filled with horror at the idea of disobedience and the fear of infringing her vow, she suffered more than it is possible to express. This trial was daily, and almost constant. Her frequent victories, and her having been ever faithful in overcoming herself, did not in the least lessen her torment. She says on this subject in a letter to her director: "I confess to you, Rev. Father, that my Divine Saviour conducts me by a way entirely opposed to my inclination. I have a strange aversion to all employments, especially to the parlour and to writing letters. Yet I must sacrifice myself continually in these things, as my Saviour gave me no repose, until I bound myself by an express vow to obey blindly in all this, showing my repugnance as little as I could possibly help. I feel now more difficulty than formerly; but I embrace this cross, together with every other that it may please my Saviour to honour me by laying upon me. I confess that if I were to be a single moment without suffering, I should think He had abandoned me."

To these pains and interior struggles Jesus Christ added another sort of mortification, which He Himself prescribed. He at first ordered her to fast on bread and water for fifty days, in honour of His fast in the desert. In this command the Son of God seemed to wish rather to try her obedience than her mortification. The sister promised to observe this fast if consistent with the submission she owed to her superior. Mother Greffier, who wisely preferred the common rule to extraordinary practices, refused her consent. Jesus Christ made known to His servant that her obedience was as agreeable to Him as the sacrifice itself; and in place of the fast which was not permitted her, He made her understand that it would be pleasing to Him if she passed the fifty days of abstinence without drinking, that by this penance she might honour, as much as was in her power, the burning thirst that He suffered upon the cross, and that mystical thirst, with which, according to St. Augustine, His Heart was consumed for the salvation even of His executioners, and which He preserves until the end for the salvation of sinners.

This abstinence appeared to Sister Margaret more severe than the first which had been proposed to her. It was so on account of her infirmities, which, as we' have before related, caused so ardent and continual a thirst, that nothing could satisfy it. The superior, to whom she gave an account of what her Spouse required, appeared at first to approve it, and permitted her to begin this terrible abstinence. But when she saw her daughter undertake it with joy and execute it with courage, in the hope by this bodily thirst to satisfy that which her soul felt for suffering, she ordered her after some days to interrupt her abstinence and to take some refreshment.

The sister obeyed with simplicity, but though forbidden to continue this practice, she had not been
forbidden to try by her prayers to obtain permission
to perform it, and her repeated requests were so
effectual, that Mother Greffier at length determined to allow her to do what Jesus Christ had
ordered, reserving to herself the office of watching
over her health, and being ready to make her discontinue this abstinence whenever she should find it
prejudicial to her. Sister Margaret then recom-
menced the practice, and passed fifty entire days
without drinking. The Son of God, whose Will it
was to confirm by the event the truth of the order
He had given to His spouse, supported her strength
in such a way, that during all that time her health,
though weakened by so many infirmities, did not
appear to suffer from the inconceivable thirst which
she endured so long.

This heroic act of patience and mortification was
the last of which Mother Greffier was witness. She
had reached the end of her superiorship, and was
succeeded by Mother Mary Christina Melin, who was
elected in the month of May 1684.

BOOK VI.

MOTHER MELIN IS SUPERIOR. SISTER MARGARET IS
CHOSEN MISTRESS OF THE NOVICES. HER CONDUCT
IN THIS EMPLOYMENT. FIRST BEGINNING OF THE
DEVOTION TO THE SACRED HEART OF OUR LORD
JESUS CHRIST. THE OPPOSITION IT MET WITH.

The change of superior was another cross for
Sister Margaret. One less perfect would have
rejoiced at the change, but it afflicted the servant of
God, because she foresaw that the salutary rigour
of her late superior would now cease. Indeed,
Mother Melin, who was a professed nun of the
house of Paray, and who had witnessed all the
wonders wrought in the person of Sister Margaret,
brought to her superiorhip nothing but esteem for
this religious, whose virtue had been so thoroughly
tried, whilst the former superiors had come into
office full of prejudice against the extraordinary
ways in which she was conducted. Mother Melin,
who believed these ways to have been sufficiently
put to the proof, regulated her conduct towards
Sister Margaret by the profound veneration she had
long felt for her virtue. Sister Margaret was soon
afflicted, and deeply so, at the loss of her who had so
liberally satisfied her desire of suffering and humiliation. The regret she felt is painted in lively colours
in a letter which she wrote to Mother Greffier some
months after her departure:

"My much honoured and dear mother," said she
to her, "how can it be otherwise than that my
soul, with its many defects and miseries, should be
eager for humiliation and suffering? But when I
remember that you at least did me the favour sometimes to nourish it with this delicious bread, bitter
though it be to the natural taste, and that now I
am deprived of this happiness, without doubt because
of the bad use I made of it, I am overwhelmed with
grief. I assure you in all sincerity, that nothing
attached me so strongly to you as this conduct, of
which I cannot think, my dear mother, without feelings of the most tender gratitude towards you.
You could not give me a more agreeable proof of
true friendship, than by humbling and mortifying so
imperfect a person as myself. Though you may not
have done enough, considering the cause I gave
you for it, yet that little comforted me, and
softened the bitterness of life, which becomes insupportable to me without suffering, as I ever see
my Divine Master on the cross. Ah! dear mother,
how hard it is to live without loving! and how can
one love a crucified God, without living and dying
with Him upon the cross? I seemed to live in
security under your guidance, because you had the
charity to oppose my inclinations. Alas! I have
become unworthy of these favours. Yet the love of
humiliation increases within me, and I know not if
it is because I no longer suffer anything. I could
not resolve to ask for length of days, as you coun-
selled me, excepting with the condition that they
should be all employed in honouring the Sacred
Heart of Jesus by humiliation, silence, and suffering."

It was thus that Sister Margaret judged of superiors with regard to herself. Those she appeared to
love the most, were those from whom she received
the greatest contradictions. What an admirable
lesson for some religious who are obedient to those
they like, and indocile to those they dislike; who
esteem superiors in proportion as they are loved and
caressed by them, and are often regulated in their
choice by this detestable motive. They choose
through self-love those who are appointed solely
for the purpose of teaching them to subdue self-
love.

Mother Mary Christina Melin did not confine her
regard for Sister Margaret to simple esteem; she
thought it her duty to appoint her to the principal
employments of the house, and this kind of cross,
which the humble sister bore with more pain than
the worst infirmities, was imposed on her in all its
rigour. Until now they had hardly entrusted her
with the meanest occupations about the children or
the sick, and then always as subordinate to every
other who served in the same office. With feelings
of alarm she found herself suddenly chosen for the
first employments of the house; and some months
afterwards, when the mistress of the novices was
taken ill, this charge was confided to her by Mother
Melin. We will say nothing of the pain which this
caused to the humble Sister Margaret; the vow
which she had made to conquer her repugnance in
these matters, and to accept everything without
excusing herself, sufficiently proves her aversion to
offices of distinction, and her confusion and sorrow
when called to this important one. She submitted, however, without answering, complaining, or

making fine speeches about her unworthiness; and
confined herself to mourning in the presence of her
Divine Spouse, deriving from His Sacred Heart the
means of worthily fulfilling her office, and especially
of leading the novices who were entrusted to her
in the ways of holy love, and courageous perfection. It was from this sacred source that she drew
the spirit in which she formed her pupils. It is
right to make known the method she pursued in
order to succeed in her undertaking.

Her first object was to obtain the friendship of
the novices and to gain their confidence. A gentle
and affable manner, charity in assisting them in their
difficulties, assiduity in serving them in all things,
carefulness in anticipating their wishes, readiness to
receive and listen to them, tenderness in compassionating their sorrows, in a word, all the little attentions which friendship inspires and charity requires,
were employed by her and produced abundant fruit.
Moreover, she studied with care the capacity of
their minds and the extent of their gifts, that she
might lead them by the path to which God called
them, and that thus they might all arrive by the
way proper to each at that self-renunciation so highly
recommended by our Lord, that death to all earthly
things, in which consists the true spirit of religion,
and particularly of that holy order which these young
hearts aspired to join.

What she reproved in them with the greatest
severity were sloth and indifference in the observance
of the rule, frivolity either in speech or manner, vain
excuses to avoid humiliation, reasoning and murmuring when obedience was required, the subtle
arts of vanity, which seeks itself or takes delight in

itself, and especially that tenderness towards self which causes one easily to complain or to set a high value upon what one does or suffers. All these weaknesses, only too much neglected by those who form young people to piety, appeared to her so many germs of self-love, which it was of the utmost importance to root out early. Above all, she could not endure those tender attachments and particular friendships which young people believe they may contract innocently, and into which they permit themselves to be drawn incautiously by sympathy of disposition, conformity of age, or habitual intercourse. These particular friendships appeared to the skilful mistress what they in truth are, the most certain obstacles to perfection, and even to the performance of the duty of common charity.

To lead the novices or postulants to the practice of the noble and courageous virtues with which Sister Margaret desired to inspire them, she required them to give an account to her with simplicity and frankness of their inclinations and difficulties, their progress and their dislikes, their failings and their fidelity. The confidence which they soon learnt to feel in their mistress gave them wonderful facility in doing this, and also gave their holy mother continual opportunities of imparting to them a cordial love of religious perfection. To each she prescribed practices suitable to her character and disposition, and to make them more easy, she required nothing which she did not first perform herself, in order to animate them by her example. In directing them she often made use of that supernatural light which God gave her concerning their interior and secret dispositions. In the sequel we shall see the testi-

mony that several of these novices have rendered to
the gift of prophecy and discernment of spirits possessed by their holy mother, which they had frequently experienced.

God had several times given her a supernatural
knowledge of the state and dispositions of the
novices, long before she had charge of them as their
mistress.   Mother Greffier, in the testimony she
bore to the wonders which God had performed in
His servant, has deposed, that during the time she
was superior, she was several times in great difficulty
on the subject of the vocation of some postulants or
novices, and that Sister Margaret had then very
clearly foretold what would happen to each of them.
She assured her of some, that they would succeed in
their good design, notwithstanding the apparently
insurmountable difficulties which would present
themselves; of others she said that they would be
saved, not in the order of the Visitation, but in
some other congregation which she pointed out;
again, of others she maintained that they would never
flourish in the soil of the Visitation, because they
were not planted there by the hand of the Lord, and
that they would themselves leave it through the
Blessed Virgin's protection of this holy order.
When the servant of God made these predictions,
their accomplishment often appeared very uncertain,
sometimes even very improbable; yet the event
always verified the prophecy, and Mother Greffier,
who was the confidant of the prediction, was also
the witness of its fulfilment.

Sister Margaret was not deprived of this supernatural knowledge when she conducted the noviciate,
therefore it was not astonishing that she should pro-

duce so much fruit in this holy and difficult employment. But without saying more in detail of these
predictions, of which we shall speak hereafter, it will
be useful to repeat some of the counsels she gave
her novices, so as to lead them by secure ways to
perfection. She permitted them to explain to her
their difficulties in writing when they found it more
agreeable than by speaking, or when the time or the
rules of silence did not permit it ; it was also frequently in writing that the holy mistress gave them
her answers. They took great care of the counsels
written by the hand of their mistress; and a great
number of them, who were living at the time when
the juridical informations were taken touching the
holy memory of Sister Margaret, delivered up
these precious papers, which may serve for the instruction and sanctification of religious. It is with
this view that we now proceed to transcribe some of
them.

INSTRUCTIONS GIVEN TO A NOVICE.

"You have given me great pleasure, my much
loved sister, by writing to me, and you ought to be
certain that my affection for you, and my wish to be
of service to you, makes me find pleasure in what
you consider a trouble ; the desire that you show of
belonging entirely to God sweetens everything to
me. I am much pleased that our Lord invites you
to abandon yourself to Him, as a child throws itself
into the arms of a good father, who is powerful
enough to preserve him from danger. Take then
these words to yourself, 'If you become not as little
children, you shall not enter into the kingdom of

heaven.' The practice of this consists in becoming
little through true humility of heart and simplicity
of mind. It seems to me that by these two virtues
you will arrive at the perfection which God requires
of you.

"The first will keep you annihilated in perfect
forgetfulness and contempt of yourself. You will
receive cheerfully, and as coming from the hand of
your heavenly Father, all the contradictions and
humiliations which befall you. Without stopping
to consider second causes, look only to His loving
Heart, which will never permit His adorable hand
to execute anything in regard to you, but what is
conducive to His glory and your own sanctification.
Because He loves you, He will often furnish you
with means of suffering, either by creatures or
through yourself; but in whatever manner this may
be, respond only *by silence and submission, saying,
' It is my heavenly Father Who has done it; that is
enough for me.'

" To begin this perfect abandonment, you will on
Thursday after holy Communion, make an entire
sacrifice of your own will to God, reserving to yourself no control over it, and asking pardon for the
bad use which you have made of it. You will sacrifice to His Sacred Heart your free will, asking
through that divine Heart the grace to live for the
future as if you were deaf, blind, and dumb.

" Deaf to the suggestions of self-love, to words by
which charity is wounded, and in one word, to whatever can sully the purity of your heart.

" Blind to the defects of others, in order not to
judge them; and especially that you may permit

yourself to be conducted in everything by holy obedience, without reply and without reflection.

"Dumb, so as never to speak of yourself, either in the way of praise or excuse. Remember that when you do the one or the other you make yourself an object of contempt in the eyes of the angels. When a wish to excuse yourself arises, say to yourself, 'Jesus was innocent, and He was silent when He was accused, and I, who am so often guilty, shall I dare to justify myself?'

"When thoughts of human respect attack you, say to yourself, 'No, my God, I will do neither more nor less, from a regard to creatures; since I wish only to please Thee, it is enough that Thou seest me everywhere.'

"As for your prayer, think when going to it, that you accompany our Lord on His way to the Garden of Olives, and unite yourself to His holy dispositions and intentions. When you find yourself negligent, or your thoughts wandering, make this reproach to yourself: 'What, my soul, canst thou not remain these few moments with Jesus?' Then return simply to your subject without stopping to consider what were your distractions, and at the end of your prayers offer to the Eternal Father those of His Son, to repair your own deficiencies. In short, contrive in some manner that the principal fruit you draw from prayer may be love, humility, and simplicity.

"In every action follow the example of your crucified Saviour, who never sought His own glory, but that of His Father. Let your glory consist in humiliation and contempt, and when they come upon you, say, 'Behold what is my due.' Keep your heart in peace whatever may happen ; be troubled at nothing, not even at your faults; be humbled on their account and correct them quietly, without being discouraged or cast down. God dwells in peace. As to the rest be courageous in seconding all God's designs upon you, by abandoning yourself entirely to His love. I conjure you to be inviolably attached to the exact practice of all your holy observances, and to make your dwelling in the Sacred Heart of Jesus. When you have committed any fault, take from this adorable Heart something to repair it; place there whatever you do, seek there all that you want; and in all your sufferings unite your heart to the Heart of Jesus crucified."

To another, who was frightened at finding in herself so many evil inclinations, she said :

" You give me pleasure, my dear sister, by so sincerely laying before me the inclinations which torment your poor heart, to lead it to evil, and to prevent you from giving yourself entirely to God. I trust that they will not succeed, and that by the resistance you will offer, with the help of grace, they will be an occasion of great merit for you. You see, I must not flatter you. You will receive nothing without fighting for it, and if I may say so, at the very point of the sword; that is to say, you must be of the number of the violent who take heaven by force. But be of good courage; grace will not be wanting to you, nor the assistance of the Heart of God, Who wishes to save you. Remember that He gives you this sight of your faults and miseries through the excess of His great love for you, and because He wishes to lead you to a high state of perfection ; but you will only reach it by an entire and perfect renunciation of all things, and especially of yourself. You should live from day to day in perfect self-denial, even of those things which are given you for your use, and deprive yourself of them when you feel an affection for them, though they may appear to you of little importance. Our enemy cares not with what he holds us enchained.

"In the second place, be persuaded that whatever makes you most vile and abject in the eyes of creatures, is that which will render you most agreeable in the sight of God. He will soon reject you if you become vain, and are filled with a high estimation of yourself, and a desire of being esteemed by others. Abjections and humiliations are often the more felt on account of their being inconsidera-ble and unnoticed; but they will elevate you to God if you support them with patient sweetness and equality of mind."

To another who described the fears which troubled her, and who consulted her upon her manner of prayer, she thus wrote:

"I will simply tell you what I think, my dear sister, of that which gives you so much pain. I believe that this fear which our Lord gives you is the effect of His very great love for you. For see-ing that His love is not sufficiently strong within you to make you fly evil, He mingles fear with love, that the two together may have the desired effect. Ever then preserve a loving fear, which will make you do good and avoid evil; in all you do renounce every intention but that of pleasing God. In your greatest trials renew your vows; and be assured that what has most power to weaken the grace of love in your heart, is its too great attachment to creatures, and the love of pleasure. You must die to all this, if you wish pure love to reign in your heart. You must also destroy the love of your own will, which much displeases our Lord. He permits you to feel this disgust for prayer, and the practice of virtue, because you take too much pleasure in communion with and reliance on creatures. You will remedy your defects only by doing continual violence to yourself; you will never find true peace until you perfectly renounce yourself, as it is God's Will you should do. Labour then with fervour; for there is no other way by which you can arrive at perfection. Forgetfulness of yourself and love of abasement, are the most certain means of attaining it. This manner of prayer is good; continue it in perfect conformity to the good pleasure of God, whether He consoles or afflicts you. Do not be distressed at all those fears of hell, but make frequent acts of hope and confidence in the divine goodness, which will never abandon you."

To another who experienced great interior troubles:

"Be comforted, my dear sister, and fight generously, for I hope the Sovereign Pastor will not lose His beloved sheep. He only permits the infernal wolf to attack us, that He may have a reason for rewarding us, and may bestow Himself as the prize of our victories. Thus we ought never to be discouraged, or permit ourselves to be disquieted. If we are humble, these troubles will raise us as much in the sight of God, as they abase us in our own eyes. If you are alone, kiss your crucifix; if not, press your cross upon your breast, and say, 'O my Saviour, I disavow with all my heart whatever passes within me contrary to Thy holy love; I cheerfully accept all the painful positions in which it shall be Thy pleasure to place me; I love and cherish my cross, for the love of Him Who has given it to me, and I desire only the accomplishment of Thy holy Will. Whenever I kiss Thy cross, it is to show Thee that I submit to mine.'

"But, in the name of God, let us not pass so much time in reflecting upon our troubles, either at the time we feel them, or when they are over; let us consider them as little as possible, for they have never less power to injure us than when we treat them with contempt.

"Do not attach yourself to spiritual sweetness, for that will not last long; but seek God by faith, and think that He equally deserves our love, whether He afflicts or consoles us. If He gives you any sweetness in your exercises, you should believe that it is to dispose you to taste of His chalice by humiliation, mortification, or in some other way.

"Be careful not to miss communion; we cannot give a greater joy to our enemy than by withdrawing from that which deprives him of all the power he would have over us.

"Be attentive to despise thoughts of vanity, and faithful in never excusing yourself. Remember never to disapprove, accuse, or condemn any but yourself, so that your tongue, which is destined to utter the praises of our Lord, and which so often serves as a passage to conduct Him to your heart, may not become the instrument of Satan. Remove from your thoughts all idea of doing more or less than what is comprised in our holy rules and constitutions; never neglect any of them, for it is in

18

this way alone that we can gain the Heart of Jesus Christ."

To another who was under the same trial :

"Believe me, my dear sister, you must not allow yourself to fall into despondency under the little trial by which it pleases God to prove you. Conform your will to His, and abandon yourself entirely to Him. It is His desire that you should be peaceful and constant in your troubles and dryness, without disquieting your mind by seeking means to relieve your uneasiness, as you have done. You must remain as you are, since it is the Will of God. Of what use is it to torment yourself as you do? Only remove whatever He shows you to be an obstacle in the way of His love. It is His Will that you live in entire deprivation of everything but Himself, of all that might satisfy your inclinations and engage your affections; for according as you clothe yourself with these things, He will in the same measure despoil you of His graces. The esteem and applause of creatures is very dangerous for you; do nothing to attract it. Avoid flattering tongues and human respect, which you basely prefer to the love you owe to your Lord. I believe that it is His holy intention to keep you low and little by this kind of trial, because humiliation is necessary for you; every other way has dangers for you. You ought to look upon it as a great favour when any occasion of humiliation and annihilation occurs."

To another, who had committed a fault, and had not at once revealed it with simplicity:

"I am much pleased, my dear sister, that our Lord has shown you this obstacle to your perfection without my intervention, and I hope that He will

Himself make you understand the importance of it better than I could have done. But remember that it is not enough to know your fault, if you do not resolve to amend it by generous detachment from all things. Be certain that it is the devil who prevents you from seeing this, lest you should break the tie which attaches you to himself, and hinders you from uniting yourself faithfully to the Heart of Jesus Christ. But our Lord will retire from your soul if He finds you attached to any other than Himself. If you fail in simplicity, you will lose the friendship of that divine Heart. He will leave yours as a barren land which produces only thorns and thistles. Labour faithfully at the mortification of your spirit and your senses; make yourself humble and simple, if you wish to be acknowledged as a true daughter of Jesus Christ."

To another, who had laid her resolutions before her:

"I find nothing to add to your note but to urge upon you the faithful practice of all it contains, endeavouring to neglect nothing by which you may become conformed to your crucified Spouse, in whatever the faithful observance of your rules will permit. Live in a loving abandonment of yourself to the care of Providence; banish all the reflections of self-love, that you may entertain yourself simply with the Heart of Jesus Christ, attain to the purity of His holy love, and enter into all His holy intentions.

"Act and suffer in silence. Ever keep your soul in peace. Whatever disposition God may make of you, be not disturbed, but leave Him to do as He pleases, uniting yourself to all His holy intentions.

This is what it seems to me He wishes from you;
for the purity spoken of in your note includes the
absence of every voluntary imperfection that would
sully your heart, which is destined to be the throne
of your Beloved. Abandon yourself to love without
reserve, and be careful to profit by the occasions of
mortification and humiliation which occur, that they
may unite you more closely to your Lord."

To another, who had asked her to give in writing
something which would arouse her fervour:

" I will, my dear sister, say a few words to you,
since you wish it. I do so cheerfully, in the desire
that you may belong entirely to our Lord Jesus
Christ. He appears to me to require from you great
fidelity in making the sacrifice of whatever He will
show you is most agreeable to Him, though it may
cost you much; for it is impossible to be saved without suffering and sacrifices; and as Jesus is jealous
of your heart, and wishes to possess it entirely, you
also must be jealous of His, by loving Him, if possible, more than any one else. And as love produces
conformity to the person loved, you must, if you
wish to be loved by Jesus, become humble and
gentle like Him; His humility will teach you to
rejoice when you are despised, and to be silent when
you are accused, saying to yourself, 'Jesus autem
tacebat;' 'Jesus was silent.' "

To another, who had a great fear of suffering:

"Live, my dear sister, entirely abandoned to the
love of our Lord Jesus Christ, permitting yourself
to be governed by His loving Providence, without
asking anything or refusing anything. But always
hold yourself in readiness to act or to suffer at the
least sign of His Will, through the obedience you owe

to those who represent Him.   Under all circumstances regard God and not creatures; this will make
you receive with equanimity from His adorable hand,
the sweet and the bitter, consolations and mortifications, blessing Him in all and everything. Maintain
inviolable fidelity to all our holy observances, however minute they may appear, for by this means you
will gain the Heart of your good Father who loves
you tenderly.   Fear nothing as long as you are
faithful; commit no wilful fault; remember that
being the spouse of a crucified God, you ought to
sacrifice yourself to Him, in order that He may
establish His kingdom in your soul; His kingdom is
a kingdom of peace in the midst of suffering. Cherish
a grateful remembrance of His benefits towards you,
for they are very great."

To another, who had been deficient in humility,
and had acquired it by the practice of honouring
the humble life of Jesus Christ in the Blessed
Sacrament:

"Your note, my dear sister, more than ever con-
firms me in what I said to you on the subject of
humility, which is the certain way of your salvation.
You cannot leave this road without losing the
friendship of our Lord Jesus Christ. He will raise
you to Himself in proportion as He sees you little
in your own estimation. Do then everything by
love and humility; you are doubly bound to do so,
by the lot which has fallen to you of honouring the
humble life of our Lord Jesus Christ in the Blessed
Sacrament. You should then offer yourself to Him
as a worthless creature to its Creator, to receive
whatever it shall please Him to bestow, without His
finding the least resistance on your part. You

must be assiduous in humbling yourself, and pleased
when others assist you in doing so. Never avoid
opportunities of humility, and those occasions which
may make you vile and abject, either in the sight
of others or in your own. Because Jesus Christ
loves you, He will often provide you with these
opportunities; for it is by them that you will become
more closely united to His divine Heart, to which
you ought to endeavour to conform yourself. You
will do this by becoming gentle and humble as He
was, being silent under accusations, and more especially when by speaking you might attract the vain
esteem and approbation of men; for the Lord often
rejects what they esteem the most, and His Spirit
rests only upon the humble of heart. Use every
effort to maintain this humble spirit, and if through
frailty you fall, do not be distressed, but humble
yourself for not having been humble, and repose
peacefully with love and confidence in the goodness
of the Heart of Jesus Christ. I entreat Him to
make you entirely His, and to give you grace to be
faithful to Him, according to the views He will
impart to you when it shall be His pleasure to do
so."

Such were the counsels of the mistress, and the
sentiments with which she inspired her novices. By
the nobility and elevation of soul that we remark in
all these different counsels, we may form some judgment as to the interior feelings and degree of perfection which the writer had attained. Without the
least intention of doing so, she described herself in
these several letters, and showed how much she
esteemed and loved the virtues of which she so ad-
mirably pourtrayed the excellence, and to which

she so skilfully pointed out the way. There is
neither art, nor effort, nor affectation in her style; it
flows naturally from the feeling of the heart; and a
heart to which holy and sublime views have become,
as it were, natural, must possess in a very eminent
degree those virtues of which it teaches the practice;
especially that powerful and courageous humility
which delights in being lowered, forgotten, or despised,
and which fears nothing so much as esteem and
applause. It is to this point that she incessantly
led her novices, because it was her favourite virtue,
and the one most calculated to render her pupils
conformable to Jesus Christ, who was "meek and
humble of heart."

Agreeably to the principles of this humility, Sister
Margaret, though so learned in the art of forming
novices, did not trust to her efforts nor her talents
alone. It was in good faith that she believed herself
only calculated to spoil everything and destroy
the work of God. She constantly invoked His aid
by prayer, and recommended to Him all those who
were confided to her, entreating Him to be Himself
their guide. She laid before Him their wants, their
state, their imperfections, and their difficulties. To
their sanctification she consecrated her mortifications, communions, and all her good works, and she
never ventured to reprove or advise them without
having first taken lessons or advice from the Heart
of Jesus Christ.

No noviciate was ever more animated with the
spirit of fervour and holiness, and never was there
seen more of that spirit of simplicity, charity, and
obedience, which forms the peculiar characteristic of
the Order of the Visitation. It was through this

holy mistress that that house was renewed in spirit, and became one of the most fervent of the whole Order, after having been much relaxed in the practices of perfection, as we have seen by the opposition which Sister Margaret met with for so long a time. The entire reform of the house cost her much, as we shall see in its proper place, but it took its rise in the holiness with which the mistress inspired her novices. This admirable fervour is maintained to this day, and the spirit of the servant of God is perpetuated in the religious whom she formed. A great number of them were alive when that house was under our charge. In the visits which we repeatedly made, we witnessed with admiration a courage for penance, an ardour for humiliation, and a zeal for perfection, beyond what one is accustomed to find in the most regular houses, and the divine fervour which we admired in these holy sisters, appeared to us to prove the eminent virtue of her who had instructed them, as much as all the wonders of which they gave us information, and to which they had borne witness.

Of all the means which the holy mistress employed to inspire her disciples with an ardent love of our Lord Jesus Christ, the most efficacious was the devotion to His Sacred Heart. It was through their ministry that she began to spread this devotion; and God, Who is pleased to establish the works of His power by the weakest instruments, willed that this holy devotion, now so accredited, authorized, and extended, should have no other beginning than the fervour of a poor religious, unknown to all the world, and no other support than the innocent simplicity of a troop of young novices in an unknown country town. And yet this holy devotion, which, opposed so strongly at its birth, and almost stifled in its cradle, as we have seen, and shall see further in the sequel, is established, like the gospel, by the contradictions which it has endured. Like the grain of mustard seed spoken of by Jesus Christ, which has the smallest beginning, it has become a large tree, wherein the birds of heaven find rest.

It was long since the Son of God had made known to His servant that the devotion which He had revealed to her would at length meet with success; that she would even establish it throughout the world, and particularly in the Order of the Visitation. Though there might be little prospect of this event, the servant of God expected it without fear; she hoped even against hope; and that word of God which was every day being fulfilled in her suffer-ings, she believed would be equally infallible with regard to all His other designs. Whilst Father Colombiere was still alive, she once wrote to him, that should she see the whole world in arms against this devotion, she would not despair of its being established, because she had received assurances of it from the mouth of her Saviour. He had not only prophesied the success of this devotion, but also the opposition it would meet with; and it was by this prophetic light that the servant of God several times predicted, that in the diocese of Autun, where she lived, this devotion would experience the longest opposition, which has been verified by the event. It was established in France in all the houses of the Visitation by permission of the bishops, when it was refused to the convents in the diocese of Autun, and particularly to that of Paray. It was only in the

year 1713 that they were at length fully permitted
to celebrate the festival, and obtained the approbation of the mass in honour of the Heart of our Lord.
Thus, according to Sister Margaret's prediction, the
diocese and the house which first witnessed the
prodigies performed by God to authorise this devotion, were the last to render public and solemn
homage to the divine Heart of our Lord Jesus
Christ.

But if this house was by the authority of superiors
so long deprived of this consolation, it has that of
having seen the first beginning of this holy devotion. It was the novices who by their fervour procured for it this advantage, and who on the following occasion were the first to consecrate themselves
to be for ever the victims of the Sacred Heart of
Jesus, the adorers of His wonders, and the imitators
of His love.

Sister Margaret had been mistress of the novices
for nearly a year when this occasion presented itself.
One Friday, in the year 1685, when the Church celebrated the memory of St. Margaret, the novices
wished, on account of its being their mistress's
festival, to give her some mark of their gratitude and
love. The humble mother having become aware of
this, begged them to pay to the Heart of Jesus
Christ the honours they had intended to bestow
upon her, and to offer to Him the nosegays they
wished to present to her. The novices entered immediately into the holy views of their mistress, and
with all the eagerness with which her fervour had
inspired them, each endeavoured to excel the other
in dressing up a little altar in the hall of the noviciate. There they placed a little piece of paper on

which they had roughly drawn the Heart of Jesus Christ surrounded with flames, to express the ardour of that excessive charity which He has felt for us, as says the apostle. Afterwards they surrounded the holy picture with all that innocent simplicity could imagine to be most becoming for its decoration.

If this simple altar had nothing precious in the sight of man, the victims who there offered themselves were without doubt agreeable to the eyes of God. Sister Margaret was the first to prostrate herself before this symbol of the love of Jesus Christ, consecrating herself generously to the worship of His divine Heart with a transport of fervour that only a seraph could describe. The innocent flock followed her example, and responded to the fervour of their mistress, prostrating themselves at her side, and each in her turn consecrating her heart to the love of the adorable Heart of Jesus Christ. After some time of recollection and prayer they all arose, and the mother then proposed that each of them should write the act of their consecration to the Sacred Heart of Jesus Christ, as they had conceived it in the simplicity of their fervour. They joyfully complied with the wish of their mistress, who, to take part in the offering of these daughters, as well as to make it more beneficial to them, added some words of her own to the writing of each, according to the particular disposition of their souls, as far as God had made it known to her. Of all these devout consecrations she made, as it were, a precious bouquet, which was without doubt agreeable in the sight of Him, Who alone knows all the merit of innocence and fervour.

To procure a greater number of adorers for the Heart of Jesus Christ, the mistress sent to several of the oldest among the professed nuns whose piety was known to her, to invite them to take part in the devotion of the noviciate. The novices undertook the commission with eagerness, but met with no success; messages and solicitations were unanimously rejected. Some sisters, forgetting themselves for the moment, replied only by making fun of the mistress; others answered by unseasonable lectures; and one amongst them, whose eminent piety had united her more closely to Sister Margaret, declared against her on this occasion more loudly and vehemently than the rest. "Go, tell your mistress," replied she to the novices who invited her to the noviciate, "go, tell her that the best devotion is the observance of our rules and constitutions; it is this which she ought to teach you, and that you ought to practise." There were but two or three sisters who, from complaisance as much as from fervour, joined the innocent group of the first disciples of the Heart of Jesus Christ.

The poor novices, humbled by the manner in which their message had been received, returned to the noviciate, and thinking it prudent to conceal all that was offensive and contemptuous in the answers which had been made, they only said that so and so could not come. But the holy mistress, to whom God had revealed what had passed, and what would in the end happen with respect to this devotion, replied immediately, and in a prophetic tone, " Say rather that they will not come; but the Heart of Jesus Christ will know how to attract them. He will have everything done by love and nothing by

constraint ; we must wait the time He has appointed,
and that time will surely come." We shall see
shortly how the prediction was fulfilled. Meanwhile the mistress, losing nothing of her recollection
and fervour, nor of her tranquillity, continued to
discourse with these innocent victims of the love of
Jesus Christ, and of the sacrifice they had made of
themselves to this divine love. During the remainder of the day she varied the exercises of piety
by which she had suggested that they should keep it
holy ; she animated them by her words and example;
her air, her countenance, and all her exterior senses
seemed to partake of the interior recollection in
which she was absorbed, and shed into the hearts of
the novices a portion of the ecstasy and heavenly
joy with which the soul of their mistress was transported. Never was there a festival more holily or
more agreeably celebrated ; and, the Heart of Jesus
communicating to the hearts of His new adorers a
portion of the love with which it is consumed, they
began to taste consolations and delights which were
before unknown to them.

As for the fervent mistress, she seemed to possess
all the fulness of the treasures of this adorable
Heart. She beheld the happy firstfruits of the
establishment of a devotion of which she foresaw in
spirit all the progress and fruit ; and delighted at
having been enabled already to form a society of
these innocent souls, in which the Heart of Jesus
Christ should be adored in a particular manner, she
exclaimed in the excess of her joy, " No, my dear
sisters, you could not have offered me a more heart-
felt gratification than you have done in paying
homage to the divine Heart of Jesus Christ, by con-

secrating yourselves entirely to Him! How happy
you are, that it has pleased Him to make use of you
to begin the practice of this devotion. Let us continue to pray that He may reign in all hearts. Ah,
how it rejoices me that this Heart of my Divine
Master will be known, loved, and glorified! Yes,
my dear sisters, it is the greatest consolation that I
can receive in my life, to see Him reign everywhere.
Let us love then, but let it be without reserve and
without exception; let us give everything and sacrifice everything to obtain this happiness, and we shall
have all in possessing the Heart of God." In conclusion, as she never separated suffering from love,
she said, "Jesus Christ desires to be all things to
the heart that loves Him, but this will be only in
suffering for Him."

The heavenly joys which the mistress and novices
had tasted in this holy festival, were soon crossed by
contradictions. God, Who willed that the spirit
which animated Sister Margaret should be tried in
every way, and that the devotion she was so anxious
to introduce, should triumph over all the obstacles
raised against it, permitted that these obstacles and
contradictions should be then carried as far as they
could go. When what had passed in the noviciate
was known throughout the community, the murmuring was as general as if the most holy laws of religion had been violated. The less devout freely exercised their wit and malice against the servant of
God; the more spiritual piously condemned her conduct, on the plausible pretext of its being necessary
to blame novelties. They said haughtily, that it was
not for little novices, nor even for their mistress, to
establish new devotions; that nothing was more

dangerous than to admit singularities, however pious
they might appear; that it was directly against the
rules of the institute of the Visitation, and especially against the eighteenth Constitution, which
says, "Let no one burden herself with prayers or
offices under any pretext whatever, excepting those
which are prescribed by the rule." To this constitution they gave the most rigorous interpretation,
and the one most opposed to the undertaking of the
servant of God. These modern Pharisees crowded
around their superior, and eagerly pressed her to
interpose her authority to put a stop to what they
called a scandal, a danger, and a novelty; and that
there might appear to be some charitable feeling in
what was so contrary to the spirit of charity, they
declared that they were favouring the mistress of
the novices by not demanding that she might be
either deposed from her employment or punished for
her rashness.

Mother Melin regarded the conduct of the mistress with more moderation and discernment. She
was of so perfectly sweet a disposition, that she was
commonly designated the true daughter of St. Francis of Sales. With her usual gentleness she received
the impetuous attack of her unruly daughters. Long
experience had made her acquainted with Sister
Margaret's holiness, and she also knew by how many
prodigies God had countenanced that devotion, of
which He was Himself the author. But whatever
might have been her inclination to support it, she
thought it her duty for the sake of peace to confine
this devotion to the noviciate alone. She forbade
the mistress to attract or to associate to it any other
religious, or to place in view without her permission

any image or representation which might inspire this devotion; in a word, to take any step which might renew the commotion which the former proceeding had caused. She only permitted her to exercise her pious practices with her novices for her own consolation.

The obedience of the mistress equalled her fervour. She submitted to this rule without reply, as she had borne without complaint the reproofs of some and the ridicule of others. It was only in the presence of Jesus Christ that she poured out her heart, and the feelings with which it was filled in this time of contradiction. These feelings were divided betweeen the joy of suffering and the fear that God might be displeased by this opposition. "I place in Thy hands, O my Jesus," said she, "the care of defending Thy cause, whilst I suffer in silence." Our Lord caused her to hear these words in the depths of her heart: "I will reign, notwithstanding My enemies and all that oppose Me." He then made her understand clearly that in spite of all these obstacles, the sacred treasures of His Heart would be manifested to the whole Order of the Visitation; that the daughters of that congregation would pay a particular worship to it, which would be infinitely agreeable to Him; that it was His pleasure to bestow this privilege upon them above all others; and that being enriched with this treasure, they would share it with the rest of the world without losing any part of it themselves. This is what Sister Margaret wrote in confidence to Mother de Saumaise at this time, and the original letter, which is preserved, bears witness to the prophecy. Indeed, its accomplishment began before the year was out, even in the house of Paray, and was attended by circumstances which rendered it still more miraculous. We shall see this in the sequel; but Sister Margaret was first to endure the measure of suffering and humiliation, which by the decree of God was to precede the consolation she would 'receive from the propagation of this devotion.

In truth, if the mistress of the novices carried her obedience to the superior's orders even to scruple, several of the sisters were not such scrupulous observers of the rule of charity. The joy of having triumphed over Sister Margaret, and of having drawn from the superior an order which seemed to tax her with temerity, inflated the hearts of these indiscreet religious. The new devotion was constantly chosen as the subject to enliven their conversations, and as the object of their jokes. Others made it a point of duty to lecture Sister Margaret, and their reproofs were not the less bitter and humiliating for being serious and clothed with an appearance of reason. Some of them threatened to denounce her to the superiors of the entire order, and to draw from them a severe correction. But her heroic courage was not to be subdued by their reproaches, nor terrified by their menaces. We shall best see her feelings during this storm, by transcribing what she wrote to Mother Greffier:

"I could not occupy myself," said she, "with anything but the Sacred Heart of Jesus. I should die content if I could procure it some honour, even though it should cost me an eternal punishment. It is sufficient for me that I love Him and that He reigns. Because of the opposition I meet with, I have often

19

been upon the point of ceasing to speak on the subject, but the vain fears by which Satan endeavoured to discourage me have been so severely reproved, and afterwards I have been so fortified and encouraged, that I have resolved, cost what it may, to carry out to the utmost what I am allowed at present to do with the sisters of the noviciate, who are warmly attached to the devotion. Yet," she continues, " if obedience did not permit this, I would give it up entirely, because to it I defer all my views and feelings." This good religious had learnt from her Divine Master to prefer obedience before everything else. She was impressed in His school with the maxim which devout and pious souls cannot too often hear, that if, according to the Holy Spirit, "obedience is better than sacrifice," it is also a much more secure road than that pointed out by the most clearly-proved revelations, and the most miraculous ways.

Mother Greffier, to whom Sister Margaret wrote so confidingly, was then superior of the convent of Semur in Auxois; she had been elected by this convent at the close of her six years of superiorship at Paray. We have seen already how much and in how many ways she had opposed Sister Margaret's devotions, and with what contradictions she had tried her during the time of her superiorship. In souls filled with the spirit of the world, and in those who spare their self-love and endeavour to mingle it with their devotions, this conduct would have produced a lasting antipathy. The superior would have endeavoured to justify her rigour, by the contempt of her who had been the object of it; and the religious, so often humbled and ill-treated, would have endeavoured to defend herself, or at least would have complained and murmured. But the Spirit of God, which animated these two hearts, used what would have disunited others less perfect, as a means of cementing their friendship more closely. The sincerely humble nun ever preserved towards this severe mother a tenderness and confidence which nature could not inspire, and which art was unable to counterfeit; and the enlightened superior, who had been austere from reason, and incredulous from prudence, preserved when absent a high esteem for her disciple and a close intimacy with her. Moreover, she became as ardent a lover of the Heart of Jesus Christ as she had formerly appeared to be opposed to that devotion.

She now wished to testify this to Sister Margaret, and what she did was eventually the cause of the miraculous propagation of this much opposed devotion. Sister Margaret had given her an account of all that had passed on the subject, and had related with the utmost simplicity all that happened in the noviciate on the festival. Mother Greffier wished to give her dear daughter a mark of friendship that would be agreeable to her; she therefore ordered a skilful painter to represent the Heart of Jesus Christ surrounded with flames, emblematic of the charity with which this Divine Heart is consumed. It was environed with a crown of thorns, the symbol of the sufferings which were the fruit of His love, and which ought also to consecrate ours. Mother Greffier sent this picture appropriately framed to Sister Margaret, feeling sure that it would be well received by her; and thus the promise of the Son of God began to be accomplished,

that it would be by its strongest opposers that His
Divine Heart would be honoured, and the devotion
to it accredited and extended.

We may judge what were the transports of Sister
Margaret when she saw this treasure, and was permitted to receive and keep it. A miser would not
rejoice more over a pile of gold, nor an ambitious
man over new honours and dignities. The unex-
pectedness of the gift increased the pleasure, and
her surprise was tenfold when she learned from this
holy superior, that the whole community of the
daughters of the Visitation of Semur united with
her in honouring the Divine Heart of the Saviour of
the world. We will now give Sister Margaret's
answer:

"I expected, my dear mother, that you would tell
me to give up all thoughts of introducing this devotion to the Sacred Heart, and to think of it only as
a vain effect of my imagination; and consequently I
kept my mind in a submissive state, because I give
little credence to anything that comes from myself.
But when I saw the representation you have sent
me of that only object of our love, I seemed to
begin a fresh existence. I was previously plunged
in a sea of sorrow and suffering, and God has
changed it into so great peace and submission to
all the dispositions of His heavenly providence in my
regard, that I feel as if nothing were capable of
troubling me. My only desire is to procure glory
for this Sacred Heart, and how happy should I
esteem myself if I could do some service to it. You
can, my dear mother, assist me much by reassuring
my poor and feeble courage, which is frightened at
everything. But I wander from my subject. It

seemed to me then, that several names were written on that Sacred Heart on account of their desire to honour it, for which cause He will never permit them to be effaced, but He did not tell me that these friends would meet with no crosses, for it is His Will that their greatest happiness should consist in tasting the bitterness of sorrow. Could it be ever possible that we should not wish to love Him with all our strength in spite of all contradictions? These are not wanting to us, as you know, but I am resolved either to die or to conquer every obstacle, with the assistance of this adorable Heart. I cannot tell you the consolation you have afforded me in sending this beautiful picture, as also in being willing to help us by joining with your community in our devotion. This news caused me ten thousand times more joy than if you had put me in possession of all the treasures of the earth."

Thus the community of the Visitation of Semur was the first which enjoyed this devotion, which was so much opposed in the place where it took its rise. We shall soon see the house of Paray in its turn coming forward to embrace it, but it was the Will of God that fresh trials should prepare the sister for this consolation. It was also His Will, in order either to increase the merit of His servant, or to show us how heroic was her courage, that she should make choice of these trials, and that she preferred them to the happiness of the angels. We learn this from a letter written by Sister Margaret to Mother Greffier, to whom she relates at length the singular favour which God bestowed on her on this occasion. The following is the letter exactly as Mother Greffier preserved it:

"I am unable to express my joy, my dearest mother, at the growth of the devotion to the Sacred Heart of my Saviour; it seems to me that I live only for that object. There sometimes burns in my heart so ardent a desire to make Him reign in all hearts, that I feel as if there were nothing I would not do or suffer for that end ; even the pains of hell, without sin, would be sweet to me. On one occasion, if I do not deceive myself, when burning with this desire in presence of the Blessed Sacrament, I was shown the ardour with which the seraphim are consumed with such exquisite delight, and I heard these words: ' Wouldst thou not rather enjoy their bliss, than suffer, humbled and despised, in order to contribute to the establishment of the reign of My Heart in the hearts of men?' Upon this, without hesitation, I embraced the cross, studded with thorns and nails, which was presented to me, and with all the affection of which I was capable, I said unceasingly, 'O my only Love, the accomplishment of my desire would most please me ; and I would much rather suffer, in order to make Thee known and loved, if Thou wilt honour me so far, than be deprived of this pleasure, even to be placed among these burning seraphs.' "

Her choice was granted. The sufferings which the servant of God endured at this time were extreme, both from bodily infirmity and contradictions. Everything was against her, even contrary to the will of those who compassionated the suffering state of this patient soul, and their support and consolation served only to aggravate her grief and increase her troubles. Yet her fervour grew with her sufferings; she supported all with joy, because she

knew that these sufferings contributed to bring
glory to the Heart of Jesus Christ, and to procure for
Him the homage she desired by the establishment of
this devotion. She usually expressed her courageous
disposition in this state by these two verses, which
she often repeated to herself, or uttered to those who
pitied her sorrows :

"Je veux tout souffrir sans me plaindre :
L'amour de mon Sauveur m'empêche de rien craindre."

At this time she wrote down her feelings of gratitude for her crosses, which she received from the
hand of God as if they had been favours. "What
shall I render to Thee for all Thy benefits, O my
God! How excessive is Thy goodness towards me,
in allowing me to partake of the food with which
Thou feedest Thy saints. Ah! without the cross
and the Blessed Sacrament, I should not be able to
live or support the length of my exile in this valley
of tears. I wish not for a diminution of my sufferings; the more my body is weighed down, the more
does my spirit feel true joy and liberty in attending
and uniting itself to my suffering Jesus. What can
I desire more than to become a perfect copy of Jesus
crucified? It rejoices me when His sovereign Goodness employs a multitude of workmen in labouring
according to His Will in the accomplishment of His
work. He sometimes tells me, 'I do thee great
honour, My child, in using such noble instruments
to crucify thee. My Father gave Me up into the
hands of executioners to place Me on the cross; and
to effect the same purpose in thy regard, I employ
persons who are consecrated to Me, into whose
power I deliver thee. In gratitude for this, it is

My pleasure that thou shouldst offer up all thy sufferings for their salvation."

A new persecution arose at this time against our patient religious, and it was one of the most violent which she experienced during her life. In the convent of Paray, there was a young lady of high birth who had been placed there in childhood. It was her father's wish that she should become a religious, and she, not having the courage to resist him, concealed her antipathy for the convent under an external piety which deceived the most experienced. Interested parents are often found who sacrifice some of their children for the establishment of the others, and who, abusing their authority over the young hearts entrusted to their care, make them, contrary to their inclination, embrace a state to which God has not called them. Such criminal designs are but too easily accomplished when parents meet with weak and unenlightened superiors, who by complaisance, or avidity for a tempting dowry, consent to admit into their house those unfortunate victims whom God repulses, and who sometimes find only despair and damnation where so many others walk in the safe and secure path to their eternal salvation. It sometimes happens that the more holy superiors are themselves deceived, and that those who are so cruelly treated by their parents, so skilfully hide their repugnance during their noviciate, that superiors cannot take too much care in discovering this kind of forced vocation, which eventually is the cause of many disorders in religious houses.

The father of this young lady was unhappily one of those just described. For the establishment of his children, it was convenient that this one, who was less beloved than the others, should, by her religious profession, renounce her share of the property. Too timid, and too complaisant, the unhappy girl concealed in the depths of her heart the aversion she felt for the convent, which she did not dare to make known. From fear of falling into the hands of an irritated father, she went through, as if from her own wish, the usual preliminaries for obtaining admittance to the noviciate. She was admitted without much precaution, and apparently conducted herself in the accustomed trials with sufficient fervour. She was faithful to all the regular observances, and besides, as her character was gentle, she soon gained the esteem and friendship of the community. The constraint she put upon herself was so well concealed, that it was an easy matter to be deceived by her; but Margaret, who so often saw the future in the Heart of Jesus Christ, could not be long without discovering what lay hidden in the heart of her postulant. In truth, she did see it; she ascertained by prudent trials that this daughter was neither sincere nor called to the religious state, and at length thought it her duty, after wise delays, to warn the superior of her discovery, and through her the relations of the young lady.

The father, who was irreligious enough to force the vocation of his children, was unreasonable enough to be offended at the information given him. He looked upon the dismissal of his daughter as a personal affront, and to oblige the superior to keep her, he employed the same means which he had used to influence his daughter, namely, haughtiness, severity, and menaces. A part of the community were terrified by this conduct, for he was a man of power and influence. They feared his resentment, which they considered so much the more dangerous, as the young girl still dissimulated her antipathy, and protested the sincerity of her desire for the religious life. But the firmness of the mistress of the novices was an obstacle which could not be overcome, either by the father's anger or the human respect of the sisters. At length the young lady herself requested her dismissal, and the father was then obliged to take her back; but his anger was excited against the house, and in particular against the mistress of the novices, whom he regarded, not without foundation, as the originator and sole cause of the affront he considered himself to have received. He spoke of her unsparingly on all occasions. He made it a crime in the convent to have so much confidence in a religious, whom he openly treated as a visionary and a fool. The weight of this nobleman's authority influenced a number of persons, for people are always ready through human respect to yield to the passions of the great, or to believe evil without examination. There was nothing talked of in the country but the prejudice, obstinacy, and imprudence of the mistress of the novices, and her virtue, prayers, and practices were cried down. Several persons of distinction came to the parlour for the express purpose of insulting her. They treated her to her face with the most marked contempt; they told her haughtily that she must be deposed from an employment of which she was incapable, and added that they would appeal to episcopal authority to oblige the superior to dismiss her. Some even carried their violence to such a height, as to tell the frightened nuns that the

house could only reestablish its reputation by condemning the imprudent mistress to prison.

A religious of high birth and great reputation for
piety was at that time in the town. Too ready to
believe what was the subject of animadversion in
society, and also much prejudiced in favour of the
family in question, he entered warmly into its resentment, and believed it his duty from pious motives to do so. He said he was bound in conscience
to undeceive the public, which was seduced by the
apparent sanctity of Sister Margaret. He cried her
down everywhere as a hypocrite, asserted that her
devotion was only hypocrisy or delusion, and believed himself lenient in treating her only as a
visionary whose brain was deranged. To what an
extent is one carried by passion when it is covered
by an appearance of piety! Conscience is deceived,
and only serves to confirm us in paths most opposed
to justice and charity, while sin hidden under the
appearance of devotion has no longer anything
which keeps us back or frightens us.

The united voices of the worldly and the devout
in blaming the conduct of the mistress of novices,
had its effect even within the house. All the virtues
of the servant of God, and the prodigies they had
witnessed, were forgotten. The outrageous attack
upon her from without, was soon taken up by the
religious within. Some from dislike to her, others
from prudence, several from affection to the dismissed girl, and human respect for her parents, willingly repeated even in her presence what was said.
They reproached and lectured her, and accused her
of ruining the house by her conduct. "The consequence will be," they added, " that no more novices

will enter; for who will confide their daughter to
one so despised, and run the risk of meeting with
the disgrace from which a girl of so illustrious a
family was not secure?" All these remarks, and
these various and continual assaults, did not move
the servant of God; her ardour for suffering and
humiliation was greater than the ill-will of all those
who were incensed against her. She saw with joy the
accomplishment in herself of all that had been predicted, and derived consolation from contemplating
the fruit which it was the Will of God to draw from
her humiliation. She acquiesced then, without murmur or complaint, presented herself wherever she
expected to meet with humiliation, and never avoided
meeting with or continuing in the company of those
proud and uncharitable religious who were pleased
to ill-treat her, and who at this moment thought
they had the advantage over her. She appeared in
the parlour at all necessary times, and whenever
she was desired. She there often listened to, and
always without justifying herself, the most outrageous things that could be said. She did even more ;
for in order to acquiesce perfectly in her humiliation, and as if to draw upon herself alone all the
indignation caused by the young lady's refusal, she
obtained permission of her superior to prostrate herself in full community at the feet of the novice before
her departure, as if she had offended her by her imprudence, and so humbly to demand her pardon for
it. It is thus that the saints revenge themselves for
the ill-treatment they experience. What a lesson
for those who, on account of an offensive word, retain an unconquerable aversion in their hearts!

The interior sentiments of the servant of God in

the midst of this persecution, are still more admirable than her conduct. Far from being irritated against the pious and highly-esteemed man who had spoken against her, she only considered and feared she was really under an illusion, since a man of so much integrity had that opinion. See what she writes on this occasion, with her usual simplicity, to Mother de Saumaise :

"I am afflicted in many ways, but the most severe trial is having to consider myself as the sport of the devil. I see nothing in myself but what is worthy of punishment, since I have not only been unhappy enough to deceive myself, but have also deceived others by my hypocrisy, though, as it seems to me, unintentionally. I can no longer doubt it after the opinion of this great servant of God. I have reason to thank God a thousand times for having sent him to me, to undeceive those who had been indulgent enough to preserve some esteem for me. What a singular obligation shall I owe him all my life for having rendered me this important service ! I can assure you nothing gives me greater consolation than to know that creatures are undeceived about me, so that I shall be able to satisfy the justice of God, and remain for ever disregarded. This thought soothes me and softens all that I endure."

This humble and admirable acquiescence in the judgments formed of her by others, renewed her uneasiness and interior pain with regard to her state. The deep conviction she felt of her unworthiness, her incapacity, and what she called her crimes, and on the other side the esteem in which she held many of the religious of whom we have spoken, and also several other pious people who had taken part against her on this occasion, excited afresh her fears of being under a delusion. She communicated her troubles to a religious of the Society of Jesus, named Father Rolin, who had been for some time at Paray, and to whom she had intrusted the direction of her soul. She consulted him in writing, so as to give him facility and leisure to reflect before God upon what she asked him. We have not this letter; but we know by the answer of Father Rolin, which was found among the papers of the servant of God, with what intentions she consulted him, and to what a height she carried her profound humility, the holy suspicion she had of herself, and the docility she felt towards those who conducted her on the part of God. It is for this reason that we here insert a part of the director's answer :

"I have read, my dear sister in our Lord, your two letters, and bless God for all the mercies He exercises in your regard; I will answer both with all the sincerity that God requires of me. The spirit that leads you is not a spirit of darkness; its guidance is good, since it is always submissive to obedience, and leaves you in repose when your superior has spoken, &c.

"In the next place you shall see my thoughts as before God. They are not devils who are enraged against you. The spirit of darkness is not the cause of the persecutions you experience, it is the Divine love which is at work, and to my great consolation, makes use of souls that are dear to Him to procure you suffering. The martyrs had not this consolation in their torments, and tyrants committed great crimes in afflicting them; but the holy souls who

obtain crosses for you, please God in the little martyrdom they make you suffer. This thought ought
to console you much. I am willing that you should
attribute whatever happens to your faults, though
all these things may be rather an effect of the goodness of God than of His justice. All the names of
reproach by which you are called, ought to cause
nothing to issue from your mouth but thanks to our
Lord and prayers for those who utter them. Do
not repent of anything you have said; a cause which
produces such excellent crosses cannot be bad. Let
them make as many complaints as they like, and
fear nothing for me. Were all that can be said
against you to be repeated to the whole world, it
would be the greatest favour our Lord could bestow
on you. Let people inform whomsoever they will,
you should rejoice at it; dismissal, imprisonment, all
proceeds from the love of Jesus Christ for you. I
ask of you a perfect self-abandonment, and a heart
ready to do and to suffer everything.

"I repeat what I have said; you are not the sport
of Satan, but of Divine Love; for it is the language
of Scripture, that sacred love is not without rigour,
whether because it is the offspring of Mount Calvary, or because it partakes of the Divine Justice,
which wishes to satisfy itself by afflicting us."

We shall see how exactly this holy religious followed the advice of her director; but we must not
forget another spiritual assistance which God prepared for His servant in the midst of her crosses.
She wrote in confidence to Mother Greffier a letter
of which the following is a part: "The heart of my
Jesus makes me always find fresh consolation amongst
the nails and thorns, with which He now keeps me

fastened upon the cross, which His love does me the favour to destine for me. Beg of Him earnestly that I may not abuse so great an assistance, but may make of it the use which He expects from me. I ask of you secresy, and the favour to tell me if I ought to afflict myself for all the sad consequences that this cross has produced, because God is much offended by them. This alone occasions me sorrow; nothing else deprives me of my peace, though I seem to be shut up in an obscure prison, surrounded by crosses which I embrace with all my heart. This is the whole of my exercise in my present state, during which the Sacred Heart of my Jesus has given me assistance which I did not expect. A great servant of God wrote to me a short time ago, telling me that whilst saying mass, he felt strongly urged to offer it every Saturday of that year for me, or according to my intention, and to be disposed of according to my desire. Now my wish is that you should have it one Saturday and I the other, and we shall still have a share in all the sacrifices that he offers. The good religious who does me this charity, is not known to me, nor I to him, except by name. This is the present that I have to make you, and it will not be disagreeable to you. But do you not admire with me the mercy of God towards His poor weak slave, in having sent me this support of prayer on the first Saturday of Lent, the time when He began to redouble the multitude and weight of the crosses with which He gratifies me? I should have fallen a thousand times under their weight, if He had not given me strength through the intercession of the holy souls who pray for me. In other respects I have never felt more peace, for which blessed be the Sacred Heart of our Lord Jesus Christ."

Whilst Sister Margaret enjoyed this peace, condemned herself in silence, and sincerely acquiesced in the humiliating judgments formed of her, God, Who justified the innocence of Susanna by the testimony of Daniel, raised up in favour of His servant as many defenders as there were novices and postulants in the noviciate. Faithful witnesses of the way in which the holy mistress had acted towards her who had been their companion, they spoke of it on every occasion, and eagerly defended her reputation with wonderful zeal, as her sanctity was well known to them. Their ardour was more displeasing to their humble mistress, than all the insults of those who illtreated her. She severely reproved her young disciples, as failing in the submission they owed to the orders of God; she told them it was self-love which was the secret motive of their ardour, and she earnestly endeavoured to inspire them with the humble tranquillity with which her own heart was filled. According to her usual custom she gave them in writing an admirable lesson, which deserves a place in this history:

"I cannot express the grief I feel at seeing you make so bad a use of this precious opportunity of giving to God proofs of our love and fidelity. It is He Himself who has permitted the invention of this cross, to prepare us for its festival; and instead of lovingly embracing it, we only endeavour to shake it off and rid ourselves of it. Not being able to succeed, we commit a thousand offences which fill the divine Heart with sorrow. Whence comes this, if it is not that we have too much love for ourselves,

20

which makes us fear to lose our reputation and the
good esteem of the world? This it is which makes
us seek to justify our conduct. We believe that we
are entirely innocent of the things of which we are
accused, and that others are guilty. We think that
they are quite in the wrong, and we in the right.
Oh, believe me, my dear sisters, that humble souls
are far from entertaining such thoughts; they always
believe themselves more guilty than their accusers
would make it appear! My God! if we knew what
we lose in not profiting by opportunities of suffering, we should be much more attentive to make a
good use of those we have. We must not flatter
ourselves; if we are not faithful on occasions of
pain, humiliation, and contradiction, we shall lose
the good graces of our Lord, Who wishes us to love
and to regard as our best friends and benefactors all
those who cause us pain, or furnish us with opportunities of suffering.

"Feel then great sorrow for having thus displeased the Heart of Jesus Christ by counteract-
ing His designs upon us, and to obtain His pardon offer to Him all the practices of virtue you
are about to perform. Abstain from speaking of
Sister N., and make no mention of her amongst
yourselves. Take care that you fall into no voluntary fault in this respect. Each of you will say
the office of the dead for the souls in purgatory,
that they may obtain for you grace to return to
the friendship of the Heart of Jesus Christ, and
enable you to establish devotion to it in this community.

"But, in the name of our Lord, let there be no
more considerations nor excuses of self-love. Let

us be silent on all occasions of mortification. Let us be charitable and humble in our thoughts as well as in our words. If you are more faithful in this, the Sacred Heart will be more liberal of His graces than He has ever been; but if, on the contrary, you fail, I will myself entreat Him to punish you. Give yourself to God, yes, and all to God; carry His cross, carry it cheerfully, joyously, courageously; otherwise you will have to render a most rigorous account of it."

In this document we see to what perfection this good religious carried the practice of humility, and at the same time what care she took to form her novices in the exercise of this holy virtue, and by what way she conducted them. It was always by love, the desire of pleasing God, and conformity to the sentiments of His divine Heart; as it was from the Sacred Heart, and in the communication of love that she drew the lessons which she gave them. Several of these nuns have borne witness, that it was commonly said amongst them that their mistress was another St. John the Evangelist, who spoke only of love and charity. They added with simplicity, that for their part, they did not resemble those disciples of the holy apostle, who were weary of hearing him always speak the same language; for that they always heard their mistress speak of this love with pleasure, because she spoke with so much unction, that it appeared always new to them.

It was then from the Heart of Jesus Christ that the fervent mistress drew that seraphic love with which she inflamed her pupils, and it was this love that inspired them with their devotion towards the Sacred Heart of our Lord. In this divine Heart she found the model of their conduct, the motives of the virtues she recommended, and, lastly, the assistance which they needed in the midst of the combats they would have to pass through in the service of God. We see in the advice she gave them the salutary use she made of this devotion, in order to lead them to perfection. We may learn not only how useful it was to them, but also how profitable it would be to those who would meditate carefully on the treasures of sanctity which are to be found in the adorable Heart of the Saviour, and whose delight it would be to learn in the infinite love with which this divine Heart is consumed, the love that we owe to Him in return. It is with this view that we are now going to transcribe some of the lessons given by the holy mistress to her novices. In her various instructions each one may find that of which he is personally in want, and the reader may possibly recognise himself in the simple picture which the wise mistress draws of the defects and vices she is so anxious to correct in her pupils.

ADVICE TO A NOVICE, TO LEAD HER TO DETACHMENT.

"The Sacred Heart of our Lord requires you to love and serve Him constantly, as some little return for the love He bears to you. He wishes you to live deprived of all which is not God, because He wishes to be your only friend, support, and delight. He will be all this to you, provided you seek it not in creatures, without, however, becoming more stiff or constrained in their regard, but mild, humble, and charitable towards your neigh-

bour. Suffer in silence, and in the love of the
loving Heart of Jesus Christ, all humiliations,
troubles, and contradictions that you may receive
in future, and never make any complaint of them;
but when they come, accept them as pledges of His
love, and, without troubling yourself, shelter yourself in the love of your own abjection. For He
delights to take up His abode in our littleness and
our nothingness; let us then be always joyful and
contented. Be faithful to all our holy observances,
without neglecting the least of them; endeavour,
nevertheless, to walk in the holy liberty of the children of God, uniting and conforming yourself to
His holy love and Will. Refer to Him the glory of
everything, without reserving for yourself anything
but weakness and poverty, contempt and sorrow.
Do not amuse yourself by perpetually devising new
means of perfection; remember that yours consists
entirely, in one word, in conformity of life and
actions to the holy maxims of the Heart of Jesus,
especially to His gentleness, humility, and charity."

To an imperfect novice who was particularly troubled on the subject of her vocation:

"It is with all the affection of my heart, which
loves you in the Lord, that I wish, in satisfying your
desire, to be able to give you all that is most useful
for the perfection that our good Master requires of
you, together with strength and courage to accomplish it. After having addressed myself to the Sacred Heart of our Lord in prayer and at communion, I will simply tell you my thoughts, which will,
I trust, profit you according to the attention you
give them.

"In the first place, do not trouble yourself to

examine whether your vocation comes from God.
You cannot doubt that you are one of those plants
that our heavenly Father has placed in His garden,
to be cultivated with His own hands, preserved by
His providence, watered by His grace, and to flourish in the odour of sweetness through the ardours
of His holy love, provided that your will courageously resist the hindrances that the enemy will
endeavour to place in your way. He takes advantage of the opposition of our corrupt nature, in
which he raises fresh repugnance, disgust, and aversion from good. Thus he endeavours to discourage
and trouble us, that we may be hindered from grow-
ing in virtue and advancing the work of our perfection. To remedy this, you must offer generous violence to yourself, by becoming more faithful to God,
your rules, and yourself.

"Faithful to God, in not disputing with grace
when it urges you to do good or avoid evil. Frequently consider that this same grace, which now so
earnestly solicits you, and which you have so often
resisted, will at length withdraw from you, and leave
you like a dry and barren land. May God keep you
from this misfortune! I believe that it will never
befall you, if when you hear His voice, you harden
not your heart. For remember, that this voice
comes and passes away in a moment, sometimes to
return no more. We seek it, and we ask for it, but
as we have before trifled with it, it now mocks us
in our turn. This is what happens to cowardly
souls, which the Lord begins to reject from His
Sacred Heart.

"In the second place, be faithful to the rules,

never neglecting anything they require, however repugnant to your natural inclinations.

"In the third place, be faithful to yourself, in judging, condemning, and imposing penances on yourself for the faults you commit. If you practise this, your soul will be reassured against its fear of the judgments of God. God loves you and wishes to save you, but by a road thickly strewn with thorns; these thorns, however, will produce roses that will never wither. It is only necessary that you sacrifice your will and all the vain amusements that occupy your heart. Keep your soul in perfect detachment from whatever is superfluous, dismissing from your heart all vain inclinations and affections, not only to creatures, but even to those of your own actions which you believe to be well done. Everything of this nature takes the place of God in you, and prevents you from finding and possessing Him; for He will only enrich you with Himself and His gifts, in the same proportion that you become empty of yourself and of all creatures. Destroy your attachment to your own will, and renounce your own judgment as often as you find the opportunity of doing so, which will, I believe, be very pleasing to God. Speak of Him with veneration, and of your neighbour with esteem, but never, or very rarely of yourself, and then always with contempt.

"Have a great confidence in God, for His mercy infinitely surpasses all our miseries; often throw yourself into His arms and on His divine Heart, abandoning yourself to do whatever He wishes. Do not be discouraged by troubles or dryness, but suffer them in the spirit of patience, as also everything else which is opposed to your inclination. I earnestly

exhort you to keep the resolutions you have made.
God will not be mocked.   He would rather you
should never promise Him anything, than that you
should be always promising and never keep your
promise.   What we have written is our own condemnation.   Have recourse to the Sacred Heart of
Jesus.   Ask counsel of Him in all your difficulties,
conforming yourself as much as possible to His
humility and gentleness towards all men, and especially cultivate a charitable feeling towards those
against whom you are tempted to feel dislike.   Love
those who humble and contradict you, for they are
more useful to your perfection than those who flatter you.   Above all things, never be guilty of a
voluntary fault."

To another novice who was more advanced in love
of perfection :

" All to the greater glory of the Sacred Heart of
our Lord Jesus Christ !   That I may follow its holy
movements, my dear sister, I will tell you as in His
holy presence, what He has informed me is His Will
concerning you.

" In the first place, it is His Will that you make
Him an entire sacrifice of your whole corporal and
spiritual being, no longer wishing to make any other
use of your powers than to procure Him all possible
honour and glory, offering Him an entire and un-
reserved gift of all that you have ever been able to
do by His grace, and may be enabled to do in future ;
' Since,' He says, ' these things are not capable of
enriching a soul which He calls to follow Him in
the ways of His holy love.'   He wishes from you
the sacrifice of your desires and your will, more
than austerity and corporal penance.   Never do

anything without the order of your superior, to
whom you owe submission and obedience in whatever she may think fit to command, after you have
shown her with simplicity all that is within you of
good or evil. This extends to everything, for one
cannot be deceived in obeying.

"I believe that the Heart of Jesus Christ will be
satisfied when you have abandoned yourself to
Him, so that He becomes the delight of your eyes,
the light of your understanding, the affection of
your will, the remembrance of your memory, and
the whole love of your heart, and you allow Him to
dispose of you according to His good pleasure. Reserve nothing for yourself but the desire of pleasing
and loving Him above all things. Banish every
thought of self-love and self-seeking, which places
so many obstacles to the operations of grace in your
soul. Walk then simply with our Lord; He will
not suffer you to be lost, for He loves you. Forgetting and despising yourself, trust entirely to Him.
Limit yourself to loving Him ; leave Him to work,
and that will be sufficient for you."

To another, whom she invites to study and imitate
the Heart of Jesus Christ :

"I have read your note, my dear sister, according
to your desire. I cannot refuse to send you a word
in answer, urging you to be more than ever earnest
in imitating the Sacred Heart of Jesus, Who I
trust will never reject you, provided you confide
humbly in His goodness. He takes great pleasure
in doing good to the poor, and instructing those who
desire to learn in the school of His holy love. He
constantly invites us to be, like Himself, meek and
humble of heart, and I believe you could do nothing

more likely to gain His approbation, or more surely make yourself His disciple, than by becoming truly meek and humble, possessing that true humility which will render you submissive to every one, and make you cheerfully, heartily, without excuse or complaint, endure in silence the little humiliations you may meet with, always thinking you deserve more than fall to your lot; and when you have failed in this respect, and shown your repugnance in some manner, do not omit to kiss the ground five times, saying these words: 'Miserere mei Deus, secundum magnam misericordiam tuam. Have mercy on me, O Lord, according to Thy great mercy.'

"Be very grateful all your life for your vocation, for it is a very particular grace, which is not given to all, and of which we shall have to render an account at the hour of death. Think much of it. To show God that you love Him, be faithful to the practice of all our observances, not neglecting one of them. I recommend to you the practice of interior and exterior recollection, which will destroy all that idle curiosity, which is the source of distractions in your exercises. I am much pleased that our Lord draws you in prayer to contemplate your vileness in the great mercy of the Sacred Heart. Entreat Him fervently to shew that mercy to you and to all sinners, of whom I am the worst. Beg of Him to give me His holy love, and to pardon me my sins."

To another, to lead her to place confidence in God:

"Often throw yourself, my dear sister, into the arms of the loving providence of Jesus, especially after holy communion, when He opens His Heart

to gain yours. Abandon yourself, and give yourself
up entirely to the power of His love, in all that you
can. Whoever speaks of pure love speaks of pure
suffering. We ought to cherish our trials and unite
ourselves to the designs which God has for us. Let
us repeat in all our troubles, ' Dominus illuminatio
mea et salus mea, quem timebo ? The Lord is my
light and my salvation : whom shall I fear ?' It is
the Will of the adorable Heart of Jesus, that the
hearts which belong to Him should be detached
from themselves and everything else. Our self-love
is so insidious that it makes us believe that it is God
whom we seek, when we attach ourselves too much
to things connected with His service. It is this
which causes us sorrow when we are obliged to give
them up, because we have sought our own satisfaction more than God. A heart which seeks Him
only, finds Him everywhere ; and as our end in becoming religious has been to give ourselves entirely
to Jesus Christ, so it is also fitting that He should
be all in all to us."

To another, who was beginning her noviciate :

" Since God has placed you in the bark of holy
religion, you have nothing to do but to abandon
yourself blindly to holy obedience, a true sign of the
Will of God towards you. In all that you do have
no other desire nor view than to please God; look to
Him only in all that happens to you, without caring
how the crosses which He lays upon you are composed. His good pleasure ought to be sufficient in all
cases. Repose upon His bosom with the confidence
of an infant; His love will take care of you. Be
humble towards God, and kind and gentle to all.
Judge and accuse yourself alone, and excuse all

others. In speaking of God, praise and glorify Him, mention your neighbour with esteem, but never speak either good or evil of yourself.

" If you wish to honour the Sacred Heart of Jesus Christ, make it the keeper of all you do and suffer, offering Him all your actions, that He may dispose of them and apply them according to His good pleasure, always uniting yourself to His holy intentions in all that you do, and in whatever may happen to you. Make your dwelling in this adorable Heart; place there all your little griefs and sorrows, and there all will be assuaged; you will there find the remedy for your evils, strength in your weakness, and a refuge in all your necessities.

"Deal with our Lord with entire confidence and simplicity ; do not amuse yourself by reflecting upon your faults; that serves only to satisfy self-love, and to discourage us. When we have done wrong, we must humble ourselves before God, entreating His pardon, and then, as our holy founder says, set to work again with fresh courage. Forget your own interests and the care of yourself, in the arms of your Heavenly Father.

" Once again, I entreat you, consider God and not yourself. The farther you remove from yourself, the nearer you will approach to God; He will take care of you, according as you forget yourself. Love to be looked upon as nothing in the house of God. Cherish and honour those who humble and mortify you ; regard them as your greatest benefactors, and say within yourself, 'If they knew me, they would see that I deserve much more.' When you are accused, think that Jesus Christ did not escape accusation, and that to follow His example you ought not to wish to do so either, even when you are not guilty of what you are accused. Besides, how many other faults have you committed of which you are not accused!

"In all the obedience you practise, remember that Jesus was obedient even to the death of the cross. Regard yourself as a poor person who receives everything from charity, and that if you were to be despoiled of everything there would be no injustice committed. In short, endeavour to conform yourself in all to Jesus your Love, to Jesus crucified; do all by love and for love; and employ the present time well, without being uneasy for the future."

To another, who suffered from great interior troubles:

"I pray the Sacred Heart of Jesus Christ, since it is not His good pleasure to make the tempest cease within you, that He will Himself be your support and your strength, that you may be firm and even tranquil in the midst of the storm. This storm should not trouble you, for it will never overthrow you. The Heart of Jesus is a good pilot; keep yourself constantly attached to it by loving confidence and great humility, though you seem only to hold on to Him by the point of your spirit, as it were, without any enjoyment or feeling. Let your enemy cry out; it is a good sign when he makes so much noise, for it is a proof that he is out in his reckoning. Resist all his suggestions by a simple disavowal, without tormenting yourself to produce sensible acts. The Sacred Heart of Jesus well knows what passes within yours; it is He who permits all these trials, to teach you to abandon your-

self to Him and to all His designs upon your soul ;
hope in His goodness, that according to the increase
of your troubles, your confidence may redouble.
Regard yourself as a tree planted by the water-side,.
which bears its fruits in season ; the more it is beaten
by the wind, the more deeply does it bury its roots·
in the earth. In like manner, the more you are
assaulted by temptations, the more deeply should
you bury your roots by profound humility in the
Heart, and according to the Heart of Jesus Christ.
I supplicate Him to surround you by His power as
with a wall, which all your enemies cannot penetrate."

To another, whose temptations were made known
to her by God :.

"Not being able to speak to you, my dear sister;
I warn you to be upon your guard, that Satan may
not have sufficient influence over your mind to make
you offend God. He will defend you from his
stratagems if you are faithful, if, after the example
of the Heart of Jesus, you are gentle and charitable
to your neighbour, have a humble and confiding
love towards God, and preserve your soul in peace,
with a courage never cast down. You are not yet
at the end of your difficulties ; but take courage, the
Sacred Heart of Jesus will be the reward of your
victories. But I must not flatter you ; I believe
that He means to try you as gold in the crucible,
that you may be placed in the number of His most
faithful servants. For this reason you must lovingly
embrace every occasion of suffering as a precious
token of His love.

"Yesterday, whilst offering you to our Lord, this
thought came to my mind: ' Let her be faithful in

the path she is treading, and suffer all without
complaint, since she cannot be admitted to the number of the perfect friends of My Heart, without
being purified and tried in the crucible.' Suffer,
then, and be satisfied with the good pleasure of God,
to which you should ever sacrifice yourself, with a
firm hope that His Heart will not abandon you, for
it is nearer to you when you suffer than when you
rejoice. Do not dwell upon yourself. Let suffering or joy be equally indifferent to you, provided
the good pleasure of God be accomplished in you."

To another, whose resistance to what God required
was known to her :

"Remember, my beloved sister, that you have a
jealous Spouse, Who will possess your heart completely or not at all. If you do not banish creatures
from it, He will retire with His love ; if you do not
quit them, He will quit you and deprive you of
Himself. There is no medium. He will have all or
nothing. His Heart is at least worth yours. Are
you not ashamed of disputing with Him a possession
which belongs to Him ? Really, I cannot understand how it is that He is not weary of your resistance ; He must have a very great love for you. Yet
He will do no nothing without your co-operation.
Think seriously of this, and no longer refuse when
He makes known to you His Will, otherwise He will
deprive you of the benefit of His graces, and leave
you in a state of great dryness. Take care for the
future to be more faithful in following the movements of His grace. Leave all, and you will find all
in the Sacred Heart."

To another, on the perfect abandonment of the
will to God.

"I willingly answer you, my dear sister, according to your desire. In the first place, you should be inviolably attached to these words of our holy founder, 'Ask nothing and refuse nothing,' but keep yourself ready and disposed to do all and suffer all in the silence of a soul perfectly abandoned to the Will of God.

"Abandoned in body; taking and receiving indifferently, health or sickness, labour or repose.

"Abandoned in spirit; cherishing dryness, insensibility, or desolation, when God wishes you to be in that state, accepting them with the same thankfulness as you would consolations, ever keeping your soul in peace, and making it act in the very nakedness of faith without noticing sensible delights, which only serve to amuse us in the way of perfection.

"Abandoned in heart; this, which is the seat of love and of the will, you ought to cause so to die in the Sacred Heart of Jesus, as to permit Him to do with you whatever may be His good pleasure, neither procuring for yourself consolation or suffering, but taking with a perfect indifference all He offers you, whatever it may be, that so you may be sanctified according to His wish.

"If you wish it, you may in your prayer keep yourself to what I have said. In the midst of the wanderings of your mind, remain in the peaceful and tranquil dispositions you have described, making your spirit simple by the single act of abandonment to the Will of God, continuing in His presence as a useless servant, and only producing acts when He shall inspire you to do so. Do not trouble yourself with the suggestions of self-love, that whisper to you that you are losing time in thus doing nothing. For the rest, let it be your principal care to renounce self, and to cast off all those thoughts of self-love which are so great an obstacle in the way of God's designs for you. Bury all your miseries in the merciful and compassionate Heart of the loving Jesus. Think no longer of anything but to love Him, and forget yourself. Take these words for your motto, 'Divine love has conquered me, it alone shall possess my heart.' "

To another, prescribing to her rules of conduct, in order to attain perfection :

"I recommend you, my dear sister, to be invariably faithful in the practice of whatever you have promised to the Sacred Heart of Jesus, in order that He may reign absolutely in yours. Be resolute in never permitting yourself to be cast down, either by your faults or on account of opposition. Always shelter yourself in the love of your own abjection, esteeming yourself happy when our Saviour furnishes you with the opportunity. Lovingly embrace that which most completely annihilates you in the sight of creatures, as the most proper and necessary means to your perfection. Vain self-love is very dangerous for you, therefore you ought to be well pleased when you are despised and forgotten.

" Be gentle, condescending, and charitable towards all, as the Heart of Jesus was amongst men, but bestow not upon your neighbour what you owe to the Heart of your loving Saviour alone.

" Be ever submissive to the Will of God, and to your superiors, permitting them to dispose of you according to their will.

"Be constant in mortifying your senses, if you wish to acquire that interior spirit and gift of prayer that I desire for you with all my heart. Ah! if you could but understand the great happiness of loving the Sacred Heart, of being engrossed with it alone, and of belonging entirely to it, you would soon despise everything else.

"Abandon yourself to Divine Providence, being ready to receive from it alike joy and sorrow, peace and trouble, health and sickness; ask nothing, and refuse nothing. Labour to attain perfect self-annihilation, and endeavour to acquire the true spirit of the Visitation, which is profound humility before God, and great sweetness towards our neighbour.

"This humility will keep you as nothing in your own sight, unworthy of all good, and of the graces and mercies of the Lord; it will make you despise the seeking of the vain esteem of creatures; it will make you rejoice when you are contradicted, humbled, or despised; and you will offer to this no other resistance than profound silence, in conformity with our suffering and uncomplaining Lord, together with an interior acknowledgment of all that you deserve for your sins.

"Sweetness towards your neighbour will make you condescending in his regard, charitable in rendering him little services, willing to excuse his defects, and bear his ill offices, and by this means you will gain the Heart of Jesus Christ. Keep yourself in this Sacred Heart as in a strong fort; you will find there strength to enable you to be neither cast down nor troubled at anything, not even at your own defects. When we see our defects, instead of being discouraged we should humble ourselves, being glad that they are known to us, and appear what they really are. This practice will keep your soul in peace, and will make your heart the throne of God, Who delights in the humble of spirit. Be well pleased that He offers you occasions of suffering, whether with regard to your neighbour or within yourself; receive them as a pledge of His love, which endeavours by these means to render your heart conformable to His.

"Employ well the time devoted to prayer and other spiritual exercises: this fidelity will support you in all your duties; and to facilitate the practice of it, make your heart the throne of the love of Jesus Christ, often retiring there to discourse with Him, to adore Him, to love Him with all your strength and might, and to listen in silence to whatever He shall say. The means of attaining this holy love is to cut off all movements of self-love, and to engraft more deeply within you the love of your own abjection.

" Place over the eyes of your soul the bandage of a holy and loving submission to God, and to holy obedience for the love of Him. True obedience allows neither of murmuring nor reflection. Go on your way, which is that of exact observance of your religious duties, which you ought not to dispense yourself from, unless charity or necessity require it, for everything else is only accessory, and ought to yield to what is marked with so much holiness in the rules, constitutions, book of customs, and directory. Study them well. Act with the simplicity of a child towards those who direct you. Conceal nothing from them, either of good or evil, and God will

bless you, for He is an enemy of all double-minded-
ness and duplicity, and there is nothing that will
make your heart more conformable to the Heart of
Jesus Christ, than sincerity and humility.

"Remain hidden in this Sacred Heart, and, as it
were, annihilated in the eyes of creatures, thinking
of nothing but how to humble yourself, and to do
well whatever obedience and your rules require of
you. Be careful not to neglect the very least of
them, for God often attaches great graces to them.
Always be disposed to do, to bear, and to suffer
everything without complaining, or even thinking
that you are hardly treated. Seek not praise or
approbation in anything you do, and if it happens
that your conduct be commended, say within yourself, 'This is not my due.' On the contrary, when
you meet with contempt, say, 'This is what justly
belongs to me.'

"Carefully destroy in yourself all views of human
respect and self-love that prevent you from becoming
interior. Remember that virtue does not consist in
making fine resolutions, nor in saying fine words, but
in putting them into effect. Fine words and resolutions will be themselves our condemnation. In
all your actions avoid haste and eagerness, endeavouring to form your exterior, as well as your interior,
upon the model of Jesus Christ and His Sacred
Heart. Always act with the same tranquillity as
if the present action was the only one you would
have to perform, and the last of your life. How great
would the purity and fervour of your soul then be in
that action!

"Full of esteem for your vocation, say frequently
with the prophet, 'What shall I render to the Lord

for all His benefits to me? I will make Him the sacrifice of my whole being as a homage of love. I choose Him for the only object of my love, the treasure of my heart, the delight of my soul. I have no other wish in this life than to study to conform myself to my crucified Spouse, and to model my heart upon His by an entire death to my own will. I sacrifice it with all my inclinations, not only to obedience, but also to show charity towards my neighbour. I will only speak of him with esteem, even though I may see him commit faults which I cannot excuse, and I will offer to God one of the virtues of the Sacred Heart of Jesus to make satisfaction for it. I will carefully keep myself buried in the abyss of my vileness by sincere self-contempt.'

"See, my dear sister, the way of being all for God, Who wishes to be the only possessor of your heart. No longer, then, withhold from Him so trifling a thing, but to-morrow, after holy Communion, prostrate in spirit at His feet, and holding, as it were, your heart in your hand, make Him an entire sacrifice of it, and a holocaust of all that you are. Entreat Him not to reject you, though you have deserved it for having resisted Him so long. In your offering reserve nothing to yourself but the sole desire of loving and pleasing Him, whatever it may cost you, for He will have all or nothing. Your heart will be all for Him, when it shall be conformed in everything to the desires, the Will, the virtues, and the love of the Sacred Heart of our Saviour."

To another, to strengthen her in desolation and interior darkness:

"You ought, my dear sister, to be filled with love and gratitude for the great mercy and tenderness which the Heart of Jesus feels for you. I recognise it still more clearly in all that you say in your letter. All that you look upon as the rigour of His justice, I regard as pledges of His loving-kindness towards you. He intends by these means, which are so contrary to nature, to detach you from yourself and all created things, to render you entirely dependent on His grace, awaiting everything from His assistance, without placing any confidence or seeking resource in yourself, or neglecting whatever may be in your power to do. Ah! my dear sister, if you could comprehend the burning charity of the Heart of Jesus Christ towards you, you would see clearly that all His dealings with you proceed entirely from love. The insensibilities which you experience are but to teach you that to be more advanced in His love, you must become insensible to all created things, and especially to the movements of self-love. He wishes you to make the sacrifice of your will as often as He shall furnish you with the opportunity, until you have so completely destroyed it, as to have no other will than that of the Divine Heart.

"All these drynesses are to teach you, that if you wish to be a fertile plant in the garden of the Heart of our Lord, you must first destroy all affection for creatures. That darkness which you experience is for the purpose of extinguishing in you those false lights of human reasoning which oppose the hidden designs of God; He wishes that you should allow yourself to be conducted, as one blind, by the hand of His good pleasure.

"That silence which our Lord seems to maintain

towards you, leaving you deprived of good thoughts, and with difficulty applying yourself to any, teaches you that if you wish to hear the voice of your beloved, you must silence entirely the thoughts and feelings of self-love within you ; after which the divine love will teach you more in that happy silence than all the eloquence of creatures. Keep yourself then in this silence; speak little to creatures, but much to God by works and suffering. Be poor and emptied of everything, and He will fill you. Lovingly embrace whatever will mortify and humble you the most; this is the way to make the Heart of Jesus triumph in yours, in spite of your pains, dryness and darkness. Keep your soul in peace, without being troubled at your defects. They serve, in the designs of God, to preserve within you the love of abjection ; for this reason, the offence against God excepted, we should be well pleased to see our faults and deficiencies.

" Once more, my dear sister, how grateful should you be to God for showing so much mercy towards you! He conducts you to Himself by the direct road, in spite of yourself. This good Master, seeing that you often quit Him to give yourself to something else, attaches you by the cords of His love, with which He draws you to Himself; and because He leads you by a steep way, somewhat rough and thorny, you look behind to see if you can find some one to smooth it for you. But it is in vain; the difficulties must be conquered, the road must be passed, since He wills it so for your purification and perfection. What have you to fear, since He surrounds you on all sides with His power, as with a wall which the enemy cannot penetrate? Remember

that nothing can support or console her for whom
God wills suffering. Abandon yourself, then, with
the generosity of a noble heart to His guidance,
since you are in the state in which He would wish
you to be, that of living without support, or friend,
or desires, other than those which He will Himself
give you. Do that, and you will live as He wishes.
Leave the future alone, and think only of employing
the present moment well. The Sacred Heart asks
you to practise sweetness and humility, to labour
and to suffer, and humbly to keep silence."

It was in this way that the mistress instructed her
novices. In all these notes, carefully preserved by
her faithful disciples, we recognise the Spirit of God,
which alone could form in her such noble, pure, and
holy sentiments. Could a simple nun who had had
no other education than that of a village and a convent, all at once speak a language as sublime and
accurate as if her pen had been conducted by God,
while He at the same time governed her heart and
all her senses? We see here no features of that
false spirituality, which under pretence of total
abandonment to God, thinks it a duty to make a
sacrifice even of love and eternity, and to acquiesce
in crime and damnation to please Him: as if the
sacrifice we make to God of our own will to be conformed to His divine Will, could possibly comprehend the sacrifice of His love and that of our salvation. In these instructions we discover no taste for
extraordinary ways ; we do not see the prudent mistress distributing rules to her disciples for arriving
at the passive state, as we find in some works of the
present day, which presume to explain the art of
attaining to that supernatural state, as if such sin-

gular favours of the goodness of God could be acquired by method and industry. Sister Margaret,
who was raised in her childhood to a high degree of
contemplation, and who conversed so familiarly with
God, knew no other road to perfection than that of
humiliation, suffering, and love. All that she taught
is reduced to this alone, because in this alone consists the whole of the Gospel. "If any man will
come after Me, let him renounce himself and follow
Me. Learn of Me, for I am meek and humble of
heart. If you become not as little children, you
cannot enter into the kingdom of heaven." See
here an abridgment of all the lessons of Jesus
Christ, and all the teaching of His spouse. He
who practises them well, always and in everything,
with love and without reserve, will attain the perfection of this life.

But what more particularly deserves notice in this
advice, is the use made by the devout mistress of the
Heart of Jesus, and of the devotion towards it. The
Sacred Heart was her treasure, as it is that of all
the faithful; and all, in whatever state they may be,
can draw from it the particular graces they stand in
need of, and the lessons which are proportioned to
their duties. This was the belief of the servant of
God in consequence of the promise made to her by
Him; and for the consolation and instruction of all
those who read this life, in whatever situation they
may be, it is advisable to relate what this holy religious has herself written on the subject:

"I know not," said she, "if there be any exercise
of devotion in the spiritual life more proper to raise
the soul in a short time to a higher sanctity, and ·
make it taste the true sweetness which is to be

found in the service of God. Yes, I say it with certainty, if it were but known how agreeable this devotion is to Jesus Christ, there is not a Christian, weak though his love for this amiable Saviour may be, who would not at once practise it. Contrive," continued she, addressing the person to whom she wrote, "contrive that all religious may embrace it, for they will derive so much assistance from it, that no other means will be necessary to re-establish the first fervour and the most exact regularity in the worst-regulated communities, and bring to a height of perfection those who already live in a well-ordered convent.

"My divine Saviour has shown me, that those who labour for the salvation of souls will have the art of touching the most hardened hearts, and labour with a wonderful success, if they are themselves penetrated with a tender devotion to His divine Heart.

"As to lay persons, they will by this means find all the assistance necessary for their state of life; for instance, peace in their families, support in their labours, and blessings from heaven in all their under-. takings. It is truly in this adorable Heart that they will find a place of refuge during their life, and especially at the hour of their death. Ah! how sweet it is to die after having had a constant devotion to the Sacred Heart of Him who is to judge us! In short, it is very clear that there is no one in the world who will not derive every kind of assistance from heaven if he have a grateful love for Jesus Christ, such as that which is shown Him in the devotion to His Sacred Heart."

In this way the servant of God, whilst instructing

her novices, pointed out an efficacious means of perfection to the faithful of every state and condition.
Happy those who, like her, taste this joy, and know
the value of the treasure they have found. It is
from the Heart of Jesus Christ that we shall obtain
all the graces, desires, and virtues which are proper
to reform ours. See the infinite love of the Heart
of Jesus Christ for His Father; the tender and compassionate love of that Heart for us ; the feelings of
deep humiliation of that Sacred Heart, which bore
within it all the confusion due to our sins ; the sentiments of goodness, compassion, condescension, and
patience towards men, towards sinners, towards its
most cruel enemies, and those of love, of eagerness
and desire for suffering and for the cross. This is
what the servant of God beheld in the Heart of the
Son of God, this what she showed to her disciples,
and what we must see there, in order to be truly
devoted to this Sacred Heart. For truly this devotion tends only to inspire love of Jesus Christ, and
through love the imitation of His virtues, feelings,
and dispositions. Precious devotion, which leads to
the most perfect love, and to the practice of the
most sublime virtues of Christianity, which have no
other end but this, and which cannot well be imagined without this object, the most sanctifying that
man can possibly propose to himself. We shall soon
see to what a new degree of perfection Sister Margaret was raised by this devotion. For this purpose
we will now return to the thread of our narrative.

BOOK VII.

THE ADMIRABLE VOW WHICH SHE MADE. THE ESTA-
BLISHMENT OF THE DEVOTION TO THE HEART OF
OUR LORD IN THE COMMUNITY OF PARAY. THE
FRUITS WHICH SHE DERIVED FROM THIS DEVOTION.
SEVERAL INSTRUCTIONS AND PRACTICES PRESCRIBED
BY SISTER MARGARET.

WE have seen how the venerable servant of God
was enlightened in conducting the novices confided
to her care, and with what discernment she penetrated the cause of their troubles, and prescribed the
remedy; yet though her penetration was so great in
the guidance of others, she was completely in the
dark as to her own trials, and could find no relief
but in an entire reliance on, and absolute obedience
to, him whom Providence had appointed to be her
director. Father Rolin, superior of the Jesuits'
house at Paray, was destined by God to direct His
servant in the last years of her life, to be a witness
of her fervour, and of the interior graces which she
received. This good religious undertook this ministry impressed with far from favourable ideas of her;
he had at first an impression against extraordinary
ways; for it was God's Will, either for the greater
trial of His servant, or to make the wonders He
wrought in her more evident, that all those who
took charge of her soul should be strongly prejudiced against her.

Father Rolin felt for some time distrustful of her,

but could not at length resist the evidence of, nor
fail to discover, the Spirit of God. The trials to
which he put Sister Margaret's virtue overcame his
suspicion, and made her merits more conspicuous,
while those which God Himself had sent her, with
which we are already acquainted, served still more
to unveil the miraculous depth of holiness within
her, and to oblige Father Rolin to support her by
his counsels under this new temptation, and to render justice to her heroic virtue.

It was only after these proofs, and after having
been well acquainted with the grace possessed by
Sister Margaret, that this father at length consented to a new vow which the Spirit of God inspired
His servant to make. But before speaking of it, it
will be well to give some short instructions written
by this servant of God with his own hand, and drawn
up in the form of rules for the guidance of his penitent. Besides being very edifying, they contain
much useful advice, and will show the dispositions
of the nun, as well as the discernment of the confessor.

"You will here find, my dear sister, the answers
to the principal questions you have put to me in the
course of the year. I will write as in the presence
of our Lord, and will notice the questions you have
put to me as they present themselves to my mind.
I think you will be able to adhere to my instructions to the end of your life. I speak with so much
the more assurance, as I am persuaded that it is God
who manifests His Will to you, though by the most
miserable of men ; the water that passes through an
earthen pipe is as good as that which runs through
one of gold.

"1. I have sufficiently seen and known your sufferings, at the very time you made known to me the mercies of God in your regard. I know what is your disposition ; be at peace ; do not torment yourself with the idea that you are a hypocrite, for one can never be that without wishing it. I do not perceive that you wish it, be therefore at rest upon this point. Put in practice what you say, that it is enough for you to love and suffer in silence. Love the spirit that leads you.

"2. Concerning writing letters and the parlour, do whatever your superior orders. Declare to her your feelings upon these two points, with indifference as to her decision. Do not refuse any employment in the house.

"3. Do not distress yourself to remember what you hear ; let loving and suffering suffice for you.

"4. I wish you to make no more general confessions ; never propose to make one to any body whatsoever.

"5. I approve of the spirit of penance which animates you ; but in the matter of austerities, do what you are permitted, and no more.

"6. It is not a mark of reprobation to have no feelings of joy or sorrow, excepting those which are inspired by the Holy Spirit which leads you.

"7. Whatever repugnance you may feel to conversing with certain persons, never let it appear. You must overcome these things when civility requires you to do so. Pray for every one.

"8. Do not attribute to hardness of heart that peace which our Lord causes you to enjoy in your crosses.

"9. Rejoice in our Lord when you are treated as

a visionary, but give no occasion for being so treated. When you say anything, say simply, 'This is my idea, perhaps I deceive myself.'

"10. I do not disapprove the hatred you have of your body; and the pleasure which you take in seeing it fail is according to the spirit of the Gospel. Let your treatment of it be guided by obedience.

"11. It seems that you are afraid of treating familiarly with our Lord. Know that it is the manner of conversing with Him, which is most agreeable to Him.

"12. When, in the letter I wrote you, I spoke to you of justifying yourself, the idea was not suggested to me by your letter; you did not say a word about it.

"13. Make your communions on Fridays as often as you are allowed.

"14. As for vocal prayers, make those which are of obligation. In regard to others, it is not necessary for you to make any. Follow the attractions of holy love.

"15. You can answer the letters that you receive, according to obedience; and as to the manner of expressing yourself, always remember the advice I have given you in my ninth answer.

"16. Keep the paper I send you, and the little note I inclose, it will be of some use to you. Read it sometimes, especially in your greatest sufferings.

"17. I approve of your making the vow you mentioned; you shall do so at the end of the retreat you propose to make on the first opportunity, but with this condition, that if at any future time this vow causes you uneasiness, it shall hold no longer, and you shall be entirely free from it, and also that your confessor shall have complete power over it, either to explain it if doubts arise, or even to dispense you from it altogether, if he judge it expedient for the glory of God and your own good."

Not only does this writing show the prudence and discernment of the director, but it also bears the strongest testimony to the admirable virtue of Sister Margaret, to the hatred she bore towards her body, and to the love of mortification and suffering which consumed her heart. We also discover in it her deep and sincere humility; far from congratulating herself and taking delight in the favours she received from God, she only saw in herself causes for fear and scruples, and was so strongly inclined to believe herself a hypocrite, that it was necessary to reassure her frequently upon this point, and this could only be done by the authority of him who directed her in the name of God.

The vow here spoken of is too edifying not to be given entire; at the same time let it be remembered, that it is not inserted with any view of exciting pious persons to make similar engagements; it belongs only to souls purified for a long time by mortification and love to take such vows; those who, tempted by presumption, would wish of themselves to make such a vow, without being drawn to it by God, and without being directed by obedience, and the counsel of an enlightened director, would expose themselves to trouble, perhaps to falls, and to infidelities prejudicial to their spiritual advancement.

But if there are few persons in a state to follow so perfect an example, all may derive some fruit

from it, either by admiring the graces God bestows
on faithful souls, and the perfection to which He
raises them, or by confounding and humbling themselves interiorly at the sight of such great holiness,
acknowledging that whatever progress they believed
themselves to have made in mortification and love,
they are still far removed from so heroic a degree of
perfection ; or lastly, by sometimes trying to practise without vow what this courageous soul engaged
herself by an explicit vow to perform for the whole
remainder of her life.

The servant of God had for a long time done so,
and it was this holy habit which made her vow not
only practicable, but easy ; yet she only made it
with the most careful precautions of prudence and
obedience. She was interiorly urged by her divine
Spouse to make this engagement ; her director and
her superior were for a long time opposed to it, but
at length, after having well examined and weighed
all the circumstances and terms, they both gave
their permission, and this sacrifice, consecrated by
obedience, was, as it were, a summary of all the
most pure and perfect virtues.

"This is," said she in the paper found after her
death, "this is the vow which I found myself urged
to make for so long a time, but which I would only
make with the advice of my director and superior,
who, after having examined it, permitted me to do
so." Behold her prudence and obedience ; and note
the inspiration of God, the profound humility, the
perfect confidence and most ardent love, in the following words, which form, as it were, the preface to
the vow : " It is only to unite myself more strictly
to the Sacred Heart of our Lord Jesus Christ, and ·

22

to engage myself irrevocably to do whatever He
makes known to me is His wish. But, alas! I feel
so much inconstancy and weakness in myself, that I
should not dare to make any promise except in reliance upon the goodness, mercy, and charity of the
loving Heart of Jesus Christ, for the love of which I
make this vow." The engagement was couched in
the following terms:

"A vow made on the Vigil of All Saints in the
year 1686, to bind, consecrate, and sacrifice myself
more directly, absolutely, and perfectly, to the Sacred Heart of our Lord Jesus Christ.

"In the first place, O my only Love, I will endeavour to subject all that is within me to Thee, by
doing whatever I believe to be most perfect, or most
conducive to the glory of Thy Sacred Heart, to
which I promise to be sparing of nothing that is in
my power, and not to refuse to do or suffer anything in order that it may be known, loved, and
glorified.

"2. I will neither neglect nor omit any of my
exercises, or the observance of my rules, except
through charity, real necessity, or obedience, to
which I submit all my promises.

"3. I will endeavour to find pleasure in seeing
others exalted, well-treated, loved, and esteemed,
thinking it to be their due and not mine, which is to
be buried in the Sacred Heart of Jesus Christ, making it my glory to carry my cross rightly, and to
live poor, unknown, and despised, only desiring to
be seen that I may encounter humiliation, contempt, and contradiction, in spite of the repugnance that my proud nature may feel to such treatment.

"4. I will suffer in silence without uttering any complaint, whatever treatment I may receive; I will avoid no suffering or pain either of body or mind, either of humiliation, contempt, or contradiction; nor will I seek or procure for myself any consolation, pleasure, or satisfaction, save that of being destitute of all sensible comfort. When presented by Providence with any of these things, I will accept them simply, renouncing any pleasure I may find in them, or that nature may take in satisfying its necessities or otherwise, not thinking whether I am satisfied or not, but only of loving my Sovereign Lord, who gives me this pleasure.

"5. I will seek no other relief than that which I find to be absolutely necessary, which I will beg with the simplicity commanded by our Constitutions. This is to free myself from the continual fear which haunts me, that I pamper and allow too much to my body, which is my most cruel enemy.

"6. I will leave to my superior entire liberty to dispose of me as she thinks best, humbly and indifferently accepting the occupations imposed upon me by obedience, notwithstanding the frightful repugnance I feel to entering the parlour or writing letters, which henceforth shall be done as if I found pleasure in them.

"7. I will abandon myself totally to the Sacred Heart of our Lord Jesus Christ, to be comforted or afflicted according to His good pleasure, being satisfied with agreeing to all His holy operations and arrangements, and looking upon myself as His victim, who should be ever in one continual act of immolation and sacrifice, according to His good pleasure, being anxious for nothing but to love Him, and to satisfy Him by acting and suffering in silence.

" 8. I will never inform myself of the faults of others; and when I am obliged to speak of them, I will do so in the charity of the Sacred Heart of our Lord Jesus Christ, considering whether I should be well pleased that they did or said the like of me; and when I see any fault committed, I will offer in reparation to the Eternal Father the contrary virtue of the Sacred Heart of Jesus.

" 9. I will consider all those who afflict or speak ill of me, as my best friends, and will endeavour to do them all the service and all the good that lies in my power.

" 10. I will endeavour not to speak of myself, or at least, very briefly; and never, if possible, either in praise or justification.

" 11. I will not seek the friendship of any creature, except when the Sacred Heart of Jesus Christ calls me to do so, to draw it to His love.

" 12. I will be ever attentive to conform and submit my whole will to that of my Sovereign Lord.

" 13. I will not willingly consent to any thought which is useless, much less to that which is bad; I will regard myself as a beggar in the house of God, who ought to be submissive to all, and to whom all is done and given through charity; and I will always think that I have too much.

" 14. As far as I can, I will neither do anything nor leave anything undone, through human respect, or vain compliance with creatures.

" 15. As I have requested our Lord not to allow His extraordinary graces to appear in me unless they draw on me contempt, humiliation, and confusion before men; so I shall consider it a great happiness when whatever I say or do is despised, censured, or blamed; endeavouring to suffer all for the love and glory of the Sacred Heart of our Lord Jesus Christ, and in conformity with His holy intentions, to which I unite myself in everything.

"16. I will be careful to render my words and actions full of glory to God, edifying to my neighbour, and salutary to my own soul; being ever faithful in the practice of the good that my divine Master informs me it is His wish that I should perform, committing, if possible, no voluntary fault; and I will never pardon any transgression in myself without first taking vengeance on myself by some penitential act.

"17. I will only grant to nature what I cannot legitimately refuse without singularity, which it is always my wish to avoid. In short, I wish to live without choice, to keep nothing, and to say always, ' Fiat voluntas tua.'

" In the multitude of these things, I felt so overcome with fear that I should fail in the performance of them, that I should not have had the courage to make the vow, if I had not been fortified and reassured by these words, which were said to me in the deepest recesses of my heart. ' What dost thou fear, since I will answer for thee, and be thy security? The unity of My love will supply the place of attention in all these various things; I promise thee that it shall repair the faults that thou committest, and revenge itself upon thee.'

" These words impressed on my soul so great a confidence and assurance that it would be so, that notwithstanding my great weakness I feared no

longer, having placed my confidence in Him who
can do all things, and from whom I hope for everything, and nothing from myself."

A vow so comprehensive and entering into such
detail, made by a person who was ill, afflicted,
contradicted, and persecuted on all sides, clearly
proves the tranquillity of her soul in the midst of
her sufferings, and the strength of her love, which
was superior to all the attacks of Satan. But the
words with which our Lord strengthened her are
very remarkable. "The unity of My love will supply the place of attention in all these various things."
May this divine lesson enter into the spirit and the
heart of those who read this. He who loves God
truly, constantly, and solely, finds in the exercise of
that love the accomplishment of all the most heroic
virtues, as occasions offer of practising them; and
draws an exactness and fidelity from the Heart of
Jesus Christ, of which our weakness would be incapable.

God never permits a sacrifice to go unrewarded.
Thus He soon afterwards crowned the fidelity of His
spouse by new favours. We will here describe one
of the most remarkable, which relates to the worship
of the Heart of Jesus Christ, in the terms used by
the servant of God in the account she gave to her
director.

"After having received my divine Saviour on St.
John the Evangelist's day, He bestowed on me a
favour, which seemed to me to be of the same nature
as that received by the beloved disciple on the evening of the Last Supper. The Heart of Jesus was
represented to me as on a throne formed of fire and
flames, surrounded by rays more brilliant than the

sun, and transparent as crystal. The wound which
He received on the cross was clearly seen. Around
this Sacred Heart was a crown of thorns, and above
it a cross planted in it. My Divine Master made
me understand that these instruments of His Passion signified that the immense love of His Heart
for men had been the source of all His sufferings ;
that from the first moment of His Incarnation, all
these torments had been present to Him, and that
from that instant the cross had been, as it were,
planted in His Heart; that from that time He accepted all the sorrows and humiliations that His
Sacred Humanity was to suffer during the course of
His mortal life, as also all the outrages to which His
love for mankind would expose Him, even to the
end of time, while remaining with them in the
Blessed Sacrament.

"He then showed me that His great desire to
be perfectly loved by men, had made Him form the
design of manifesting to them His Heart, and giving
them in these latter times this last resource of His
love, offering to them at once an object and a means
calculated to induce them to love Him with an enduring love. That in doing this He opened to them
all the treasures of love, grace, mercy, sanctification,
and salvation which this Heart contains, so that all
those who wish to render to Him and procure for
Him all the love and honour in their power, might
be enriched with the profusion of treasures, of which
this Divine Heart is the fruitful and inexhaustible
source.

"He again assured me that He took singular
complacency in seeing the interior sentiments of His
Heart and His love honoured under the figure of

this Heart of flesh, such as had been shown me, and that He wished it to be exposed in public, in order, He added, to touch the insensible hearts of men. He at the same time promised me that He would abundantly shed the treasures of grace, with which His Heart is filled, into the hearts of those who should honour Him, and that wherever this image should be exposed to particular honour, there would He bestow every kind of blessing.

" But no trouble I had ever experienced caused me so much grief as the words which I heard when this Heart was presented to me : ' I have an ardent thirst to be loved and honoured by men in the Blessed Sacrament; and yet I find scarcely any one who is eager to quench My thirst by offering Me any return.' "

It was in the same year that God bestowed on her another favour, by giving her St. Francis of Assisi as her special protector. Between this great saint and the servant of God there was a striking similarity of attraction for poverty, humiliation, and suffering, which formed the peculiar character of the saint and of his order, and was deeply engraven in the heart of Sister Margaret. She was herself astonished that she should have so great a love of these things, and yet never be satisfied nor find herself poor or suffering enough. " How is it," said she one day to her director, " that poverty and suffering have so many attractions for my heart, that I regard them as my most delicious food, and yet I suffer so little as to count it for nothing ?"

One day, then, on the festival of St. Francis, God showed her in her prayer this great saint shining with unspeakable light, and as it seemed, in more

eminent glory than the other saints, because upon
earth he had had more conformity with the poverty
and sufferings of Jesus Christ, and because he had
had the honour of bearing in his body the sacred
wounds of this divine Saviour.   God made known to
His servant that this great saint was particularly
united to His Divine Heart, and had a particular
power to obtain graces from it; that he offered
himself incessantly to the divine justice in union
with the Heart of Jesus Christ, to obtain in Him
and by Him mercy for sinners, and especially for
those religious who were relaxed in the observance
of their rules.   She saw him, as it were, groaning
and prostrate at the foot of the throne of God, to
appease His anger on account of some disorders
which had taken place in a certain religious order,
and of the relaxations which were there introduced.
These disorders were manifested to Sister Margaret,
together with the horror of God at sins of this
nature, into which persons especially consecrated to
His service fall.   It appeared to her that the prayer
of St. Francis stayed the wrath of God, who was
about to punish these unhappy religious.   The vision
ended by Jesus Christ bestowing on Sister Margaret
the favour of giving her St. Francis as her guide in
the new sufferings of which He warned her, and for
which He wished her to prepare herself.

Thus the graces she received were all marked
with these two characters; they were the reward of
past, and the preparation for new, sufferings. Such is
the order and rule of our salvation and of our perfection; all has been merited by the cross of the
Saviour, and all the favours that come to us from
His goodness, draw us nearer to this cross, and

invite us to unite ourselves more closely to it. This
was shown on another occasion to the servant of
God under a new symbol. The following is her own
account of it:

"On one occasion when my soul was in dreadful·
agony, our Lord honoured me with a visit, and said
to me, 'Enter, my daughter, into this delicious
garden, to reanimate thy languishing soul.' I saw
that this garden was His Sacred Heart. It was entirely filled with flowers, the diversity of which was
as admirable as their beauty was exquisite. After I
had looked at them all without daring to touch
them, He said to me, 'Thou mayest gather them at
thy pleasure.' Throwing myself at His feet, I said
to Him, 'O my divine Love, I wish for nothing but
Thee, who art a bundle of myrrh to me, that I would
ever carry in the arms of my affections.' 'Thou
hast well chosen,' said my divine Love; 'it is this
myrrh alone which can preserve its odour and its
beauty. This life is its time and season; there will
be none of it in eternity, there it will change its
name.'"

It is plain that Sister Margaret alluded to those
words of the Spouse in the Canticle, "My beloved
is a bundle of myrrh to me," in order to express the
ardour with which she would embrace the saving
rigour of love of suffering with Jesus Christ. But
let not these sufferings terrify His spouses; divine
love has also its consolations and its sweetnesses, as
the servant of God soon experienced when she
reaped the fruit of her troubles by the unexpected
and unhoped-for establishment of the devotion to the
Heart of our Lord.

. It was in this same year, 1686, that the predictions of this devout religious, and the promises made by Jesus Christ to her on the subject of this establishment, were at length fulfilled. If in relating the graces of which we are going to speak, and which she received in the course of this year, we anticipate the order of our history by some months, it is only that we may give without interruption an account of the beginning and progress of this miracle.

We must first recall to the reader what has been before related of the almost universal contradiction the sister met with in the house about a year before, on the occasion of the first attempt made by the novices to honour the Heart of Jesus Christ. The prejudice then shown against this devotion, far from being effaced, had only increased, if one may say so, up to this time. Reflection had confirmed the first sallies of human prudence, which had been excited at the report of this devotion; the fervent and negligent religious were alike prejudiced and determined to oppose it, and a thousand reasons made their dislike to it appear plausible.

In addition to this, the dismissal of the young lady, in which Sister Margaret had so great a share, had prejudiced against her the minds of persons both far and near. They loudly taxed her with indiscretion, imprudence, obstinacy, or hypocrisy, according to their character and humour. The less devout maliciously ridiculed her, whilst the more fervent charitably pitied her; but all united in feeling contempt for her mind and her inspirations, and in opposing her devotion. What likelihood was there that the community would receive at the hands of one so much abused and despised a devotion

which was almost universally an object of contradiction ?

Yet the Son of God had foretold to His servant,
that not only would this devotion be established in
the house in spite of this opposition, but that it
would be sanctioned by those amongst the sisters
who had been hitherto the most vehement against it.
Sister Margaret had made no mystery of the promise given her by her Spouse; the prediction was
well known in the house; no one was ignorant of
it; but it was even less believed than the devotion
itself; the whole was despised under the general
name of delusion and vision; use was even made of
the prophecy to insult Sister Margaret, and defy her
to bring about its accomplishment. The less fervent
found in this a fresh subject of ridicule against the
servant of God, and reproached her bitterly and scoff-
ingly for a prediction which appeared to them absurd.

Of all the sisters, the one who had declared herself the most openly was Sister Mary Des Ecures, a
person in other respects of extraordinary merit and
great piety, whose peculiar distinction and favourite
exercise was the most exact observance of the rules.
After having long edified the house, she at length
died in high reputation of holiness; but before her
death it was the Will of Jesus Christ that she should
promote the glory of His Heart and its worship,
though she had hitherto opposed it with all the
power and force which the esteem of the community
gave her. This religious had opposed the devotion
of Sister Margaret in good faith. She regarded her
practices as contrary to the spirit of the rule; and as
her opposition arose from pious feeling, and appeared
to her to be right, it was the more open and earnest,

and she thought herself conscientiously obliged to discredit actively devotion towards the Heart of Jesus Christ.

Yet it was this sister whom God made the instrument of establishing it in the house, and of procuring public homage to the Heart of Jesus Christ. This year, 1686, on the last day of the Octave of the Blessed Sacrament, she felt urged in so lively a manner, and by so extraordinary a movement of the Holy Spirit, to acknowledge the error in which she had been until this time, that she found it impossible to resist the attraction, and was, as it were, compelled to repair her fault, and to acknowledge the advantage of the devotion she had before held in such contempt. She vainly endeavoured in the secrecy of her heart to struggle against this impression; but grace triumphed absolutely over her repugnance and her fears, and she resolved to make reparation for her incredulity, by an acknowledgment as public as had been her opposition. In the evening she went to the noviciate to borrow of the devout mistress the miniature that Mother Greffier had sent some months before. She asked for it without saying anything of her intention, and it was lent her without question; but Sister Margaret knew by divine illumination the use that Sister Des Ecures was about to make of it, and the change that had been wrought by God in her soul. She went to pray, and made all the novices join with her in praying for the happy success of the undertaking.

The next day was the first Friday after the Octave of the Blessed Sacrament, the day which Jesus Christ had pointed out to the venerable Mother Margaret,

as the one on which it was His Will that His Heart
and His love should be particularly honoured, and in
the morning the community were greatly surprised
to see a little altar fitted up against the grate, in
the most conspicuous part of the private choir of the
nuns.   This altar was ornamented with flowers, and
with whatever both devotion and simplicity could
devise to make it attractive and rich.   In the midst
of these ornaments was placed the miniature representing the Heart of Jesus, and over it an inscrip-
tion inviting all the lovers of the Son of God to
come and unite their hearts with His, and to render
Him together the profound homage which is due to
His love for us.

When the sisters arrived in the morning to adore
the Blessed Sacrament, they approached the newly-
erected altar with much surprise, to satisfy themselves as to the object of all this pomp; but their
surprise was changed into wonder, when they discovered who was the author of this pious stratagem.
They looked at each other with astonishment, and
could hardly believe the testimony of their own eyes,
saying to one another, " Can this be done by her
who has declaimed so loudly against the devotion of
Sister Margaret?   What can have produced so incredible a change?   Is it the Heart of Jesus Christ
that has changed hers?"   This prodigy instantly
won over the whole community, and there was not
one amongst those who had been so strongly opposed
to Sister Margaret, who did not yield at last.   All
felt it a duty to bow to the influence of grace, which
changes hearts and disposes of them at its will; they
fell prostrate before the little altar, and paid their
homage to the Divine Heart of the Saviour, of which

they saw there the representation. The superior, the officers, the religious, the older sisters, and the novices, the fervent and the tepid, the friends of Sister Margaret and her critics, all were eager to adore during the whole day with one common fervour the holy love of the Heart of Jesus, to return it by offering up the feelings of their heart and their affection, and to celebrate the first festival consecrated in this monastery to the adorable Heart of Jesus Christ."

They did more. On that very day they resolved that they must have a larger and more conspicuous representation of the Heart of Jesus Christ, with the several symbols which expressed the attributes of His love in the little picture. They agreed that a large picture should be made from this design, and that a place should be found in which to deposit it, where it might be particularly honoured. It was planned that a chapel should be erected for it in the garden. All these projects were formed, agreed to, unanimously arranged, and one might almost say, executed the same day ; the purchase money for the building and the picture was almost entirely raised. The children gave the little money they had, and promised to obtain larger sums from their families. Some of the nuns, for whom their relations paid pensions, requested that they might expend what was due to them on this holy work. There was not one, even among the lay-sisters, who did not show all the generosity in her power ; they proposed to redouble their labour, and undertake more work for the advantage of the house, requesting that the profit the community would derive from it might be laid out on the projected edifice. The zeal was so

great and universal, that the undertaking, which
would have otherwise appeared impracticable in a
very poor house, was soon put in execution. The
chapel, which is beautiful, large, and highly ornamented, stands in the middle of the garden ; it was
begun very soon after the plan had been conceived, and the devout Mother Margaret had before
her death the consolation of seeing it finished, dedicated, and blessed under the name of Jesus Christ
and of His divine Heart.

Before this building was finished, the novices prepared a niche for the little picture in a conspicuous
part of the house, ornamenting it in the best manner
they could, that the nuns might more easily offer
their particular homage to the love of Jesus Christ
at the sight of the image of His Sacred Heart. This
place has since become an oratory for the convenience of those whose infirmities prevent their cross-
ing the garden to go to the chapel of the Heart of
Jesus.

What more clearly pointed out the hand of God
in this event, which may indeed be called miraculous,
was the renewal of fervour which then began in the
house, and which was brought to perfection through
the care and sufferings of Sister Margaret. The
true love of Jesus Christ was better understood when
the nuns began more particularly to adore that
love which He has for us ; prayer, modesty, silence,
mortification, and the other religious virtues, now
more carefully practised by those who had before
been negligent of them, soon made known in a
sensible manner what treasures are found in the
divine Heart of Jesus, and how large a share of
these treasures the Saviour bestows on those who

pay Him the perfect worship that His love deserves.

We may imagine the joy of Sister Margaret at
this event. Not thinking herself worthy to thank
God for it, she induced her novices to join her in
blessing God for the triumph He had this day obtained. She wrote an account of these proceedings
to Mother Greffier, saying with transport, "I shall
now die contented, since the Heart of my Saviour
begins to be known."

It was at this same time that our Lord made a
fresh disclosure to His servant of the particular
graces He destined for those who should honour His
divine Heart, and persevere in that devotion. We
find an account of this in the letters of the servant
of God. "It is impossible for me to express," she
said in one of them, "the great blessings that this
devotion draws down upon our institute, and in
particular upon those houses which obtain for it the
most love and glory. This loving Heart has shown
me that, like a beautiful tree, it is destined to take
root in our institute, and to extend its branches into
all our houses, that each may be able to gather fruit
from it according to its different taste, some more,
some less. The portion of each will be proportioned
to its labour, and the profit derived will correspond
to the dispositions of those who feed themselves with
the fruits of salvation and life, which ought to renew
in us the primitive spirit of our holy vocation. By
this means the glory of our holy founder is much increased; but it is the will of the Divine Heart that
the religious of the Visitation distribute the fruits
of this sacred tree to all who desire it, without fear
of their failing; because, as He made known to His

23

unworthy slave, He intends by this means to give
life to many, by drawing them from the road of
perdition, and thus destroying the dominion of Satan
in their souls in order to establish that of His love,
which will not permit any of those consecrated to it
to perish."

In another letter she spoke thus upon the same
subject: "Our Lord has disclosed to me treasures of love and favour for those who consecrate
and sacrifice themselves to render and procure for
His Heart all the honour and glory in their power—
treasures so great as to be beyond expression. This
loving Heart has an infinite desire to be known
and loved by its creatures, in whom it wishes to establish its empire, in order to provide for all their
wants, since it is the source of every blessing. For
this reason it desires to be addressed with great confidence; and it seems to me that there is no more
efficacious means of obtaining what we ask, than by
doing so through the ever-blessed sacrifice of the
mass."

She also prescribed in honour of the Heart of
Jesus Christ a practice which was familiar to her,
and which had been suggested to her by our Lord,
Who led her to expect by means of it the grace of
final perseverance, and that of receiving the Sacraments of the Church before death, for those who
should perform it. This was, to make a novena of
communions with this intention, and in honour of
the Heart of Jesus Christ, communicating for this
end on the first Friday of the month for nine suc-
cessive months.

In another letter to Mother Greffier she prescribed a more sublime practice which our Lord had

taught her, and which in a few words comprises a summary of perfection. "It is no small consolation to me," said she, "to see the devotion to the Sacred Heart, which evidently exists, and gains ground by its own force alone, increase so rapidly and so wonderfully. I cannot be silent on this subject. So stupid am I, that I could not write a letter if I did not speak of it. I can love no one but on condition that she loves the Heart of my Jesus, and loves and desires only what He loves. Let us then love Him, and trouble ourselves about nothing else. Behold what it is that this adorable Heart requires of its friends. 'Poverty in intention, humility in working, unity in aim.' I doubt not that you understand this better than I do."

The mother-superior of Paray, who had been foremost in the zeal shown by the community for the worship and the love of the Heart of Jesus Christ, had also a particular share in the rewards of the Son of God. This reward was appropriate to the nature of the devotion and to the love of which it was the principle and the object. Mother Margaret, in accordance with the command of Jesus Christ, told her that the trouble she had taken to build a place where His Heart might be adored with love and by love, was so pleasing to Him, that as a reward He promised her the privilege to die pronouncing an act of pure love of Him. The circumstances of the holy death of this good superior caused the accomplishment of this prophecy of the servant of God to be made known.

These divine lights and singular graces redoubled the zeal of our mistress to inspire her novices with the fervour of divine love, and to form these young

hearts upon the model of the Heart of Jesus Christ.
God blessed her labour by the fervour with which
He animated the noviciate. It was under her direction that so many religious of consummate virtue
were formed, of whom several have died in the general reputation of sanctity, while others still preserve
the spirit in which they have been educated, and are
the edification of the house of Paray. The eagerness of her novices to collect all her words and the
advice given by her, is a certain proof of the success
of the mistress. They were not contented only to
receive them by word of mouth, but they further
wished to have them written by her own hand.
With pious artifice, they complained to their mistress of the shortness of their memory, to induce her
to write what they so much wished to preserve, and
which they have in fact preserved with veneration as
precious relics. We have already given extracts from
some of these holy instructions, and will add here an
abstract of others which we cannot insert, together
with some of the observances she recommended to
them; they will be useful to pious persons, who, in
reading this Life, seek the spirit which animated the
holy mother; for as the actions of great men who
are esteemed by the world are carefully related, it is
but just to transmit the opinions of the Saints to
posterity, since it is by these noble sentiments that
they have acquired glory far superior to that with
which the world crowns its heroes.

The love of Jesus Christ and of His Sacred Heart
was always the principal object which Sister Margaret proposed to herself; it was the centre, so to
speak, upon which she formed all her exhortations;
but she wished it to be loved with that generous

love which is maintained alike in affliction and in consolation, and is ever superior to the accidents of life. "What weakness it is to love Jesus Christ only when He caresses us, and to be cold immediately He reproves us! This is not," said she, "true love. Those who love thus, love themselves too much to love Jesus Christ with all their hearts."

The fruit of this constant and uniform love was an absolute adherence to the whole Will of God, that Will which is found clearly marked through all the events and circumstances of life, since what is called in the world chance or misfortune, contradiction and disappointment, is regarded by faithful souls as the disposition of that loving Providence which watches over all and arranges all, not only according to its sovereign Will, but also according to its sovereign wisdom. It was Sister Margaret's wish that her novices should be ready at all times to bear in peace those little trials which distress and disturb imperfect souls, and even to love Him the more Who thus disposed of them for His glory, in fulfilment of His designs.

Sin was the only limit that she placed to the obedience which she required of her novices; or, to speak more correctly, she exacted an unlimited obedience, for under such holy superiors the novices were not afraid that their docility would ever be abused. She wished that they should be ready to obey always and in everything, either their holy constitutions, their superiors, or those who represent them in the different offices. She wished their obedience to be blind, and quite divested of those secret reasonings which so often degenerate into murmurings. "The soul of this obedience," she said, "consists in having no will of one's own, in refusing oneself every desire, or in not permitting oneself to have any desire which is not entirely submissive ; in being always ready to give up one's own views, lights, and inclinations, in deference to the inclinations, views, and lights of our superiors." She desired that the practice of this self-renunciation should be carried into the smallest matters, "because," said she, "nothing is little when it is sacrificed to God from a motive of pure love; and besides, though this fidelity may be a little irksome at first, it gives in the end wonderful facility to obey without repugnance on more important occasions; in addition to which, the peace of mind of a religious can only be perfect and unalterable in proportion as she practises this total and absolute self-renunciation."

The means she recommended in order to arrive at this state, was a profound humility of heart, which does not limit itself to being lowered in the eyes of others, as for this description of humility we sometimes indemnify ourselves interiorly by the proud estimation in which we hold it. She taught that the only true and perfect humility leads us to despise ourselves, and willingly to acquiesce in the contempt we meet with from others. She found the model of this humility of heart in the Sacred Heart of Jesus Christ, who, according to the prophet, looked upon Himself as "the last of men," and who bore the confusion and weight of all our iniquities. Confidence in oneself and one's own lights, pride and preference of one's own judgment to that of others, cannot subsist with this holy disposition; those also who have attained this true humility, have no longer any trouble in obeying, in submitting with the most perfect simplicity, or in conforming their judgment, and even their wishes, to the wishes and judgment of those who hold to them the place of Jesus Christ.

Another fruit of this sincere humility is detachment from all things. Of what has she need who desires nothing, who believes herself unworthy of everything, who always considers that she has more than she deserves, who receives as a real favour whatever is given to her, and thinks she ought to be in want of all things? In health and in sickness, in winter and in summer, in abundance or in scarcity, it is not difficult to satisfy a soul thus disposed, nor does she weary any one by complaints or uneasiness. From this humility arose that detachment from all things which was one of the virtues with which Sister Margaret was most anxious to inspire her novices; she feared that they might become attached to the lightest trifles, as is usual in young persons who love to receive or give, to possess or retain, and who, not daring, or not being able, to satisfy this natural inclination in important things, indemnify themselves by trifles which they collect and preserve with a care that arises from cupidity. Were it only a picture, a book, or a medal, the wise mistress wished them to deprive themselves of it as soon as they felt any attachment to it. In the same manner as, according to the rules of the order of the Visitation, the rooms, employments, places, and even clothes, are annually resigned, to be received again by lot, this prudent mistress wished her novices to draw by lot all the little necessaries for their work or their devotions, and to those who had an inclination for collecting anything, she said that the only treasure of a religious was the Heart of Jesus Christ, and that she who was not satisfied with that, was avaricious indeed.

She inspired the novices with great ardour for holy Communion, and often said that just as appetite is a mark of health in the body, so eagerness to approach Jesus Christ is a mark of fervour of heart; and though as to the frequency of communion she wished them to conform to the constitutions, and the prudent direction of their confessor, yet she said that if they did not communicate every day, they ought at least to desire it, and that she should augur ill of those who, under pretext of respectful fear or of longer preparation, deferred approaching the holy table. On this subject she said that in the composition of holy fear there were two-thirds of love. "What should we say of a child," she added, "who through fear dare not approach his father and mother, and who would hide himself from their sight?" However, she did not fail to draw great advantages from fear; she made use of it in never permitting Communion without, as it were, some sensible fruit. She taught her daughters not to communicate without having, either on the same day or the day before, made to Jesus Christ some particular sacrifice of privation and mortification, or gained some victory over their inclinations or passions.

What she above all things desired her pupils to obtain, was the spirit of recollection and silence. "A daughter of Mary," said she, "who does not love prayer, is a soldier without arms, a citadel without ramparts, a ship without provisions, or a lamp without oil. Why do we become religious, if we do not enjoy the principal occupations of that state? Why are we disengaged from all other cares which might make us useful in the world? Is it not because we wish to be entirely occupied in praying for the rest of the world, and in doing so worthily, assiduously, and constantly? We deceive the world," she continued, " if we fail in this duty, and neglect the only employment confided to us." But as the practice of mental prayer is sometimes difficult to young persons, whose too lively imagination appears incompatible with recollection, she accustomed her novices to it by degrees, advising such practices as were suited to the character of each ; but she especially instructed them that it was through mortification that we attain the spirit of prayer, and that sensual persons, who love ease and enjoyment, can only be enabled to practise this holy exercise profitably, by seeking to become through it more penitent and mortified. On this subject we will give some of the practices she recommended in order to enable them to keep themselves in the presence of God, and to fix the wanderings of the imagination, as well as some very edifying little papers that she from time to time gave her novices, either to awaken their fervour on certain festivals of the year, or to challenge them to attain certain virtues by repeated acts. Thus she wonderfully aroused in the sisters of the noviciate that holy emulation and fervour which incited them to the most heroic virtues.

" A rule for keeping oneself in the presence of God, which may be useful to those who are easily distracted, and which consists in meditating on each day of the week upon one of the wounds of our

Lord, and in being occupied with it throughout the day.

" Monday. You will take the wound of the Right Hand of our Lord Jesus Christ. It will serve as a mirror to your soul, which will contemplate itself there from time to time, to discover by comparison with the sufferings and patience of Jesus Christ the ill-regulated movements of your heart, and to find out what it is which prevents it from being truly united to Him. You will present yourself to Him as a criminal before his judge ; you will ask pardon of Him, and entreat Him to be Himself your recompense and your justification. You will say to Him from time to time, ' O Judge, full of clemency and mercy, by the merits of the rigorous sentence and unjust judgment borne against Thee, turn away from me the condemnation that my sins have deserved.' At other times you will say, ' O God, save by Thy mercy her who might be condemned with justice.' You will often repeat these aspirations during the day, and you will consider them as in the presence of this sovereign Judge, to negotiate with Him the affair of your salvation. You will show your sorrow for having offended Him by frequent acts of contrition, which you will make in secret, without interrupting your other occupations ; you will bear in the spirit of expiation whatever suffering may present itself to you, and you will perform all the actions of the day in this spirit.

" Tuesday. Your dwelling will be in the Left Hand of Jesus Christ. You will appear before Him as the prodigal son before his father ; you will reproach yourself for the poverty which your own misconduct has caused ; you will ask pardon of your Father for

having wasted His goods, by abusing His graces,
and despising His Will. You will throw yourself
with great confidence into His arms, which His love
has extended upon the cross, as if to receive His
children who return to Him.   You will frequently
say to Him, 'My God! Thou art my Father, have
pity on me according to the greatness of Thy mercy;
I abandon myself to Thee, do not reject me; the
child cannot perish in the arms of a father who loves
it and who is all-powerful.' At other times you will
say, 'O my Father, I am Thy child, make me worthy
of this title, that henceforth I may always, and in
everything, accomplish Thy holy Will, for I am
entirely Thine.' You will exercise yourself to-day
in the practice of gentleness and patience.

"Wednesday. You must retire with deep humility into the wound of the Right Foot of our Good
Shepherd. You will there contemplate what He
suffered in seeking His wandering sheep. That
sheep is yourself, and you must look upon yourself
as brought back to the sheepfold by the goodness of
the Shepherd; you will hide yourself close to Him,
that you may be safe from all fear of the wolf; the
wolf is the devil; it is also your pride and self-love.
Considering afterwards how much this Good Shepherd has done to seek you, you will thank Him for
it; you will unite your steps to His, and beseech
Him not to permit you to walk otherwise than in
the way of His love. You will say to Him, 'O my
loving Shepherd, detach me from everything created
and from myself, that nothing may ever separate me
from Thee ; I no longer wish for any other pasture
than that which Thou wilt give me.' At other times
you will show Him the wounds you have received in

your wanderings, and will say to Him, 'O my Lord, cure my wounds through the merits of Thine own; if Thou wilt, Thou canst cure them instantly.' This day wherever you go, imagine that you are following the footsteps of your Shepherd. Lose no opportunity of humbling yourself.

"Thursday. You will retire into the wound of His Left Foot. You will consider Jesus Christ as a conqueror whose wounds have gained the victory; you will regard yourself as a soldier destined to fight under the eyes of your captain, and in the same cause with Him. You will consider all the enemies which surround you; but you will only be so far terrified as to induce you to keep close to your chief; He is Himself our buckler and our strength, and He might exempt us from the combat, but He does not wish to do so, in order that by making us triumph, feeble as we are, His strength may appear in our weakness. Since then He finds pleasure in seeing us fight and conquer, let us also find our happiness in fighting with Him. Say to Him frequently, 'I am Thine, save me; I have no strength but in Thee, I shall have no other victory but by Thee; support my weakness, and I shall fear nothing.' At other times say to Him with fervour, 'My God, I suffer violence, answer for me.' And again, 'Lord, come to my aid, haste Thee to help me.' The practice for to-day will be the mortification of the slightest movement of your passions.

"Friday. You will enter into the wound of the Side of Jesus; you will retire there as a traveller seeking a safe harbour, who earnestly desires it during the tempest, and is transported with joy when he finds it. But the voyage is not ended; you will

still have to encounter storms, and to avoid the
rocks which day after day rise up before you. Jesus
will be your pilot ; abandon yourself absolutely to
His guidance ; aim at nothing but loving Him and
seeking to please Him, as travellers in a storm do
blindly whatever the pilot commands. Say to Him
from time to time, 'O my Love, save me; do not
permit me to perish ;' or, 'The waters are come in
even unto my soul, the waters are ready to swallow
me up; extend Thine hand unto me and help me.'
The practice for to-day will be to study the movements of that divine Heart into which you have
retired, and to conform yourself to it in all your
intentions and desires.

"Saturday.   You will consider attentively the
injury which Jesus Christ received from the weight
of the cross, when He carried it upon Calvary, and it
made a large wound upon His bruised shoulder.
You will reflect that the weight of your sins was
still more painful to Him ; you will represent to
yourself the dejection of mind He was then enduring, and you will reproach yourself with having reduced Him to that state, by loading Him with your
daily faults. You will be filled with wonder at the
thought of that goodness which has made Him take
everything upon Himself, and load Himself with
everything through love for you. You will say to
Him, 'O generous Friend, wilt Thou bear the whole
weight of the justice of God, and shall I take no
share of it ? Relieve Thyself by purifying me.' At
other times, 'What can I render to my God for all
the good that He has done to me, and for all the
evil that He has suffered for me ? I will take His
chalice, and I will drink it with Him, if necessary,

even to the dregs.' The practice will be mortification of the senses, depriving yourself of some pleasure, satisfaction, or convenience.

"Sunday. You will consider Jesus expiring, and
in that same moment consummating our redemption
and deliverance, of which the first-fruit was that of
the holy souls who were in Limbo. We will adore
the last movements of His mortal heart, and the last
sigh of His life, which sealed the decree of our salvation, and was the consummation of His sacrifice
and His triumph. 'O Jesus! Thine enemies are
conquered, but they hope to conquer me in their
turn; yet do Thou triumph in me to their confusion.' Say to Him sometimes, 'My God and my
Spouse, conform my heart to Thine. Thou hast
shed for me even the last drop of Thy Blood; take
for Thyself even the smallest affection of my heart,
which shall no longer be withheld from Thee; it is
due entirely to Thee.' For your practice, you will
examine your attachments, in order to struggle
against and destroy them, if they are not according
to the Will of Jesus Christ. You will often repeat
to yourself these words: 'Love reigns in suffering,
love triumphs in humility, love rejoices in unity.' "

Stations in the Sacred Heart of Jesus for every
day in the week, to occupy the sisters of the noviciate.

"Sunday. You will enter into the open Heart of
Jesus as into a furnace of love, to purify yourself
from all the spots you have contracted during the
week, and to consume this life of sin in order to live
that of pure love, a love which will transform everything into itself. This day will be dedicated to the
particular worship of the Blessed Trinity.

"Monday. You will regard yourself as a criminal who desires to appease his judge by sorrow for his faults, and who consents to satisfy his justice. In this spirit you will enter into the Heart of Jesus to shut yourself up in that prison of love, there to partake of the bitterness which overwhelmed that Sacred Heart; you will consent to be tied and bound so firmly that, in a manner, you will retain no liberty save that of loving, no light, movement, or sight save that of pure love, by which love that Heart itself is held captive in the Blessed Sacrament. By the merit of this divine captivity, you will ask relief for the souls in purgatory, and will do all your actions in the spirit of penance with this intention.

"Tuesday. You will enter into the Heart of Jesus, as into a school of which you are a disciple. This school is that in which is taught the science of the saints, the science of pure love, which causes all worldly science to be forgotten. You will listen attentively to the voice of your Master, Who says to you, 'Learn of Me, for I am meek and humble of heart, and you shall find the true rest of your soul.'

"Wednesday. You will enter into the Heart of Jesus Christ, as a traveller into a ship, of which love is the pilot, and by which you will be conducted happily across that stormy sea which you are compelled to pass before you can arrive in port. The tempests you have to fear arise from self-love, vanity, and attachment to your own will; your pilot will defend you from these if you are faithful to him, and will give you a calm and tranquil passage.

"Thursday. You will enter into the Heart of Jesus Christ as a friend who is invited to a banquet;

you will find there enjoyments which are prepared
for you, and which will surpass your desires and
your knowledge; you will be inebriated with the
delicious wine of His love, a wine which soothes the
sorrows of time, and inspires disgust for all earthly
pleasures. The friend who receives you is as liberal
as He is tender; He will say to you, 'Whatever is
Mine is thine, My merits, My wounds, My Blood,
My pains; love makes all these common between us,
but liberality should be reciprocal, and I therefore
desire to possess thee entirely without so much reserve and division.' To-day you will perform all
your actions in the spirit of love.

"Friday. You will consider Jesus upon the
cross, as the tender mother who has brought you
forth in His Heart with infinite pain; you will
repose in His arms and His Heart, as an infant in
the arms of its mother, finding there consolation and
safety; abandon yourself then to this Sacred Heart,
without so much uneasiness and care for the future;
He foresees it for you, and that is enough. Be
satisfied to love Him confidingly at the present
time, assured that you are His, and that He will
not abandon you. You will pass the day in this
spirit of abandonment as to all the events of your
life, reserving to yourself nothing but love.

"Saturday. You will present yourself to the
Sacred Heart of Jesus, as a victim, brought to the
temple to be immolated, is presented to the sacrificer; this divine Priest, by inflicting a spiritual
death, destroys the animal life, and then consuming
the victim in the fire of love, restores to it a new
and divine life. Take pleasure in fulfilling the
duties of an holocaust; love to die to the world and

all that is sensible, to be consumed in the fire of
love for the honour of God, and to find that new life
of which love alone is the soul; happy will you be if
you can then say with truth, 'It is no more I that
live, but Jesus who lives in me. He lives in me by
His love; it is in Him and by Him that I act, suffer,
and love.'

"In conclusion, would you wish to know who will
be the first to enter into this sacred abode, the
Heart of Jesus? It will be the most humble and
the most despised; she who is the most destitute
of everything will be the one to enjoy it the most;
the most mortified will be the most tenderly caressed; the most charitable will be the best loved;
the most silent will be the best taught; and the
most obedient will have there the most credit and
power."

THE LIFE OF JESUS CHRIST IN THE BLESSED SACRA-
MENT. THE MANNER OF HONOURING IT DURING
THE OCTAVE OF THE FEAST.

"1. THE LIFE OF LOVE.

"You are the beloved spouse of Jesus, and you
will honour His life of love in the Blessed Sacrament. For this object be most careful to become
pure and innocent, in order to please this divine
Spouse; in whatever you do have no other view than
this; give yourself to Him without reserve, if you
wish Him to give Himself· entirely to you. If you
desire to taste the sweetness of His loving intercourse, banish all thoughts of self-love and human
respect. You will make to-day five acts of resistance to self-love, and you will offer them to our
24

Lord when you visit Him in the Blessed Sacrament.
In communion you will make reparation to the Sacred Heart of Jesus, and you will ask His pardon
for all the unworthy communions which are made,
and which have been made, as well by you as by
bad Christians.   On this day you will deprive yourself, as far as the rule will allow, of every pleasure
and enjoyment, to obtain perfect mortification.   You
will keep half an hour's silence after Prime, to honour that of Jesus in the Blessed Sacrament.

" 2. THE LIFE OF GLORY.

" Our Lord destines you to honour His life of
glory in the Blessed Sacrament.   There He renews
His glorious Passion, by which He has established
His kingdom over all hostile powers.   He wishes
you to be associated to His royalty, for which reason you must make the cross your throne; you will
be glorious there with Him, if like Him you carry
those crosses which are presented to you, without
allowing yourself to complain of their weight or
their continuance.   You will take them indifferently
and without choice, as it shall please Providence to
lay them upon you; by this means you will reign
over all your impetuosities, your resentments and
repugnances, and you will triumph over them with
Him in His Sacred Heart.   You will make five acts
with this intention, and will offer them to the glorious Heart of Jesus when you visit Him.

" 3. THE HIDDEN LIFE.

" Our Lord has chosen you to honour His hidden
life in the Blessed Sacrament.   You will participate

in this life by burying yourself so deeply in the solitude of His Heart, that you will wish to be seen no more by any but Himself. Your greatest care will be to hide the good you do, lest you should lose it. Love to be unknown and forgotten, and when you go before the Blessed Sacrament, present to Him five acts of self-annihilation and abandonment of whatever might attract vain esteem or the attention of creatures.

"4. THE LIFE OF SACRIFICE.

" Our Lord wishes you to honour His sacrificed and immolated life in the Blessed Sacrament. There He is the victim of propitiation for our salvation. Offer yourself to His Sacred Heart as a victim that desires to be immolated with Him. He is at the same time the sacrificer; abandon yourself, therefore, to Him as a lamb in the hands of the priest who is about to immolate it; beg Him to accomplish all His designs in you, however hard they may appear to nature; sacrifice to Him all the pleasure you take in loving and being loved, approved and esteemed by creatures; you can only be perfectly associated to Jesus Christ in the state of a victim, by depriving yourself entirely of whatever you naturally love. Offer five acts of this nature to the immolated Heart of Jesus, when you visit Him in the Blessed Sacrament.

"5. THE LIFE OF GRACE.

" Our Lord calls upon you to honour His life of grace. The Blessed Sacrament is the throne of grace and mercy, and it is for the purpose of in-

viting sinners to come and ask these blessings, that
He remains always in this holy mystery. Offer
yourself to Him as a slave before his liberator, and
as a criminal who has deserved death before his king
who has delivered him from it. As such you are
entirely His, and He has a right to dispose of your
life, which is rather His than yours; reserve then to
yourself no other right than what is necessary to
love Him freely. On this day you will keep your
tongue captive and mortify yourself for its frivolity,
in order that nothing may escape you contrary to
charity or humility, either in praising or excusing
yourself. You will make five acts of this virtue,
offering them to our Lord when you visit Him.

." 6. THE LIFE OF HUMILIATION.

" Our Lord has chosen you to honour His life of
humiliation in the Blessed Sacrament. He there
veils His power and glory, and through love exposes
Himself to all the insults of heretics and false Christians. You will enter into the same spirit, offering
yourself before Him as nothingness before an all-
infinite being, as clay before the sun, to be trodden
underfoot by all the world if He so wills it. All
your attention on this day will be directed to humbling yourself, and taking pleasure in being assisted
by others to obtain this object, when they humble
and despise you. Shun nothing that presents itself,
which is calculated to render you more vile and
abject in the sight of all; by this means you will be
more strictly united to the Sacred Heart of Jesus.
You will offer Him five acts of humiliation when you
go to visit Him.

" 7. THE LIFE OF ACTION AND WORK.

" Our Lord has chosen you to honour the admirable operations of His Heart in the Blessed Sacrament. He glorifies His Father, conducts His Church, animates His saints, invites sinners, and changes hearts. As the servant of Jesus, you must labour like Him, with Him, and, if possible, as much as He did, as if you could relieve Him in the immense occupations of His Heart. How will you be able to do this, poor, weak, languishing, half-dead creature as you are? You can do it by love; love will supply everything, love will dictate to you how to act according to the designs of your Beloved. Imitate His actions in your exactness and promptitude in performing all that the rule enjoins; but like Jesus Christ you will act in exterior and interior silence, without anxiety or hurry. You will remember these words, ' Jesus was silent.' When you visit Him in the Blessed Sacrament, you will offer Him five acts of charity towards your neighbour.

" 8. THE LIFE OF CONSUMMATION.

" Our Lord destines you to honour His life of consummation in the Blessed Sacrament. A victim is entirely consumed by fire to the glory of Him to whom it is offered. Jesus in the Blessed Sacrament is, as it were, the Victim of God, and the fire of love would consume Him if He were not immortal and impassible. It is not so with us, who ought to languish and wither away with love, and be consumed even to death. Offer yourself to Jesus Christ, that if it should be His good pleasure you may be in His presence as one of the lighted tapers which are burnt in His honour, and consumed whilst contributing to the glory of God. You will abandon yourself without reserve to Jesus, that He may do what He will with you; the victim is His, and He will immolate it at the time and in the manner that He, the High-priest, knows to be best. It is sufficient for you to be ready, and to love beforehand the kind of consummation He destines for you; for the greater the suffering, the greater will be your happiness. Make today five acts of love and abandonment, and offer them to Jesus Christ.

THE ABYSS OF THE SACRED HEART OF JESUS SUITED TO EVERY STATE OF MIND.

" The Heart of Jesus is an abyss where everything may be found; it is especially an abyss of love, in which every other love should be swallowed up, above all, self-love with its evil effects, which are human respect and the desire of raising and satisfying ourselves. In burying these inclinations in the abyss of divine love, you will find all the treasures necessary for you, according to your different states.

" If you are in an abyss of privation and desolation, this divine Heart is an abyss of all consolation, in which we must lose ourselves without desiring to feel its sweetness.

" If you are in an abyss of dryness and weakness, go bury yourself in the Heart of Jesus Christ, which is an abyss of power and love, without being eager to taste the sweetness of this love until He pleases.

"If you are in an abyss of poverty and privation of everything, bury yourself in the Heart of Jesus; it is filled with treasures; it will enrich you if you permit it to do so.

"If you are in an abyss of weakness, of failings, and miseries, go also frequently to the Heart of Jesus; it is an abyss of mercy and strength; it will raise and fortify you.

"If you are conscious that you are filled with pride and a vain esteem of yourself, bury these quickly in the deep humiliations of the Heart of Jesus; that humble Heart is the abyss of humility.

"If you find yourself in an abyss of ignorance and darkness, the Heart of Jesus is an abyss of light and knowledge; learn especially to love Him, and to do only what He desires of you.

"If you are in an abyss of infidelity and inconstancy, that of Jesus is one of constancy and fidelity; bury yourself there, and you will there find a love which is constantly loving us and doing us good.

"If you feel, as it were, buried in death, go to the Heart of Jesus; you will find there an abyss of life, and you will draw thence a new life, a life by which you will regard everything with the eyes of Jesus Christ; you will act only as He prompts you, you will speak only with His tongue, you will love only by His Heart.

"If you are in an abyss of ingratitude, the Heart of Jesus is an abyss of gratitude; draw from it wherewith to offer to God for all the benefits you have received from Him, and beg of Jesus to supply for you from His abundance.

"If you find yourself overcome with agitation, impatience, or anger, go to the Heart of Jesus, which is an abyss of sweetness.

"If you are in an abyss of dissipation and distraction, you will find in the Sacred Heart of Jesus an abyss of recollection and fervour, which will supply everything, and will fix your heart and imagination by uniting them to Him.

"If you find yourself plunged in an abyss of sadness, bury the sadness itself in the Heart of Jesus, which is an abyss of heavenly joy, and the treasury of all the delights of the saints and angels.

"If you are in trouble and uneasiness, the Divine Heart is an abyss of peace, and that peace will be communicated to you.

"When you are in an abyss of bitterness and suffering, unite them to the abyss of the infinite sufferings of the Heart of Jesus, and you will learn to suffer with Him, and to be pleased to suffer.

"When you are in an abyss of fear, the Heart of Jesus is an abyss of confidence and love; abandon yourself to it; you will there learn that fear should yield to love.

"Finally, everywhere and in everything bury yourself in this ocean of love and charity, and, if possible, never depart from it, that you may be penetrated with the fire by which this Heart is inflamed for God and man, as iron in the furnace, or as a sponge cast into the sea, and filled with its waters."

SEVERAL COUNSELS TO THE NOVICES WHEN THEY
ENTERED INTO RETREAT.

1. "To prepare yourself to receive in solitude the
life of pure love, you must die to yourself exteriorly
and interiorly, by the renunciation of all tastes and
pleasures, either sensual or spiritual; as also to the
reasoning of your own judgment and attachment to
your own will. Up to this time your will has rendered you so sensitive to opposition, that your dislikes are seen at once.

"You will destroy within you the thought, 'What
will they say?' which includes all human respect and
vain compliance.

"You will no longer show your inclinations and
aversions, whatever they may be. You must die to
all too eager impulses and movements; you must
empty your heart of self and whatever is not God,
if you wish it to be prepared to receive the graces that
God destines for it. You will make fifteen acts of
these practices; your watch-word will be, ' God is
my all; out of Him all is nothing to me.'

2. "To prepare yourself for solitude, your motto
will be humility, to conform yourself to Jesus humbled, and, as it were, annihilated in the Blessed
Sacrament. You will meditate on these words, ' He
emptied Himself.' Is it not a horrible thing that a
worm of the earth should desire to be exalted, when
God humbled Himself? In elevating yourself and
seeking the esteem of others, you give up the true
character of the children of Jesus Christ to take that
of the devil, and to do what has ruined him.

"You will, then, first humble yourself for not

having been humble, though you have had so many
reasons for being so; you will next rejoice interiorly
at finding yourself despised and forgotten; you will
embrace whatever renders you more abject in the
sight of others and annihilates you in your own
eyes, in order that God may establish His reign in
your nothingness. You will take fifteen practices
of humility, and when you fail in them, you will kiss
the ground, saying, "Sacrificium Deo spiritus contribulatus; cor contritum et humiliatum, Deus, non
despicies.' Think often that it is only the humble
heart which can enter into the Sacred Heart of
Jesus Christ, to converse with Him, to love Him,
and to be loved by Him. Your motto will be, 'This
is the time to humble myself, to testify to God my
love.' "

3. "To prepare yourself for solitude, your aim
must be exterior and interior obedience. In the
first place, you will faithfully obey the movements of
grace by acts of virtue, thinking of these words :
'If to-day you shall hear His voice, harden not your
heart.' With regard to exterior obedience, you will
obey promptly, simply, without reply, and lovingly,
those who have the right to command you. You
will meditate on these words, 'I am not come to do
My own will, but the Will of Him Who sent Me.'
At the first stroke of the bell you will leave everything to listen to the voice of the Spouse, saying to
yourself, 'Jesus was obedient even unto death; I
wish to obey like Him, even to my last breath.'
You will offer fifteen practices of obedience in
honour of the obedience of Jesus in the Blessed
Sacrament. When you have failed, say the psalm
De profundis five times. If you are faithful in

doing the Will of God in this life, your own will be
accomplished throughout eternity. Watchword:
'Fiat voluntas tua.' 'Thy Will be done.'"

4. "To prepare yourself for solitude, you will
keep beforehand all your interior and exterior senses
inclosed, as it were, in the Heart of our Lord, by
the profound silence you will impose on them.
Silence within you, by the retrenchment of all useless thoughts and reflections of self-love, that you
may be disposed to hear the voice of the Spouse.
Silence on every occasion of praising or excusing
yourself, of blaming or accusing others; silence
instead of the little sallies by which our unmortified
nature shows our pleasure in joyful things, and our
dissatisfaction with evil ones. Cut off all superfluous words. Your silence will be in honour of that
of Jesus left alone in the Blessed Sacrament. He will
teach you by this means to converse with His Sacred
Heart, and to love Him in silence. If you fail in
these practices, you will say the psalm 'Miserere.'
Your motto will be, 'Jesus autem tacebat.' 'But
Jesus was silent.'"

5. "Go into solitude, to learn to leave and forget
yourself, by an entire abandonment of yourself to
the providence of the Heart of Jesus; He will be
your Director and your all. Thus all to God, and
all for God. One only heart, one only love, for one
only God."

6. "Go into solitude to repair the time you have
lost, and to employ the present better, as well as
every moment you may be in His presence, each according to the end for which He gave it. To pass
this holy time well, you must love ardently and constantly; you must abandon all to love, and leave it

to act for you, contenting yourself with persevering in it by deep self-annihilation. All from God, and nothing from self; all to God, and nothing to self; all for God, and nothing for self."

7. "Go into solitude to learn in the first place to change yourself entirely, and to live the life of Jesus Christ. Secondly, in order to conform your will to His, and to His life of poverty, you must leave yourself, by an entire renunciation of whatever gives satisfaction to nature. In the third place, you must be satisfied that if you wish to possess Jesus Christ and to dwell in His Sacred Heart, you must be willing to be deprived of everything else, and be contented with Him alone. Hearken no longer to the sentiments of your unmortified nature, nor to the suggestion of self-love, which takes delight in having, possessing, keeping, and amassing. Let nature cry out as much as it will, we are in the Heart of Jesus Christ, and we must only have what He wishes us to have, and be satisfied with His complete destitution. Let us love this Sacred Heart with a love of preference which will give us a distaste for everything else; where pleasing Him is concerned, let there be no more excuse for self-love, no more human respect or pretexts of any kind. It is better to give up everything and lose everything, than to lose the favour of this adorable Heart."

It was in this way that the holy mistress prescribed to each the necessary virtues, and those most conformable to the attraction of grace in their souls, while she also pointed out the means of acquiring them. As her novices delighted in these instructions, of which they felt the value, and as they urged

her to give them more of them in writing, she one
day in the utmost simplicity wrote the following instruction for them :

" Behold, my dear children, you force me to write
what I have said to you, particularly concerning the
Sacred Heart of our Lord ; but if you do not profit
by it, I will myself ask Him to punish you ; that is,
if you should forget or despise it. Take care, for I
warn you frequently of this; the grace that our
Lord has begun to give you, will raise you to a high
degree of perfection, provided you allow it free
course by faithful correspondence on your part.
Like the rising sun, you must advance and gather
strength as you go. Your names are written in the
adorable Heart, but as yet only with ink ; you are
but beginners, and grace comes to enlighten your
darkness, to assist you to combat and vanquish your
imperfections, especially that natural pride which
creeps in everywhere. Your names will be written
in characters of silver, when your intentions shall be
purified in the furnace of pure love, and no longer
retain anything human and earthly. But you must
not be satisfied with this; your names must be
written at last in the Heart of Jesus in characters of
gold; it is pure love that will cause you to attain to
this happiness; you will then be, as it were, holocausts
entirely consumed in the fire of holy charity, the
centre of which is the Heart of our Saviour. To
arrive there, you must suffer with love, offer continual violence to yourselves, and mortify and humble
yourselves out of love. When then you commit
some act of pride or self-love, such as excusing yourself, or endeavouring to insinuate yourself into the
esteem or friendship of creatures, or when you do

anything, either in word or action, that you would
not wish to have done to yourself, these actions are
as so many letters of your name which you thus
efface from the divine Heart of our Master.

"Finally, my dear sister, I cannot sufficiently
admire the goodness and liberality of this divine
Heart in your regard. It seems that all its treasures
are opened to enrich you, so great pleasure does it
take in doing you good; but if after this you relax
in your endeavours, and are wanting in the fidelity
which Jesus demands from you, and which you have
promised Him, I believe that He will not be less un-
sparing in severity to revenge Himself for your ingratitude; take care, for even I myself shall then
be against you. Now as love wishes for a return,
and this return can only be the same love; in order
to correspond to its desire, it must engrave its name
in your hearts, and a letter of this adorable name
will be written in characters of gold by each glorious
victory you gain over yourselves, whether by humility, mortification, or charity. Be then faithful,
constant, and ardent in the love of God; I could not
speak strongly enough of the evil which would
arise from your tepidity. I have said more than I
intended, and even more than I wished; but God
be praised for it, and may His Heart be loved and
glorified eternally. Pray for the conversion and
salvation of the sinner who writes this; she orders
you by all the power that the Heart of Jesus gives
her over you, to tell her and warn her of my defects
simply and charitably. You must each of you do
her this office of charity; I have great need of it. I
will not fail to pray especially for her who does me
this favour. God be praised."

To complete this collection of instructions given by the venerable mistress to her novices, we will here add some other practices which she proposed to them at different times, under the name of "challenges," in order that by emulation they might excite each other to a careful observance of them, and surpass each other in attention and fidelity:

CHALLENGE FOR THE BEGINNING OF THE YEAR.

"Behold, my beloved sisters, in the Heart of Jesus Christ, a word or two which He desires me to tell you from Him, because He loves you, and wishes you to begin in earnest to make Him some return for His love by purity of heart and intention, humility and charity; these virtues will make you the objects of His loving complacency, and cause Him to reign in your hearts. My children, I must not flatter you, your names are yet only written there faintly; and besides, we have blotted out this faint writing by our want of purity of intention. But it is the Will of Jesus that we should this year labour in earnest to engrave them firmly by these three practices, which He Himself makes known to you through His poor slave. The first is purity of intention; the second, humility, that is, humility of heart in all your actions; the third, simplicity, without any admixture of your own earthly interests in your wishes and desires. He does not wish me to bind you to any number of acts; He leaves that to the ardour of your love; He wishes to see by this means which of you loves Him the most."

CHALLENGE FOR LENT.

"Behold, my beloved sisters, a little challenge which I consider necessary for you at this holy time of Lent, that you may live conformably to our holy observances, and render yourselves worthy of receiving abundantly the graces of the Sacred Heart of our Lord.

"You will show your love for Him if you are faithful in not making use (as our constitutions say) of your eyes, ears, or tongue, except for His love and service. For this end you must inclose yourself in His Heart as in a little solitude, to find there recollection and silence, mortification of all your senses, and, in short, a new life of spirit and love.

"You will destroy within you the curiosity of your eyes; and turning them from all useless things, you will fix them upon yourselves, upon the movements of your own heart, and upon the Heart of Jesus Christ. Of this you will make five acts.

"You will destroy your inclination for speaking by never saying anything unnecessary in places and times of silence. In conversation no expressions of complaint or murmuring, no slighting words of others or disapprobation of their actions. You will say nothing in your own praise, or in justification of your defects; as to obedience, let there be no replies, and never show your repugnance nor your inclinations. You will make fifteen acts of these practices.

"You will curb the vain curiosity of your ears, by refusing to listen to what would give them pleasure or cause distractions. You will do this five times,

and each time you will say, ' O Sacred Heart, I die
to this pleasure, to live only to Thy love.'

"Thus, my dear sisters, you will die entirely to
yourselves during this holy time of Lent, to rise
again with Him. Those who are the most faithful to
these practices, will be the most loved and caressed
by Jesus, and will obtain the greater gift of prayer,
at which we only arrive by true mortification."

CHALLENGE IN PREPARATION FOR THE FEASTS OF THE BLESSED SACRAMENT, AND OF THE SACRED HEART OF JESUS CHRIST.

" In the first place, on awaking, you will represent
to yourself the Heart of Jesus full of goodness,
which watches over you. You will consecrate to
Him your body, your soul, your heart, and all that
you are, to be used for nothing but His glory.

"In prayer, you will unite yours to that which He
makes for us in the Blessed Sacrament. In your
office, you will in like manner unite yourself to those
praises which Jesus offers to His Father in the
same Sacrament. In hearing holy Mass, you will
unite yourself to the intentions of the Heart of
Jesus immolated for us, praying Him to apply to
you His merits, according to His Will.

"On the way to the refectory, you will replace
yourself in the adorable Heart, if through distraction or weakness you have quitted it. You will
take in Him spiritual refection, begging Him to
nourish your soul with His love, and to give you a
greater relish for this nourishment of your soul, than
for all earthly food.

" When you go to recreation, offer up all your

25

words to be united to the Divine Word, Who is the Eternal Word of His Father, that you may say nothing except for His glory; you will take care that your tongue, the path by which He so often passes into your heart, may not be sullied by any raillery, complaint, or criticism, so as to wound charity. You will be more anxious to give pleasure to the Heart of Jesus than to your own; and in order to do what will most please Him at some cost to yourself, you will joyfully receive the contradictions, mortifications, and humiliations which may befall you.

"You will unite your silence to that which Jesus maintains in the Blessed Sacrament, and, like His, your silence will not be unprofitable.

"Jesus is poor in the Blessed Sacrament; He is there despoiled of the brightness of His glory and of His riches, that you may learn to be deprived, like Him, of all splendour and earthly goods. Jesus obeys the priest, good or bad, without showing His horror of the vile hands and corrupt hearts which then consecrate and receive Him; in like manner you will obey in all things, without showing your repugnance, but repressing your own judgment.

"When you have committed any fault, after having humbled yourself for it, take the opposite virtue of the Heart of Jesus, and offer it in expiation to the Eternal Father. You will do the same with regard to faults that you see others commit.

"Keep yourself in the presence of God, considering the virtue and operations of Jesus in the Blessed Sacrament in whatever you do, according to the relation they bear to your different exercises. Offer these holy dispositions to God, to supply those which are wanting in you, and in reparation for your faults; and when you suffer anything, rejoice in being conformed to the opprobrium and injury which Jesus suffers in the most Blessed Sacrament. Endure your interior dryness and desolation, in honour of that which He experiences from men; offer the hunger and thirst you suffer, in honour of that which Jesus feels for our salvation; the heat of summer will bring to your remembrance the fire of love by which this Divine Heart is consumed, and so of other things.

" Never indulge in any coldness of feeling towards your neighbour, or the Heart of Jesus will feel the same towards you; when you take pleasure in recalling the slights you think you have received, you induce our Lord to recall to His remembrance your sins, which His mercy had made Him forget.

" When you feel unable to conceive any good thought in prayer, offer to the Eternal Father those of the Heart of Jesus in the Blessed Sacrament, that they may supply all that you ought and would wish to do. You will do the same in confession and communion.

" When you genuflect before the Blessed Sacrament, you will say to yourself, ' May everything bow before Thee, O infinite greatness! May every mind adore Thee, may all hearts love Thee, may every will be submissive to Thine.' When kissing the ground, you will say, ' This is to render homage to Thy greatness, humbled, and, as it were, annihilated in the Blessed Sacrament.' "

FOR ALL SOULS' DAY.

PRACTICES FOR THE RELIEF OF THE SOULS IN PURGATORY.

" It seems to me, my beloved sisters, that the following is the way most agreeable to the Heart of Jesus Christ, to acquit yourselves of the promise you have made to Him in favour of the holy souls in purgatory.

"In the first place, you will, as usual, enter into this divine Heart, consecrating yourselves entirely to Him, with all that you do, say, or think. From prime until mass, make five acts of purity of intention, with as many of adoration, uniting them to those rendered by Jesus to His Father in the Blessed Sacrament. You will offer them to satisfy His justice, atoning by the purity of His Sacred Heart for the defects of purity of intention in these poor souls, for which they now suffer.

" Between holy Mass and recreation, make five acts of interior silence, and unite them to that of Jesus in the Blessed Sacrament. Offer all the masses which are celebrated in the holy Church, to appease the justice of God ; you will also adore Him in all hearts which have had the happiness of communicating.

"During dinner make five acts of mortification, and unite them in the same manner.

"At recreation, make five acts of charity, with five acts of the love of God ; you will unite them to the burning charity of the Heart of Jesus Christ, to atone for the defects of charity in these poor souls, who are suffering in expiation of them. You will be exact in maintaining silence until vespers. You will make five acts of this, uniting and offering them as the preceding, with nine acts of love.

"Between vespers and the evening recreation make five acts of modesty and attention to the presence of God. At the evening recreation you will make as many of sweetness and condescension towards your neighbour, with the same intentions. But pride owes the heaviest debt to the justice of God; you will therefore make as many acts of humility as you can, uniting them to that of the divine Heart of Jesus Christ.

"In the evening you will offer all you have done during the day, begging our Lord to apply the merit of it to those suffering souls, whom you will at the same time pray to obtain for you the grace to die in the love of Jesus Christ, and to live in such a way as to correspond to His Will without resistance.

"I load you perhaps too much, but do not make yourselves uneasy, and act with simplicity. When you cannot perform these practices in one manner, do them in another; but if you can set at liberty some of these poor prisoners, how happy you will be in having them as advocates in heaven to plead for your salvation."

CHALLENGE FOR THE TIME OF ADVENT.

"Our challenge for Advent shall be to unite ourselves in heart and spirit to the Blessed Virgin as often as we can, in order to render homage to the Incarnate Heart by loving and adoring with her in silence God made Man in her womb.

"In the first place, you will make five offerings to the Eternal Father, of the sacrifices which the Sacred Heart of His divine Son offers Him by His charity on the altar of His holy Mother's heart; you will at the same time beg of Him that all hearts may be converted and given up to His love. You will make five acts of self-renunciation, saying, 'Sacrificium Deo spiritus contribulatus.' 'A sacrifice to God is an afflicted spirit.'

"In honour of the humiliation of this adorable Heart, make five acts of humility, keeping yourself in the profound abyss of your nothingness; you will be well pleased to be despised and humbled; you will utter no word of vanity nor even of excuse; you will not seek to be loved and esteemed except by the Heart of our Lord; that He loves you is sufficient, and will indemnify you for everything. You will adore Him nine times, saying, 'Venite adoremus et procedamus ante eum.' 'Come, let us adore and fall down.' Or, 'Et Verbum caro factum est,' &c. 'The Word was made flesh,' &c.

"You will make five acts of interior and exterior silence, rejecting every useless thought from your heart, cutting off all superfluous words, and keeping your senses collected and attentive to mortification.

"In honour of the sacrifices which Jesus offered to His Father whilst concealed in the womb of His Mother, as upon an altar, on which to be continually immolated to the divine justice, we will make three offerings of the three powers of our souls, keeping them as it were annihilated in those of the soul of Jesus Christ.

"Our understanding will be swallowed up in His, by being satisfied with the knowledge that He has given us, and dismissing from our thoughts all vain and useless knowledge regarding the actions of our neighbour.

"We will keep our memory hidden in that of Jesus, limiting ourselves to the recollection of Him, or of what will lead us to self-abjection, of which we shall embrace every opportunity.

"Our will shall be entirely conformed to His, leaving Him to ordain for us whatever is most to His glory, whether He makes it known to us through our superiors or by means of His holy inspirations, saying always, 'Not my will, but Thine.' We will endeavour to keep all our desires confined within those of Jesus. Between each exercise we will make three acts of love, and three of adoration and contrition, saying often, 'I adore and love Thee, O Divine Heart of Jesus, living in the heart of Mary; I conjure Thee to live and reign in all hearts, especially in my own, and to consume it with Thy most pure love. God be praised.'"

Such are in part the practices taught and prescribed by the pious mistress to her novices, in order to raise them by degrees to religious perfection. She did not recommend them all, or at all times, to the same persons; she distributed them according to the occasion and the degree of their strength, proportioning the observances to the capacity of each, and leading them by degrees from one exercise and practice to another, according as it was necessary to awaken their attention, or occupy their fervour. Should any one desire to adopt these several practices all at once, and to bind themselves without discretion to observe them all, they would run the risk of fatiguing their head, and exhausting their health by overloading their mind. Every one should select from them such as are suited to their capacity and state, to be practised according to their strength; they ought especially to be guided by the prudent counsel of a director. Yet this detail into which we have entered may be useful, insomuch as it teaches us in the first place to recognise the spirit of God, which is clearly manifested in these counsels, which are so wise, so pure, and so full of the true spirit of the Gospel. Secondly, to admire the work of God, which raised a simple uneducated nun to the knowledge of the most sublime truths, and which guarded her pen from error in the many writings she has left. In the third place, to be confounded at seeing ourselves so far removed from that perfection to which all Christians should constantly aspire, especially those consecrated to God in the religious life.

The novices, as we have said, carefully preserved all these pious writings of their holy mistress, and kept them after her death, as one keeps the relics of saints. It is this respect which has preserved for us so many precious monuments of the fervour and wisdom of the mistress of novices. They, however, were not the only persons who had recourse in their difficulties to the inspirations of the servant of God, who received written advice from her, and carefully preserved it; those who had formerly been opposed to her, took delight in consulting her, hearing her, and receiving from her hands written instructions, which they also preserved. It is through them that other documents, instructive and often prophetic, have been handed down to us, from which we will here make a selection.

To a tepid nun, who had recommended herself to her prayers :

" I must tell you, my dear sister, that in praying for you, the following idea has been communicated to me: the Sacred Heart wishes to establish its empire and the reign of its love in your heart, but you destroy it to establish that of His creatures ; He will not, however, permit you to find true peace except in the perfect abandonment of, and detachment from, these same creatures. You will obtain this by avoiding them, and you will be victorious by combating them. Learn then to resist and fight, for you will acquire nothing without trouble, and the prize is only awarded to the conqueror. I entreat the Sacred Heart of Jesus to make you a conqueror, for mine cherishes you fondly, though attached to the cross where it is impossible to do anything but suffer; but its only desire is to love in suffering, and to suffer in loving. This is all my ambition."

To another, whom she particularly loved on account of her virtue :

" Yes, my dear sister, it is in this Sacred Heart that we shall be wholly His, although it may cost us much. Keep faithfully the promise you have made Him, and He will not reject you, so long as you are submissive to Him in all the states in which He may place you, without being either troubled or cast down. In a word, if I thought that you were not a friend of this divine Heart, you could never be a friend of mine, because it is my wish as much as possible to love only what Jesus loves, and to shun whatever is not agreeable to Him."

To another, who suffered much, both interiorly and exteriorly:

"Since our Lord wishes you to honour His life in the Blessed Sacrament, you must constantly carry the cross He lays upon you, whether interior or exterior, without the least complaint, or being weary of its length or weight. Is it not enough for you that it is selected by the hand of a friend, whose loving Heart has decreed from all eternity that you should be His victim, immolated and sacrificed, without resistance, to all His adorable designs? You must stifle all petty resentments, all passion, and every vain desire to love and be loved, esteemed and applauded by men, if you would be faithful to the Heart of our Lord Jesus. To make Him triumph in your heart, you have at present only to keep the promises you have made Him, whatever so doing may cost you. I believe this is what He requires of you, that you may not lose His friendship. Let nothing trouble you; keep your soul in peace in the midst of all your repugnances and drynesses. In this state He only asks of you acts of abandonment and perfect submission; nothing displeases Him so much as your troubles and depressions. What do you fear? Is He not all-powerful to support you? And why have you so little confidence in Him? Leave Him to act; and as for yourself, be content to suffer in loving Him. He wishes you to love Him above all, and with an entire forgetfulness of self. Think no more of the opinion of any one, but let it be your only aim to satisfy the Heart of Jesus in the way that He will teach you. He loves you, and will not permit you to perish whilst you have confidence in Him ; He will make you feel His power in due time."

To another, who allowed herself to be carried away by her eagerness of disposition :

"I remembered you at the Holy Communion as I promised, but our Lord wishes me to say that He is not satisfied with you; that if you are not more attentive to moderate your little sallies and impetuosities, you will oblige Him to withdraw from your heart. But take care to do as He desires, otherwise you will become as wicked as you now wish to be good. If you will take my advice, you will undertake five practices every day; you will mortify your hastiness three times, and your antipathies twice daily until the feast of our Lady's Presentation, thus to dispose yourself to receive the favours Jesus designs for you in your retreat. I believe our Lord loves you singularly, for if it were not so, He would have left you longer in your faults. Confide in His goodness, and be not troubled or cast down. When you have fallen voluntarily, do penance for it immediately."

To another, who was very fervent in the love of Jesus Christ:

"Remember that if I die before you, you will take my place before the Blessed Sacrament, and there entreat pardon for all the irreverences and outrages our Saviour has received from me; if God has mercy on me, I promise you that I will not forget you, and will do for you all that is in my power. In the meanwhile, be assured, my dear sister, that there is nothing I would not do, with the exception of sin, for your advancement in holy love. Let us love one another in the Heart of Jesus Christ; let us love Him for one another; let us love Him under all circumstances, and let our watchword always be, 'Fiat voluntas tua.' 'Thy Will be done.' 'Love, and do whatever you wish,' says St. Augustine; for who has love, has all, and does all by love, in love, and for love; and it is love which gives value to everything. Love will not have a divided heart; it wishes for all or nothing; love will make all things easy to you. Never forget Him whose love made Him die for you; but you will not love Him till you know how to suffer in silence."

BOOK VIII.

SEVERAL MIRACULOUS FAVOURS BESTOWED BY GOD ON SISTER MARGARET. HER GIFT OF PROPHECY, AND SUPERNATURAL LIGHTS UPON DIVERS SUBJECTS. WONDERFUL PROGRESS OF THE DEVOTION TO THE HEART OF JESUS.

THE true character of piety may be easily recognised in the instructions and practices given by the devout mistress to her novices, which we have collected in the preceding book. They speak throughout of nothing but love and suffering. The love of Jesus humbled for us, the love of humiliation in order to resemble Jesus; in a word, she had learned to be humble and meek of heart, as the Heart of Jesus Christ was itself full of meekness and humility. To accustom her novices to have this divine model ever before their eyes, and to be constantly conformed to it by love, she had given them a little picture of the Heart of Jesus, which they handed by

turns to one another ; she who had it, wore it secretly upon her heart the whole day, which was for
her one of recollection and fervour ; during it she
made several acts of those virtues which are dearest
to the Heart of Jesus, and was occupied as much as
possible in caressing, as it were, by love, the Heart
of her Beloved, mourning interiorly over the misfortune of those who do not know Him, and earnestly beseeching Him to establish His kingdom in
all hearts, by inflaming them with the sacred fire of
charity.

It was thus that the mistress used the devotion to
the Heart of Jesus for the sanctification of her
novices, at the same time that she made the education of her novices serve for the increase of this
devotion. We shall feel less surprise at her success
in both these designs, if we reflect on the extraordinary favours with which God blessed her labours
and rewarded her fervour. As we have already said,
Sister Margaret knew the depths of the heart, predicted the future, and manifested the most secret
thought when it would promote the glory of God
and the sanctification of souls. The examples of
this which we find both in the investigation made
since her death, and in the writings of her superiors and other trustworthy persons, are innumer-
able.

One of the nuns deposed that having recommended her brother, who was an officer in the king's
army, to the prayers of Sister Margaret, she foretold
some days afterwards, that he would at the hour of
death receive a very singular favour from God.
The event justified the prediction. This officer was
wounded in the head at the siege of Landau, by a

blow which would, in the course of nature, have
killed him on the spot, but to the astonishment of
the army-surgeons, he lived for two days in the possession of his senses, and received the sacraments
with edifying piety.

Another has related that she had for a long time
endured a pressing fear, which very much distressed
her when she was about to approach the sacraments;
she recommended her trial to the prayers of Sister
Margaret in general terms, and at the end of a few
days the servant of God said to her: "The Spirit
who directs me, urges and obliges me to tell you
that your fears are displeasing to our Lord, because
He wishes for more love and confidence from you;
and more especially He wishes you not to abstain
from holy Communion." The sister took note of
the exact words as coming from God Himself, since
she saw plainly that God alone could have discovered
her secret; and being faithful to this advice, she
found the repose which she had hitherto sought in
vain.

Two Ursuline nuns of the convent of Paray, who
were in their youth educated at the monastery of
the Visitation, have likewise deposed to the supernatural knowledge that Sister Margaret had in
their regard, and which she had imparted to them.
One relates, that being a pupil under the care of
the servant of God, she wished, by way of amusement, to plant a fruit-tree, promising herself, as she
said, to eat the fruit of it some day. "It is not
worth while," said the mistress to her, "for you will
not be a religious in this house." Appearances
were, however, against this, both on account of the
girl's own inclination and the wish of her parents,

who were anxious that she should be a religious in this house rather than in any other. She also relates that there were there at that time fourteen other children, of whom she had heard the mistress say, that only two would remain with them. It happened as she had said, but she could only know it then, said the religious who made this deposition, by supernatural light.

Through one of Sister Margaret's brothers we have become acquainted with two other events as instructive as they are wonderful. The first concerns his wife, and the second another brother. His wife one day urged him to take her to Paray, to see the servant of God, their sister. When they were in the parlour, Sister Margaret, according to her custom, spoke with them only on edifying subjects. Madame Alacoque, who up to that time had been too much attached to the world, was so touched with the conversation of her sister-in-law, that she began to shed tears. Her husband was astonished at this, and even reproached her, but Sister Margaret, who knew the cause of this salutary sorrow, said to her brother, "Permit her to weep, for these are good tears." Monsieur Alacoque, under these circumstances, thought it advisable to leave his wife alone with Sister Margaret, that she might speak with confidence and freedom. The servant of God then asked her sister-in-law what was the cause of these sudden tears, and if she could do anything to comfort her? The lady replied, "Yes, you can." "How?" "By asking my salvation of God, whatever may be the price." "Have you well considered this?" replied the religious. "Yes," said her sister-in-law. "I will then beg your salvation of God, as

if it were my own," said Sister Margaret; "but
God informs me that it will cost you much." Madame Alacoque, impelled by her fervour, said courageously, "It does not matter, I submit entirely to
His Will."

Monsieur Alacoque, who loved his wife exceedingly, and who had withdrawn on account of the
uneasiness that her tears caused him, returned some
hours afterwards to seek the servant of God, and
hear from her the cause of the sudden and excessive
grief of his wife. Sister Margaret very simply related what had passed, and told him that the
next day she should begin a novena for her sister-in-
law. "Both of you will have need of patience,"
added she, in an inspired tone, "therefore earnestly
beg this virtue of God." Monsieur Alacoque avows
in his relation of this event, that these words terrified him, but he dared not, or could not ask more.
He retired with his wife to Bois Ste. Marie, a little
town of Charolois, of which he was perpetual mayor,
and a few days after their arrival, his wife was seized
with such an acute pain in her head, particularly in
her face, that she could scarcely bear it, and uttered
continual cries.

The physicians and surgeons of the place employed the usual remedies for her relief, but without
success. After several weeks of trial and suffering,
they acknowledged to the patient that they knew nothing of her complaint. Monsieur Alacoque called
in others from the neighbourhood, who said the same
thing, after having tried all the remedies known to
them. He says himself that he employed twenty-
four, and that they all equally confessed their impo-
tence or their ignorance. In the meanwhile the

pain of the poor sufferer increased to such a degree,
that she could not refrain from uttering lamentable
cries day and night, demanding relief and not being
able to obtain it. Her husband took her to the
waters of Vichy and Bourbon, which, though beneficial to others, only increased her pain, and the
celebrated physicians of these frequented places,
confessed, like the others, that the malady was unknown to them. Monsieur Alacoque, hoping to
find some relief at Lyons from the skill of the physicians, took his wife there. All those of the town
were called in one after another, and consulted together several times ; but all was of no avail, to the
great disappointment of the invalid and her husband,
who relates with great simplicity the quarrels he
had with the physicians of that town, when in his
anger he reproached them with their ignorance.

While all this was going on, Sister Margaret, who
had heard of her sister-in-law's attack, and of the im-
patient anxiety of her husband to procure her relief,
was grieved that they should both place so much
confidence in the art of the physician, instead of
trusting absolutely to Divine Providence, and that
they appeared so anxious for a cure, which, according to the designs of God, they were not to obtain.
She wrote to her brother reproaching him for this,
and often repeated that there was no remedy for
the evil which was so painful to the wife, and so
ruinous to the husband, but entire patience and
absolute submission to the Will of God. More
than a year passed, and yet the family could not
resolve to enter heartily and absolutely into the
holy and courageous views of the servant of God ;
they wearied her by reiterated requests for prayers
26

and novenas, but in a different spirit from that
which God required, and questioned her anxiously
as to the length and result of the disease. At
length she wrote to them in these terms:

"In truth, my dear brother, I know not what
more to say to you. I am deeply grieved to see
that all the prayers that our community, and other
good souls of my acquaintance, constantly unite
with me in offering up for my dear sister and yourself, have not been able to obtain a moment's patience for you; this result I attribute to my sins.
Yet this is all that God wishes from both of you,
submission to His Will, and patience to bear this
trial with sweetness, and not to allow yourself to
have recourse to those things which do not please
Him. I thought I had said enough in the two preceding letters, if you had reflected on it, to make
you see, that as it is the Will of God she should
suffer this pain for her salvation, it is in vain to seek
human remedies for it. They will be of no use; for
who can counteract the Will of God, which is always
accomplished whether it pleases us or not? To
speak plainly, the salvation of this poor sufferer
depends on this pain, and the good or bad use she
makes of it; and she should not even wish to know
whether it will be of long or short duration. Let
her leave that with God, to whom she should make
a sacrifice of her life, to return it to Him when He
may please to take it. With tears in my eyes I
most earnestly exhort you to follow this advice, because I know that God has sent her this illness as a
proof of His love and desire to save her, and that
He could not give her a greater mark of His anger
than by curing her. When salvation is at stake, we

must do everything, suffer everything, sacrifice and abandon everything. Behold, my dear brother, what the most lively grief, and the share I take in your affliction, permits me to say to you. As to prayers, it seems to me that I cannot do more for you. Our much honoured mother has caused various novenas to be made with this object, and takes much interest in your sorrow. As to myself, I am unable to express the surprise I feel at your want of submission and patience, which gives me extreme pain. Make another vow to St. Francis of Sales in her behalf; cause nine masses to be said, to obtain for her patience and detachment from the things of this world. Let her remember that the last time I saw her, she told me to ask her salvation of God, whatever it might cost her, and it is now too late to retract. But, my dear brother, though God wishes to save us, it is His Will that we should contribute our part towards it, otherwise He will do nothing; for this reason we must resolve to suffer. This is a fruitful seed-time for eternity, where the harvest will be abundant. Do not lose courage; trials suffered with patience are worth a thousand times more than any other austerity, and this is what God at present demands of you. I embrace a thousand times the dear invalid," &c.

This wholesome advice had some effect, but that tranquil and absolute abandonment to the Will of God which Sister Margaret required, could scarcely find place in hearts accustomed to look upon afflictions with human eyes. At length Sister Margaret told them plainly, that the pain would not cease until the sick person was entirely resigned to the Will of God. She submitted in the end; and the fervour with which she had demanded her salvation of God at any price being once again renewed within her, she acquiesced with courage in the infirmity, which was the price God required from her; and abandoning herself to His Will, henceforth renounced all search after human remedies. God was contented with this sacrifice, for which He had been waiting, and the very next day after having made this devout act of resignation, Madame Alacoque died with great sentiments of piety, and thus the prediction of the servant of God was fulfilled.

Another of her predicions, also related by her brother, concerned a cousin who was a nun, and ended more mournfully. This religious was young, and of a trifling, frivolous character, more so perhaps than was becoming the gravity of her profession. She went accompanied by M. Alacoque, curate of Bois Ste. Marie, to see Sister Margaret, and whilst this devout religious entertained them with pious and holy subjects, she enlivened the conversation by pleasantries. The curate was annoyed at this, and remarked to the too lively religious, that it was not agreeable to the grave dispositions of his sister; but Sister Margaret, who heard this reproof, replied to her brother, "Let her laugh, these are her last enjoyments." The young nun either did not hear these words, or else made no account of them. A few days afterwards she returned to her convent, and on arriving there was seized with an illness which carried her off in five days.

The curate of Bois Ste. Marie experienced in his turn the miraculous power of his sister. He fell dangerously ill, and his case was thought to be hopeless; his brother, who witnessed the fact, and has deposed to it, relates that he sent an express to Sister Margaret, entreating her prayers. In the meantime the sick man grew worse; he suffered from a kind of suffocating catarrh, in which he was without feeling or motion. His teeth were so tightly closed that they were obliged to break one in order to give him medicine. Sister Margaret, after having prayed for him, told the messenger that they were to give the sick man some drink, in which they had dipped a note she gave him. This note contained an invocation of the Sacred Heart of our Lord. She added that the sick man would not die. God had made known to her that it was His Will to make use of this good priest in the establishment of the devotion to the Heart of Jesus Christ, to which he applied himself very efficiently and with great zeal after his cure. To the great astonishment of the physicians, an unexpected change took place as soon as they had made him take what the servant of God had prescribed; and this cure was the beginning of the holy and edifying life which he led until death, following exactly his holy sister's advice.

These prodigies could not remain secret; they excited the confidence of a number of persons who came to consult Sister Margaret upon their interior troubles and spiritual needs; some even carrying their curiosity so far as to ask her prayers for their deceased relations, and to question her with simplicity as to the state of their souls in another life. These visits, consultations, and requests offended her humility. She would have wished to see nobody, and said sometimes with dismay, " Do you suppose I know what passes in purgatory?" Yet she could not refuse to obey her superior, who ordered her to answer simply according to what God communicated to her, and those who visited her always carried away some spiritual fruit from her conversation and counsels.

It was particularly on the subject of the establishment of a hospital at Paray, that she was often consulted by pious persons of the town of both sexes, who had undertaken to found this useful institution. This project was at first strongly opposed, as almost always happens with pious undertakings. Men of worldly prudence were ever ready to see difficulties to this establishment, and to call it impossible. Some, through pride, pique, or whim, offered opposition, but the greatest obstacle of all was want of money and endowment. On Sister Margaret being consulted, she assured them that the enterprise would succeed against all appearances. She several times supported the flagging courage of pious persons, who were cast down by the opposition they met with. She gave advice according to the difficulties which presented themselves, with a prudence which seemed miraculous in one who had scarcely any knowledge of worldly affairs; but the Spirit of God, which loves to confound the wisdom of the world, can give light and prudence to whom He will, and by His divine wisdom can supply the want of human experience. Sister Margaret had so great a share in the establishment of this hospital by her predictions and counsels, that it is now looked upon as her work, and her memory is revered there as much as in her own house.

This house of the Visitation, as we have before remarked, renewed its fervour by the establishment of the devotion to the Heart of our Lord; but it still cost the servant of God much suffering. We have related in the fifth book how God required Sister Margaret to pray, suffer, and do penance for the souls in sin or tepidity, whose state He manifested to her. Those who cost her most tears and suffering, were the religious of her own convent. The sanctity which now reigns in the convent, and the fervour which the memory of the servant of God has left there, allows me to record unreservedly the faults of several of the religious of that house, and not to conceal defects which have been so gloriously repaired; besides which, these defects could never be imputed to those who are now there. At that time, though there were some holy nuns in that numerous community, there were many others, as we have seen, who cared little for perfection, and were very negligent in the duties of piety. There were not, it is true, those crying disorders, and those divisions, which scandalize the world, and the community always passed for being edifying and regular. But what satisfies and even edifies men, is not always sufficient to satisfy the Heart of God. Jealous of the purity of His spouses, and of the fruit of His graces, He is irritated by coldness as well as by infidelity, and He casts from Him the negligent heart. Those sisters, who thought they had nothing to reproach themselves with, and whom the world in truth reproached with nothing, were regular in the performance of the principal observances, but despised the lesser ones as trifles. Jealousies, murmurs against superiors, ridicule of their neighbour, little self-indulgences, the love of vanity and whatever nourishes it, curiosity regarding worldly things, and little attachments, were looked upon as they are

in many relaxed communities, as faults pardonable to
human weakness, or as necessary comforts.

These relaxations were happily repaired by degrees through the devotion to the Heart of Jesus
Christ, and the example and care of Sister Margaret,
but still more by the suffering she endured for the
sanctification of her sisters. God had prepared her,
and prescribed the manner in which she was to
sacrifice herself to His justice, when He showed her
that His anger was ready to punish sinners, who
are known only to Himself; and who, on account of
their profession, pass for saints in the eyes of men,
who cannot fathom the heart. We think it right
here to quote what our Lord revealed to His servant
in her retreat of the year 1684, as she herself related
under obedience to her superiors:

"Whilst attentively considering in prayer the
only object of my love in the garden of Olives,
plunged in the sadness and agony of a sorrow which
was truly loving, and feeling within me a strong
desire to share His anguish, He said lovingly to me,
'It was here that I suffered more than in all the
rest of My Passion, beholding Myself abandoned
both by heaven and earth, and loaded with the sins
of all men. I appeared thus before the holiness of
God, Who without any regard to My innocence,
bruised Me in His fury, and made Me drink the
chalice which contained all the gall and bitterness
of His just indignation, as if He had forgotten the
name of Father, in order to sacrifice Me to His
anger. There is no creature who can comprehend
the greatness of the torments I then suffered; and
it is this agony which the soul feels, when, standing
before the tribunal of the divine holiness, which

weighs heavily upon it, this infinite holiness breaks, overwhelms, and buries it in its just fury.' He afterwards added these words, ' My justice is irritated, and ready to punish secret sinners by open punishment, if they do not quickly do penance. I will make known to thee when My justice is ready to strike these criminals; it will be when thou feelest My holiness weigh heavily upon Thee. Thou must then raise thy heart and hands to heaven by prayers and good works, continually presenting Me to My Father as a victim of love, immolated and offered for the sins of the whole world; placing Me as a strong and safe rampart between His justice and sinners, to obtain mercy, by which thou shalt feel thyself encircled, when I am disposed to show favour to any one of these sinners. Then thou must offer Me to My Father, in thanksgiving for the mercy He exercises towards them. Thou shalt even know when a soul has the grace of final perseverance; for I will give thee a share in the songs of joy which the blessed utter in heaven; and all shall be through the communication of My love.' "

Sister Margaret had, on more than one occasion, to make the sacrifices our Lord required, and the consolation of knowing that they were not in vain. God only manifested His anger against these imperfect religious, in order to excite within her a lively desire of obtaining mercy for them; and being desirous of showing them favour, it was His Will that this grace should be the fruit of His faithful lover's fervour and suffering. We will simply give the account she has left in writing :

" On rising one morning, I seemed to hear a voice, which said to me, ' The Lord is weary of waiting, He wishes to enter into His barn to sift His wheat, and separate the good grain from the bad.' I took no notice of this; I even turned my mind away as from a distraction, to apply myself to my usual morning exercises; but the holiness of God, presenting itself before me as if it would annihilate me, once more made me hear His voice, which said, 'My chosen people secretly persecute Me, they have irritated My justice, but I will make manifest their secret sins by visible punishments; I will sift them in the sieve of My holiness, to separate them from My beloved, and having done so, I will surround them with that same holiness which stands between sinners and My mercy; when thus imprisoned by My holiness, their conscience shall remain without remorse, their understanding without light, and their heart without contrition; and at length they will die in their blindness.'

" Then discovering to me His loving Heart torn and pierced with blows, He said, ' See the wounds which I receive from My chosen people; others are satisfied to strike My Body, but these attack My Heart, that Heart which has never ceased to love them. My love will at length give place to My anger, to punish these proud souls who are attached to earthly things, who despise Me, and love what is contrary to Me, who leave Me for creatures, who fly from humility to seek self-esteem, and whose hearts are empty of charity, so that there remains to them only the name of religious.' "

Another time the Son of God made known to her what He endured from an unfaithful religious receiving Him in holy Communion; and to represent by a symbol the contempt He felt for the hypocritical prayers of such an indevout soul, He presented Himself to His servant with His eyes closed and His hands upon His sacred ears, as if neither seeing nor hearing, and said to His spouse that it was in this way He entered the sullied heart of her who had received Him in Communion. He added, 'I shall not listen to what she says to Me, neither will I regard her misery, that My Heart may not be touched, and may be as insensible for her, as her's is for Me."

On another occasion, He showed her a nun on the point of falling into this state of hard-heartedness, on account of the contempt with which she treated the favours of God. "Look," said He to her, "behold a soul which is about to fall into the state I have described; if she again abuses the favours I have to bestow on her, I will surround her with the holiness of My justice, that hearing she may not hear, and seeing she may not see, and may be insensible also to her own misery."

One day, she accompanied the Blessed Sacrament, with the rest of the community, to the chamber of a sick nun. The Son of God then showed Himself to His spouse, dragged, as it were, violently into the room; He addressed the priest who performed this duty, and said to him, " Cease to force Me, I suffer violence." The servant of God, penetrated with the most intense sorrow at this sight, went away weeping to hide herself, lest her grief should betray her secret. She retired into a corner apart to relieve by sighs and tears the sorrow of her heart, and when the ceremony was over, Jesus Christ presented Himself to her, and said, " Permit Me to repose in thy

heart, to console Myself for the violence My love
has made Me suffer."

Another time after holy Communion, He showed
Himself to her, wearing a crown of nineteen thorns,
which pierced His head in a very painful manner.
He told her that He came that she might draw these
thorns from Him, which, said He, have been driven in
by the many proud actions of a faithless spouse. This
sight afflicted the servant of God so much the more,
as she knew not how she could extract these dreadful thorns. Yet this object did not quit her, but
pursued her everywhere. She went to explain her
difficulty to her superior, who ordered her to ask our
Lord to point out the way in which she could relieve
Him. Jesus Christ approved of the obedience of
His spouse, and the counsel of the superior, and told
Sister Margaret to make as many acts of humility as
He had received wounds, to honour by these acts
the humiliations of His life on earth. The holy
sister returned to give an account to her superior of
the order she had received, which caused her a fresh
embarrassment; "For," said she, "I am myself full
of pride, how then can I relieve my Saviour from
what pride has made Him suffer?" In this belief,
she had not discovered that she was thus making
one of the acts prescribed to her. The mother left
her in her simplicity, and ordered her to offer to our
Lord all the practices of humility which should be
made in the community that day. The docile religious executed this command, and our Lord revealed
to her that the offering had been infinitely agreeable
to Him.

On another occasion God revealed the interior
dispositions of some of the religious who were about

to receive holy Communion with her. The sight so terrified her, and filled her with such a dread of communicating unworthily, that she wished not to communicate that day. The superior would not permit this, and ordered her to present herself at the altar. She then, out of obedience, communicated, and immediately after communion our Lord appeared to her, wounded and disfigured, as He was in His Passion, and said, "I have found no one willing to give Me a place of repose in the state in which I am. Five souls consecrated to My service," He added, "have treated Me in this way. I have been forcibly drawn with cords through narrow places, stuck with points and thorns which have thus torn Me." Sister Margaret did not at first perceive the meaning of these words, but Jesus Christ made her understand soon afterwards that these cords, and the violence they had done Him, were His love itself, and the promise He had made to give Himself to us in the blessed Eucharist ; that those narrow places were the ill-prepared hearts of the sisters who had received Him in Communion; and that the sharp points and thorns were the proud feelings of these souls who were careless about acquiring perfection.

It was not only the sad state of some particular religious, which was the object of Sister Margaret's sufferings and prayers, but the too common coldness of the community, which excited the anger of God and afflicted His spouse. Since the time that He revealed to her His wrath against them, they were the usual object of her prayers and sighs. Once on the feast of the Visitation, whilst she was praying with more than usual fervour in the choir of the

Church, when no office was being performed, she
saw the Son of God accompanied by the Blessed
Virgin and an infinite multitude of angels, who
trembled in His presence, because He appeared irritated. The devout religious understood what it was
that excited His anger. She redoubled the fervour
of her prayers, and our Lord seemed to say to her
with anger, "Speak no more of them, they turn a
deaf ear to My voice; they destroy the foundation
of the edifice; but if they attempt to raise it upon a
strange foundation I will overthrow it." Then the
Blessed Virgin, with all the blessed spirits, threw
themselves at the feet of her Son; she interceded
for the community, saying that they were the daughters of her heart, and she entreated mercy for them.
The Son of God received her prayer with a serene
countenance, but added, "Shall I suffer on your
account the abuse they make of My favours? Shall
I suffer their contempt of My spirit of humility and
simplicity? This spirit would keep them hidden in
Me; but they overcome it by the spirit of pride,
which breaks the ties of charity, and divides what I
have united."

The Blessed Virgin redoubled her entreaties and
demanded a short delay, for the conversion of these
faithless souls to the spirit of their vocation; which
delay was promised. As soon as this favour was
granted by the Son of God, the Blessed Virgin herself drove away the demon, who seemed only waiting
for the moment when the sentence of justice should
be pronounced, to seize on his prey. This enemy of
mankind, full of fury and vexation, immediately
raised so violent a tempest, that it seemed as if the
Church would be thrown down. He only suc-

ceeded, however, in tearing down the curtains and rods of the choir grating, saying, "It is thus I would have overthrown them all, if they had not been supported by a column against which I have no power." The noise made in the Church was so loud, that a sister who was stationed with Sister Margaret before the Blessed Sacrament, being seized with terror, was rising hurriedly to run away, when Sister Margaret called her, and said with a tranquil air, " Fear nothing, it is over, there will be no more of it," which words, while they reassured the terrified sister, made her also understand that Sister Margaret had had a vision.

Some time after this the Blessed Virgin appeared again to the servant of God, seeming as if fatigued with some great labour. In her hands she held several hearts covered with wounds, and said to her, " See what I have just taken from the hands of the enemy, who sported with them at his pleasure ; but, alas ! there are still some who take his part against me."

From this day till the autumn, Sister Margaret had no particular revelation upon the same subject ; but when her time of retreat came, she related as follows what passed on the second day of it:

" The second day of my retreat, when before the Blessed Sacrament, where I was preparing for confession, the sight of my sins, by which I had so much dishonoured God, threw me into such great confusion and deep sorrow, that I did not cease weeping for the five or six hours that I had the happiness to employ in this holy exercise. After that, my Divine Love presenting Himself to me, said, ' My child, wilt thou sacrifice to Me the tears which thou hast shed, to wash the feet of My beloved which are sullied in following a stranger?' 'Oh, my Lord!' replied I, 'Thou knowest that I have sacrificed everything to Thee, and have reserved nothing to myself of all that I do, except the desire of pleasing Thy Sacred Heart.' Another time when I was in the same state, He made me the same request, telling me that it was for the soul of His beloved who had fallen into sin, and who had a desire to be released from it. Still I did not understand who this beloved was. A third time He appeared to me making the same request, saying that His beloved was in purgatory. He then asked me if I knew who His beloved was? That it was the community of the Visitation, which should have but one heart and one soul; that the purgatory of which He spoke, was the retreat into which the religious had just entered. He added, 'My daughter, give them this last warning from Me, that every one may consider within herself, and profit by the grace which I present to her through the intercession of My holy Mother; those who will not profit by it shall remain as dry trees which produce fruit no longer; yet they shall be capable of receiving some light from My holiness of justice; a light which, whilst it enlightens the sinner, often hardens him; which discovers to him the misery of his situation, without giving him any conquering grace to withdraw him from it; in this state he either falls into despair, or into insensibility as to his own unhappiness. This is one of the most rigorous chastisements with which the holiness of My justice punishes the impenitent sinner.'"

Sister Margaret gave an account of all to the mother superior, whose exertions, together with the

tears and austerities of the servant of God, had so
much influence, that the community profited by
these warnings and threats. Already the devotion
to the Heart of Jesus had aroused their fervour, and
Jesus Christ had said in this last vision, that His
beloved who had fallen into sin had a desire to leave
it. She was in some sort already pure, since she
had only to wash her feet, according to our Saviour's
words in the Gospel, "He that is washed, needeth
not but to wash his feet;" but that perfect purification which the victory over earthly affections, figured
by the feet, imports, is one of the obligations of the
beloved and the spouse. Let those who neglect to
sigh after that purity, learn hence to fear the menaces
of their heavenly Spouse, who often punishes our in-
dolence in not profiting by the abundance of the
graces which we enjoy through His goodness, by
depriving us of them. The greater part of the religious who composed the community of Paray profited by this counsel, but a small number, who were
engrossed with themselves, did not yet enter into
the spirit of simplicity which characterises the true
daughters of St. Francis of Sales. It was for their
instruction that Sister Margaret had the following
vision some months after the retreat.

Being in prayer on the feast of St. Francis of
Sales, she shed plentiful tears for the sanctification
of the members of the institute, and in the bitterness of her heart invoked her holy founder. He
presented himself before her, accompanied by the
venerable Mother de Chantal, and addressing his
holy co-operator in the establishment of his order,
he said, "God has commanded me to visit all the
convents of my institute; He has assured me that

27

all those whom I recognise as my true daughters,
shall be received by Him as His spouses.   To fulfil
this command, I have done nothing but visit the
hearts of the superiors, within which all those of the
daughters of the Visitation should be enclosed;
whether they are good or bad, they represent the
person of Jesus Christ, and all religious who are
separated from their superiors, will be rejected by
Him.   There is one community which has given me
much joy, since in it I found only three, and in
another only five, who have not been placed in the
number of my daughters; but there is also one
which causes me great sorrow, for a third part of
the sisters were such as I could not recognise as my
daughters."   The servant of God, in relating this
vision, adds that Mother de Chantal seemed to
answer very distinctly, that all the evil arose from
want of simplicity, in which they were defective; for
that walls which leave their foundation will soon be
overthrown.   "I felt," added the blessed foundress,
" so much pain when on earth, at seeing a daughter
of the Visitation deficient in simplicity, that I would
rather she had pierced my heart.   Let every superior," continued she, " do all in her power to re-
establish this holy virtue of simplicity, as well as
that of humility ; for if there is not a speedy amendment, God will punish them severely."

Sister Margaret begged the holy founder to make
her understand more particularly what the faults
were which they committed against simplicity.   "It
is," said he, " that they are not perfectly sincere in
accusing themselves of their sins; they justify themselves by accusing others; in a word, they seek their
own glory and not that of God.   Now they who so

act, become objects of laughter to the devil, who
after having puffed them up with self-esteem, looks
upon them as empty vessels fit only to be used as
playthings.   Curiosity also," added St. Francis of
Sales, "does much evil; she who gives herself up to
this fault, falls into forgetfulness of God and of
herself."

The servant of God pressed the holy founder to
teach her a way of remedying what displeased God
so much, and he answered that the most efficacious
means his daughters possessed of rising from their
sins, was the Sacred Heart of Jesus Christ, and the
love they might draw from it; that having this divine
Heart as their defender and support, they would be
guaranteed from the danger with which His faithless
spouses are threatened; he added again, that by this
divine Heart they would be preserved from yielding
to a strange spirit, full of artifice and pride, which
would seek to destroy the spirit of humility and
simplicity; but that Satan would make use of this
unhappy spirit to ruin others.   We see but too truly
now the accomplishment of this prophecy, made forty
years ago.   We see into what excesses the spirit of
curiosity, and want of simplicity and submission,
have precipitated some religious communities.   That
of Paray profited so well by the devotion to the
Sacred Heart of Jesus Christ, and the light given to
Sister Margaret, that the nuns who had been a cause
of sorrow to their holy founder, were eager to regain
his favour, and that of their Spouse, by following his
spirit, which was established in them by simplicity
and obedience, and that in so solid a manner, that
they have not been lost in the day of temptation,

and the spirit of curiosity and rebellion against the vicar of Jesus Christ has found no entrance there.

It was thus that the devotion to the Heart of our Lord worked a wonderful change in this community, in answer to the tears and sufferings of Sister Margaret; her patience and humility triumphed over all, and the Son of God changed the hearts which began to honour His. He spread amongst them love of religious perfection, and zeal to acquire it; but in proportion as they opened their eyes to the sanctity of their obligations, they discovered the merit of her who had drawn down so many blessings from God. Contradictions and contempt changed into veneration for her. They spoke of her as a saint, and listened to her words as oracles. This veneration was carried to so great a length, that even while she was living, the sisters would, unknown to her, collect anything that had been used by her, to keep as a relic, and one of the nuns who lived in her time has deposed that when her hair was cut, the boarders eagerly requested their mistress to allow them to preserve it.

A lay-sister experienced the advantage of this pious confidence even in the lifetime of Sister Margaret. In the first days of her probation, she had wounded her leg with a hatchet when cutting some wood. She concealed her pain, fearing the nuns might send her away, and endured it for several weeks with a constancy as heroic as it was imprudent; but a second accident caused the wound to re-open, and she began to be anxious for its cure. As she could no longer hide either the pain or the danger she was in, she had recourse to God, and felt confident that if her leg could but touch the

habit of the saint, of whom she had heard so many
wonders, she should be cured. She succeeded in
doing this without the knowledge of the servant of
God, and found the next day that she was entirely
cured. She thought herself bound in gratitude to
confide her cure to Sister Margaret, whose humility
was alarmed at the information, and led her to use
all her influence in persuading the postulant to keep
her secret to herself.

We have already spoken of the confidence placed
in the prayers of this holy sister, in behalf of the
souls of the departed. This was founded upon
several supernatural lights which God gave her on
this subject, and which deserve to be related, not
only because they are wonders which it has been the
Will of God to perform for His servant's glory, and
with which He rewarded her particular devotion for
the relief of souls in Purgatory, but more especially
because these illuminations and revelations contain
very wholesome instructions for those who wish to
find in this history what alone they ought to seek,
namely, their own edification. Sister Margaret, as
we have seen, had a most tender and compassionate
affection for those who satisfy the justice of God in
Purgatory; the sufferings of these holy souls were
one of the things which most excited her fervour,
and often inspired her with a great desire of practising austerities for their relief, as far as she was
allowed to do so.

Once, on new year's day, she prayed very earnestly for three persons lately deceased, two of whom
had been religious, and the third a secular. Our
Lord presented all three to her, and said, " Which
dost thou wish Me to give thee?" The servant of

God, humbling herself profoundly, begged our Lord to make the choice Himself, according to His good pleasure and greater glory. He then released the soul of the secular person, saying that He had less compassion for the souls of those who had been religious, because in faithfully practising their rules they had had more opportunities of meriting, and of expiating during life their daily faults.

Another time our Lord showed her a number of souls, who, for having been during their life estranged from their superiors, and for having had misunderstandings with them, were undergoing punishment, and deprived of the assistance of the Blessed Virgin and the saints, and of the visit of their guardian angel. Several of these souls were destined to remain a long time in terrible flames; some amongst them had no other marks of their predestination, than not hating God; others who had been in religion, and who during their life had had little union and charity with their sisters, were deprived of the benefit of their prayers, and received no assistance from them.

"I learned from Sister Margaret," says Mother Greffier, in her Memoir, "that two religious, for whom she prayed after their death, were shown to her in these prisons of divine justice; but the one suffered incomparably greater pain than the other. The former complained bitterly that by her faults, which were contrary to that mutual charity and holy friendship which ought to reign in religious communities, she had, among other punishments, drawn upon herself the loss of the prayers that the community offered to God for her. She only received relief from the prayers of three or four persons of the same community, for whom she had had less affection during life. This suffering soul also accused herself of too great facility in taking dispensations from the rule and community exercises; finally, she deplored the care she had taken on earth to procure relief and comfort for her body. She at the same time made known to our dear sister, that in punishment for these three faults, she had suffered three furious assaults of the devil during her agony, and that each time thinking herself lost, she had been upon the point of falling into despair, but that the Blessed Virgin, for whom she had always had a great devotion, drew her each time from the grasp of the enemy.

"The other religious who suffered less, asked for no relief, at which Sister Margaret was astonished, but she was told that this soul was not permitted to ask for assistance, because she had failed to correspond with the attraction God had given her to go to Him by pure suffering, and that in opposition to this she had anxiously sought relief.

"Sister Margaret was on another occasion praying for two persons of consideration in the world, when one of them was shown her as condemned for several years to the pains of Purgatory, notwithstanding the solemn services and the great number of masses that were said for her; all these prayers and suffrages were applied by the divine justice to the souls of some families subject to her, who had been ruined by her want of charity and equity in their regard; and as these poor people had left nothing after their death to obtain prayers, God supplied them in this way.

"The other was in Purgatory for as many days as

she had lived years upon the earth. Our Lord
made known to Sister Margaret, that amongst all
the good works this person had performed, He had
had particular regard to certain humiliations she had
received in the world, which she had endured with
a truly Christian spirit, not only without complaint,
but even without mentioning them, and that in reward for this He had been mild and favourable in
His judgment." These are the words of Mother
Greffier, who was wisely suspicious on the subject
of the extraordinary graces which Sister Margaret
received, and who only acknowledged their truth
after many trials.

Mother Greffier has related another fact which
deserves a place here, since it regards a person in
whom the whole order of the Visitation is interested.
Mother Philiberte Emmanuel de Montoul, superior at
Annecy, whose memory is in veneration, and whose
holy life was the edification of the whole institute,
died on the 5th of February, 1683, in the time of
Mother Greffier's superiorship, and was particularly
recommended by her to the prayers of Sister Margaret.   After some time, she told her superior that our
Lord had shown her that this soul was very dear to
Him, because of her love and fidelity in His service,
and that He had prepared an ample reward for her
in heaven, after her purification in Purgatory was
ended.   He also showed her this soul receiving
great relief in her sufferings, from the suffrages and
good works which were every day offered for her in
the order.   Sister Margaret was praying again for
this holy superior on the night of Holy Thursday,
when our Lord caused her to see her placed, as it
were, under the chalice which contained the sacred

Host, and receiving a share in the merits of His
agony in the Garden of Olives. On Easter-day,
which that year fell on the 18th of April, she saw
her ready for heaven, desiring and hoping soon to
enjoy the sight and the possession of God. At
length, on the Sunday of the " Good Shepherd," she
saw her sweetly lost and swallowed up in glory,
melodiously singing the favourite song of the servant of God; "Love triumphs, love reposes, love
rejoices in God." Thus we see that this holy and
fervent superior, who was animated with the pure
spirit of the institute, died on the 5th of February,
in the reputation of sanctity, but only entered into
the enjoyment of glory on the 1st of May, as was
revealed to Sister Margaret; God, in order to purify
her, deferring her happiness for eighty-six days.   So
long a Purgatory for so fervent a soul, is a lesson
for all cowardly and idle persons, who think
they do too much for the service of God, and who
pride themselves on the lightest practices of penance. What time and what suffering will not be
necessary to expiate their faults in Purgatory !

God not only revealed to His spouse the state of
the souls for whom she prayed, but sometimes destined her to suffer for these afflicted souls, by making her share in their pain. These sufferings, which
God only knows, and of which St. Augustine says,
they are wonderful but true, " miris sed veris
modis," were communicated to Sister Margaret
in a manner no less wonderful, and no less true.
We only know what she relates of them, and it will
be instructive and edifying to those who read this
life, since they can thus learn the severity of God's

justice towards certain faults, which our tepidity
makes us regard as light ones.

Sister Margaret being one day before the Blessed
Sacrament, a person all on fire suddenly appeared
before her, and his burning heat penetrated her so
powerfully, that she thought herself consumed with
the same fire. She did not recognise him, but his
state caused her to shed many tears. The suffering
soul then told her that he was a Benedictine monk
of the convent of Cluny, who a short time before
had been prior of the convent of Paray, when she
had once confessed to him, and he had given her
some consolation by allowing her to receive holy
Communion. In his sufferings, God had permitted
him to address himself to Sister Margaret, that he
might obtain relief by her prayers. He then requested that she would offer for him, and apply to
him, all that she should do and suffer for the space
of three months. He then disclosed to her three
reasons for the great suffering to which he was condemned. The first was that he had been too much
attached to his reputation, which had sometimes
made him prefer his interest on this point to the
true glory of God. The second was his want of
charity towards his brethren. The third was a too
natural affection for creatures, and the manifestation
of it in spiritual conversations with them; "which,"
said he, "much displeased God."

Sister Margaret promised that if she could obtain
permission, she would perform what he asked. It
was granted, but her promise did not deliver her
from the sight of this afflicting spectacle, which
never left her during all that time. She seemed
incessantly to see this religious near her, and

communicating fire to the side of her on which
he appeared to remain, and in all this half of
her body she felt such intense pain that she wept
almost continually. The superior, who knew her
state, and the cause of her pain, found that nothing
gave her any alleviation but ordering her some penances, as disciplines, &c., which holy practices appeared to give relief both to the religious and
the sister. At the end of three months they were
both delivered from their sufferings, for Sister Margaret saw this holy religious ascend to heaven full of
joy, after having testified his gratitude, and assured
her that he would protect her before God.

We will insert here what Sister Margaret has
related of a similar event, which also procured her
much suffering. "I saw in a dream," said she, "one
of our sisters who had been dead for some time.
She told me she suffered much in Purgatory, but
that God had just made her experience a grief
which surpassed all her pain, by showing her one of
her near relations precipitated into hell. Upon
these words I awoke, and felt my whole body so
bruised, that it was painful for me to move. As we
are not to think of dreams, I took no great notice
of mine, but this religious made me do so in spite of
myself, for she gave me no repose from that moment,
and said to me incessantly, 'Pray to God for me,
offer Him your sufferings, united to those of Jesus
Christ, to relieve mine, and give me all that you do
until the first Friday of May, and then communicate
for me.' With the permission of my superior I did
so; yet the pain which this suffering nun communicated to me increased to such a degree, that it overwhelmed me, and I could obtain neither relief, nor

repose. Obedience obliged me to retire to bed to take rest, but I was no sooner there than I seemed to have her close to me, saying, ' Thou art at thine ease in bed, look where I am lying, and what intolerable evils I suffer.' I saw that bed, and it makes me tremble even now whenever I think of it. Above and beneath were sharp-pointed and fiery nails, which entered into the flesh; she told me this punishment was inflicted on account of her idleness and negligence in observing the rules. ' My most intense pain,' added she, ' is caused by the agony of my heart, for the murmuring and dissatisfied thoughts which I entertained against my superiors; my tongue is eaten by vermin, and it is continually being torn out, for the words I have uttered against charity, and for my little attention in keeping silence. Ah! how I wish that all souls consecrated to God could see my horrible torments. If I could show them what is prepared for those who live negligently in their vocation, they would indeed keep their rules in a different manner, and would be most careful not to fall into those faults which have caused me so much suffering.' I burst into tears at this sight, whilst the suffering soul continued thus : ' Alas! one day of exactness as to silence, on the part of the whole community, would cure my parched mouth; another, passed in the practice of holy charity, would heal my tongue; a third, spent without murmuring or dissatisfaction with the superior, would relieve my agonizing heart; but nobody thinks of me.' After having made the communion as she requested, she told me that her horrible torments were much diminished, but that she was still to remain in Purgatory for a long time, to suffer the punishment due to those who live with tepidity in the service of God. However, I found myself released from my sufferings, which she told me would not diminish until she was relieved."

In truth, it is only from Sister Margaret herself that we learn the detail of these revelations and apparitions; but the well-attested prodigies, and the miracles juridically proved, as we have seen elsewhere, remove all doubt as to those other marvels, which we only know through her fidelity in giving an account of them to her superior and confessors. Besides which, the constant and tried humility of this holy religious deprives the most incredulous of any reasonable suspicion that she invented these things, especially as they, far from attracting the admiration of those to whom she related them, procured her, on the contrary, nothing but continual humiliation. Happy those who, not listening to the vain objections urged by incredulity, learn from these various recitals how just and rigorous are the judgments of God, and guard themselves against His severity by an exact fulfilment of all their duties, and by a truly penitent and laborious life, for we shall find the pain we would spare ourselves in this life through sloth or effeminacy, increased a hundred fold in the next.

But if there are still some who are determined to put themselves in opposition to these miraculous events, we would use against them the reasoning employed by St. Augustine, on the subject of the propagation of the Gospel. This astonishing propagation of a law so contrary to human sense and reason can only be the effect of the miracles of its first preachers. But those who deny that they performed miracles, are compelled to acknowledge a greater one, namely, the propagation itself, without the assistance of prodigies; for it is more difficult to believe that religion can have triumphed in a few ages over the errors and prejudices of all nations without any miracle, than to believe that this astonishing triumph has been rendered easy by the miracles of those who preached the Gospel.

It is the same with respect to the blessed Mother, and the devotion to the Sacred Heart of our Lord Jesus Christ that she has established. We see clearly that all the wonders God has worked by His servant, or on her account, have been so ordered in the designs of His providence, as to accredit this devotion by her means. Here is a woman, without birth, credit, or power, without even understanding, if one may say so, since what she had was buried under her profound simplicity; who from the obscurity of a cloister, where she is humbled or treated with contempt, gives rise to a devotion that is adopted by the whole world in a few years. For the establishment of this devotion, God used the same means that He formerly employed for the establishment of the faith, that is to say, the word of simple and unlettered persons, who having of themselves neither power nor knowledge, find their all in the power of God, who accredited their words by His miracles; and in the same way that the faith has been spread by miracles, so also they have been the cause of the wonderful propagation of Sister Margaret's devotion, which had no other support than that of a woman despised by every one. But if some say that these miracles are incredible, and are not inclined to believe them, we answer

with St. Augustine, that it is still more incredible
that without a miracle, a person so contemptible in
the eyes of the world, should have had such prodigious
success.

In truth, when the sanctity of the venerable Sister
Margaret had triumphed over the obstacles she met
with from her superiors and sisters, the devotion to
the Sacred Heart of our Lord, which was at length
established in her convent with the concurrence of all
the religious, soon spread elsewhere, together with
the reputation of the servant of God. Wherever
she was mentioned, the devotion she had originated,
and the object of that devotion were also spoken of;
and the wonders related of this holy religious excited the confidence of the people and animated their
fervour. In a few years the poor convent of a little
town served as a model to the whole world; and
every one was eager to copy what had been practised
with so much fruit in that little place.

The festival was soon established in almost all the
convents of the order of the Visitation, and celebrated with the greatest solemnity. From that
time this devotion has ever increased; and as there
is scarcely a nation to which the order of the Visitation has not extended, the holy religious who com-
pose it have carried and spread over all countries
the fame of a devotion which awakens fervour and
the love of God in all hearts. It has crossed the
seas, and been carried into the vast regions of Asia
and America, where religion has been preached by
the Jesuit Fathers; with the truths of faith, they
have inspired their fervent neophytes with the love
and worship of the Heart of Jesus Christ, the beginning of their salvation, and of the graces He works

in them.   Thus again is accomplished a prediction of the servant of God, who said several times
that the worship of the Heart of Jesus Christ
would be established in all the world, and that the
Fathers of the Society of Jesus were destined by
God to fulfil these His designs.   She made Mother
de Saumaise acquainted with this in the year 1689,
and the original of her letter, with many others,
which prove the truth of these several predictions,
has been preserved in the convent of Paray, and
laid before the ecclesiastical commissary in the
juridical information, which we have already mentioned.

This devotion also increased daily throughout the
whole of Europe ; in the year 1726, it was reckoned
that more than three hundred societies had been
established in less than thirty years, in France,
Flanders, Piedmont, Italy, Germany, Poland, Bo-
hemia, the Indies, and China.   All these societies,
formed under the title of the Sacred Heart of our
Lord, and designed to honour this divine Heart
with especial worship, have been erected by the
authority of the Holy See, and with the approbation of the ordinaries, with indulgences obtained
from Popes Innocent XII., Clement XI., Innocent
XIII., and Benedict XIII. now reigning.   All kinds
of communities, secular and regular bodies, even
chapters of cathedral churches, have been eager to
see these devout associations formed amongst them.
The fruit they have produced in all hearts, and the
graces with which they have been blessed, have been
the only means employed by God for the propagation of this devotion.   Temporal powers, human
motives, or political intrigues, have had no share in

it; it was the Will of God that this miraculous propagation, like the first beginning of the devotion,
should appear visibly to be His work, and He caused
it, by the secret springs of providence, to triumph
over contradiction, criticism, and the indifference of
tepid souls; as He had already, by the humility of a
religious without name or support, overcome all the
obstacles she met with in her convent.

God, who only permits evil in order to accomplish
His merciful designs, and who disturbs the whole
world in order to give birth to His elect by means
known to Himself, allowed Provence to be ravaged
by pestilence in 1720. This terrible scourge was
employed by Him for the glory of Sister Margaret's
devotion. The town of Marseilles was the first attacked by this plague, which in a few months carried off half the inhabitants. Monsignor Henri
Francis Xavier de Belsunce de Castelmoron, bishop
of Marseilles, seeing the insufficiency of human
remedies, thought it his duty to have recourse to
Him who holds in His hand the keys of death and
hell, and in order to interest the merciful Heart of
our Saviour in favour of His flock, he determined to
assuage the anger of God by the merits of the Sacred
Heart of His Divine Son.

This pious and courageous prelate, in whom
France beheld with admiration a new St. Charles
by reason of his boundless charity, and a new St.
Hilary by his zeal for the defence of the faith, hoped
to find in the public worship of the Heart of Jesus a
remedy for the evil, and his hope was not disap-
pointed. He exhorted all his people to enter into
the same spirit, and ordered that the feast of the
Sacred Heart should henceforth be solemnised on
28

the Friday after the octavo of Corpus Christi, as one of the greatest festivals of the year. On All Saints' day, after a long procession, in which he walked barefoot, and carried the Blessed Sacrament, he made a solemn and public consecration of himself and his whole diocese to the Sacred Heart of Jesus.

It was evident that his prayer was heard. From that day the plague which had been so violent, began to diminish rapidly, and in a short time it ceased entirely, as the magistrates of the town acknowledged and declared in an authentic public act. Still more marked protection was afterwards extended by God to the fervour of the bishop and his people.

In the month of May, 1722, the plague, which had been long thought to be entirely extinguished, broke out afresh in the town, and threw it into great consternation. The Heart of Jesus Christ was the happy resource of the holy prelate. At his solicitation all the magistrates made a vow to go every year in the name of the town to the church of the Visitation, on the day fixed for the feast of the Sacred Heart of Jesus Christ, there to honour this divine object of our love, to receive the holy Communion, to offer a candle of white wax weighing four pounds, ornamented with the town escutcheon, and, finally, to assist at the general procession which the prelate proposed to establish for ever on this same day. This vow was pronounced publicly before the altar of the Cathedral Church, by the first of the municipal magistrates, in the name of the corporation, on Corpus Christi, previous to the procession of the Blessed Sacrament; the Bishop holding Jesus in his hands, and the magistrates kneeling before Him. All the people approved the vow, of which, with lively faith, they hoped to reap the benefit.

This vow was heard in a manner which was the admiration, as well as consolation, of all the town. From that day the sick were cured, and those who were in health preserved. Panic, which in these fatal scourges often causes more evil than the scourge itself, gave place to entire confidence; the inhabitants of the town believing themselves safe under the protection of the Saviour's merciful Heart. The plague was so entirely stopped, that six weeks afterwards the Bishop of Marseilles, in a letter which he wrote to excite gratitude to God for so visible a miracle, said, " We actually enjoy such perfect health, that, what is without example in a town so large and thickly populated as this is, we have scarcely had any deaths, or sickness of any kind in Marseilles for some time."

It was in remembrance of this second favour, which seemed still more sudden and miraculous than the first, that the bishop established for ever a general procession on the day of the feast of the Heart of Jesus Christ. All these facts are verified by the letters of this prelate, and the acts of deliberation of the body of municipal magistrates of the town of Marseilles. At Aix, Arles and Toulon, the same festival was established on account of the same scourge, and its establishment was attended with the same result as at Marseilles. It has since been extended to several other places, and the devotion still continues to increase every day in all parts, thus contributing to awake the fervour of the faithful.

Let us consider then, what an unknown woman, despised and repulsed by her own companions, shut up in an obscure convent, in a corner of the world, has accomplished by her fervour, or rather what God has accomplished by her. Can we refuse to recognise the finger of the Almighty in such events? Whoever recollects that it was a simple nun of the Convent of Mont-Cornillon, near Liege, that God formerly employed to excite the people, the bishops, and at last, the Sovereign Pontiff himself, to cause the festival of the Blessed Sacrament to be celebrated in the whole Church, will be less astonished at the wonders we have just related, and at the devotion of the religious of Paray becoming a resource in public calamities. The Spirit breathes where He will, and communicates Himself to whom He pleases, and as He pleases; and if He chooses the less illustrious of the world, and what appears most contemptible to those who only esteem human greatness, for the instruments of His wonders, it is because He would confound the wisdom of the wise, and show that everything, even the power and prudence of men, is so subordinate to His supreme power, that without them and in spite of them, He causes His designs to triumph. And if on the sad occasions we have just described, the faithful have found greater relief from their temporal evils in the invocation of the Sacred Heart of the Saviour, than in all human remedies, it is because God would teach them by these miraculous events, that they may still more surely find in this same Heart, an efficacious remedy against their own tepidity, and a certain means of obtaining from His goodness the graces and virtues necessary to work out their salvation.

BOOK IX.

SHE IS MADE ASSISTANT. HER LAST SICKNESS AND
DEATH, AND THE MIRACLES PERFORMED
AT HER TOMB.

WHILST the devotion towards the Sacred Heart
of Jesus Christ grew every day in the Community
of Paray, and piety and fervour likewise increased
sensibly, so also the holiness of Mother Margaret
appeared to augment daily. Before this she appears
to us so excellent, that nothing could be added to
her sanctity; but the Heart of Jesus, infinite in
love and in riches, has always treasures to bestow,
and Mother Margaret received them in profusion
during the few years preceding her death, after the
establishment of her devotion. God crowned His
former graces by other favours, one of the first of
which was the care He took to relieve her from a
trial which had been the most severe she had ever
experienced.

The extraordinary things that passed within her,
had not only been an occasion of persecution by
others, but had also produced interior alarm and
inexplicable trouble of mind in this holy nun. As
she often heard it said that she was a hypocrite, a
fanatic, a false devotee, that she was the sport of the
devil, and that she yielded to delusion, she could not
believe that so many people were deceived on this
subject, and taking the part of her calumniators
against herself, she was brought almost to doubt the

truth of the favours of God, and to fear that she was
in a state of perdition. The Son of God had compassion on these trials, which were caused by the
humility and love of His servant; He was anxious
to calm her fears, and to be Himself her director in
order to reassure her. The advice He one day gave
her on this subject deserves to be related, and the
lesson He gave her upon the marks whereby to distinguish the true favours of His Spirit from the illusions of the devil, is so beautiful, that it is impossible not to acknowledge that it was eternal Truth,
and uncreated Wisdom that spoke to her. This is
the way in which this humble nun gives an account
of it.

" In the fear I have always felt that there might
be illusion in the graces I received from God, it has
been the Will of my Sovereign Master to give me
certain marks by which I can easily distinguish what
proceeds from Him, from what proceeds from the
devil or self-love, or any other natural cause.

" In the first place He told me that these graces
and favours would always be accompanied by some
humiliation or mortification on the part of creatures.

" Secondly, that after having received any of these
divine communications, of which my soul is so unworthy, I shall feel plunged into an abyss of nothingness and interior confusion, which will occasion
me as much grief at the sight of my unworthiness,
as I shall have received consolation through the
liberality of my Saviour; thus stifling all vain complacency and all feelings of self-esteem.

" Thirdly, that these graces and communications,
whether for myself or others, will never produce the

least feeling of contempt for any one ; and that whatever knowledge they may give me of the interior of others, I shall never esteem them less, though their miseries may seem very great, but shall only be led thereby to feel sentiments of compassion, and to pray earnestly for them.

" He added, that these graces, however extraordinary they may be, will never hinder me from observing the rules, and obeying blindly ; and He assured me that He had so subordinated them to obedience, that if I removed myself from it in the slightest degree, He would withdraw from me, with all His favours.

" Finally, that this spirit which directs and reigns over me with so much power, will lead me to five things:

" 1. To love my Saviour Jesus Christ with exceeding love.

" 2. To obey His example perfectly.

" 3. To suffer incessantly for His love.

" 4. To be willing to suffer, if possible, without its being perceived.

" 5. To have an insatiable thirst to communicate, and to be before the Blessed Sacrament.

" It seems to me that the graces I have hitherto received have produced these effects in me."

Thus speaks the servant of God in a paper in her own handwriting, which is still kept, and which her director, who had exacted it from her by obedience, carefully preserved as a useful lesson to all those who direct souls. The fervent religious, immediately afterwards, and without any connection, added these words : "As for the rest, I see more clearly than the day, that a life without the love of Jesus Christ is the greatest of all miseries." In these unnecessary words, the transport of love which animated her may be easily recognised. All is love; all reminds her of love; to those who love ardently everything is an occasion of speaking of the beloved object.

In the meanwhile, as we have remarked, consideration for the servant of God increased in the house, together with the devotion to the Heart of our Lord. Each one thought herself indebted to her prayers for the change she experienced in her own heart; and this return of consideration and regard for a person so long despised, may be counted as one of the wonders which God worked on her account. A nun who was formerly the object of the hatred of some and the compassion of others, and who had seemed to be the sport of the greater part of the sisters, one to whom they had not thought fit to entrust the least employment, became in the eyes of these same sisters, who now acted justly towards her, capable by her prudence of directing the house, and undertaking the first offices.

In the year 1687, Mother Melin having been continued in the superiorship, thought that she could not find a more efficacious help in directing the community, than by choosing Sister Margaret for her assistant; this choice was as much applauded by the community as it would have been censured, and perhaps opposed, a year before. Mother Margaret was at this time relieved from the care of the novices, as her infirmities would not allow of her uniting the two employments. Before quitting the noviciate she left this instruction:

"As my last advice, my dear sisters, I conjure you with all the affectionate earnestness of which I

am capable, and by all the love you bear to our
Lord Jesus Christ, to be always faithful to Him,
keeping the promises you have made Him. Do
nothing intentionally that you know will displease
Him, neglect nothing that you believe will be agreeable to Him, in order that He may not be constrained
to limit His designs upon you, and to withhold the
graces He is willing to bestow, if you do not keep
them back by your ingratitude. This would be a
great suffering to me, for there is nothing I am not
ready to undergo in order that you may be united to
the Heart of our Lord Jesus, and that He may
reign in you. Therefore I deliver you up to His
care, and His loving direction. I entreat you to do
the same, and to give yourselves up entirely to Him,
saying often to yourselves, ' Since this Divine Heart
is mine, what can I want? If I am entirely His,
who can injure me?' Make an oratory of your
heart, there to adore and love the Heart of your
Divine Spouse.

"Enter this oratory three times in the day. In
the morning, to render your homage of adoration
and sacrifice to this adorable Heart, as to your
Sovereign and Redeemer; consecrate all that you
do and suffer to Him, as also your whole being, that
you may only use it in loving, honouring, and glorify-
ing Him; unite all that you do to Him, and to His
holy intentions, renouncing whatever is contrary to
them.

"At noon, you will enter there to render your
homage of love and prayer; you will disclose your
poverty and your necessities, and all the wounds of
your soul to Him, as to one who is the Sovereign
remedy for them.

"In the evening, enter there once more, to offer Him your homage of gratitude and thanksgiving for all His benefits; entreat His pardon with lively sorrow for your ingratitude, and make a firm resolution to die, rather than to return to your unfaithfulness.

"Make, as it were, a crown of all the practices you have performed during the day, and offer them to Him in reparation for the pain He has suffered from the thorns of your sins; beg of Him to repair the evils you have done by the good He has done in you. Afterwards, that you may lie down and repose in safety, enter into the sanctuary of the loving Heart of Jesus, shut yourself up there with the key of tender confidence, and abandon yourself entirely to His care.

"When you feel agitated and troubled by any fear, say to your soul, 'What dost thou fear? Thou carriest the Heart of Jesus and His love; this is the treasure, the strength, and the delight, of heaven and earth.' When you are suffering, say, 'I wish to suffer everything without complaining; the Heart of my Jesus prevents me from fearing anything.'

"When you wish to pray, enter into the Heart of Jesus as into a sacred desert; you will there find wherewith to render to God what you owe to Him, by offering the prayer of our Lord Jesus Christ, to supply for yours. You will love God with the love of this Divine Heart; you will adore Him by its adorations; you will praise Him by its praises; you will work by its operations; and you will wish for nothing but by its will.

"If you are faithful to this Divine Heart, it will

be a source of all good to you, but if, on the contrary, you abandon it by your ingratitude, it will
become as insensible to you. Adieu, my dear sisters;
let us belong entirely to the beloved of our souls,
let us give to Him our whole heart, love, and affections. I earnestly desire for you the pure love of
this Divine Heart, and that you may be consumed
by its most ardent flames. Remember that it is to
Him you have made so many promises, and He
cannot be mocked. Be invariably constant in fulfilling your promises, whatever it may cost you.
No more affection for creatures, nor for self, but all
for that Divine Heart in the care of which I have
placed you."

Such was the last advice of Mother Margaret to
her dear disciples. It contains a summary of all
her others, and is, as it were, an abstract of all
perfection. This divine seed did not fall upon an
unfruitful soil; of this the holiness of these faithful
novices, and the fervour of the community, were sufficient proof. The new assistant animated them by
her example; in spite of her infirmities, she was the
first in everything; the most obedient and the most
humble, notwithstanding the rank her employment
gave her, and the pre-eminence which drew upon
her the universal confidence of all her sisters.
Those who had been the most opposed to her, who
had even ill-treated her, distinguished themselves
from the rest by the confidence they placed in the
holy assistant, and by the earnestness with which
they asked her advice, in order that they might follow it, and thus successfully aspire to perfection.

This esteem and confidence became so general,
that the community had thoughts of making her

superior when the six years of Mother Melin's superiorship should come to an end ; and indeed she was proposed with two others, at the election of 1690. Our Lord warned her of this proposal. On the Holy Thursday of the year in which the election is made, He appeared to her, presenting a cross which she eagerly accepted, not yet comprehending what this cross signified. After having made the sacrifice and submitted herself to it, she learnt that they intended to make her superior, and complained of it to our Lord: "Is it possible," said she to Him, "that Thou wilt permit a creature such as I am to be exposed at the head of a community? I beg of Thee as a favour to remove this cross from me; I submit to every other one." Our Lord yielded to her request, and Mother Catharine Antoinette de Levi-Chateaumorand was elected in the place of Mother Melin. The first favour which Sister Margaret asked of the new superior, was to retire from the charge of assistant, in which she knew this wise superior wished to leave her. This request displeased our Lord, and He reproved her for it the same day at evening prayer, saying, "What! I have yielded to thy will, and for the love of Me wilt not thou do violence to thyself?" These words pierced her to the heart, and she went immediately to find the superior, to ask her pardon, and assure her that she was ready to do whatever she ordered. She remained then in this employment, but it was for no long time, as the election preceded her death but a few months.

Finally, in the midst of so many crosses, austerities, trials, and sufferings, the bodily infirmities of Sister Margaret gradually increased, and her soul acquired the measure of its merit, and advanced towards the day of its reward. God gave her knowledge of her approaching death, as she herself mentioned in plain terms to some of her sisters: "I shall die this year," said she, "because I no longer suffer anything." She spoke thus two months before her death. She told others that she should die soon, because her life hindered the great benefit our Lord intended to draw from a book of devotion to His Sacred Heart, "which Father Croiset," said she, "will have printed." This religious having learned what the servant of God had said of him, was utterly astonished, for he had communicated his design to no one. He afterwards fulfilled that part of the prophecy which concerned him, by giving to the public a book which bore this title. The remainder of the prophecy is being every day fulfilled by the spiritual fruit which is drawn by so many souls from this book, of which several editions have been already exhausted.

Yet the heart of Mother Margaret, which longed only for eternity, and rapidly advanced towards it, seemed already to be inflamed with the ardour of the saints with whom she was so soon to be associated. Her words were animated with an entirely new fervour, and she spoke of God with more liberty, grace, and transport than ever. Even tepid souls were forced, so to speak, to enjoy her conversation and to delight in it; they loved to approach her whom they had so long been unable to endure. The discourses of this holy lover of Jesus were only upon His love, and that which we should have for Him; upon the happiness of submitting our heart to His good pleasure, and upon the joy we experience in pos-

sessing Him and being absorbed in Him for all
eternity.

She not only seemed to share with the seraphim
their love and ardour, but she began to taste something of that heavenly peace with which these blessed
spirits are inebriated. God had at last established
in her heart a calm which surprised her, and she no
longer suffered from her infirmities. Her humility
was alarmed at this. Ever ingenious to conceal
from herself whatever consolation there might be
for her in the favours she received from God, she
had recourse to her director, in the fear of being
seduced by a deceitful calm. "I know not," said
she, in a note written to him shortly before her
death, "I know not what I ought to think of the
state in which I now am. Until now I have had
three desires so ardent, that I regarded them as
three tyrants, which compelled me to suffer a continual martyrdom, without giving me a moment of
repose." We have before seen what these desires
were, and how they tended only to suffering and
humiliation. She continues, "At present I find myself in a cessation of all desire which astonishes me;
I fear that this peace may be an effect of the tranquillity in which God sometimes leaves faithless
souls. I apprehend that by my great unfaithfulness
I may have drawn this state upon me, which is
perhaps a mark of reprobation, for I declare to you
that I am unable to desire or wish for anything
more in this world. Sometimes I could wish to
afflict myself, but I cannot; I only feel a perfect
acquiescence in the good pleasure of God, and an
ineffable delight in sufferings. The thought which
from time to time consoles me, is that the Sacred

Heart will do all for me, if only I place no obstacle in the way. It will wish, love, and desire for me and in me, and will supply for all my faults."

The servant of God thought it her duty to pre-pare for her last passage by a more strict retreat. She obtained permission to make one of forty days, which she began, about the festival of St. Mary Mag-dalen. We have remaining a fragment she then wrote under obedience, giving an account of her interior dispositions. It was either never con-cluded, or the conclusion has been lost. We give here what has been preserved, as containing the last sentiments of a soul, so heroic in love and humility.

"Since St. Mary Magdalen's day, I have felt ex-tremely urged to reform my life, in order to make myself ready to appear before the holiness of God, whose justice is so formidable, and whose judgments are impenetrable. I must then always keep my ac-counts ready that I may not be surprised, for it is a terrible thing at the hour of death, to fall into the hands of the living God, when, during life, we have by sin withdrawn from the arms of God who died for us. To carry out then this salutary purpose, I pro-pose to make an interior retreat in the Sacred Heart of Jesus Christ. I expect and hope for all the as-sistance of mercy which is necessary for me to effect this. In Him I place all my confidence, since His excessive goodness never fails to lead me, when I address myself to Him; on the contrary, He seems to take pleasure in having found a subject so miser-able, mean, and needy as I am, to fill my nothing-ness with His infinite abundance. The Blessed Vir-

gin will be my good Mother, St. Joseph and our holy
founder will be my protectors.

"The first day of my retreat I was occupied in
thinking whence this great desire for death could
proceed, since it is not usual with criminals, such as
I am before God, to be pleased to appear before
their judge, a judge too, the holiness of whose justice penetrates even to the marrow of the bones,
from whom nothing can be concealed, and who
leaves nothing unpunished. How then, my soul,
canst thou feel so great a joy at the approach of
death? Thou thinkest only of ending thy exile, and
art transported in imagining that thou wilt soon
leave thy prison. But, alas! take care that from a
temporal joy, which proceeds perhaps from blindness
and ignorance, thou art not plunged into an eternal
sadness: and that from this mortal and perishable
prison thou dost not fall into those eternal dun-
geons, where there will be no more place for hope.
Leave then, O my soul, this joy and these desires of
dying to holy and fervent souls, for whom great
rewards are prepared; and let us, whose works
allow us to expect nothing but punishment, if God
were not still more merciful than just in His dealings with us, let us consider what will be our fate.
Wilt thou be able, my soul, to support for eternity
the absence of Him whom thou so ardently desirest
to enjoy, the loss of whom causes thee such excessive pain?

"My God, how difficult is it for me to settle this
account, since I have lost my time, and know not
how to repair it. But in this difficulty, to whom
can I apply but to my adorable Master, who of His
great goodness has been willing to undertake this

for me? It is for this that I have placed before
Him all the articles upon which I am to be judged,
namely, our rules, constitutions, and directory;
by these I shall be justified or condemned. After
having placed all my concerns in His hands, I
experienced a sweet peace at His feet, where He
kept me a long time buried as it were in my own
nothingness, there awaiting His sentence of the
miserable criminal.

"The second day, all that I had been, and all that
I then was, was presented before me as in a picture:
but where indeed could be found a monster more
deformed and horrible to the eye? I saw there no
good, but so much evil, that it was a torment to me
to think of it. It seems that everything condemns
me to eternal punishment for the great abuse I have
made of so many graces, to which I have been so
unfaithful. O my Saviour, who am I, for whose
repentance Thou hast waited so long; I who have a
thousand times deserved to be buried in hell through
the excess of my malice? As many times hast
Thou prevented it by Thine infinite goodness. Continue then, my loving Saviour, to exercise Thy
mercy upon this miserable subject. Thou seest that
I cheerfully accept all the pains and punishments
which Thou mayest be pleased to inflict upon me in
this life, and in the other. I feel so much sorrow
for having offended Thee, that I could wish to have
suffered all the punishment due to sin, as a preser-
vative from it, before I had committed any, rather
than have offended Thee so many times. I desire
not to be spared any part of that vengeance which it
may please the divine justice to exercise upon this
criminal, if He will only not abandon her to herself,

29

and punish her for her past sins by new falls. Do
not deprive me, O my God, of Thy love for ever!
as to the rest, do with me as Thou pleasest. I tell
Thee all that I have, and all that I am. All the
good that I can do cannot repair the least of my
faults except through Thee. I am insolvent: Thou
knowest it well, my Divine Master. Put me in
prison; I consent, provided it be in Thy Sacred
Heart; and when I am there, keep me a close captive, held by the chains of love, until I have paid
all that I owe Thee. And as I can never do this, so
do I wish never to leave that prison."

This fragment, written by her own hand, makes
us regret the remainder which has not been preserved. What were the feelings of this holy soul,
who, at the beginning of her retreat, carried the
rigour of her examination and the fervour of her
contrition so far? What a lesson for us! The
saints tremble at the sight of the slightest imperfections, and weep for them bitterly; how can we be so
insensible in the midst of so many sins!

The long retreat of Mother Margaret was soon
followed by her last sickness. She had been failing
for some time, and her indisposition increased in
the month of October of this year. Notwithstanding her weak state, and although she had made in
the month of July the long and extraordinary
retreat of which we have just spoken, yet in October
she desired to go through the exercises of the annual
retreat with the rest of the community, who, according to the custom of the institute, usually made it
at that season. Her turn was appointed by the
superior, and the day was fixed, but on the evening
before, she was attacked by a slight fever, and she

knew immediately that it was the signal given her
by her Spouse, to make known His coming. One of
the sisters, finding that the fever appeared trifling,
and being accustomed to see her overcome more
violent maladies in order to attend to the common
exercises, asked her if she thought she could enter
upon the retreat. The Mother Margaret replied
sweetly, " Yes, but it will be the great retreat."
The religious who deposed to this fact in the information, understood that she spoke of her approaching death.

The next day her weakness was so great that she
was obliged to keep her bed. The physician was
called, the same who had so long witnessed her different infirmities and their miraculous cure, and
who sometimes said, that as these infirmities were
caused by divine love, medicine could provide no
remedy for them. Accustomed to see her weak and
languishing, and now finding her with only a slight
fever, he considered the illness of little consequence,
and assured the sisters that she would not die. She
thought otherwise, and seeing near the bed a sister
who had made her noviciate under her, she told her
plainly that she would die of this illness; she then
requested her good offices, especially in the time of
her agony, "For it will be," she added, "in your arms
that I shall expire." This daughter, who was young
and of a timorous nature, replied that she could not
render her this last service. The mother persisted in
assuring her that it would be as she said, and that
she would feel no fear. She had foretold the same
thing five years before to another religious, and the
prediction was verified in both cases.

In spite of the assurance given them by the physician, and the confidence they placed in his skill, the community still felt great uneasiness at hearing a nun, whose sanctity was so well known, speak of her death with so much certainty. They repeatedly entreated the physician to watch closely the symptoms of the disease. He readily consented, for he had long respected the virtue of the holy religious, and he came several times in the day to examine her; but the more he saw of her, the more he was confirmed in the opinion that there was nothing dangerous in the attack. Mother Margaret, who knew what would be its end, thought only of redoubling her fervour at the approach of her Spouse, of occupying herself lovingly with God, and of rejoicing at the happiness she hoped for, of being soon absorbed in Him. It was of these wishes that she discoursed incessantly with the sisters who came to visit her.

This illness, which made so little outward show, was accompanied by interior sufferings, of which neither the cause nor the violence were known. Notwithstanding the pains taken by Sister Margaret to hide them, and never to complain of them, one of the sisters discovered that she endured much, and was eager to give her some relief. The courageous religious thanked her for her good offices, saying, "that the few moments remaining to her were too precious not to derive profit from them; that in truth she suffered much, but not enough to satisfy her desire." She added, that "she found so great a satisfaction in living and dying upon the cross, that however ardent the desire of enjoying her God might be within her, she would have still greater satisfaction in remaining in the state in which she was until the day of judgment, if such were the good pleasure of God."

The sincerity of these heroic sentiments may be known by the carefulness she showed throughout her illness to profit by all the opportunities of suffering which presented themselves; she was always satisfied with what was ordered for her, and given to her. The remedies, sometimes a greater burden to the sick person than the disease itself, drew from her no complaint, nor any mark of repugnance or disgust; she received with indifference whatever was given her to eat, good or bad, cold or hot, were it even scalding, and she appeared as insensible to these things, as if she had already no body. She was once asked what she wished for to excite her appetite; she replied with simplicity that she knew nothing about it, and that what they gave her was too good for her.

This tranquillity, in addition to the confidence of the physician, reassured the community, whom the first idea of danger had alarmed. They no longer talked of allowing the invalid to receive the last Sacraments. Indifferent as she was to everything else, she was most anxious to receive the holy Viaticum, and asked for it with earnestness; but they saw so few marks of danger, that they thought it right to defer it, and told her there was no hurry. She entreated that she might at least communicate, since she was still fasting; this was the morning of the day which preceded her death. The favour was granted her, and we may imagine with what transports of love and fervour she received the holy Communion. In intention she received it as Viaticum,

and after the ceremony she said to one of the infirmarians, that it was for the last time.

It was the Will of God that before her death she
should pass though a last trial of interior sufferings.
The peace which she enjoyed in her heart, and the
consolation with which her soul was as it were inebriated, were suddenly changed into inconceivable
terror of the judgments of God. The thought of
death, which until then had been her delight, excited
feelings of alarm in connexion with the divine
justice. These were so sensible, that her whole
body was seen to tremble; to reassure herself, she
pressed upon her heart the crucifix she held in her
hands; she uttered deep sighs, and was often heard
to repeat these words with tears; "Mercy, my God,
mercy!" One of the religious, who witnessed this,
has said, "that she told her that one of the subjects
of her fear was the sight of the bad use she had
made of her time, which she thought had not been
employed sufficiently well to obtain her salvation."

Thus God consummated the purity of this
favoured soul, or rather, He wished by this example
to teach us to watch over the purity of our own
hearts; for if the judgments of God appear so terrible to the saints, what should be the fear of those
who serve Him with coldness?

Mother Margaret then remembered, that after
her death some of the papers she had written in
obedience to her directors or superiors would be
found, in which, by their order, she had given an
account of the singular graces she had received.
Her humility made her fear that these favours would
be known by their means, and to prevent it, she
begged the infirmarian to go and burn them all.

The sister could not resolve to do so; she represented to the invalid, that she ought out of obedience to place these writings in the hands of the mother-superior, and sacrifice her inclination to what should be ordered. At the word obedience, the invalid had no longer any wish, and as she saw that this sister was overcome at the thought of the loss the house would soon have to sustain, a loss that would be felt more sensibly by her than by any one, on account of the friendship that existed between them, the servant of God consoled her, repeating what she had formerly said, that her death was necessary to the glory of the Heart of Jesus Christ. Thus this humble nun was persuaded that her infidelities were an obstacle to the reign of this devotion; but her prediction had another meaning which the event has manifested, and which her humility hid from her. Indeed, it was by the recital of the wonders that God had worked in her and by her, that this devotion spread; and this recital could not be made till after her death. Thus her death gave occasion to Father Croiset to add to the book which he caused to be printed, the compendium of the life of the servant of God, and so was necessary for the glory of the Heart of Jesus Christ.

She said also to the same infirmarian, that if God showed her mercy, she should feel the effect of her prayers. The religious mentioned three things in particular which she begged her to obtain of God for her. The dying mother gave her promise, and the sister has deposed that she received sensible proofs of the venerable mother's protection, in the three things she requested.

The last day of Sister Margaret's life began, and

yet no one could be persuaded that she was about
to die so soon. Even on that morning the physician
said that she would not die of that illness. The invalid quietly replied, "You will see." She was told
that the superior had sent to apprise her family of
her illness, on which she said that she could not see
them, and added, "Let us die and sacrifice everything to God." In the meanwhile her strength
began to fail visibly, and in the same degree increased
the ardent longing of her soul for heaven. She
often repeated, "I will sing the mercies of the Lord
for ever." At other times she said, "What do I
desire in heaven or on earth, but Thee only, O my
God?" An oppression came upon her, which made
it impossible for her to remain lying down. The infirmarians placed her in a sitting posture, and supported her in that position so as to enable her to
breathe, and to relieve her breast from the interior
fire which consumed it. "I burn," said she, "I
burn; alas! what consolation if it were with divine
love! But I have never loved my God perfectly."
Then addressing the infirmarians who supported her,
she said with humility, "Ask pardon of God for me,
and love Him yourselves with all your hearts, in
reparation for all the moments in which I have not
done so." She said again, "What happiness to
love God! O what happiness! Love then this
Love, and love Him perfectly." She said these
words with an ardour and transport which showed
what sort of fire it was that consumed her, and how
medical science knew it not.

As the weakness of the invalid increased, it was
feared that she would soon pass away, and the superior sent to beg the physician to return. This was

about five o'clock in the evening, but as soon afterwards the weakness seemed entirely to have passed
off, and the invalid appeared much relieved, the physician persisted in saying there was nothing to fear,
for that her pulse had scarcely changed. When she
again begged for the holy Viaticum, the physician
decided that she must wait till the next day; but
there was no tomorrow for her. She then said to
Sister Claude Rosalie de Farge, who was near her :
" Happily I foresaw this ; I thought they would not
believe me to be so ill ; and therefore the last time
I communicated, (which was the day before,) God
gave me grace to receive Him as my Viaticum."
As she was then very quiet, the sisters went to the
community exercises, and there remained only one
infirmarian with the servant of God, who employed
this time of comparative solitude in speaking with
her of the excess of God's love 'towards His creatures. She gave her some advice concerning perfection, and asked her afterwards if it was thought she
would last long. The sister replied, that according
to the opinion of the physician, she would not die of
that illness, but that she herself did not believe she
would live beyond the next day. "Ah, Lord !" cried
the servant of God, " when wilt Thou take me from
this place of evil ?" She then added, "I rejoiced at
the things that were said to me; we shall go into
the house of the Lord, (Ps. cxxi. 1.) ; yes, I hope
that through the love of the Heart of Jesus Christ,
we shall go into the house of the Lord, and that
soon." She said at the same time to the religious
who attended her, that when she saw her in her
agony, she wished her to call the superior, and beg
her to cause the Litanies of the Heart of Jesus, and

those of the Blessed Virgin, to be recited near her
bed, and especially to invoke for her, her guardian
angel, St. Joseph, and the holy founder of the Visitation.

She had scarcely finished these words, when she
was seized with a convulsion, which seemed to indi-
cate that her agony was come. The infirmarian was
anxious to fetch the mother-superior, but another
sister who had entered the room a few minutes before, thought it would only be a passing weakness,
and prevented the infirmarian from doing so. The
dying religious said to her, " Let her go, it is time
she should." The superior arrived, and gave orders
that the physician should be fetched immediately,
but the servant of God prevented her, saying, " My
mother, I have no need of any one but God alone,
and to lose myself in the Heart of Jesus Christ."

The sisters ran in, and surrounded her bed, overcome with sorrow and melting into tears. The
dying religious collected all her remaining strength
to console them, and to recommend them to belong
entirely to God, entirely and without reserve, assuring them that when admitted into IIis presence, she
would be grateful for all the affection she had received from her sisters. After this, seeing near her
one of the sisters in whom she placed most confidence, she begged her to write to Father Rolin, a
Jesuit, formerly her director, to conjure him from
her, to burn whatever letters and writings he had of
her's, and to preserve an inviolable secrecy about all
that he knew concerning her; she demanded the
same favour of the mother-superior, and particularly
requested her to arrange so that she should not be
spoken of in the order in any other way than in ask-

ing for the usual suffrages. But these efforts of her humility were useless; she desired to remain unknown in the tomb, as she had always wished to be hidden in life; but how is it possible to hide what God wishes to manifest for His glory and for the edification of His saints? The proud love to be brought forward, and are confounded when they meet with contempt and forgetfulness; the humble conceal themselves as much as possible, and God perpetuates their glory to the end of the world. It happened thus to His servant, for her superiors and directors published the wonders which God had wrought in the soul which they had tried so long, considering, as the Scripture says, "that it is glorious to publish the works of the Most High."

In the midst of her agony, the servant of God lost neither her consciousness nor her presence of mind; after making the request just mentioned to her superior, she warned her that it was time to give her Extreme Unction. She received this Sacrament with all the devotion and fervour with which her soul was penetrated, being able to pronounce nothing but the names of Jesus and Mary, because the heat of her breast stifled her respiration. It was in pronouncing these sacred names, and during the fourth unction, that she gently expired, according to her prediction, in the arms of Sister Francis Rosalie Verchere, and Sister Claude Rosalie de Farge, whose mistress she had been in the noviciate, and to each of whom she had predicted separately, that they would perform this charitable office. Though they were neither of them infirmarians, and were not the first to arrive in the sick chamber, yet chance, or rather the providence of God, arranged that the word of His servant should be fulfilled. These two young sisters supported her in their arms during her agony, and it was thus that she rendered her soul to God, on the 17th of October, 1690, between seven and eight o'clock in the evening. She was forty-three years, two months, and twenty-four days old.

The physician whom they had gone to seek, arrived at length when she had just expired, which made him say, "that since Sister Margaret had lived by miracle in the midst of so many mortal and desperate diseases which it was impossible for her to resist naturally, he was not surprised that by a new miracle she should die without any appearance of real disease."

As death had less share in the separation of her soul than divine love, it seemed to respect her body; her countenance, far from being changed and disfigured, appeared more majestic and beautiful than before ; the terror and fear which the bodies of the dead usually inspire, and which seize upon all who approach them, were unknown here to the youngest and the most timid. All were eager to approach the holy body, and to pray near it; they found a kind of enjoyment and consolation in remaining near it, as if to collect the remains of that spirit of fervour which had animated it, and it was difficult to choose from amongst those who offered to pass the night there. There were none who did not weep bitterly, and reproach themselves with not having esteemed the saint enough, and for having profited so little by her example, and who did not from friendship and esteem shed over her bitter and sincere tears, such as are seldom shed from other than interested motives.

The report of this precious death was soon spread in the town, and the sorrow was not less there than in the community. Everywhere there was mourning, as for a public calamity, and people cried aloud in the streets, "The Saint is dead!" The doors of the church were no sooner opened on the following morning, than it was filled with an eager crowd of people of all classes, who came either to find consolation in seeing the servant of God once more, to have recourse to her protection by invoking her aid, or to obtain something which had belonged to her, to keep it as a relic. All begged for something, and it was difficult to satisfy so many, for this faithful lover of poverty had died in so great a deprivation of everything, that nothing was found in her cell but her bed, the book of the rules, and her discipline. Several other instruments of penance would have been found, if some time before her death the superior had not ordered her to give them all to her, an injunction which she had obeyed without hesitation.

However, to satisfy the devotion of the people, the sisters caused her body to be touched with the chaplets and other things which each presented for that purpose. Two sisters were thus occupied from morning till evening, and could scarcely get through the duty. Her funeral took place on the evening of the 18th of October, with an extraordinary concourse of ecclesiastics and persons of note. Those who came into the house, according to custom, for the interment, imitated the devotion of the people; each wished to take away some relic of the deceased saint, even cutting off pieces of her habit or veil, and one of them having taken away the little crucifix she held in her hands, steadily refused to return it to the house, saying it was the most precious treasure that he could leave to his family.

This general fervour was not of that transitory nature which passes away in a few months. It is nearly forty years since the death of this holy religious, and her memory is still held in benediction throughout the country. People from all parts flock to her tomb, either to invoke her protection, or to thank God for the favours for which they consider they are indebted to her intercession; and they receive with gratitude portions of the earth where she is buried, or fragments of the bier on which she was laid.

What principally contributes to feed this devotion, is the number of miracles by which God has honoured the memory of this devout lover of His Sacred Heart. It is thus that God crowned the humility of His servant, and that she who had no other ambition than to be unknown to all the world, or to be known only to be despised, is raised to the highest glory to which man can arrive upon earth, which is, to become the object of the veneration and worship of the faithful. The extravagant adoration of the Roman Emperors vanished with the smoke of the funeral pile that consumed their ashes; all their power could not guarantee them from the contempt into which they fell after their death; whilst a poor, simple, despised woman, unknown to all the world, becomes the object of the veneration of men; time which buries others in oblivion, only increases her glory; she overcomes death, the elements, and disease, even twenty-five years after she is interred, and she, who seems to be no more, still works wonders. God alone can thus honour His elect and His servants. We have given sufficient proofs that it was IIis Will to load His humble servant with glory; if they do not satisfy the incredulous, a greater number would not convince them more fully. It is enough for us that pious persons, for whom we write, find in them wherewith to strengthen their piety, and learn by these miracles, not only to judge of the holiness of the venerable Mother Margaret, and of the solidity of the devotion instituted by her, but also to imitate the sublime virtues which have merited so many favours, and to derive from that devotion the fruit which they ought to gather from it. That holy devotion tends only to the love of God, to kindle that love in our languishing hearts, to make us act and suffer in that spirit of love, to induce us to consume ourselves, so to speak, in the fire of that sacred love; a love which will be our happiness in heaven, and our holiness upon earth. Happy he who tastes and practises it; but as for him "who loves not the Lord Jesus Christ, let him be anathema."

BOOK X.

COLLECTION OF SOME OF HER WRITINGS OF DEVOTION.

———

CANTICLE IN HONOUR OF THE BLESSED SACRAMENT.

C'EST dans la sainte Eucharistie.
Où j'ai trouvé mon vrai tresor.
Jésus pour m'y donner la vie,
S'y tient dans un état de mort.
    C'est à l'ombre de cette hostie,
Qu'il a blessé mon pauvre cœur,
Pour lui communiquer sa vie,
Il s'en est rendu le vainqueur.
    S'il ne falloit rien que ma vie
Pour recevoir ce Dieu d'amour;
Helas ! que je serois ravie,
De la donner cent fois le jour.
    Si pour avoir ce Dieu que j'aime,
Il faut un parfait dénuëment :
Je quitte tout, jusqu'à moi-même
Pour Jésus au Saint Sacrement.
    Si mon Epoux veut la souffrance,
Pur amour ne m'épargnez pas :
Car pour avoir sa joüissance,
Je veux souffrir jusqu'au trépas.
    Pourquoi me cacher votre face,
Puisque je ne veux plus que vous?
Helas ! que faut-il que je fasse,
Eloigné d'un objet si doux ?
    Coupez, brûlez, c'est ce que j'aime,
Contentez-vous à mes dépens :
Si ma douleur devient extrême,
L'amour allége mon tourment.

Il est une fournaise ardente,
Qui brûle sans se consumer.
Helas! que je serois contente,
De m'y pouvoir toute abîmer !

Le cœur pur qui vous sert de couche
Combien goûte-t-il de douceur ?
Mais le cœur soüillé qui vous touche,
Ne trouve en vous que des rigueurs.

Pour calmer la sainte justice,
Jesus s'immole chaque jour :
Pour nous délivrer du supplice,
Il fait ce prodige d' amour.

L'ame pure y trouve la vie
Le pécheur y trouve la mort :
Tous deux avec la même hostie,
Eprouvent un different sort.

Amour du ciel et de la terre,
Venez, pénetrez dans mon cœur :
Faites de moi un beau parterre,
Tout rempli de fruits et de fleurs.

Je suis une biche harassée ;
Qui cherche l'eau avec ardeur :
La main du chasseur m'a blessée ;
Son dard a percé jusqu'au cœur.

Souffrir, aimer, c'est mon délice ;
Je ne veux plus d' autre plaisir.
Le plaisir même est un supplice,
Et la souffrance est mon desir.

Je veux tout souffrir sans rien craindre,
Mépris, douleur, peine et travaux.
Quand on aime, peut on se plaindre ?
L'amour adoucit tous les maux.

Perdez-moi en vous, ô ma source !
Comme une goutte dans la mer.
Aimer et mourir sans ressource,
Car toute le reste m'est amer.

ACT OF CONSECRATION TO THE SACRED HEART OF JESUS CHRIST.

Adorable Heart of my loving Jesus, seat of all virtues, inexhaustible source of every grace, what didst Thou see in me, to induce Thee to love me with such an excess of love, whilst my heart, sullied with a thousand sins, felt only indifference and coldness towards Thee? The extraordinary testimonies of Thy love for me, even when I did not love Thee, make me hope that Thou wilt accept the proofs I now wish to give Thee of my love. Look favourably then, O my loving Saviour, upon my desire to consecrate myself entirely to the honour and glory of Thy Sacred Heart; accept the gift I make Thee of all that I am; to Thee I consecrate my person, my life, my actions, my pains and sufferings, wishing henceforth to be a victim consecrated to Thy glory, already burning, and one day, if it please Thee, to be consumed entirely in the sacred flames of Thy love. I offer Thee then, O my Lord and God, I offer Thee my heart, with all the feelings of which it is capable, trusting, and ardently desiring, that it may be during my whole life perfectly conformed to the dispositions of Thy Sacred Heart. Behold me then, O Lord, entirely devoted to Thy Heart, and to Thee. O my God! how great are Thy mercies towards me! O God of Majesty! what am I, that Thou shouldst deign to accept the sacrifice of my heart? It shall henceforth be all Thine, no creatures shall divide its affections with Thee, for they are not worthy to do so. From this time, O my loving Jesus, be Thou my Father, my Friend, my

Master, and my All; I wish to live only for Thee.
Receive, O loving Saviour of men, the sacrifice made
by the most ungrateful of creatures to Thy Sacred
Heart, in reparation for the offences I have committed up to this hour by corresponding so ill to its
love. I give Thee little indeed ; but at least I give
Thee all that I can give, and whatever I know Thou
desirest of me; and when I consecrate to Thee this
heart, I intend never to take it back again.

Teach me, O my loving Saviour, perfect forgetfulness of self, since that is the only way to find the
entrance I so much desire into Thy Sacred Heart ;
and since henceforth I shall do nothing but for Thee,
grant that whatever I do may be worthy of Thee.
Teach me what I ought to do to attain the purity of
Thy love; give me this love, and let it be ardent and
generous.	Give me that deep humility, without
which it is impossible to please Thee ; and perfectly
accomplish in me Thy holy Will, in time and through-
out all eternity.	Amen.

REPARATION TO THE SACRED HEART OF JESUS CHRIST.

Most adorable and loving Jesus, ever full of love
for us, ever touched with our miseries, ever eagerly
desirous to impart Thy treasures to us, and even to
give Thyself to us; Jesus my Saviour and my God,
who by an excess of the most ardent and wonderful
love, hast placed Thyself in the condition of a victim
in the adorable Eucharist, where a million times a
day Thou offerest Thyself in sacrifice for us ; what
must be Thy feelings in that state, when, notwithstanding all this, Thou findest in the greater part of
men nothing but coldness, forgetfulness, ingratitude,

and contempt! Was it not enough, O my Saviour,
to have chosen the most painful way to save us,
though Thou mightest have testified Thine excessive
love at much less cost? Was it not enough to have
abandoned Thyself for a time to that cruel agony,
to that tremendous sorrow, caused by the sight of
our sins, with which Thou wert loaded? Why wilt
Thou still expose Thyself day by day, to all the
indignities of which the blackest malice of men and
devils is capable? Ah, my God, and my ever blessed
Redeemer, what are the sentiments of Thy Sacred
Heart, at the sight of all this ingratitude and these
sins! With what bitter sorrow must Thy Heart
have been overwhelmed at so many sacrileges and
outrages!

Touched with an extreme regret for all these insults, behold me prostrate and annihilated before
Thee, to make reparation in the sight of heaven and
earth for all the irreverence and insults that Thou
hast received upon our altars since the institution of
this adorable Sacrament. With a contrite and humbled heart, I ask Thy pardon a thousand times for
all these insults. Oh that I were able, O my
God, to water with my tears, and wash with my
blood, all the places where Thy Sacred Heart has
been so grossly insulted, and where the signs of Thy
divine love have been received with such strange
contempt! Oh that I could by some new kind of
homage, humiliation, or annihilation, repair so many
sacrileges and profanations! Oh that I could for
one moment be master of the hearts of all men, to
repair in some sort, by the sacrifice I would make
of them to Thee, the forgetfulness and insensibility
of all those who have not chosen to know Thee,

or who, having known Thee, have loved Thee so little!

But, O my loving Saviour, what covers me with still greater confusion, and ought to make me grieve the most, is that I have been myself amongst the number of these ungrateful beings. My God, Thou seest the bottom of my heart; Thou knowest the sorrow I feel at my ingratitude, and my regret at seeing Thee so unworthily treated. Thou knowest my earnest desire to suffer anything and do anything to repair these offences. Behold me then, O Lord, with a heart broken with sorrow, humbled and prostrate before Thee, ready to receive from Thy hand whatever Thou shalt please to exact from me in reparation for so many outrages. Strike, Lord, strike; I will bless and kiss a hundred times the hand which shall inflict upon me so just a punishment. Oh that I were a fit victim to repair such injuries! Oh that I could water with my blood all those places where Thy sacred Body has been thrown upon the ground, and trampled under foot! Too happy, if I could by every possible suffering repair so many outrages, so much contempt and impiety. But if I do not deserve this favour, at least accept the sincere desire I feel for it. Receive, O Eternal Father, this reparation that I make Thee, in union with that made by the Sacred Heart on Calvary, and that which Mary made to Thee herself at the foot of her Son's cross. In consideration of the prayer that this Sacred Heart offers to Thee for the same object, pardon me the commission of so many indignities and so much irreverence, and by Thy grace render efficacious the intention I have, and the resolution I make, to omit nothing in my power in order

to love ardently, and to honour in every possible
way, my Sovereign, my Saviour, and my Judge,
whom I believe to be really present in the adorable
Eucharist. I intend henceforth to show by my respect in His presence, and by my assiduity in paying
my court to Him, that I believe Him to be really
present. And as I make profession of honouring
especially His Sacred Heart, it is also in this same
Heart that I wish to pass the remainder of my life.
Grant me this favour, that at the hour of my death
I may give up my last sigh in this same Heart.
Amen.

ASPIRATIONS OF A SOUL THAT ARDENTLY DESIRES HOLY COMMUNION.

Great God! whom I adore, veiled under these
humble appearances, is it possible that Thou hast so
lowered Thyself as to take possession of this contemptible dwelling, that thus Thou mightest come
into my house and remain corporally with me?
The heavens are unworthy to contain Thee, and
Thou art satisfied with these poor and weak species,
that Thou mayest be ever with me. O inconceivable
Goodness! could I ever believe this, if Thou didst
not Thyself assure me of it? Could I dare to
believe that Thou wouldst deign to enter my mouth,
to repose upon my tongue, to descend into my
body? Thou willest it then; and to incite me to
come, Thou promisest me a thousand benefits, O
God of majesty! But, O God of love, would that I
were all understanding, to know this mercy, all
heart to feel it, and all tongue to publish it! What
a God must Thou then be, thus to create me to be
the object of Thy love, and the subject of Thine in-

effable goodness? The angels never cease to behold
Thee, they desire this favour even while enjoying it;
and shall I not wish to possess Thee? Since it
pleases Thee, O my loving Saviour, and since my
wants compel me to desire it, and Thy goodness permits me, I will open to Thee my heart, my mouth,
my tongue, and my breast. Come, come, O divine
Sun, I am plunged in the horrible darkness of ignorance and sin; come and enlighten this darkness,
and cause the divine light of Thy knowledge to
illumine my understanding. Come, O loving Saviour;
Thou didst once deliver Thyself up entirely to draw
me from hell, but since I have fallen back miserably
under the slavery of sin, come yet once more to
break my chains; burst my fetters, and set me at
liberty. Come, O charitable Physician of my soul;
after Thou hast bathed me with Thy Blood, and
rendered me by baptism more holy and healthy than
I deserved to be, I have through my own fault contracted a thousand dangerous diseases, which bring
disgust to my heart, fear to my mind, and death to
my soul. Come, then, and heal me; I need it more
than the paralytic whom Thou didst ask if he
desired to be cured. Yes, my God, I wish it sincerely; but Thou who knowest the coldness of this
desire, by Thine infinite mercy increase it within
me. Come, O most faithful, but most tender and
gentle of all friends, come to my assistance; she
whom Thou lovest is faint, and dangerous and
mortal infirmities oppress her; Thou knowest them,
O my Saviour, Thou who readest the depths of my
heart. If until now I have been insensible to my
misfortune and thoughtless of my danger, now by
Thy grace I complain, I cry out, I feel my wants,

and implore Thy assistance; by Thy incomparable love, and by Thine own words, I entreat Thee to come and help me. Come, and never permit me to give Thee reason to quit me. Come, O life of my heart, O soul of my life, O only support of my being! O Bread of Angels, incarnate for the love of me, delivered up for my ransom, and prepared for my nourishment, come and make me grow quickly, come to support me powerfully, come to satisfy me abundantly, come and make me truly live by Thee, in Thee, and for Thee! Ah, my only beloved, if a body were to be deprived of its soul, how earnestly would it seek the soul, how ardently would it call upon it to return. Have I so little feeling of the union between Thee and me, that I am not aware that without Thee I am a body without a soul? Come, then, O my God and my All, come and animate once more my languishing soul, which sighs after Him who is the light of its beauty, the principle of its movements, and the source of its life. O Jesus, my Love, I conjure Thee to absorb all my thoughts, and draw my heart from all created things by the power of Thy love. O Love, more ardent than fire, and sweeter than honey, grant that I may die consumed with the ardour of Thy fire, as Thou hast been willing to die of love for me. O Lord! so wound this ungrateful heart in every part, and pierce it thoroughly, that it may no longer be able to contain anything earthly or human, but be filled with the fulness of Thy love alone, since it is Thine, and wishes to be Thine eternally. Amen.

PRAYER FOR HOLY MASS.

Eternal Father, permit me to offer Thee the Heart of Jesus Christ Thy dearly beloved Son, as He Himself offers it to Thee in sacrifice. May it please Thee to receive this offering for me, with all the desires, feelings, affections, movements, and acts of this Sacred Heart. They are all mine, since it is immolated for me, and henceforth I wish to have no other desires. Receive them in satisfaction for my sins, and in thanksgiving for all Thy benefits. Receive them in order to grant me through its merits all the graces which are necessary for me, especially the grace of final perseverance. Receive them, as so many acts of love, adoration, and praise, which I offer to Thy Divine Majesty, since it is by it alone that Thou art worthily honoured and glorified. Amen.

ACT OF LOVE.

O most loving Heart of my only beloved, being unable to love and glorify Thee according to the extent of the desire Thou hast given me, I invite all heaven and earth to assist me, and I unite myself to the burning Seraphim in order to love Thee. O Heart, burning with love, why dost Thou not set heaven and earth on fire with Thy pure flame, to consume whatever they contain, that all creatures may breathe only Thy love. Oh make me suffer or die, or at least change my heart entirely, and consume me with Thy most ardent heat, that I may love Thee perfectly. O divine fire, O most pure flames from the Heart of My only Love, burn me without compassion, consume me without resistance. Alas! why dost Thou spare me, since I am only fit to burn, and only deserve fire? O Love! O Love of heaven and earth, come into my heart and reduce me to ashes! O devouring fire of the Divinity, come and dissolve me, burn me, consume me in the midst of Thy pure flames, which cause those who die in them to live.

PRAYER TO JESUS IN THE BLESSED SACRAMENT.

It is to honour Thee as Victim in this Sacrament of love, that I come to Thee, O divine Jesus, entreating Thee to be pleased to be my Sacrificer, immolating me upon the altar of Thy loving Heart. But as this victim is guilty in every way, I beseech Thee, O my divine Sacrificer, to purify and consume it in the ardours of Thy divine Heart as a perfect holocaust, to give me a new life of love and grace in Thee! O my sweet Jesus, only love of my heart, sweet pain of my soul, and blessed martyrdom of my flesh and body, all the favour I ask of Thee to honour Thee as Victim, is that I may live and die the victim of Thy Sacred Heart, by an utter aversion for all that is not Thee; a victim of Thy love, by all the sorrow and desolation of which mine is capable; and a victim of Thy body, by the abandonment of everything which gratifies mine, through hatred of this criminal flesh, which I desire to crucify for the love of Thee.

COMMON CONSECRATION OF THE SISTERS OF THE
NOVICIATE TO THE SACRED HEART OF JESUS.

Lord Jesus, holy and sweet Love of our souls, who
hast promised that where two or three are gathered
together in Thy Name, there wilt Thou be in the
midst of them, behold our hearts united in one
accord to adore, praise, love, and please Thy most
holy and Sacred Heart, to which we dedicate and
consecrate ours for time and eternity, for ever
renouncing all love and affection which are not
in the love of Thine adorable Heart, desiring that
all the wishes, aspirations, and desires of our
hearts may be always conformable to the good
pleasure of Thine, which we wish to satisfy as
much as we can. But as we can do no good
of ourselves, we beseech Thee, O most adorable
Jesus, by the infinite goodness and sweetness of
Thy most Sacred Heart to support ours by confirm-
ing them in the resolution we have made to love
and serve Thee, that nothing may ever separate and
disunite us from Thee, but that we may be faithful
and constant in this resolution, sacrificing to the
love of Thy Sacred Heart whatever may give vain
pleasure to ours, and amuse them idly with the
things of this world. We confess that all is vanity
and affliction of spirit, except loving and serving
Thee, our God and Saviour; we desire henceforth
no other glory than that of belonging to Thee as
slaves of Thy pure love; no other desire nor power
than that of pleasing and satisfying Thee in everything at the expense of our own lives.

And since, O divine Mary, thou art all powerful

with this Sacred Heart, obtain for us that it may receive and accept this consecration which we now make of ourselves in thy presence and through thy hands, protesting that we will be faithful to it, being assisted by its grace and thy prayers, which we entreat thee never to deny us.   Amen.

THE END.

RICHARDSON AND SON, PRINTERS, DERBY.